TELEGRAPH TO THE EAST

TELEGRAPH TO THE PAST

Best wishes,

Ben Grantham

A DRISCOLL NOVEL

BEN GRANTHAM

An imprint of Spitalgate Press

This is a work of fiction. Any references to actual historical events, characters, or locations are used fictitiously. Other names, characters, places and incidents are the product of the author's imagination. Any resemblance to historical events or persons, living or dead, is purely coincidental.

ISBN 978-1-9193511-1-7

bengranthamauthor@gmail.com

For George, James and Alfie,
who are yet to read my book

Contents

1 1889, Harton, Lancashire 1
2 1899, Kirk Allerton, Yorkshire 9
3 1912, Dublin, Ireland 15
4 1914, Hamburg, Germany 21
5 1915, New York City, USA 26
6 1915, Frankfurt University, Germany 34
7 1916, Burnley Lancashire 40
8 1916, Egglescombe, Lancashire 45
9 1916, Frankfurt, Germany 50

Timeline Two

10 1916, Wilmersdorf, Berlin 56
11 1917, Frankfurt, Germany 62
12 1917, St Annes-on-the-Sea, Lancashire 68
13 1917, St Annes-on-the-Sea, Lancashire 74
14 1917, Egglescombe, Lancashire 79

Timeline Three

15 1916, Wilmersdorf, Berlin 88
16 1917, Wilmersdorf, Berlin 98
17 1917, Manchester University, Lancashire 107
18 1917, Manchester University, Lancashire 116
19 1917, St Annes-on-the-Sea, Lancashire 122
20 1918, Rusholme, Lancashire 129
21 1918, Rusholme, Lancashire 138
22 1918, St Annes-on-the-Sea, Lancashire 144
23 1918, St Annes-on-the-Sea, Lancashire 149
24 1919, St Annes-on-the-Sea, Lancashire 154
25 1919, Manchester, Lancashire 159
26 1919, Northern France 165
27 1920, West Prussia, Germany 172

28 1920, Manchester University, Lancashire ... 180
29 1921, Kirk Allerton, Yorkshire ... 187
30 1921, Kirk Allerton, Yorkshire ... 193
31 1921, Rusholme, Lancashire ... 200
32 1922, Liguria, Italy ... 206
33 1922, Schöneberg, Berlin ... 213

Timeline Four

34 1920, Schöneberg, Berlin ... 220
35 1921, Kirk Allerton, Yorkshire ... 228
36 1921, Hendon, Middlesex ... 237

Timeline Five

37 1920, Rusholme, Lancashire ... 243
38 1920, Friedrichshain Hospital, Berlin ... 250
39 1920, Aberystwyth, Wales ... 256
40 1921, Manchester, Lancashire ... 265
41 1921, Kirk Allerton, Yorkshire ... 271
42 1923, The Pennines, Lancashire ... 278
43 1923, Kirk Allerton, Yorkshire ... 284
44 1925, Armley Gaol, Leeds, Yorkshire ... 291
45 1925, Armley Gaol, Leeds, Yorkshire ... 297
46 1925, Liverpool, Lancashire ... 304
47 1925, Dublin, Ireland ... 311
48 1926, Kirk Allerton, Yorkshire ... 319
49 1926, El Monte, California, USA ... 329
50 1926, El Monte, California, USA ... 335
51 1926, Kirk Allerton, Yorkshire ... 340
52 1926, Kirk Allerton, Yorkshire ... 346
53 1927, Schöneberg, Berlin ... 352

Introduction

In 2011, scientists at CERN thought they had discovered particles travelling faster than light. This later turned out to be false when faults were found in their equipment, but it posed the question - what if their findings had been correct? What impact might that have had on the accepted view of world history? Could there be alternative versions of history that we are totally unaware of. The premise that history might change as a result of such a discovery was the inspiration for Telegraph To The Past.

The idea for a Hermes device came from real-life experiments conducted by scientists such as Max von Laue, Nikola Tesla and Albert Einstein. In 1907, Einstein wanted to show how faster-than-light signals could lead to a paradox of causality, described in 1910 by Einstein and Sommerfeld as a "telegraph into the past". The reference for his original paper is *Einstein, Albert (1907). "Über das Relativitätsprinzip und die aus demselben gezogenen Folgerungen" [On the relativity principle and the conclusions drawn from it]. Jahrbuch der Radioaktivität und Elektronik. 4: 411–462.*

Hans Paasche, Karl Gareis, Matthias Erzberger, Walther Rathenau and hundreds of other German politicians and pacifists were assassinated by Organisation Consul in the early days of the Weimar Republic. In the twenties and thirties there were many failed attempts to kill Adolf Hitler, including the one that took place in a Munich Hofbräuhaus, in November, 1921.

Telegraph To The Past is a work of historical fiction that tells the story of James Driscoll, a brilliant but troubled young scientist.

Ben Grantham, 2025

1

Harton, Lancashire
July 1889

In the days and weeks to come, Father Gabriel McCarthy would be described as a kind and gentle soul who had devoted his life to the service of God. His victims knew better, and on one of the hottest nights of the summer, on the outskirts of a sleepy market town in the Bowland Forest, one of them lay in wait. The gluttonous priest spent the evening in the Waggon and Horses public house in Harton village, devouring two large helpings of a tasteless shepherd's pie, washed down with several glasses of red wine. McCarthy suffered from gout, and the mile-long walk home was challenging for him in daylight. In his drunken state and on this moonless night, it would have been treacherous without the light from his paraffin lamp. On the main road, he waved goodnight to a fellow drinker and hobbled up the woodland path that led to his cottage. Kevin Schmidt, a former student at Harton Green Catholic Seminary, waited patiently in the darkness, with murder in his heart.

Kevin's grandparents had brought their young family to England from Bavaria in 1839, at a time when friendly relations existed between the two nations. They had opened their first German butcher's shop the following year, and when their son Jürgen was old enough, he worked there on weekends. As the business became successful, they were able to take on a number of Saturday girls. One of them took a shine to Jürgen, and they eventually married. Eighteen years and two children later, she was bored with her life and her husband. One day in 1885, she went shopping and did not return, having run off with one of the Schmidt's suppliers, a pig farmer from the Rimrose Valley.

Kevin Schmidt was thirteen at the time, and he never forgave his mother. Her departure resulted in a noticeable change in his behaviour, particularly at school. The anger that burned inside him led to fights with other boys, but discipline at Harton Green was strict, and no one cared why he was causing trouble. The beatings meted out by Father McCarthy in the name of corporal punishment were bad enough, but they were the tip of the iceberg. No one would have believed Schmidt, had he complained about the abuse that took place in the priest's private quarters. Any thoughts he may have had of becoming a priest evaporated at the hands of Father McCarthy. The shame and guilt he carried with him was almost too much to bear, and he contemplated suicide many times. In the end, shame turned to rage, and a burning desire for revenge. By the age of seventeen, he couldn't take any more. If he stayed at Harton Green, he would eventually be hanged for murder. Rather than return for another excruciating year, he stole some valuable church artefacts and made sure he was caught, guaranteeing his expulsion.

Schmidt could not bring himself to tell his father the truth, concocting an unlikely story about being framed by another boy. Jürgen Schmidt was just relieved to avoid the shame that would have followed, had anyone in Liverpool found out. No one ever mentioned the incident again, and his wayward son started to work in the family business. This gave him access to some fearsome butchery tools, and he started to daydream about the ways in which he could inflict pain on McCarthy, rejecting them all on the basis that he was bound to get caught.

In the past twelve months, two unrelated events set Kevin on a path that would shape the rest of his life. When a Victorian travelling circus came to Liverpool, it featured a boxing exhibition by Jem Mace, the English former world heavyweight champion. This inspired him to join the Vauxhall Lads' Club in Liverpool, where he learnt the Queensberry Rules and started to make a name for himself by taking on and beating much older boys.

A few weeks later, Kevin's grandfather Hans died at the age of seventy-three. Kevin was very close to his *opa*, an eccentric former marine in the German navy who had lived on a narrowboat on the Leeds and Liverpool Canal for as long as he could remember. Hans used to take him on canal trips from an early age, and taught him all manner of useful skills, from hunting, shooting and fishing to setting fires and tying knots.

'*Opa* wanted you to have these,' said his father, handing him a box and a large canvas bag. Inside were a pair of binoculars and his grandfather's' old A-frame ridge tent, which he claimed to have used while climbing the Matterhorn. Kevin loved his grandfather's stories, but he was never sure whether any of them were true.

With the arrival of summer came an idea. Crazy as it seemed, he could not get it out of his head, and gradually the idea became a plan.

He told his father he was going fishing and set off in the family's horse and trap. In the hills above Harton, he spent the next week watching the comings and goings of Father McCarthy. When the priest went out, Schmidt followed a forest path down to the cottage, where he prised open a rear window and climbed inside. While there, he had a good look around and, satisfied that his plan would work, left the way he came, leaving the window unlocked.

He returned two days later. Late in the evening, he watched as the light from McCarthy's lamp weaved its way homewards. He melted into the shadows and withdrew a cosh from his belt. The drunken priest made a rather noisy entrance and placed the lamp on a hook by the fireplace. A slight, scraping sound, from the direction of the kitchen, made him stop and peer into the shadows, shuddering at the thought that it might be a rat. Too late, a raised arm loomed out of the darkness. Before he could react, he was knocked to the floor by a heavy blow. When he came to, he was lying on the path outside his front door. He wrinkled his bulbous nose at the smell of paraffin.

'Remember me, Father?' asked his assailant in a quiet but menacing voice.

McCarthy opened his eyes to see a dark shape standing over him. 'Who are you? What do you want? I have nothing of any value here.'

'You used to teach forgiveness, Father. "Be kind and compassionate to one another, forgiving each other, just as in Christ, God forgave you." Well, he might have, but I haven't. This is your Judgement Day. The Devil's come a-calling!'

'What do you mean? Who are you?' he squealed, the fear rising inside at the realisation that he was soaked in the combustible liquid.

'Who am I?' he replied angrily. 'Just one of your boys who walks with the Devil because his God deserted him. You really don't remember me, do you? You should have been more careful, Father. When they find you, it's going to seem like a terrible accident.' Schmidt swung the paraffin lamp above him, its light reflecting a malevolent glint in his eyes.

'What do you want?' whimpered McCarthy, now terrified.

'As you die, I want you to think about what you did to me and the others. I'm Kevin Schmidt.' Recognition flickered in the priest's eyes, but at that moment, his assailant dropped the lamp, which smashed at his feet. Within seconds, McCarthy was engulfed in flames, his agonised screams echoing into the night as he sank to the ground, skin and clothing melting in the intense heat.

Schmidt watched the old man burn, recalling a line from James 4. "There is one lawgiver, who is able to save and to destroy: who art thou that judgest another?"

No longer a boy, he was McCarthy's judge, jury and executioner, meting out justice without pity or remorse.

Returning to the cottage, Schmidt covered his tracks and left through the rear window with more than a hundred pounds, found stuffed under a mattress. He planned to leave England, at least until the heat died down, so to speak. It would be several days before McCarthy was missed, and another couple of weeks before his charred body was discovered. The newspapers would report that a tragic accident had befallen a respected local priest after a night's drinking. By then, Schmidt would be thousands of miles away.

He was surprised at how easy it had been to take someone's life. He had felt no fear, and certainly no sympathy for his victim. If anything, he felt exhilarated by what he had done, and it made him think about evening other scores.

When he was ready to leave, he told his father he was going to America to seek his fortune. Using McCarthy's money, he purchased a second-class ticket in the name of Kevin Winter, for the maiden voyage of the RMS *Teutonic*. He figured that his paternal grandmother's maiden name would give him a fresh start and hinder any future efforts to track him down in the United States.

On the transatlantic crossing, he became more than a little envious of the way the first-class passengers were treated. He almost wished he had spent the extra money, even though someone of his age and background would have attracted unwelcome attention in such opulent surroundings.

As the *Teutonic* neared its destination in the early hours, Winter went up on deck to catch a glimpse of New York's newest landmark, the Statue of Liberty. Less than three years earlier, Bartholdi's colossal sculpture, a permanent symbol of freedom, was erected on Bedloe's Island, watching over the ships arriving in New York Harbour. Winter peered through the early morning mist but, disappointingly, there was only a faint gleam from the statue's torch.

New York City
August 1889

Winter's first day in New York was almost his last. At the White Star Line dock, someone gave him directions to a comfortable hotel on Canal Street, where he slept for the rest of the day. Venturing out onto the dark and gloomy street that night, the sound of river traffic made him yearn for home. The constant smell from the gas works and factories may have been unpleasant, but it was infinitely preferable to the stench of the night soil man's cart as it made its way down the street. On his eastward journey towards the bright lights of the city, several ladies of the night made themselves known to him. Brazen and unkempt, none were in the first flush of youth, and they were deeply unattractive to Winter, who was far more interested in his stomach. A church clock struck ten as he turned south, walking towards the smell of cooking and passing a sign that read Baxter Street.

Ahead of him, in an alleyway between Baxter and Mulberry Bend, Nico Varese was fighting for his life. The girl he was with was Irish, and the couple were followed into the alley by her brother and two of his mates. This evening was not going to end in the way Nico had planned. Winter cautiously made his way towards the sounds from the alley. A young woman ran past him, crying and adjusting her clothing. He peered into the gloom and, as his eyes adjusted to the darkness, observed a fistfight in full swing. There was more than one Irish voice among the cursing and shouting. Winter heard the word *goombah*, though he had no idea what it meant. The fight was three against one, but the three were worse for drink and the one was holding his own, until a blow from behind knocked him to the ground. Now they were kicking him mercilessly and Winter decided he could not stand idly by and allow them to kill their quarry. He strolled into the alley as casually as he could and mustered up his best Dublin accent.

'Now then lads, I've just seen a copper along the street. You'd best be away outta here.'

'Go way, yer langer! Dis is no business of yours.'

'Ah come on now, lads, that's no way to talk to someone who's trying to keep you out of trouble, now is it?'

At that, the largest of the three youths walked menacingly towards Winter and threw a wild punch. He ducked underneath it and landed an uppercut that stopped the lad in his tracks, followed by a right hook that laid him unconscious on his back. Seeing his friend on the ground, the second assailant aimed a kick at Winter, who grabbed his ankle and twisted hard, making him yelp with pain. Holding onto his leg, he drove him backwards into a brick wall and watched him sink to the floor.

'Attento!' The warning came from the target of the original attack.

Just in time, Winter turned to see the third attacker coming at him with a knife. He moved inside the lad's thrust, catching his wrist with his left hand and his elbow with his right. Raising his right arm so that his elbow was locked in front of him, he lifted him straight up into the air. The elbow gave way with a sickening snap, and the unfortunate youth screamed in agony. He staggered off into the night, his anguished cries reverberating from the alley walls.

'Are you alright there?' said Winter, offering a hand to the Italian and helping him to his feet. He could see that they were about the same age.

They shook hands and his new acquaintance said, *'Mi chiamo Nico.'*

'Micky who?'

'What? No ..., my name is Nico.'

'Pleased to meet you Nico. I'm Kevin. Kevin Winter.' He had dropped the Irish accent.

'You're English? Well, we're in the wrong part of town, so we better get outta here! *Andiamo!* I was doin' fine on my own you know.'

'I could see that. They were definitely starting to tire.' They both laughed.

'Where d'you learn to fight like that?'

Thinking about Jem Mace, a wry grin spread across Winter's face.

'The circus,' he replied.

On that hot, summer's night in New York, Winter could not have imagined the impact his actions were to have on his future. Nico Varese parted company with him outside his hotel and he never expected to see him again, but the following day, a knock on the door would change everything. Standing there was a tough looking, middle-aged man. Winter thought he had been tracked down by his adversaries from the night before.

'Can I help you?' he asked, trying not to sound nervous.

'Your name Winter?'

'Who wants to know?'

'*Ciao*, Kevin!' cried Nico, stepping out from behind the older man, who now had a broad grin on his face.

'I'm Nico's father, Moe,' he said. 'How yer doin,' kid?'

'Pleased to meet you, sir.'

'I wanna thank you for lookin' after my boy.'

'Papa!' protested his son.

'Nico tells me you're lookin' for work. How'd you like to work for me?'

By earning the gratitude of a New Jersey hood, Winter had unwittingly changed his life. From being a stranger in a foreign land with no money, he now had the offer of a job.

'What would I have to do?'

'Just run a few errands to start with. We'll see how it goes. You can stay with us until you find a place of your own.'

It didn't take him long to figure out that the job was anything but legal. It didn't matter to him, because for the first time in his short life, he felt a sense of belonging. Apart from the killings, he was soon doing the same work as Moe's other soldiers and within a few short months, he was one of his most trusted men.

In his first few years in New Jersey, he progressed quickly from running errands to money collection and the occasional robbery or kidnapping, alongside Nico and a couple of more experienced soldiers. His *caporegime*, Tony Insalaco, was a squat man with little hair and no discernible neck. He took Winter under his wing and taught him what it meant to be a mafia associate. There was an unwritten but unbreakable code of conduct that all associates had to obey in order to survive.

'Follow the rules and you'll do just fine, kid,' he said. 'Always treat the people you work for with respect. The same goes for the wives. Look at one of them the wrong way and you're in deep trouble. Oh, and stay away from the cops. Even being seen with one could get you killed.'

Winter heard stories about drive-by shootings that had gone wrong, often resulting in the deaths of innocent bystanders. The perpetrators didn't know who they were working for, so the police were never able to link them to the Vareses, but Winter thought there was a more effective and less risky way to eliminate your enemies. He acquired a Springfield rifle and practised with it day and night, until he was an expert marksman. Insalaco recognised his abilities and sanctioned his first hit, a local politician who was starting to become a problem. As he was leaving his house, Winter shot him from a distance of more than four hundred yards. He had made his bones, and several such killings would follow, but despite a growing reputation as a reliable assassin, he could never rise above the rank of associate, due to a lack of Italian blood.

By the turn of the century, the Vareses had forged links with an Irish republican organisation known as *Clan na Gael*. They were an American offshoot of the Irish Republican Brotherhood, a secret organisation dedicated to the establishment of an independent, democratic republic in Ireland. Moe saw a business opportunity, supplying them with arms for use in the fight against the British, but he wanted a man on the ground in Ireland who could be relied upon. Winter was the obvious choice. As Moe's man in the British Isles, he earned more money than he could ever have dreamed of, and spent much of it on wine, women and song.

2

Kirk Allerton, Yorkshire
October 1899

In the north-west of England, Ellen, the wife of George Driscoll, Lord of the Manor of Kirk Allerton and a wealthy millowner, gave birth to twin boys at home. Set in twelve acres of land that straddled the border between Lancashire and Yorkshire on the outskirts of the village, home was Allerton Manor, an imposing Georgian manor house, where six generations of the Driscoll family had lived since Benjamin Driscoll built a water-powered mill at Welbeck in 1747. The family were well respected in Kirk Allerton for their philanthropy, most notably through the funding of Driscoll Cottage Hospital, named after Henry, George's late father.

Alfie Driscoll was older than his brother James by twenty minutes. Their mother doted on them and spent every waking minute talking and reading to the boys when they were very young. It soon became apparent that both children were gifted and, as they developed, it seemed as if they were trying to outdo each other at every stage of their young lives. Alfie spoke his first words at four months and James followed suit a week later. James walked at six months, Alfie at seven. Alfie played the piano at three years old, and James began to read at the same age. At five, James could write and had a large vocabulary, while Alfie was good at arithmetic and beat his mother at chess for the first time. James became interested in science and could name the major constellations at six years old.

Ellen was immensely proud of both her boys but frustrated that their father seemed oblivious to their talents. George spent so much time at work that he really didn't have time for family matters, although, as a gifted pianist himself, he allowed Alfie to play duets with him. It was not something that his son enjoyed, as his father would scold him whenever he made a mistake.

In the early years of the twentieth century, Europe was in political turmoil. The Ottoman Empire had lost territory to Russia, France and Italy, and seen several nations gain independence or autonomy. Russia had strong ties with France and formed a military alliance to counteract the perceived threat from the Austro-Hungarian Empire, which was also in decline. To protect themselves against future attack, Austria-Hungary formed a Triple Alliance with Germany and Italy.

The British Empire was the largest in history and Britannia ruled the waves. In Germany, the envious Kaiser made plans to build a navy capable of challenging the British. Aware of the German threat, Britain formed a Triple Entente with Russia and France in 1907. It was widely accepted that such alliances were necessary for the preservation of peace in Europe. To the Driscolls, living in a place that felt like heaven on earth, and with a business that was booming, life was perfect and there was no indication that things would ever change.

When the boys were five years old, Albert Einstein, a lowly patents clerk in Switzerland, published four papers in the scientific journal, *Annalen der Physik.* They would become the foundation stones of modern physics and included his special theory of relativity, which changed the scientific community's understanding of space, time, mass and energy forever. The papers were so revolutionary that 1905 became known as Einstein's *annus mirabilis,* or miracle year. James Driscoll would not learn about his theories for several years, but they were destined to shape the course of his life.

Welbeck, Yorkshire
August 1907

James thought his lungs were going to burst as he fought frantically to reach the surface. He was starting to lose the fight when strong hands reached down and pulled him out of the river. He caught sight of Alfie's limp body being tossed and turned in the turbulent water a short distance away, his jaw broken and his face a bloody mask.

Ten minutes earlier, the boys had been sitting on the hillside, basking in the summer sun and looking down upon the huge, red brick building on the opposite side of the river. Their father George owned the Welbeck cotton mill, as had his father and his father before him.

'Do you think mummy's going to be all right?' asked James.

'She'll be fine. People break bones all the time'.

The boys had just returned home from a week with their mother Ellen at their grandparents' guest house on the Welsh coast. The holiday was cut short when Ellen tripped and fell, breaking her ankle. George sent his chauffeur Ralph to bring them home, but there was no one to look after them. Accompanying their father to work was an adventure, but the boys soon became bored sitting in an empty office. It was too noisy and dusty for them to stay inside on such a warm day, so George had sent them out to play, with strict instructions to stay away from the river.

Alfie got to his feet. 'Can't catch me, Jimmy' he laughed as he ran off up the hill. Never happy to let his older brother get the better of him, James was on his feet and after him in a flash. Alfie veered off the track to his left and, with James in hot pursuit, doubled back on himself, scampering towards the riverbank at the bottom. The track became steeper, and he had to lean back and dig his heels in to slow himself down. Behind him, caught up in the chase, James failed to spot the danger until it was too late. He let out a frantic cry as he lost his balance and tumbled head over heels down the hill, past Alfie and into the swirling waters below.

The Thurwell, as it reached the foot of the Pennines, was a dangerous stretch of river. It was the very reason the Driscoll mill had been built there long ago, when its main source of power was the water wheel that now stood silent and still.

Without hesitation, Alfie dived in to save his twin, only seeing the submerged rock as his body broke the surface of the water. He felt a sudden, agonising pain and saw a flash of red as his chin took the brunt of the impact, before he mercifully lost consciousness.

James was convinced that his brother was dead as he watched his body being lifted from the water and placed face down on the ground. As luck would have it, one of the millworkers had seen an artificial respiration technique being used when his niece almost drowned in a water-filled quarry a year earlier. James watched transfixed as the man knelt astride Alfie's lifeless body and started to apply pressure to the lower part of his chest. Within a couple of minutes, he coughed and brought up a large quantity of water, gradually regaining consciousness as his father arrived breathlessly on the scene. Later, in a Manchester hospital, his jaw was realigned and fixed in place with a wire ligature. The procedure was so skilfully carried out that the only lasting sign of his accident was a crescent-shaped scar under his chin. Although James was uninjured, the incident left him with a morbid fear of water.

In the summer of 1910, George returned from a business trip to America on the RMS *Mauretania*, bringing with him a telescope that James had seen advertised in *The Astronomical Journal*. He used it to observe and document the arrival of Halley's Comet, which he calculated was travelling at more than 150,000 miles per hour. George was impressed when he subsequently read the same figure in *The Times*.

Later that year, the twins were sent to Egglescombe, an independent, fee-paying boarding school for boys. It was located on the outskirts of the village of the same name, not far from Burnley, a large Lancashire cotton town. There, they shared a dormitory with two boys named Freddie and Harry. At the end of their first week at the school, James paid a visit to the village shop. On his way there, he noticed a group of six local lads in a field to his right. They were a year or two older than James and were amusing themselves by throwing stones at a stray dog. Before he could react, he saw Freddie charge into the middle of the group, knocking one of them over. Unsurprisingly, he was then set upon by the lad's mates. James saw Freddie's spectacles go flying as he curled up in a ball on the ground, trying to protect himself from the kicks and punches that were raining in on all sides. James sprinted towards the melee and yelled at them to stop. Although they were older, he was tall and well-built for an eleven-year-old, and his arrival made all but one of them scatter, despite their superior numbers. His sole adversary threw a wild punch that missed James by a foot, before being winded by a punch to the stomach that made him stagger off in the same direction as his mates.

James helped Freddie to his feet and gave him a handkerchief to stem the blood that was flowing freely from his damaged nose. 'That was very brave of you,' he said.

'Or stupid,' he replied, 'but that poor dog wasn't hurting anyone, and I can't stand cruelty to animals.'

'Still, it took guts to do what you did.'

Freddie squinted at him and said, 'Have you seen my glasses? I'm blind without them.'

James found them in the long grass and handed them to him. The lenses were thick and round, and when Freddie put them on, they gave him an owl-like appearance.

'Thanks for saving my bacon,' he said.

'I didn't do much,' said James, 'but I've found that bullies aren't that brave when you stand up to them. Talking of bacon, are you hungry?'

'Starving!' said Freddie. 'I was on my way to the sandwich shop in the village.'

'I'd better come with you, then, just in case those lads come back.'

Freddie Taylor was seven months younger than James, and might have remained a casual acquaintance, had it not been for his appearance, which made him an obvious target for school bullies. James liked the fact that he never backed down in front of them. On one occasion, he overheard him dealing with a particularly annoying thorn in his side.

'Someone told me you're the happiest kid in the school, on account of ignorance being bliss and all that,' he said. Unfortunately, when the bully realised it was an insult, he hit him. James made sure it wouldn't happen again by sitting next to Freddie in class. It was the start of an unlikely friendship. James excelled at sport and was academically brilliant. He loved science and literature, which explained his love of science-fiction. Freddie was the complete opposite, although he enjoyed football and cricket, if only as a spectator, and was good at mathematics.

The Driscolls' other roommate was a boy by the name of Harry Milburn, a mine owner's son from the Weardale Valley in County Durham. Harry shared James' interest in science, and they soon became firm friends. James was fascinated by an ornament that Harry used as a paperweight. It looked as if someone had taken a pile of bright green, transparent glass cubes and squashed them into one big lump.

'Where did you get that?' asked James when he saw it on the desk one morning.

'From my dad,' replied Harry. 'They call it fluorite. It's from one of the mines up where I live. They use it to make iron.'

'It looks amazing,' said James.

'If you think that's amazing, watch this,' said Harry. He opened the curtains, and light flooded into the room. James had heard of fluorescence, but he'd never seen it before. He watched, spellbound, as the crystal began to change colour from green to bright purple.

'Wow!' said James, who wanted to know how something so astoundingly beautiful could simply be lying in the ground, waiting for someone to dig it up. His interest in crystals would endure for the rest of his life.

3

Dublin, Ireland
April 1912

After more than twenty years working for the Vareses, Winter was as busy as ever, running guns between New York and Dublin. Just before Easter, he arrived in the Irish capital with the latest cache of weapons, destined for delivery to his Irish nationalist contacts. He checked into a hotel for the night, before crossing the river and heading south in search of refreshment. One of his favourite haunts was The Long Hall pub, where an impromptu group of musicians was playing Irish fiddle music. It was getting late, and he was thinking of heading back to his hotel when the band struck up again, accompanying a young woman who sang a poignant Irish ballad. Admittedly he'd had a few drinks, but he thought her voice was the most beautiful thing he had ever heard. Before she left, he persuaded her to let him buy her a drink.

Maureen O'Neill was an innocent but spirited Catholic girl of eighteen, whose parents had been taken by tuberculosis in 1911, leaving her with nothing but their cottage in Tullybay, on the Donegal coast.

'Where did you learn to sing like that?' asked Winter.

'I don't remember,' she said. 'My daddy said I was born singing and dancing.'

'You've never had any lessons?'

'No, but I sing in a musical society back in Donegal. Why do you ask?'

'Because with a voice like yours, you could make a career out of singing.'

'Ah, get away with you,' she replied. 'What are you after?'

'Nothing, I swear, but I know people in this city, and you could really go places.'

'Do you think so? I just like singing.'

'I tell you what, let me make some enquiries. I'll see you back here tomorrow night. What do you say? You won't regret it, I promise.'

'What have I got to lose? I'll be here anyway,' she said.

The following evening, Winter kept his promise. He had secured her an audition for regular paid work, singing in one of the swankier bars in the city centre. To help her in the short-term, he gave her money for food and clothes. She was dazzled by his wealth and charm, and despite the twenty-year difference in their ages, they had a steamy, short-lived affair.

Maureen was the reason that he failed to arrive in Queenstown until the afternoon of the eleventh of April, just in time to see the RMS *Titanic* disappearing over the distant horizon. He left Ireland the following day on its sister ship, the RMS *Celtic*, and only discovered how close he had come to death when he arrived in New York to learn that the great liner had sunk on its maiden voyage. Maureen O'Neill had unwittingly saved his life. She had also fallen in love with him, but his constant travelling took him away for weeks at a time. In the end, she became tired of waiting and they drifted apart.

Across Europe, the nineteenth century had been relatively peaceful, and the expectation was that nothing much would change. In 1912, the wars that broke out between the Ottoman Empire, Greece, Serbia, Montenegro and Bulgaria were not expected to spread outside the Balkans. Britain had reaped the benefits of the industrial and scientific revolutions, and Sir Edward Grey, its Foreign Minister, believed that the nation was, "entering a period of calm, and again, continued progress and prosperity."

Winter did not share that view. In April 1914, he entered Wynn's Hotel on Abbey Street in Dublin, where he was due to see a man about some guns. For the past ten years he had operated a legitimate import-export business in Ireland, a cover for the illicit distribution of guns, alcohol and just about anything else that made money for the Vareses. In the main, the people he dealt with were Irish nationalists, committed to the defence of Ireland against British rule. Wisely, in his line of work, he had adopted an Irish accent rather than his native Liverpudlian tongue.

He first saw her in the hotel foyer, struggling with her bags. When he went to her assistance, she smiled warmly at him, and something unspoken passed between them. The look on her face told him that she liked what she saw. Nico sometimes used the phrase 'kiss-me-eyes,' but until that moment, Winter hadn't fully appreciated its meaning. He guessed that she was in her late thirties, a few years younger than him. Over a drink, he discovered that her name was Sinéad, and she was there for the first meeting of the Irishwomen's Council, an Irish republican paramilitary organisation that was prepared to use force to achieve its aims. He was a sucker for a southern Irish accent which, together with lush brown hair that cascaded down onto her shoulders, a fiery temper and those eyes, made her irresistible. It was no surprise that they ended up in bed together before the night was out.

It was the start of a tempestuous love affair that suited them both. There were no awkward questions about who the other one was seeing, nor any expectation of long-term commitment, and they would meet up whenever they were both in Dublin, with no strings attached.

In June, the assassination of Archduke Franz Ferdinand of Austria by a Bosnian Serb set in motion a chain of events that resulted in the First World War. As a result of historic alliances, Germany found itself doing battle with Russia and France. Britain was under pressure to take sides, because of its naval agreement with France and a long-standing commitment to safeguard Belgium's neutrality. Although many were still fighting for its independence, Ireland was British, and many Irishmen went to war. Winter knew that if he ever took up arms, it would be for his father's homeland.

The Oval Bar, just along the street from Wynn's Hotel, was one of the most popular public houses in Dublin. It was a favourite haunt of Abbey Street journalists and the Irish Republican Brotherhood, who could meet there without causing suspicion. One day in July, Winter entered the bar, absent-mindedly patting his jacket pocket to make sure the gun was still there. Moving slowly through the lunchtime throng, he scanned the sea of faces until he saw him, sitting with his back to the wall at the far end of the bar. He moved to within six feet of him before their eyes met.

'How are yer, Martin?' he shouted. 'Can I buy you a Guinness?'

Martin McKenna, his contact for the supply of weapons, nodded impassively. Winter took two pints of the black stuff over to McKenna's table and sat next to him, facing the room. The Irishman regarded him menacingly. 'You're late! Where are they?'

'There was a mighty storm, Martin. You must have read about it. The ship ran aground in Cork harbour and its cargo washed ashore. By the time my men got there, the local Gardai were everywhere. We're gonna have to shut it down and look for another route.'

'How long's that gonna take?'

'Who knows?' said Winter. 'It took months to set up last time.'

'Ah feck! We need those guns,' said McKenna angrily.

'Keep it down, will you?' said Winter in a low voice. 'You don't know who's listening.'

'You'd better not be messin' with me,' he replied. 'Now, drink up. There's someone wants to meet you.'

McKenna led the way to an upstairs room, its only occupant a frail-looking, middle-aged man with very little hair, other than a thick, unruly moustache. He was reading a copy of the *Irish Worker*. The man turned and looked Winter in the eye.

'This is Tom Clarke,' said McKenna. Winter knew of the Irish Republican's reputation as a fierce revolutionary leader in the fight against English rule, but he would never have guessed it from his appearance.

'A pleasure to meet you, Mr Clarke.'

'Mr Winter. Take a seat. You can leave us now, Martin.'

Once McKenna had left the room, he continued. 'I have a proposition for you, if you're interested.'

'What sort of proposition?'

'One that could earn you a lot of money.'

'Tell me more,' said Winter.

'I've been talking to a man called Franz Kuhle. He's a senior officer in the German navy and he wants to recruit agents to provide information on the movement of British ships and troops.'

'Spies? What made you think of me?' asked Winter.

'I can't think of anyone who's better qualified, Mr Winter, or should I say Mr Schmidt?'

He raised an eyebrow. 'The name's Winter and I'm Irish, Mr Clarke.'

'Now, if that were true, we would not be having this conversation. I know more about you than you think.'

Winter stared at him and held his gaze for several seconds. There was something in Clarke's manner that hinted at an iron resolve, and it was Winter who blinked first. Looking down at the floor, he dropped the Irish accent and said, 'Your information is very good, Mr Clarke, but I go by the name Winter now.'

'Very well. This could make you a rich man, Mr Winter.'

'I'm listening.'

'There's a war coming, and Germany has very little information on what the British are up to. Herr Kuhle is offering a large sum of money to someone who can establish a network of spies in Britain.'

'How much money?' asked Winter.

Clarke handed him a piece of paper. Winter glanced at it and whistled softly under his breath.

'What would I have to do?' he asked.

'Recruit other spies, train them and give them the equipment they need.'

'I wouldn't know where to start,' said Winter.

'That's why you're booked on a ferry to Liverpool tomorrow,' said Clarke, pushing a folder across the table.

Winter examined the contents of the folder. It contained tickets for the following night's sailing to Liverpool and a ferry timetable for the Hull to Hamburg ferry, together with contact details for a location in the German city, where he would meet a man known simply as *Herr Doktor*.

He turned his attention back to Clarke, saying, 'I'm sorry, what does this have to do with my associates in America?'

'I wondered how long it would take you to ask that,' said Clarke. 'War is coming, Mr Winter, and neither side is prepared for it. They don't have enough shells, because they don't have enough cordite, and they don't have enough cordite because they don't have enough acetone.'

'I'm afraid I don't follow,' said Winter.

'I happen to know through my friends at Trinity College that a solution is brewing, literally.'

Winter had no idea what Clarke was talking about. 'You've lost me,' he said.

'Synthetic acetone, produced by fermentation. A process very similar to the way we brew beer. Scientists are working on it in Manchester, but right now their own government has no idea. Once they find out, they will take control of the process and our opportunity will have gone. It will give them an advantage in the war, but one they will struggle to press home.'

'Why's that?'

'Because the process requires large quantities of raw materials such as starch. The British don't have nearly enough, but the Yanks do. With your help, our friends in America are going into the acetone business, Mr Winter. They just need you to supply them with the process.'

'Why would I want to help them help the British?'

'You wouldn't, and neither would I. They're going to sell it to the Germans.'

Clarke's words hung in the air. Winter enjoyed the irony of the British nation losing a war through the deeds of its own scientists. 'So, let me get this straight. On my way to Hamburg, you want me to break into a laboratory in Manchester and steal the process?'

'Not quite,' said Clarke. 'One of Martin's men is in Manchester now, talking to a man who's prepared to steal the process.' Taking an envelope from his jacket pocket, he handed it to Winter. 'Your instructions are in there. You'll be in Hamburg for a week, returning via Manchester. By the time you get there, everything should be arranged. Our thief wants four grand, which will be wired to your account by Mr Varese. You're going to give it to him in exchange for the process. All you have to do is get it and take it to Nico.'

'What's in it for me?' asked Winter.

'That depends on your powers of persuasion. When you've paid him, whatever's left is yours.'

'Alright, I'll do it.'

'Very good. Get yourself away now, and when you see your family, tell them to get the hell out of England. Your kind will not be welcome when British soldiers start dying.'

That evening, Winter met up with Sinéad. He'd had many casual relationships with attractive women, most of whom wanted more than he could give. Sinéad was different, and in the short time they had known each other, they'd become friends as well as lovers. He had to admit that he could imagine settling down with her one day, but when she revealed that her brother's name was Martin McKenna and he was in town looking for guns, Winter turned down her invitation to meet him for a drink. Martin already thought that Winter had screwed him. The news that he had done the same to his sister might not go down too well.

4

Hamburg, Germany
July 1914

While in Hamburg, Winter was taught radio communications, codes, ciphers and sabotage techniques. He took to espionage like a duck to water and returned to Britain with all the skills and equipment needed to spy for Imperial Germany.

In Manchester, he woke to the news that Great Britain had declared war on Germany, following its refusal to remove troops from Belgium. He stood at his hotel window, drawing heavily on a cigarette as he looked out across the grimy, grey city. Well before the appointed hour, he was sitting in a corner of the coffee lounge in the Victoria Hotel. From his vantage point, he could see everyone who entered the room. His contact had been instructed to carry a green bag and walk to the centre of the room. At a minute to eleven, there he was, a tall man with a green bag, sporting a beard, moustache and spectacles, eyes darting around the room nervously. Winter smiled at a disguise so obviously false that others might well notice. He waited to make sure the man had not been followed, before walking across to greet him.

'Try to act naturally,' he said as they shook hands. 'Pretend we're old friends.' The man followed him back to his table and they sat down.

'Do you have the money?' he asked.

'I have a gun,' replied Winter, 'and a thousand pounds in my pocket. I advise you to take the money.'

Anger flashed in the man's eyes. 'The deal was four thousand. I need that money.'

'Why? Do you owe people, pal, or are you just being greedy?'

'I'm not your pal, and that's none of your business! I'm taking a huge risk here. Three thousand is as low as I'll go.'

'I'm sorry, the best I can do is two. Take it or leave it.'

'I'll leave it, thanks. If that's the best you can do, this meeting is over.' He rose from his seat, adding, 'You've wasted your time. I'll bid you good day, sir.'

'Two and a half.'

He sat down again. Winter took five rolls of money from his pocket and placed them on the table. Checking that no one was looking, the man took each one and checked it before dropping it into his bag. Taking out an envelope, he pushed it across the table.

'Everything you need is in there, but as I told your friend, the process has not been perfected yet. Do I have your word that this is not going to fall into the wrong hands?'

'No, you don't. That's a question you really should have asked before we agreed a price. But, seeing as I like you, I can tell you that it will aid the war effort. Good day to you, sir.'

The man remained in his seat until well after Winter had left. Although he knew it was wrong, he had convinced himself that no one would be hurt by his actions. Still, from the moment he agreed to sell his employer's fermentation process, he couldn't sleep for fear of being caught. Had he known his treachery was going to help the enemy, he would not have been able to live with himself. Never before had he done anything remotely illegal and now the deed was done, he could not stop shaking from a mixture of fear and exhilaration. Once he had calmed down sufficiently, he left the hotel and hurried off in the direction of his bank.

His mission accomplished, Winter headed for Liverpool. His father Jürgen had lived on his own in a small apartment above his shop, ever since his wife left him. She had pleaded with him to take her back when her lover disappeared without a word in the late eighties, but he never forgave her.

'*Verschmutzte Ware*,' he would say. 'Soiled goods.'

He was overjoyed to see his eldest boy after such a long time. Winter raised the subject of leaving England, but his father would not hear of it.

'I have a life here, Son. Good friends, loyal customers, why would I want to leave?'

'Things are changing, *Vati*.'

'I can look after myself, don't you worry.'

That evening, Winter found his younger brother Dieter in a more receptive mood.

'Everything's different,' he said. 'I can see it in their eyes. The way they look at me, people I've known for years.'

Dieter and his father had a German surname, displayed prominently above each of their shops. Schmidt's German Butchers were well known in Liverpool.

'Ailbhe said Esther was bullied in the street yesterday. I don't want that for my girls. There's already talk of internment for known German troublemakers, and I don't exactly get on well with the police.'

'That's because you keep getting drunk and punching them!'

'Maybe, but I want you to make me a promise. If the worst happens, will you take Ailbhe and the girls to Ireland?'

'Yes, of course. I have a place on the west coast where they'll be safe, but let's hope it doesn't come to that. I have some business to take care of in America, but I'll be back in two or three weeks. Let's see how things look then.'

New York City

A quarter of a century after Winter first set foot in New York, he was back and this time he'd planned to travel first-class. He was hugely disappointed to discover that the SS *Philadelphia* had downgraded its passenger accommodation. In Hoboken, he met with his old friend Nico and handed over the documents.

'What's the deal?' said Winter. 'How're you gonna get this stuff to Germany. You know there's a naval blockade in place?'

With a mischievous grin on his face, Nico replied, 'There's ways round a blockade, or should I say under?'

'Submarines?'

'*Si*. We gotta place in Florida, but that don't concern you. Listen, Papa asked me to give you something.' Reaching into a desk drawer, he pulled out an envelope and handed it to his friend.

'Thanks, Nico,' said Winter, pocketing the envelope without opening it.

'Now, get yourself back across the pond while you still can.'

Later, in his hotel room, Winter opened the envelope to find a wad of pristine hundred-dollar bills, wrapped in a bill strap, on which was written, "Well done, kid." He counted them out, one hundred images of Benjamin Franklin. It was more money than he had ever seen in his life. Spreading the notes out on the bed, he laughed aloud as he rolled around on them. For several days, he forgot all about home, becoming a rich tourist with a stylish new wardrobe and a beautiful woman on each arm, courtesy of Nico. After war was declared in England, news came that the government had passed the Aliens Restriction Act, condemning 'troublesome' Germans to internment for the duration of the war. It was time to go home and keep his promise to Dieter.

Liverpool, Lancashire
August 1914

When he arrived back in England, his father Jürgen confirmed his worst fears.

'They made us register as German,' he said. 'Before we could leave, they took Dieter into another room and that's the last we saw of him. I was told he's in a camp at Handforth. I've asked Ailbhe to move in here with the children, but she's not keen.'

'That's okay, I promised Dieter that if anything happened, I would take them to Ireland where they'll be safe. I think you should come too.'

'I've already told you, I'm not going anywhere. If Ailbhe leaves, she'll lose the shop. How will she manage?'

'I'll take care of it, *Vati*.'

Winter told Ailbhe to pack and be ready to leave in a couple of days. He secured Dieter's butcher's shop, took down the sign, and boarded up the windows. Having paid the land agent a year's rent in the hope the war would soon be over, they said goodbye to Jürgen.

'If things get too bad, come to Ireland,' said Winter.

'I'll be fine, *mein sohn*,' said Jürgen. Something in the tone of his voice told Winter that the discussion was at an end, but he could tell that his father was worried.

'Take care, *Vati*.'

'And you take care of my granddaughters for me.'

Egglescombe, Lancashire
September 1914

When the Driscoll twins returned to school that autumn, the war was the main topic of conversation, for the first week at least. Most boys were excited about it, reflecting the wave of nationalist fervour that was sweeping the nation. No bad news had been reported yet, so they were unaware of the early German successes at Mons and the river

Marne. In October and November, more than 200,000 soldiers were killed or injured while the opposing armies fought themselves to a standstill at Ypres.

Had they known all this, Alfie and his friends Tommy and Stan might not have been quite so keen to do what they did next. They were all members of Burnley Boys Club and in November, they saw a poster of Field-Marshal Lord Kitchener, resplendent in dress uniform and handlebar moustache, sternly pointing a finger above the words "Your Country Needs You." It seemed to be aimed directly at Alfie, and he left that weekend, never to return.

James was handed a note, left with the school porter by his brother. It explained that he had gone home to ask for his father's permission to join the Burnley Pals, a volunteer battalion. He apologised for not telling James, but he knew that he would have tried to stop him. He ended by saying that he would not be gone long, as he was sure the war would be over by the spring.

James was furious when he realised that his father had allowed Alfie to join up at the tender age of fifteen. He would never have done the same, as he thought war was wrong and his conscience would not allow him to take anyone's life. He feared for Alfie's safety and did not share his confidence that the war would be brief.

By the spring, it became clear that James' pessimism was justified. Early German successes had faltered in Belgium and France, resulting in trench warfare that would continue for years. The war was not going to be over quickly.

5

New York City
April 1915

Winter returned to neutral America, but this time he travelled in style, sharing a first-class suite on the RMS *Lusitania*, the pride of the Cunard fleet, with a girl he referred to as Mrs Winter.

He had lost touch with Maureen O'Neill after their fling in Dublin. He might never have seen her again had he not discovered, through his rebel contacts, that she was on the run after witnessing the murder of a Garda officer. Winter managed to find her before anyone else. To save her life, he hid her for several months at a remote location near Glendalough in the Wicklow Mountains.

They rekindled their relationship there but, as time went by, she became more and more disenchanted with her sanctuary. Winter would come and go, leaving her alone for weeks on end, so it felt more like a prison to Maureen. He spent a lot of time in Dublin, much of it with Sinéad, secure in the knowledge that Maureen was safe, albeit unhappy. He knew what would happen to her if she ever tried to return to her previous life, so he hatched a plan to set her free, once and for all. She needed money, so he bought her cottage for a generous sum before putting the word out that she had died from TB. Then, armed with false papers, she posed as his wife on the Atlantic crossing.

In New York, one of Nico's men met them at the dock and drove them to the Waldorf Astoria, where Nico was waiting. Their entrance was met with admiring glances from many of the men in the hotel lobby. Winter was well aware that they were not for him.

'*Ciao*, Kevin!' Nico's greeting raised eyebrows throughout the lobby, but he either didn't notice or didn't care.

The two friends embraced, and Winter said, 'Can I introduce you to my wife, Edith?' He was keeping up the pretence for the benefit of anyone who might be listening. 'Edith, this is Nico, one of my oldest friends.'

'Hello,' she replied coyly.

Nico looked into her eyes, took her hand and kissed it. '*Sei bellissima*, Edith.'

After she had gone to their room to deal with the luggage, Kevin and Nico sat down to talk.

'She's a beautiful girl, Kevin. When did you get married?'

'We didn't,' he whispered. 'Her life was in danger back in Ireland, so I helped her get away. She has papers that say she's Edith Banks, but that's not her real name. She wants to be an actress and a singer. I was hoping you could help her to make a new start over here.'

'*Nessun problema*. We have good contacts here 'n' on the west coast.'

'Thank you. She has no family in Ireland, so I'm putting my trust in you.'

Nico raised his eyebrows in mock innocence. 'Don't worry, I'll look after her.'

'You'd better. Listen, I'm leaving on Saturday. Maybe we could meet up on Friday night?'

'*Ottimo!* I'll be in touch.'

Across the Hudson in Hoboken, Maurizio Varese stood with arms folded, looking down from a sixth-floor window at the majestic sight of the *Lusitania* at its dock.

'Shame,' he murmured.

'Boss?' enquired Fabrizio Lippi, one of his trusted capos.

'*Non importa*. Now, tell me about Florida.'

'We had a few teethin' problems at first, but now it's runnin' smooth as silk. We're almost up to full production 'n' we're shippin' a hundred thousand gallons a quarter. That's a profit of more than half a million dollars a year.'

'Half a million?'

'Yeah. Best thing of all, the feds are none the wiser. We got ten miles of coastline an' a coastguard on the books, so no one ever comes snoopin' around.'

'Good, but we need to make the most of it while we can. See what you can do to increase production.'

'Yes, Boss.'

It was Winter's last evening in New York, and he sat in the hotel bar, drinking whisky with Nico.

'Where is she now?' he asked, referring to Edith.

'I've set her up in a nice little apartment in Manhattan.'

'That's a long way from Hoboken, isn't it?' asked Winter, concerned that she wouldn't know anyone in the big, unfamiliar city.

'Nah, it's only an hour away, but it's just around the corner from the Academy of Dramatic Arts. We know someone who can get her into a class there. If she's good enough, I'm told there's no better place for an actor to learn their craft.'

Winter relaxed a little. He couldn't have asked for more from his friend. 'That sounds perfect, Nico. Thank you. Can you check she's alright from time to time? I don't want to see her get hurt.'

'*Nessun problema.* She's very lucky to have you looking out for her.'

'Yeah, well, she's a good kid, but she's a bit naive. Take good care of her, please.'

'I already said, no problem. Don't worry.'

'Alright, thanks.' Nico seemed to understand how important Edith was to him. 'You should come visit me in England some time,' said Winter.

'Maybe, when the war is over. What time do you leave in the mornin'?'

'Early. *Lusitania* sails at ten and I've got a first-class ticket! I'll have to check out of here by seven at the latest.'

'Leave it to me. I'm gonna stay here tonight, and Papa will take care of the bill. Come on, let's get drunk.'

On the morning that Lusitania sailed for England, Nico, much the worse for wear, was woken by the incessant ringing of the telephone. Eventually, he hauled himself from the couch and walked unsteadily over to the desk.

'Hello.'

'It's me,' said Moe. 'Put the kid on the line.'

Nico shuffled into the bedroom. He returned, saying, 'He must have gone already.'

'*Merda!* You gotta stop him. Tell him not to get on that boat!'

'What's wrong, Papa? And it's a ship, not a boat.'

'What's the difference? Listen, that ship ain't gonna make it. Get down to the docks and tell him to find another ride. One that ain't British!'

Half an hour later, after shoving a wad of cash into the receptionist's hands, Nico jumped into a cab and headed for Pier Fifty-Four. He could see that people were already on board, so he bribed a porter to help him. They found Winter in the first-class lounge, talking to an American couple in a bogus upper-class English accent. Nico decided to play along with the pretence.

'Excuse me, sir. I have a message from the Ambassador that requires your immediate attention.'

Winter was nonplussed, but he excused himself and followed Nico to the promenade deck. 'What's so urgent that it got you out of bed before lunchtime?'

'Papa says it's not safe to travel on British ships anymore.'

'Really? He knows this for a fact?'

Nico unfolded a copy of the *New York Times* and read out a warning notice from the Imperial German Embassy. 'It says "Vessels flying the flag of Great Britain, or of any of her allies, are liable to destruction."'

'They wouldn't dare attack the *Lusitania*, would they?'

'Yes! Listen to this. "Travellers sailing in the war zone on ships of Great Britain or her allies do so at their own risk." If Papa says it's goin' down, it's goin' down, 'n' you don't wanna be on it when it goes.'

'We need to warn people.'

'Fuggedaboudit! You wanna cause a panic? They've read the warnin's, but still they want to board a British ship. We have to leave now.'

In fact, leaving the ship wasn't quite as easy as he thought, due to the large number of passengers transferring onto the *Lusitania* from the RMS *Cameronia*, which had just been requisitioned as a troop ship by the British Admiralty. Eventually, Winter and his luggage made it onto the SS *New York*, and he said his final goodbyes to Nico. The *New York* was a much older, slower ship, but worse than that in Winter's view, it had no first-class accommodation. It did have a comfortable lounge, where he met an elderly lady who looked vaguely familiar. Only when a steward said, 'How are you today, Miss Terry?' did he recognise Ellen Terry, the greatest English actress of the Victorian age. At the last minute, she had given up a complimentary suite on the *Lusitania*. Winter introduced himself, and found her to be friendly and approachable, not at all what he had expected. He remembered thinking how beautiful she had been in her youth. Now in her late sixties, she was still a graceful, striking woman, with a charming smile and a voice that had a soft, almost musical tone.

‘My daughter asked me not to take the *Lusitania*, Mr Winter. The beds on this ship may not be as comfortable, but I suppose, on the whole, they’re preferable to the seabed!’

Winter laughed. ‘Well, despite the warnings, I find it hard to believe that Germany would attack a ship with so many American passengers on board, Miss Terry. All that would do is drag America into the war on Britain’s side.’

‘I hope you’re right. We don’t want another *Titanic* now, do we?’

‘Funny you should say that,’ said Winter as he pulled a card from his inside jacket pocket. It was his unused ticket for the *Titanic*, which he always carried with him for luck.

Ellen Terry stared at it with disbelieving eyes. ‘Where on earth did you get that?’ she said.

‘It’s mine. I missed the boat, thankfully.’

‘Well, aren’t you the lucky one?’ she laughed.

At dinner that evening, a generous tip persuaded the head waiter to seat him at one of the private side tables, rather than in the cafeteria style saloon alongside three hundred other passengers. There he continued his conversation with Ellen Terry.

‘Is there a Mrs Winter at home?’ she enquired.

‘No, but I just left someone in New York who played the part of Mrs Winter very well. She’s going to the Academy of Dramatic Arts to become an actress.

‘How interesting, what’s her name?’

Winter hesitated, almost imperceptibly. ‘Edith Banks.’

‘I have a daughter Edith. She used to be an actress too. Why don’t you give me your friend’s address and I’ll pass on some tips?’

‘That’s most generous of you, Miss Terry, thank you.’

Off the West Coast of Ireland

Although the *New York* was flying an American flag, Winter became nervous as the ship approached the war zone around the British Isles. Due to the ever-present threat of mines and the worry that a careless U-boat captain might make a mistake, he took to wearing a life jacket and spending more time on deck, watching for the tell-tale sign of a periscope. His fears would only have been heightened, had he known of German attacks on more than twenty British-flagged ships since he had left New York.

On its approach to Liverpool, a rumour spread throughout the ship that the *Lusitania* had been attacked and sunk. A handful of senior crew members knew this to be true from radio communications, but they kept the news from the passengers to avoid panic setting in. There was no sign of the great liner at its landing stage. Any hopes that it had already left Liverpool were dashed when the captain called for a minute's silence to allow people to pay their respects to those lost at sea. Winter had narrowly escaped a watery grave for the second time in three years.

It was a sombre group of passengers that disembarked from the *New York* that morning. With a porter leading the way, Winter headed towards a taxi rank, where he took a cab to the Adelphi Hotel. As he waited to check in, he picked up a discarded copy of the previous day's newspaper. The front-page headline confirmed the unthinkable.

DESTRUCTION OF THE LUSITANIA

SUNK OFF IRISH COAST BY GERMAN PIRATES

NO WARNING

1,978 PEOPLE ON BOARD

FEARED LOSS OF OVER 1,400 LIVES

SURVIVORS AT QUEENSTOWN

A shiver ran down his spine at the realisation that, had it not been for Nico, he would probably be dead.

Later that afternoon, he took a cab to Moor Road in Liverpool. He wasn't in the mood for talking, but the driver had other ideas. 'Rum do about Lusi, sir,' he said.

'Who's Lucy?' asked Winter.

'It's what we call ..., sorry, called the *Lusitania*. This is her home port.'

'I know. I switched to another ship at the last minute.'

'You was in America? Well, you're lucky you weren't here last night, sir. There was rioting all over this part of the city.'

'Rioting. Why?'

'Anything German. Shops, anyone with a German name, you name it.'

Winter was astonished. 'Because of the *Lusitania*?'

'Yeah, I heard that someone was killed in Moor Road.'

The colour drained from Winter's face and there was tension in his voice as he asked, 'Who?'

The driver shook his head. 'No idea. All I know is that it happened outside a butcher's shop.'

'Please God, no! Get me there as quick as you can!' cried Winter.

'What's up?' said the cabby, alarmed. 'You think it might be someone you know?'

'Just step on it!'

In Moor Road, a young woman with a pram was standing outside the shop, talking to a policeman. The windows were smashed, and the sign proclaiming "Schmidt's German Butchers" was daubed with red paint. Winter jumped from the cab and ran across the road towards the policeman.

'Now then, sir, you can't come in here.'

'This is my father's shop. Where is he?'

'What's your father's name, sir?'

'Jürgen Schmidt.'

The policeman's demeanour changed. 'You're German?'

'English,' said Winter. 'I was born here.'

'Forgive me. I'm sorry, sir, but your father had an accident last night.'

'Is he alright?'

'No, I'm afraid he died.'

Winter staggered towards the officer, placing a hand on his shoulder to steady himself. 'What sort of accident?'

'There's been trouble in the city since the *Lusitania* was sunk. From what we can tell, your father's shop was targeted by a mob, and he was knocked to the ground.'

'That doesn't sound much like an accident to me.'

'According to his sister, he seemed alright at first, but then he collapsed. He was dead by the time the ambulance arrived.'

Winter bent over, hands on knees, struggling to take in what he was being told. 'Aunt Mitzi was with him?'

'I believe so. She's inside if you want to speak to her.'

Winter went into the shop, which had been completely ransacked. In the back room, his aunt was sweeping up the mess. She burst into tears at the sight of a friendly face, and they hugged each other for several minutes. 'Who did this, Mitzi?'

‘I don’t know, Kevin,’ she sobbed. ‘I recognised one or two faces, but there were too many of them.’

‘What do you mean, you recognised them? Who were they?’

‘Some of them were his customers, but they acted like animals. It was awful.’

Winter was filled with a terrible rage, but he spoke quietly. ‘If you see them again, will you point them out to me?’

‘Why, what are you going to do?’

‘I grew up here. I thought these people were our friends, but I was wrong. Believe me, you don’t wanna know what I’m gonna do.’

The sinking of the Lusitania provoked outrage around the world and turned public opinion against Germany. 128 Americans died, resulting in calls for America to enter the war, which it would have done had Germany not agreed to stop sinking passenger ships without warning.

Without American support, the Allies were losing the war. The Gallipoli campaign, designed not only to capture Constantinople but also to enable Allied ships to sail through the Dardanelles, ended in failure in January 1916 after eleven months. On the Allied side, more than 50,000 men were killed, with another 90,000 missing or wounded. The Ottoman Empire lost even more men and was seriously weakened, but succeeded in defending its land.

6

Physics Department, University of Frankfurt
May 1916

Max von Laue was a professor of theoretical physics at the University of Frankfurt. In 1912, he was responsible for the successful diffraction of x-rays by crystals, for which he would receive the 1914 Nobel Prize for Physics. Two years later, his students were using the same techniques to explore the internal structure of crystals, revealed by the distinctive patterns they left on photographic plates.

Max was preparing to leave at the end of a long day when there was a knock on the door.

'Come in,' he said.

Anna Dransfeld, one of his undergraduates, stood hesitantly in the doorway. 'Good afternoon, Professor, do you have a moment?'

'Of course. Fräulein, how are you settling in?'

'Very well, thank you,' she said nervously. Anna had jumped at the chance to take the place of one of the many male students who'd left university to enlist in the Imperial German Army.

'It's Anna, isn't it?' She nodded and looked sheepishly at the floor. 'Don't be shy, Anna. My students can ask me anything. In this office, there are no stupid questions, only stupid answers, and I promise, I don't bite! Now, what can I do for you?'

She smiled and looked the professor in the eye. 'I fear this may simply be ignorance on my part, but I've been getting some rather strange results from one of the crystals you gave me.'

'Really? Which one?'

'The magdalite, Professor.'

Max was somewhat embarrassed to recall that the specimen had lain forgotten in a box since its discovery in a Bavarian cave six years earlier. He'd only noticed it when looking for a slide rule and, on a whim, had included it with the samples to be analysed by his students.

He gathered his things together and headed for the door. 'Tell me what happened, Anna.' She described an experiment that had been carried out hundreds of times on dozens of different crystals. What she told him stopped him in his tracks.

‘That’s simply not possible, Anna,’ he said. ‘There must have been something wrong with the photographic plate.’

‘That’s what I thought, so I repeated the experiment with a new one. It happened again.’

‘Alright, let’s give it another try, shall we?’ said Max. They returned to the lab, where he checked the apparatus and selected a new plate, from a different batch this time. When he repeated the experiment, Anna saw his bewilderment and knew she had witnessed something very unusual.

Before he left, he said, ‘I’m at a loss to explain this anomaly, Anna, but rest assured, I shall get to the bottom of it.’

By the following weekend, Max was forced to admit defeat. He called Einstein, the only man he thought capable of offering an explanation.

‘Max, my friend, how’s life in Frankfurt?’ asked Einstein.

‘Frustrating, Albert,’ he replied. ‘In fact, that’s why I’m calling. I’m struggling to make sense of the results of an experiment that I’ve performed many times before without any issues, and it’s driving me mad.’ Max told him what he had witnessed.

‘That’s intriguing,’ he replied.

‘Why don’t you come to Berlin and bring the crystal with you?’

‘I wish I could, Albert, but Magda’s having the baby in a few weeks’ time. I can’t leave her.’

‘Alright, then I’ll come to Frankfurt at the end of term.’

‘Thank you, that’s much appreciated.’

Two weeks later, Einstein travelled to Frankfurt. Max described Anna’s experiment and its outcome in detail. ‘Nothing like that has ever happened before, Albert.’

‘And the only difference between that and the previous experiments was the crystal?’ asked Einstein.

‘Correct. What we observed was impossible, yet there must be an explanation.’

‘Yes, there must. Where did the crystal come from?’

‘The Nördlingen caves in Bavaria. We were there several years ago, just after we got married.’

‘That’s the crystal you named after Magda, isn’t it?’ Max nodded. ‘What did you call it?’

‘Magdalite.’

‘Ah, yes. Do you think I might be able to borrow it to carry out my own tests?’

Reluctantly, Max handed over a small box. ‘Please take great care of it, Albert. It’s the only one I have.’

When Einstein returned to Berlin, he left his newspaper behind. Max sat in his living room to read it, although he knew the German press was heavily censored to protect morale. Had the reporting been truthful, he would have been shocked to learn the true level of German losses in Northern France, as the Battle of Verdun entered its fifth month. The same newspaper had described the sinking of the *Lusitania* a year earlier as “an extraordinary success.” Max knew that the huge loss of innocent lives was an escalation that was unlikely to help his nation’s cause in the long run. Like Einstein, he was a pacifist and, almost two years into the war, both men knew too many former colleagues and students who had been killed or were now missing in action.

Pas-de-Calais, France
July 1916

Alfie Driscoll stirred as the sun came up on a dry, bright morning, unsure whether he’d slept at all. The previous evening, the Burnley Pals Battalion had completed a gruelling march towards the constant sound of shellfire. They took shelter in Monk Trench, some distance behind the British front line, where they tried to get some sleep.

Shortly after seven, the Pals were called forward. Alfie and his friends Tommy Bradshaw and Stan Grimes waited anxiously for the order to advance, smoking cigarettes and telling jokes to keep their spirits up. At a little before half past seven, Captain Riley blew his whistle and they were up and over the top, marching forwards through their own front line and beyond into no-man’s land. The Battle of the Somme had begun.

Kirk Allerton, Yorkshire

Later that same day, Alfie’s brother James was the only passenger to leave the train at Allerton Station. He was suffering from a headache that had been bothering him all morning. James was almost seventeen and yet, as far as he could recall, it was the first headache he'd ever had. The bright sunshine was making it worse as he carried his cases up past The Fleece public house and across the bridge over the river that bisected the village. Nestled in the Thurwell Valley, Kirk Allerton was quintessentially English, full of timber-framed, thatched cottages with ivy-clad walls. The bell tower of Holy Trinity Church dominated the skyline as it had for the past three hundred years. A lone horse and cart made its way sedately up the main street. A visitor could have been forgiven for thinking they had travelled back in time, had it not been for the bright red Edwardian postbox, standing incongruously outside the sub-postmaster's house.

He skirted around the village green, waving to some old men who were playing quoits, before turning left into the lane that took him past the church and home to Allerton Manor. It was a house full of happy memories, but without Alfie it was a lot quieter.

James burst through the front door and dropped his cases in the large, imposing atrium, admiring the grand double staircase that led to the galleried balcony above. His mother Ellen stood there with outstretched arms, beaming down at him. He bounded up the stairs two at a time, and she greeted him with a hug.

'My, you've grown.'

'You always say that, Mother,' he replied, but it was true. He was now six feet tall and blessed with a powerful, athletic frame. 'I'm so sorry about Uncle Mike.'

On the last day of May, Ellen Driscoll's brother Michael had been killed at the Battle of Jutland when his ship, HMS *Warrior*, was hit by enemy shellfire. The German Navy had attacked the British fleet in a failed attempt to break its blockade.

Ellen's emotions were still raw, and James' words were all it took to make her cry. Burying her face in a handkerchief, she said, 'Your father's expecting you. He's in his study.'

He grimaced. George Driscoll was a Yorkshireman born and bred, with a reputation as a hard-nosed, straight-talking businessman who did not suffer fools gladly. James had impressed his father with his knowledge of the machinery and processes that turned raw cotton into yarn, yet although he was sure that his youngest son would make a very fine engineer one day, he had never offered him any encouragement or praise. His attitude towards children was that they should be seen and not heard, and James was still intimidated by him.

He loitered outside the study door for a while, wondering how his father was going to react to his latest school report. He knocked nervously.

'Come in,' said George brusquely.

James took a deep breath and opened the door. His father ambled from behind a large mahogany desk and walked across the room towards him.

'Nah then.' It was his stock greeting, and legend had it that he once addressed Edward the Seventh in the same way when attending a Manchester Wool Merchants' Banquet. Father and son shook hands, much too formally for James' liking.

'Sit yourself down,' said George. 'Let's have it.'

James took a seat, pulled a crumpled envelope from his jacket pocket and handed it to his father. Inside was a glowing school report that any parent should have been proud of. James had achieved top marks in every subject, and for good measure, his sporting achievements were impressive. He was naturally talented at most sports, with the notable exception of swimming. At the annual sports day, he became the first boy from his school to run the mile in under four minutes and forty seconds, a record that would not be broken for another twenty years. Unsurprisingly, given several summers spent working on his uncle's farm, he was immensely strong for his age and easily came first in the shot put. He was a member of the school football and cricket teams from the age of fourteen, prompting Mr Heath, his sports master, to tell anyone who would listen that he was good enough to play for Lancashire. On one memorable occasion, he made the mistake of sharing his opinion with George Driscoll.

'Never mind bloody Lancashire, he's almost good enough to play for Yorkshire!'

George grunted and waved the report in James' direction. 'Only to be expected,' he said. 'That's what your brother gave up to fight for his country.' The implied criticism was hardly subtle, and James was summarily dismissed.

Attracted by the smell of freshly baked bread, he wandered into the large kitchen at the rear of the house where his mother was setting the table.

'I'm starving!' he said. A ploughman's lunch was placed on the table in front of him, and he devoured it as he read his brother's latest letter home. After war broke out, Alfie had asked his father's permission to lie about his age and enlist, when only fifteen. George chose not to stand in his way because, even though he had never served a day in his life, he firmly believed that a spell in the army was exactly what his boys needed. Alfie looked older than his years and easily met the height requirement of five feet three inches. His patriotic act marked the end of an idyllic childhood in a part of the world where nothing much ever happened. The Driscoll boys were alike in so many ways, with the notable exception of their views on war. Full of youthful idealism, James believed that killing was simply wrong, whatever the justification. Alfie disagreed, arguing that tyranny could only be defeated by force. He went off to war while James stayed at school, earning his mother's gratitude and his father's contempt. It never occurred to George to ask his wife for her opinion.

Alfie had written the letter in May, but wartime censorship meant that it contained no clues as to his whereabouts. In fact, there was far more information in the local newspaper, which was able to report on the experiences of returning soldiers who had been injured in battle. This was how James had learnt about the massive casualties being incurred in the battle for Verdun, to the east of Paris, where a German offensive had been building since February. He kept this news from his mother and hoped that his brother had been posted elsewhere.

Alfie was able to confirm that he was still with Tommy and Stan, and that where they were wasn't a patch on Yorkshire. The three friends were now a part of Z Company in the 11th Battalion, East Lancashire Regiment.

He asked his brother to pass on his regards to Tommy's sister Molly, if he should happen to see her. James wondered how long it was going to take to break the enemy's resistance. Until Uncle Mike's death, life in rural Yorkshire had seemed a million miles away from the war that raged on three continents, but it felt much closer now.

7

Burnley, Lancashire
July 1916

The letters from the War Office began to arrive towards the end of the month. Along the cobbled streets of Burnley and hundreds of other towns and villages throughout the land, they dropped through the letterboxes of thousands of families. Harold Bradshaw came home from work to find his wife Betty in a terrible state. Their letter contained the dreadful news that their beloved Tommy was missing in action. Like so many other families, the Bradshaws closed their blinds and prayed for the safe return of their son. Harold's daughter Molly went to the town hall every day to look at the casualty lists. No matter how often she looked, there was no mention of Alfie Driscoll, Tommy's best mate and the love of her life.

One evening, Walter Grimes, Harold's next-door neighbour, called in to see him. Betty and Molly stopped folding sheets to listen.

'I thought you'd want to know I've had a letter from our Stan.'

''Ow is 'e?'

'He were shot in t'leg. He'll never play football again, but the doctors have saved his life and hopefully his leg.'

'He'll be coming 'ome then?'

'Aye, but that's not why I'm here. I'm sorry, Harold, but he reckons after getting wounded, he saw your Tommy and Alf fall under fire.'

Betty collapsed onto the sofa and Molly ran from the room in floods of tears. She lay on her bed and clasped Alfie's latest letter to her chest, weeping bitterly for the first boy she had ever truly loved. Tommy had broken his promise to look after him and keep him safe. Her anger turned to anguish as she realised that, for a fleeting moment, she had been angry with her courageous brother.

Official confirmation that Tommy was missing followed at the weekend. Stan's letter home arrived before the letter from the War Office, which was hardly surprising in the circumstances. More than 19,000 British troops were either dead, missing or wounded on the first day of the Battle of the Somme alone. Molly hoped against hope that Tommy and Alfie were among the wounded. The following Sunday, she persuaded her father to take her to see Alfie's family.

She had met them once before and wanted to let them know she was praying for their son. Kirk Allerton was only about twenty miles from Burnley, but the Bradshaws had to take two trains to get there. They arrived at lunchtime on a fine summer's day, walking up through the village to the manor house. There they found Ellen Driscoll watering the flowers in her rose garden. Harold cleared his throat and called across to her.

''Ello, Mrs Driscoll. Me and Molly wanted to say 'ow sorry we were to hear about Alfie.'

For a second or two, Ellen didn't react, but when she realised what Harold had said, the watering can fell from her hand. She staggered and dropped to her knees, and an unearthly wail came from deep within her. Clearly, they'd made a terrible mistake.

'Did you not know?' cried Molly. 'I'm so sorry. 'E were with me brother Tommy when they were shot, but they might still be alive for all we know. We found out Tommy were missing days ago.'

They took the distraught woman inside and sat with her while a kitchen maid made a pot of tea and the housekeeper telephoned George, who was working seven days a week at the mill. James was away playing cricket in a neighbouring village, and nobody seemed to know which one. It was decided to wait and tell him when he got home. Sitting in a kitchen that was larger than the entire ground floor of their terraced house, the Bradshaws tried their best to comfort a weeping Ellen.

George Driscoll was raised in a home devoid of love and affection. As a young boy, he spent as much time as possible in the company of his maternal grandfather, Tom Morgan, a man who was different in every way to his father, and who he adored. When Tom died, George incurred his father's wrath for crying in public, and the need to maintain a stiff upper lip was drummed into him. He could not remember ever seeing his father show any emotion, a trait that was unfortunately passed down from father to son.

When he arrived, Harold and Molly were surprised at how calmly he took the news. He thanked them for coming and arranged for Ralph, his chauffeur, to take them back to Burnley in his Rolls-Royce. He sent the rest of the household staff home until further notice, leaving the Driscolls to wait for news alone. Ellen dreaded having to tell James.

When he returned that evening, George summoned him to his study and informed him in a very matter of fact way that Alfie had been shot and was probably dead. Then he announced that he had work to do and told James to shut the door on his way out. Out of sight of his family, George downed several glasses of malt whisky and broke down in tears.

James was overcome by a mixture of grief and guilt, but he tried to cling to the hope that Alfie was only wounded and would soon be coming home. He lay on a bed in the room they had shared as children. The light from the waning moon highlighted the flower pattern on the curtains, and he remembered how it used to scare his brother, who could see faces where none existed.

James tossed and turned, thinking about the way his father had broken the news to him. Crying had always been frowned upon in this house, but surely today was an exception. Had he no feelings at all? James was tormented by the thought that his father blamed him in some way for what had happened. Would things have been any different if he had been there, alongside his brother? Would they both have been killed? He began to feel angry at his father's reaction. Was that what he wanted? Would he have cried then?

He turned onto his side and sobbed until he had no tears left. All that remained was an empty feeling that left him knotted up inside. He must have dozed off at some point, but he was awake at first light. He got up, dressed quietly, and left the house by a side door. It was a calm, peaceful Sunday morning as he walked down the lane to the village, the silence broken only by the cooing of a pair of wood pigeons in the trees ahead. He sat down on a wooden bench next to the cricket pavilion and watched the sun rise on the far side of the valley, casting long shadows across the village green. In front of the church was a wizened old alder tree, under which he once sat with Alfie while their late uncle scored a century against Scarthwaite, a rival village, before the war. The boys spent the rest of that day recreating his innings while playing their own game behind the pavilion, taking it in turns to 'be' Mike Jackson. Now Alfie was missing, life might never be the same again. James thought about the cruel twist of fate that had befallen his family and cried for the second time that morning, relieved there was no one around to see. For the remainder of the summer, he dropped out of village life altogether, avoiding any contact with other people. The only time he left the house was to go running in the hills, where he could be sure of being alone.

On a rainy day towards the end of July, George was dealing with the post when he came across a letter from the regimental record office. Inside was a pre-printed sheet, overtyped with his son's details. It confirmed that Private A Driscoll was killed in action on July 1st, 1916, "in the field, France." Underneath this appalling news was a message:

> By His Majesty's command I am to forward the enclosed message of sympathy from Their Gracious Majesties the King and Queen. I am at the same time to express the regret of the Army Council at the soldier's death in his Country's service.
>
> I am to add that any information that may be received as to the soldier's burial will be communicated to you in due course. A separate leaflet dealing more fully with this subject is enclosed.

Two days later, another letter arrived. It was handwritten by a Major Carlson of the East Lancashires. It stated that Alfie died bravely in the service of his country and added the Major's sympathies to those of his King and Queen. Enclosed with the letter was a discoloured envelope that had been found on Alfie's body by a member of his battalion. George did not want Ellen to see the bloodstains, so he never told her about it. The dried blood made it difficult to read, but the gist of it was that Alfie hoped he had done his duty and did not regret giving his life for his country in a just cause.

In Burnley, Molly also received a blood-spattered letter, but hers had simply been placed in a fresh envelope. There was no covering letter. She took it to her room and sat on the bed, where she read its heartbreaking contents over and over.

My darling Molly,

What a strange thing it is to be writing this letter, knowing that if you are reading it, I am not coming home and will never see your beautiful face again. I hope I did my duty and did not let anyone down. The days we spent together were some of the happiest of my life. I know you will make someone a wonderful wife one day and have lots of children, but I hope you sometimes think of me. Don't grieve too long for I am in a better place. Know that my last thoughts were of you.

Your Alfie

George and Ellen struggled to deal with their son's loss. George had always liked a drink, but now he drank too much and, when drunk, was bad-tempered and aggressive. Ellen knew to keep out of his way at such times. They married when she was eighteen, but theirs was a marriage of convenience. George wanted an heir, and she was pressured into marrying a wealthy but much older man by her parents.

She blamed herself for allowing Alfie to join up in November 1914, when he was almost three years too young for armed service overseas. At that time the Imperial German Army was five times larger than that of the British. Recruiting officers were turning a blind eye to almost anyone who met the height requirement, especially when the odd half-crown changed hands. Ellen remained silent when George told her that a spell in the army would toughen Alfie up. The war, he said, would be over in a matter of months. The death of her younger brother Mike made her realise just how wrong he was. She had written to the War Office, asking for the return of her sixteen-year-old son, but she was still waiting for a reply. She was tormented by the thought that, if only she had voiced her fears earlier, her darling Alfie might still be alive. She did not sleep much and, when awake, spent hours at a time in his room, untouched since the day he left. The only thing that gave her any comfort was to be alone with her thoughts, amongst his things.

8

Egglescombe, Lancashire
September 1916

The Battle of the Somme cost more than a million British, French and German lives, and the impact on families across Europe was devastating. In communities like Burnley and Accrington, the annihilation of the Pals' battalions amounted to the loss of a whole generation of young men. It was almost impossible to find someone who had not been directly affected in some way, and at the end of it all, the Allied armies had advanced less than seven miles.

A short film about the conflict was being shown in cinemas across the nation. James travelled to Welbeck to see it, and Molly watched it with her father in Burnley. All three were hoping to catch a glimpse of their loved ones. Soldiers were shown leaving the relative safety of their trenches to face the German guns, but there was no way of telling who they were. One poor man fell within seconds, with the camera recording what may have been his final moments for posterity. James didn't think he looked tall enough to be Alfie, but he couldn't watch any more. He was haunted by the image for weeks afterwards.

When the truth began to filter through about British losses, newspapers started publishing daily casualty lists. On this, the first day of term at Egglescombe, the headmaster stood at the front of the hall with a sheet of paper in his hand. He read out a list of former pupils who had either died or were missing in action. It included Alfie Driscoll and Tommy Bradshaw. During that autumn term, James' classmates noticed a significant change in his personality. Gone was the larger than life, outgoing Jimmy, and in his place a sad, introverted loner with little interest in the company of others. He often couldn't sleep but when he did, the nightmares were never far away. In them, he invariably relived the childhood incident when he fell into a river and Alfie nearly died, trying to save his life. Since that day, his fear of water had never left him.

As a child, James had been fascinated by the adventure novels of Alexandre Dumas and Robert Louis Stevenson. His mother instilled in him a love of reading that saw him devour the works of Dickens and Conan Doyle. His favourite story, *Mike* by PG Wodehouse, was about a schoolboy cricketer with the same name as his late uncle, Mike Jackson.

His recent, self-imposed isolation had given him plenty of time to pursue his passion. He was an avid reader of HG Wells and Jules Verne, whose novels transported him to imaginary worlds where he could escape the grim reality of his own life for a while. On a Thursday night in October, he had spent the evening reading *The Time Machine* and went to bed in the early hours. When sleep came, so did the nightmare, but on this occasion, grotesque creatures prevented him from surfacing. They grabbed him by the neck, hair and arms, pulling him downwards. He could feel their teeth nipping at his neck as he struggled and then broke free, slowly crawling out of the water and looking up into Alfie's smiling face. He was beckoning him, saying, 'Come on, you can do it.'

When he woke, it took him a few moments to realise that it had been a dream, and several more to recognise the creatures as Morlocks. Thankfully, they existed only in Wells' imagination, on the printed page and in James' nightmares. He turned onto his back, trying to remember the details of a dream that had already faded, save for Alfie's face and words. The pain of his brother's loss was still raw, a kind of emptiness in the pit of his stomach that never seemed to go away. His imagination conjured up all manner of agonising, lingering deaths, nightmarish visions that would not leave him. He could only hope and pray that his brother's death had been quick and painless.

Fighting back the tears, he sought out the early morning peace and tranquility of the Lancashire fells. He always saved the toughest run for the end of the week, so on that Friday morning, six miles of intense effort brought him to the top of Egglescombe Rigg. He usually found that running helped him to think more clearly and get rid of any negative thoughts, but not today. Today was his seventeenth birthday, but that only served to remind him that it would also have been Alfie's. Looking down on the mist-covered valley below, with a sheer drop in front of him, he thought how easy it would be to jump. One step and all his troubles would be over.

At the last moment, he lost his nerve. What if he survived the fall? He would probably be crippled for life. He took a step back from the edge. Had he really been ready to end it all? There were times when he didn't seem totally in control of his own actions, and it scared him. What would his death have done to his poor mother?

For some reason, the words from his dream came back to him. When he was trying to get out of the water, the meaning of 'you can do it' had seemed obvious. Now, he remembered the idea that came to him while reading *The Time Machine.*

Wells had written about time travel as fiction but, as far as James knew, no one had ever shown it to be impossible. Could someone really go back in time and prevent a disaster? Could he go back and persuade Alfie not to bear arms? Was that what his dream meant? He sat down on a rock and began to think about the possibilities of a world in which he could travel through time. He recalled a quote by the Roman historian, Pliny the Elder, who once posed the question "How many things are looked upon as quite impossible, until they have been actually effected?"

After returning to the valley floor by a more circuitous, but much less deadly route than the one he had contemplated earlier, he went in search of his housemaster. Charles Lucas was James' favourite science teacher, and the only person he felt comfortable discussing the subject of time travel with. Lucas knew that the loss of James' brother had affected him deeply. His schoolwork had suffered, and his behaviour was worrying. He was irritable and prone to aggressive confrontations with other pupils, who now avoided him. When he was fifteen, one of Lucas' colleagues had described James as being "built like a brick outhouse," but that was no longer the case. Although he went running every day, he often skipped meals, so it was not surprising that he had lost weight. Lucas had been wondering whether it was time to seek professional help.

James' teachers had long described him as having an "inquisitive mind" and a "fertile imagination". They hated it when he asked challenging questions in maths and science classes that they were unable to answer. One commented that "James has a tendency to flights of fancy that must be curbed if he is to fulfil his potential." Charles Lucas, however, was not so dismissive. There was something different in the way James thought about the world. In class discussions, he would always be the one to ask, 'Why not?'

When asked about time travel, Lucas said, 'Have you considered the consequences should it ever become possible? Just imagine it! It's something my colleagues and I have discussed.'

'I've only really thought of it as a way of changing the past for the better, sir.'

'That's all well and good, but what if someone went back and met themselves when they were young? What if, by changing something that happened in their past, they set in motion a chain of events that resulted in the death of their younger self? What would happen to that person? Would they cease to exist?'

'If I ever find out, I'll let you know, sir!'

Lucas was tempted to tell James he was wasting his time, but he understood his desire to change the past. 'What do you know of a young German physicist by the name of Albert Einstein?' he asked.

'He wrote *The Theory of Relativity*. I know it's divided opinion among scientists, but that's about all.'

'Well, he seems to be rewriting the laws of physics, and he's written about the possibility of time travel. I think his view was that it's impossible, but why don't you make that the subject of your project for this year? You might be able to find out more in the school library. I should warn you though, anything German may well have been removed by now.'

With Britain at war for almost three years, anti-German feelings were running high. People with German-sounding surnames lived in fear of retribution, and even pets such as dachshunds and German shepherd dogs were not safe. It was a fear that would soon force the Royal Family to change its name from Saxe-Coburg-Gotha to Windsor.

Fortunately, the school librarian had a more enlightened outlook. In the section marked Natural Sciences, James quickly found a pristine copy of a book whose German title translated to *About the special and general relativity theory: (Commonly understood)*. In a matter of weeks, and with the help of his Modern Languages teacher, he translated the entire book into English.

Given the widely held view that Einstein's theories were too complex for most scientists to understand, James was surprised at how much he could grasp. He was fascinated by Einstein's theories and inspired by the elegance of his equations, but if he was right, then the amount of energy required to accelerate an object to the speed of light was so vast as to make time travel impossible for all practical purposes.

One of Einstein's early works looked much more promising. It discussed the possibility of sending faster-than-light signals back in time, something Einstein called a "telegraph to the past." This was not time travel as Wells had imagined it, but transmitting information sounded a lot safer than sending someone into the ether in a time machine. James let his imagination run wild, choosing to ignore the rather fundamental question of whether anything could ever travel faster than light. Other questions occupied his thoughts. If he succeeded in sending a message, who on earth would be there to receive it? If he sent it far enough back to warn of impending doom, might that save Alfie? How far was far enough? He imagined a signal travelling further and further back in time. Would it remain strong or, as he suspected, slowly fade away until it ceased to exist altogether? If there was a limit to how far messages could be sent, then time was of the essence. Alfie died over a year ago and James couldn't bear the thought that he might succeed in his quest, only to find that a warning message could not be sent far enough back in time. His mind was made up and his future was settled. He clearly had an aptitude for science, and becoming an engineer would not bring Alfie back.

9

Frankfurt, Germany
December 1916

It was six months since Einstein had visited the von Laues. One morning, following a sleepless night with a teething baby, Max received a call. Einstein shouted down the line, 'It's solved!'

'Hello, Albert,' he said drowsily. 'What is?'

'The crystal!'

Max was suddenly wide awake, his pulse racing. 'You have an explanation?'

'Yes! A wise man once said, "When you have eliminated the impossible, whatever remains, however improbable, must be the truth."'

'Aristotle?' suggested Max.

'No, Sherlock Holmes. When you said it was impossible, you were forgetting the fourth dimension.'

'You're speaking in riddles, Albert,' said Max. 'What do you mean?'

'Come to Berlin and I'll show you. Can you be here by tomorrow afternoon?'

'If the trains are running, yes,' he said excitedly. 'I'll see you then.'

The Battle of the Somme was over, but it had cost the German Imperial Army half a million men. It was running short of reinforcements, so other than the *Kanonenbahn*, the main line from Metz in the south to Berlin, trains to the capital were few and far between. A call to his father in Pfaffendorf provided Max with a solution. Julius von Laue was a retired military administrator, who knew that *Kanonenbahn* trains still passed through Koblenz, just across the Rhine from his home. Max took Magda and their son Theodore to Koblenz by local train. They stayed with his father, who was meeting his grandson for the first time, while Max caught a train to Berlin.

Berlin, Germany

Max arrived in time to find a guesthouse for the night. After attending a service at Berlin Cathedral in the morning, he headed south to Wilmersdorf, arriving at Einstein's apartment shortly before two. The friends embraced and Einstein led the way towards the kitchen. Max couldn't help noticing that he looked gaunt.

'Are you alright, Albert?' he asked. 'You don't seem yourself.'

'I'm fine,' he said dismissively. 'Just a little tired. Now, there's someone I'd like you to meet.' A man appeared in the doorway. 'This is my good friend, Moritz Katzenstein. He's a brilliant doctor, but a terrible sailor.'

'Says the man who gets lost on the River Spree!' laughed Moritz. Max liked him instantly.

Katzenstein was one of the finest surgeons in Germany and a professor at Berlin University, where he met Einstein for the first time. After an exhausting few months working under terrible conditions in frontline military hospitals, he had been given two weeks' leave. Although he had saved many lives, he had seen countless young men die. Einstein's invitation to meet Professor von Laue and take part in 'a little science experiment' was a welcome and intriguing distraction on his last day before returning to duty.

After Einstein congratulated Max on becoming a father for the first time, there was an awkward silence, only broken when he said, 'You can talk freely, Max. Moritz knows about the crystal. I invited him here today as an observer.'

'Very well,' he replied uncertainly.

'Just remember that I'm not a scientist,' said Moritz. 'Try not to use too many long words, Albert.'

'I'll do my best,' said Einstein. Turning to Max, he said, 'Did you know that a quarter of a century ago, Nikola Tesla demonstrated the production of an incredibly bright beam of light to the Royal Institution in London?'

'No,' said Max, 'but it doesn't surprise me. He has quite a reputation for the spectacular.'

'Well then, do you remember the thought experiment I presented on sending faster-than-light signals into the past?'

'Yes. You called it a Telegraph to the Past.'

‘That’s right, but until your crystal came along, it was nothing more than a theory.’

‘So, what’s changed?’ asked Max.

‘I found an application for Tesla’s beam of light!’

Max felt the hairs stand up on the back of his neck. ‘Well, are you going to tell me what it is, or are we going to stand here all day?’ he asked.

‘Come with me, both of you,’ said Einstein, as he led the way into his study.

‘Now, Max, from what you told me in May, I realised that there could only be one explanation. Before I tell you what it is, would you please choose a number between zero and fifty?’

‘I’d rather you just told me what you know,’ protested Max as he sat down in an armchair.

‘Humour me, Max, please. A number?’

‘Very well, thirty-nine,’ he said.

‘Perfect,’ said Einstein. The two men watched him scribble on a sheet of paper, before walking to the far corner of the room, where a large canvas cloth was draped over a triangular wooden frame. When he removed the cloth, they could see an array of scientific equipment, attached to the frame, which straddled a table.

‘This is Hermes,’ said Einstein. The equipment bore a strong resemblance to the apparatus that Max had used for his own award-winning experiments.

‘Why Hermes?’ asked Moritz.

‘It seemed appropriate,’ he replied. ‘The messenger of the Gods?’ Then, turning to von Laue, he said, ‘I know this needs no introduction to you, Max, but I’m going to describe it for Moritz’s benefit.’ He pointed to a large glass tube, which was connected to a switch by a lead. ‘This tube is a mercury vapour lamp, which needs time to warm up before it can be used. The other one, the one fastened to the table by two brackets, is a resonance tube containing the crystal and two curved end reflectors.’ Pointing to a hollow box containing tinted glass, he said, ‘In between the tubes is a filter. Are you with me so far, Moritz?’

‘Well, I can see two tubes and a box, so I suppose so, but what on earth is a resonance tube?’

‘It’s something that I saw being used at the university to amplify sound waves,’ said Einstein. ‘I’m simply using it for light rather than sound.’

'That's clever,' said Max.

'When I press this switch, the lamp emits ultraviolet light, which passes through the crystal.'

'So, what's the box for?' asked Moritz.

'It absorbs shortwave light but allows longwave to pass through. When longwave light hits the crystal, its particles are stimulated to a higher level of energy, causing it to fluoresce and produce a beam of blue light.'

'What does that have to do with sending a message back in time?' asked Max.

'I'll come to that,' said Einstein. 'Using the same device, I can also produce a bright red beam by removing the filter to allow shortwave light through.

'That doesn't sound safe, Albert,' said Max. 'Shortwave can be very dangerous.'

Handing a pair of goggles to both men, Einstein said, 'You're right, which is why you need to wear these. I had them specially made by Rodenstock in Munich. The amber glass protects your eyes from shortwave light.'

'Alright, so you can create blue or red beams of light,' said Max, 'but for what purpose?'

Pointing to the resonator tube, Einstein said, 'When a beam of light is created, it is repeatedly reflected by the concave surfaces of the reflectors, which constantly refocus the beam.'

Max was becoming exasperated. 'I'll ask you again, Albert. Why? What does this have to do with sending messages to the past?'

'Everything, Max!' he replied triumphantly. 'Magdalite is not like other crystals.'

'I already know that,' he replied testily, 'but why?'

'Because the light beams it produces are travelling faster than the speed of light!'

Max was stunned by this revelation. 'But you always said nothing could do that.'

'No, Max, I did not, but I have often been misquoted. What I said was that, for a particle to accelerate to the speed of light, an almost infinite amount of energy would be required. That does not apply to magdalite particles.'

'Why not?'

‘Because they are already travelling faster than light and have been from the moment of their creation. No acceleration is necessary.’

Max needed time to digest this bombshell, but Moritz had questions of his own. ‘Where does the light beam go?’ he asked.

‘It doesn’t go anywhere,’ said Einstein, ‘but it does travel back in time.’

‘Then how can you see it?’

‘Magdalite is phosphorescent, Moritz, so the glow left by the beam remains visible long enough to be seen.’

‘So, how far back will it travel?’

‘I don’t know. The beam will eventually run out of energy, of course, but that is not the problem.’

‘What is?’ asked Moritz.

‘Hermes,’ said Max, realising that Einstein’s invention had a fundamental flaw.

‘That’s right,’ said Einstein. ‘The fact that Hermes did not exist until last Thursday. Prior to that, there was no crystal to amplify the beam and nothing to contain it. We cannot send messages any further back than the thirtieth of November. That means that, for example, we couldn’t send a message back to 1913 in order to prevent the war. Even if we could, I wouldn’t know where to start.’

‘And presumably,’ said Max, ‘Hermes will only continue to work as long as it remains in the precise position it now occupies?’

‘Correct,’ he replied. ‘If you were to move it, even by a fraction, you would break the beam and have to start from scratch.’

‘But, given what you’ve just told us, it could still be used to change the past?’ asked Moritz.

‘I think it’s time for a demonstration,’ said Einstein. He consulted his handwritten sheet and said, ‘I’m going to press this switch six times at one-minute intervals. I will have to remove and replace the filter, so we’re going to need the goggles.’

When they were ready, he pressed the switch. Within a few seconds, the room was bathed in a red glow that faded after about fifteen seconds. He replaced the filter and pressed the switch again. This time the glow was blue. He repeated the process another four times to create another blue glow followed by three reds. ‘Okay, you can take your goggles off now.’

‘So that’s it?’ said Max. ‘With the greatest of respect, Albert, what proof do we have that anything went back in time?’

Earlier That Day

When Moritz arrived at a little after ten, he brought canned meat and real coffee, something that Einstein had not seen in Berlin since the imposition of a naval blockade in 1914. It was infinitely preferable to the coffee substitute that he kept in his larder. The two men went into his study, where they talked about sailing and music, before the conversation turned to the huge losses being suffered on both sides in France. Moritz didn't want to relive the horrors he had seen at the front, so he changed the subject.

'Why did you invite me here, Albert?' he asked.

Einstein came straight to the point. 'I need a witness to an experiment I'm going to conduct when Max gets here.'

'So why ask me here so early?' asked Moritz.

Einstein winked mischievously. 'It's hard to explain, but all will become clear.' He went on to describe Max's x-ray experiments and his call regarding the magdalite crystal.

'And you don't know why the pattern appeared before the x-ray was fired?' asked Moritz.

'I didn't then, but I do now. Would you like to see something remarkable?'

Moritz nodded. 'Wouldn't anyone?'

In a corner of the room was a device, covered by a canvas cloth. 'When I remove the cloth,' said Einstein, 'we're going to see a sequence of six coloured lights. It doesn't matter when we begin the observation, as each light passes through each and every moment in time. They're continuously striking the crystal, so we will always see it fluoresce until the beam has passed.' Handing Moritz a sheet of paper and a pencil, he continued. 'All I need you to do is record the colour of each beam as it arrives.'

10

Timeline Two

Wilmersdorf, Berlin
December 1916

Einstein removed the cloth with the flourish of a magician and a red glow illuminated the room. It was followed by a blue glow a minute later. When the last light faded away, he replaced the cloth. Moritz had written Red, Blue, Blue, Red, Red, Red on the sheet. He handed it to Einstein, who wrote a one or a zero underneath each colour.

'Thirty-nine!' he announced with aplomb. Then, taking another sheet, he wrote a message on it, removed a book from his bookshelf and opened it at page thirty-nine. After folding the sheet of paper in half and tucking it inside at the same page, he returned the book to the shelf and draped the cloth over the device.

'Time for lunch, I think,' he said as he turned to face Moritz.

'Why don't we take it down to the park?' asked Moritz.

As they wandered round the only green area within a mile of Einstein's apartment, they saw several workmen digging up flowerbeds, as others were preparing to plant vegetables.

'This was bound to happen,' said Moritz. 'Berliners can't eat flowers.'

The naval blockade was working.

When Max arrived in the afternoon, the three of them entered the study and Einstein asked him to choose a number. He chose thirty-nine.

Einstein unveiled the device, saying, 'This is…'

'Hermes?' Max's interruption took them all by surprise.

'What made you say that?' asked Einstein.

'I have absolutely no idea. Was I right?'

'Yes,' he replied. With a hint of a smile, he added, 'That's very interesting.'

Max was going to ask why when Moritz said, 'Why did you call it Hermes?'

'It seemed appropriate,' said Einstein. 'The messenger of the Gods?'

'So, are you going to show us what it can do?' asked Max.

'I don't need to,' he replied.

'Why ever not?' he asked. 'I thought that's why you invited me here.'

'It was, but you've already seen it working.'

Max looked at him as if he had lost his mind. 'No, I haven't,' he said. 'Is this one of your little jokes?'

'No. I'm deadly serious. You simply don't remember it happening.'

'Is that all you've got to say?' he asked. 'If I can't remember it, what proof is there?'

Einstein went to the bookshelf and reached for a copy of his new book on relativity.

'I'm told this is a very effective cure for insomnia,' he chuckled. 'Now, would you be so kind as to open the book at page number thirty-nine?'

Max did as he was asked and found a folded piece of paper.

'Can you tell me what's written there?' said Einstein.

Unfolding the paper, Max read aloud. 'It says "To Max, from your friend now and in the future, Albert Einstein."'

'There's your proof, Max.'

Max was nonplussed. 'Why can't I remember you sending this message?' he asked. 'It doesn't make any sense, Albert.'

'That's a good question. Marcus Aurelius once compared time to a river. I think that sending a message back along that river created a new branch at the point where the message was received. That might explain why we have no memory of what happened before, because we are on the new branch, although…'

'Although what?' asked Max.

'You remembered the word Hermes. A sort of déjà vu, perhaps?'

Max sat down to mull this over. When he stood up again, he said, 'One more question, Albert. Why this crystal? What makes it different to all the others?'

'Ah, therein lies the mystery, but I think I have an answer. There is an as yet unproven theory that a large meteorite hit the earth millions of years ago, creating the Nördlingen crater in Bavaria. The impact would have deposited all manner of celestial material in the ground. The intense heat and pressure would have generated a huge amount of energy, causing a sudden and colossal metamorphosis in the earth's crust.'

Max's eyes lit up. 'I don't think that's just a theory, Albert,' he said excitedly. 'When Magda and I were in Nördlingen, the buildings shimmered in the light. Professor Sauer in Stuttgart told me that the town was built from suevite rock, containing carbon. He believed that the impact of an asteroid instantly transformed the carbon into millions of tiny diamonds.'

'Well, as unlikely as it may sound, I think that impact was also the moment of creation for your magdalite, and heaven knows how many other minerals, exhibiting characteristics that we don't normally find on earth.'

Max put his hands together and steepled his fingers, deep in thought. 'If what you are saying is true, the implications for mankind are extraordinary.'

'I know. Imagine how much good we could do if we knew in advance when something bad was going to happen.'

'Or how much damage!' said Moritz.

Einstein raised an eyebrow. 'Such pessimism, Moritz,' he sighed.

'No, Moritz is right, Albert,' said Max. 'If this secret fell into the wrong hands, the consequences would be unthinkable.'

'I know. That is why we must keep it to ourselves until we have decided what to do. You must stop your students from experimenting with crystals, Max.'

Lancashire
February 1917

Twenty miles to the north-west of Manchester, on the freezing cold banks of a reservoir near the village of Garside, Kevin Winter sat by a woodland campfire. The riots that followed the sinking of the Lusitania had robbed him of the one person he respected and admired. The subsequent murders had the police scratching their heads. Over a two-week period, four local men were stabbed to death within a mile of the Moor Road butcher's shop. Fear had spread throughout the city at the prospect of a serial killer, dubbed the "Liverpool Ripper" by the press, but the murders stopped after the fourth killing. The police failed to link the deaths with that of Jürgen Schmidt, even though all four had been his customers. They were the only men that Mitzi had managed to identify from that fateful night. She knew very well who had killed them, and she was proud of him.

The quality of the information passed to the Germans in the nine months following his father's death resulted in Winter's promotion from head of the German spy network in the north-west to command of their entire British network. Such recognition gave him little comfort. The Battle of Verdun had ended in December with the French declared the victors, but apart from the huge loss of life on both sides, nothing had changed much in the ten months since it started. In January, the United States severed diplomatic ties with Germany after it announced the resumption of unrestricted submarine warfare. Winter knew that if America declared war, it would be the beginning of the end for his father's homeland.

With a bottle in one hand and a gun in the other, silent rage boiled inside him as he thought about the hand that life had dealt him. Although McCarthy had been Irish, it was the British church that had enabled him to commit his heinous crimes and rob Winter of his childhood. The internment of his brother and the manner of his father's death at the hands of a baying Liverpool mob had only served to cement his hatred of all things British.

Egglescombe, Lancashire
April 1917

By the end of the Spring semester, James was starting to come to terms with the loss of his brother, but the grief never left him, making him distant and unapproachable. Freddie Taylor invited him to spend the Easter break on the Lancashire coast with him and his family, but he didn't really want the company of others. Out of a sense of duty to his father and his struggling business, he returned to Allerton Manor to help the estate manager at the height of the lambing season.

There was no expression of gratitude from his father, who had little interest in farming. In fact, there was no real acknowledgement that James was even there. George was drinking heavily again. The atmosphere in the old house was unpleasant, and not just from the sickly smell of stale whisky hanging in the air. It soon became apparent that his parents had stopped speaking to one another, and James decided to keep well out of the way.

Returning from a punishing run to Allerton Edge one morning, he entered the house by the rear door, hoping not to be seen. Unfortunately, George had seen him coming across the fields and they met in the hallway. James could smell the whisky on his breath and realised he had started early. He had also decided to lay down the law. He eyed his son malevolently.

'Nah then, lad.'

'Father?'

'You're coming to work with me tomorrow. Seeing as you didn't have the bottle to join up along with your brother, I don't see why you should be wasting your time round here when there's work to be done. I've got machines standing idle with nobody to fix them since Horace went off to war.'

James didn't rise to the bait. He had put up with his father's self-righteous disapproval since Alfie left. Yes, the mill had lost a lot of men due to conscription, but there was nowhere to export cotton to, so the need to fix idle machines was not as urgent as his father made out.

'But Father, I'm not interested in working in the mill. I've decided to apply for a place at university.'

'I'm not talking about any old job. You're going to take over from me one day. I've had a word with the principal of Welbeck College, and you'll be studying engineering there in your spare time.'

James knew it wasn't the right time to mention it, but he found himself saying 'I want to study physics, not engineering.'

'What bloody good is physics if you're working at t'mill?'

'You're not listening. I don't want to work at the mill. Ever.'

'Well, you're bloody well gonna, so you'd better get used to the idea.'

'No Father, I'm not. I've made up my mind and you're not going to stop me.'

'Oh, am I not? Well, we'll see about that, lad. You'll do what you're bloody well told, or you'll not get another penny from me. Then see how far you get!'

'That's not fair!'

'Aye, well, life's not fair, Son.'

'Oh really? Is that what you said to Alfie when you let him go off and get himself killed?' James knew instantly that he'd overstepped the mark, but he'd had enough.

George's face turned a deeper shade of red, veins throbbing in his temples. 'Why you little… How dare you talk to me like that!' he roared. He was a big man, but he was badly out of shape and suffering from the effects of half a bottle of Glenfiddich. He took a drunken step forward and attempted to throw a punch, losing his balance and barging into James. Instinctively, he pushed him away, causing him to stagger backwards and fall onto his back in the hallway. He was beside himself with rage as he struggled to his feet.

'Get out of my house and don't come back!'

James ran upstairs. His mother, alarmed by the raised voices, followed him into his room. 'Whatever's happened?'

'Ask him!' he shouted, grabbing an old leather portmanteau bag from his wardrobe and stuffing some clothes into it.

'What are you doing?' she cried, the panic rising in her voice.

'I can't stand it here anymore, Mother. I have to go.'

Ellen ran downstairs to confront her husband. 'You must stop him! I've already lost Alfie and Mike. I can't lose James as well!'

'Stop your mithering, woman! I'm not having him telling me what's what in my own home.' George stomped off into the library and slammed the door, making a beeline for the whisky bottle once more.

James appeared in the hallway and his mother ran to stop him, screaming, 'Where will you go?'

He put the bag down and hugged her. 'Don't worry about me, I'll be fine. I'll let you know where I am when I get settled. Goodbye, Mother.' Freeing himself from her grasp, he picked up his bag and left. Ellen sank to the floor and lay there on the cold tiles, sobbing.

11

Frankfurt, Germany
April 1917

Max woke to the shrill, jangling sound of the telephone in the hallway. He threw on a robe, made his way downstairs and lifted the receiver.

'Hello.'

A female voice said, 'I have a long-distance call for you.'

There was a delay on the line, before a man spoke in hushed tones.

'Max?'

'*Ja*, who is this?'

'It's Moritz. Can you come to Berlin? It's happening.'

Max winced at the news he'd been dreading. 'I'll be there tonight,' he said, and the line went dead.

When he was ready to leave, he loaded his Audi Tourer with the last cans of gasoline from his garage. Wartime fuel shortages meant he would not make it home again, but if all went to plan, that would not matter. After saying an emotional goodbye to his wife Magdalena, he headed north, doing his best to avoid the largest potholes in the unpaved roads. Passing through the village of Dransfeld, he was reminded of Anna, the student whose observations had turned his well-ordered life upside down less than a year ago.

The "Ride of the Valkyries," from Wagner's opera *Die Walküre,* was such a stirring piece of music that, without even thinking about it, Max had begun to drive faster, using up more of his precious fuel than he intended. Try as he might, Max couldn't get the tune out of his head, but as soon as he realised what he was doing, he slowed down, hoping that there would still be enough fuel to get him to Berlin.

In Magdeburg, more than a hundred miles from his destination, he stopped briefly to pour the last can of gasoline into the fuel tank. Shivering from the biting cold, he pulled a scarf over his mouth and ears before continuing his journey. Without a heater, it was almost as cold inside the car as out.

On the outskirts of the capital, the Audi coughed and spluttered to a halt on a wide, tree-lined boulevard in the Grunewald district of Charlottenburg. The sun was setting, and he was still more than four miles from his destination. Max cursed aloud. Why hadn't he driven more slowly?

Stepping out into the icy April air, he shivered. The chill wind made it seem even colder. Stamping his feet in a vain attempt to generate some warmth, he continued his journey on foot.

An hour later, he stood outside the open door of an apartment block near the opera house on Bismarckstrasse. The residents' names, listed on a metal plate, revealed his destination to be an address on the top floor. He crossed the lobby and entered the dark, dingy lift. With a high-pitched whirr, it creaked into life, slowly screeching and squealing its way to the fourth floor. At the door to Apartment 403, he knocked and heard movement inside.

The door was opened by Moritz, who said, 'What took you so long?'

'Hello, Moritz,' said Max wearily. 'I ran out of fuel. I've been walking for ages.'

'You'd better come in and warm yourself. It's freezing out there.'

Max didn't need a second invitation. He followed Moritz into a spacious living room where a log fire was burning. Still wearing his coat, he stood in front of the dancing flames, hands outstretched, feeling the heat slowly seeping back into his body.

'How is he?' he asked.

Moritz placed a hand on Max's shoulder and spoke with the weary demeanour of a man who had seen too many good men die. 'Still in a coma, Max. He's dying, and he doesn't have long left.'

'Is there nothing you can do?' he asked.

'It's too late for that. If I'd seen him when he first became ill, I could have told him it was more than a mild liver complaint. The diet he was on doesn't seem to have helped at all. He's lost more than thirty kilos in the last three months.'

Max rubbed the back of his neck, wondering what could have caused this man to lose over a third of his body weight? 'Do you have any idea what's wrong with him?'

'It could be any number of things,' said Moritz. 'He has a raging fever, not to mention low blood pressure and an increased respiratory rate. I need to look inside to be sure, but he may be too weak to survive the operation.'

'What's the alternative?'

'There isn't one. I have to take the risk, but I'm going to need your help.'

Bemused, Max turned to face him. 'What do you mean?'

'Well, I can't operate without an anaesthetist.'

'I don't understand.'

'You're going to assist me, Max,' said Moritz.

Shocked by the suggestion, Max backed away from him. 'Are you mad? I'm a physicist, not a physician! Why can't we take him to a hospital?'

'You are just going to have to trust me when I say nobody can know what we're doing. I can show you what to do and we can both keep a close eye on him while he's unconscious.'

'And if something goes wrong?'

'Then we could both end up in prison.'

'This is madness!' Max protested, putting his head in his hands. 'It's been a long day, and I can't think straight. I need to sleep.'

Moritz showed him to one of the bedrooms. 'You'll be getting a crash course in anaesthetics in the morning, so get some rest. Good night, Max.'

It was still dark when Moritz woke his guest after a fitful night's sleep. 'Coffee?'

'Real coffee?' he mumbled.

'Yes. I know a man who knows a man.'

Max couldn't remember the last time he'd seen real coffee, let alone tasted it. He ambled through to the living room, where a mug of the steaming, black liquid sat on a low table. Lifting the mug to his mouth, he closed his eyes and savoured the rich aroma.

'Get a move on, we have a lot to do,' said Moritz.

'Okay, but just answer me one thing. Why does he need anaesthetising if he's in a coma?'

'Because I don't know whether he can feel anything, and I don't want to take that chance.'

Max's shoulders sagged and, for the first time, he started to panic. 'This is not right,' he said.

'It's his only chance, and I can't do it on my own.'

Max had hoped to avoid the impending ordeal, but he realised that he had no choice if the man was to survive. 'Where are we going to do this?'

'Come with me.' Moritz led the way to a room at the rear of the apartment. It looked like a kitchen, but without a cooker. In the centre of the room, two metal tables stood at right angles to each other. A variety of gleaming medical instruments were arranged in a neat row on the smaller table, while an assortment of cylinders, tubes and bags hung from a portable stand next to it.

Max saw the anaesthetic equipment for the first time. Ashen faced, he ran to the sink and threw up. Moritz waited patiently for him to compose himself, wondering how he was going to react to the sight of blood.

'Take some deep breaths. You can do this,' he said, although from the way Max was shaking, he doubted it.

'This is crazy!'

'Ok, let's take a break. Go and have a cigarette and we'll try again when you've calmed down a little.'

Max returned to the living room and opened a window. He stood there for several minutes, smoking a cigarette and breathing deeply in a vain attempt to relax. He was grateful for the respite, but strongly suspected that his part in this insane affair was not going to be as straightforward as Moritz was making out.

Twenty minutes had passed when he ventured back into the operating room, but the sight of the equipment set his nerves on edge again.

'We're going to practise this for a while,' said Moritz. 'I want you to think of it as you would a science experiment.'

He showed Max how to administer the ether, and how often. Then he demonstrated how to inflate the patient's lungs with oxygen by squeezing a bag.

'Do it exactly the way I've shown you,' he said. 'Too much oxygen and the patient could end up with a collapsed lung. Too little and he could die from lack of oxygen in the blood.'

'You're not helping,' said Max.

'It's not as difficult as it sounds. You have two hours. Do it again and again, until it's second nature.'

Before the two hours was up, Max decided that he knew what to do, even if he doubted his ability to do it. He found Moritz in the kitchen and said, 'Let's do this before I lose my nerve again.'

They went to the bedroom where their unconscious patient was lying on a hospital trolley. Between them, they wheeled him into the operating room and slid him onto the table. Max followed Moritz to a sink in the corner of the room. After washing their hands and putting on clean white gowns, they were ready. Moritz placed a face mask over his patient's face and began to administer the anaesthetic. A dry, sweet smell rose into the air. Once he was sure it had taken effect, he handed over to his reluctant assistant.

Max averted his eyes as Moritz made a skilful midline incision. Every fibre of his being was telling him to get out of that room. Worried that the sight of blood might be too much for him, he forced himself to concentrate on the man's face, avoiding the gruesome evidence of Moritz's handiwork. The simple fact was that if he stopped what he was doing, their patient would die. The responsibility was almost overwhelming, and his hand began to cramp up from nervous tension. After what seemed like an eternity, even though only half an hour had passed, Moritz looked at Max through wire-rimmed spectacles, a grim smile on his face. 'I can find no evidence of cancer. It's something else.' He continued his examination for several more minutes, then moved round the table and turned off the oxygen supply.

Shock registered on Max's face. 'What the hell have you done?'

'I'm sorry, but I have no choice. He has more than one problem that will undoubtedly kill him. I can't help him until I find out precisely what's wrong.'

'And how are you going to do that?'

'Trust me,' said Moritz in the calm, friendly manner he had used to reassure many a worried patient over the years. 'Carry on with the ether as before.'

Though dubious, he did as he was told. Fifteen minutes later, the convulsions started, and the man took his last breath soon after.

Max stumbled away from the table with his head in his hands. 'You've killed him!'

'Max, I need you to listen carefully to what I say. If anyone finds out what we've done, we could both go under the axe. Take a break, have a smoke and a cup of coffee, and I'll explain.'

Back in the living room, Max chain-smoked, trying to comprehend what he'd just seen. He eyed Moritz with anger and suspicion. 'Why did you turn off the oxygen?'

'From what he told me, I knew that the only way I could help him was to carry out an autopsy to establish the precise cause of death.'

'How on earth could that help him?' asked Max, his exasperation clear.

'He would have died anyway. When I last spoke to him, he asked me to make him a promise. If I couldn't save him, I should find out exactly what had killed him. He said that if I did that, you would know what to do.'

Max put a hand to his forehead, and exclaimed, 'Of course! How could I have been so dim? You need to do your autopsy.'

'Very well, but I need you to record it for me.'

'Will I have to watch?'

'No, you can sit with your back to me if you want, as long as you write down everything I say.'

'Okay, let's get this over with.'

For the next three hours, Max sat and took notes while Moritz methodically removed and examined the man's internal organs, describing what he saw at every stage. Although he didn't see what Moritz was doing, the sounds of sawing and cutting were bad enough. Max didn't understand much of what was said, but he did his best to write it down word for word. When the autopsy was over, he asked, 'What happens now?'

'I'm going to get cleaned up. Then we need to talk.'

Max remained in the operating room and eventually plucked up the courage to take a last look at the body. White and European in appearance, the large head was out of proportion with the painfully thin, short body. Crisp, frizzy black hair framed a face dominated by a large, bulbous nose, underneath hooded eyelids that gave him a rather doleful expression. 'Goodbye, my friend,' said Max, kissing Einstein on the forehead. He was only thirty-eight years old.

12

St Annes-on-the-Sea, Lancashire
April 1917

James woke in a cold sweat, his heart pounding as the train shuddered to a halt. He knew the feeling well, for the dream had haunted him now for ten years. He took one of the tablets his mother had given him and massaged his temples, trying to ease the throbbing that would often be there when he woke up. As a child, he had never suffered from headaches, but now they were a regular occurrence. He rubbed his eyes and looked out of the window as the station guard blew her whistle. The sign behind her read "St Annes-on-the-Sea." It was his stop! Scrambling to grab his possessions, he was forced to jump from the slowly moving train, earning some well-chosen words from the guard. He thought better of asking her for directions to the pier and tried to remember Freddie Taylor's words. 'We're easy to find,' he'd said. 'When you get to the seafront with the pier in front of you, turn left and walk along South Promenade for about half a mile, until you see a house called Holmleigh on the left.'

It was pouring with rain when James left St Annes railway station, and he was drenched by the time he knocked on the Taylors' front door half an hour later. His unheralded arrival was a surprise to Freddie's parents, but once he'd introduced himself, they seemed genuinely pleased to see him. Len Taylor was the manager of a local bank and spent most of his spare time in his garden. His wife Irene's involvement with the St Annes Ladies' War Support Group had resulted in the couple's first row in twenty-five years of marriage, when Len came home from work to find a vegetable patch where his flower beds had been. It was Irene's way of doing her bit to increase wartime food production, but she had neglected to consult her husband, who didn't speak to her for several days.

The warmth of the Taylors' welcome contrasted sharply with the frosty reception James had received at home. After a hot bath, he sat in front of a roaring fire with a mug of cocoa and explained his sudden change of mind to Len and Irene.

'I needed to get away,' he said. 'Since my brother died, things haven't been the same.'

‘It must have been very difficult for your parents,’ said Irene.

‘It was, but it seems to have driven a wedge between them. I don’t think they said a word to each other while I was there. Mother just sits in Alfie’s room for hours on end, and Father’s drunk all the time.’

‘Well,’ said Freddie, ‘you can forget all about home while you’re here.’ After his parents had left the room, he added, ‘The only fly in the ointment is Alice.’

‘Alice?’ queried James.

‘My sister. She’ll be home from university tomorrow. If you’ve got any sense, you’ll keep well out of her way. You won’t like her, she’s as dull as ditchwater. Always got her head in some book or other.’

James didn’t see what was wrong with that. ‘I always wanted a sister,’ he said.

‘Good, you can have mine!’

When she arrived the following afternoon, Alice was less than happy that a stranger was staying for the holiday. She was two years older than her brother, and James’ first impression was that she was rather distant and aloof. The boys seemed to be an irritation to her, and she invariably left the room when they entered, thereby missing their scintillating discussions on the prospects for cricket and football after the war.

The weekend news headlines were dominated by America’s entry into the war after a couple of months in which German U-boats had sunk more than a million tons of merchant shipping. James was pleased to hear Len Taylor say that it was a major turning point in the war, which he was confident would be over before the year was out.

Ignoring sub-zero temperatures and an icy wind blowing in off the Atlantic, James went for a run along the beach every morning, and Freddie was shamed into accompanying him. As the Easter weekend approached and conditions slowly improved, they spent more and more time outside, kicking a ball around for as long as Freddie could be bothered. Not the most athletic of boys, he preferred to sit on a bench with his comics and sweets.

On Easter Monday, the boys were playing football on the sands, when Freddie twisted his ankle and fell on top of James. He couldn’t put any weight on the injured limb, so James picked him up and carried him the two hundred yards to his home. Approaching the house, he saw a concerned Alice watching from the front step.

'Can you hold the door open, please?' he shouted. She stood aside as he effortlessly carried her brother's ample frame up the steps and into the hallway. She examined Freddie's swollen ankle and made him comfortable on the living room sofa.

'Lie there, and I'll get you a drink,' she said tenderly.

Seven years at an all-girls' school had not prepared Alice for the sight that greeted her when she walked into the kitchen. James was standing by the sink, stripped to the waist, with water dripping from his muscular chest and arms.

'Do you have a towel?' he asked innocently. 'Freddie fell over on the beach, and I'm covered in sand.'

Alice's face was as red as the dress she was wearing, so without saying a word, she turned and went to get a towel from the airing cupboard. There, she paused, reminding herself that James was the same age as her little brother. She had to admit that he seemed a lot older, but she hoped he hadn't noticed her embarrassment. When she returned, he was still trying to reach a patch of sand that was clinging stubbornly to his back. Fighting to retain her composure, she said, 'You've missed a bit.'

'Where?' he asked.

'Here, let me.' She took a deep breath and wiped his broad shoulders and back with a flannel, before handing him the towel, which was clearly too small for the task.

'Thanks,' he said gratefully. She smiled and stood there, until she realised that she was gawping.

'Erm, I was going to make Freddie a cup of tea. Would you like one?'

'Yes please, I'm parched.'

Freddie was still lying on the couch when his parents returned from a walk along the promenade.

'Oh, Freddie,' said his mother. 'What have you done this time?'

'I think it's just a sprain,' said James, 'but he should get it looked at.'

'The surgery is closed today,' said Len. Turning to Freddie, he said, 'If we can get you into the car, I'll nip you down to the hospital.'

With Freddie lying across the back seat of his father's Rover, they set off, leaving Alice and James alone in the house. There was an awkward silence between them, as each desperately tried to think of something to say.

When the others returned, Freddie's ankle was heavily strapped. 'You were right,' said Irene. 'It's a bad sprain. He'll have to keep his weight off it for a week or so.'

James couldn't resist making fun of his friend's lack of athletic ability, and was delighted when Alice joined in. 'The only time I've ever seen him run was to the sweet shop!' she laughed.

'Shut up, Stringbean!' was Freddie's feeble response. His sister was tall and willowy, and she hated the nickname. Frowning, she bowed her head and looked self-consciously at James, who winked, making her giggle. Although she was painfully shy, something about him put her at ease, and he clearly enjoyed teasing her brother as much as she did. The next time Freddie made fun of her appearance, she was ready for him.

'To look at you,' he said, while lying on the couch, 'anyone would think there was a famine in Lancashire.'

'To look at you, anyone would think you caused it!'

His face reddening, Freddie lay there helplessly as James roared with laughter. Within a year, talk of famine would be no laughing matter, when supplies of basic foodstuffs such as meat, butter and cheese ran short.

With her brother incapacitated, Alice felt obliged to spend more time with their guest.

'It would be rude to leave him on his own,' she told her mother, who smiled knowingly. 'What's that look for?'

'Nothing, dear,' said Irene, still smiling.

The more time James spent in Alice's company, the clearer it became that she was the most intelligent girl he'd ever met. They would sit by the fire and discuss their ambitions for the future. She was almost two years into a mathematics degree at Manchester University and wanted to pursue a career in astronomy when she graduated. She was saving up for a telescope, and he told her she could borrow his until she could get one of her own.

'So,' he said, 'you will have studied Newton and the motion of bodies in space?'

'Yes, and mutual attraction.'

He couldn't tell whether it was an innocent remark but, to his horror, he began to blush and had to look away. When he looked back, Alice was looking at the floor and her face was bright red. Eager to change the subject, he said the only thing that came into his head.

'I've been studying Einstein, and I have this crazy idea that I could be the one to discover time travel. Does that sound ridiculous?'

Her answer was unexpected. 'Not at all,' she said. 'How thrilling would it be, to be the first person in the world to discover something amazing?'

'Exactly!'

'What makes you think time travel might be possible?'

'It all started when I read *The Time Machine*,' he said.

'HG Wells?' she replied. 'That's just fiction, James, but okay. Let's assume for a moment that, one day, someone figures out how to travel through time. What would they do?' she asked.

'What do you mean?'

'Would they tell the world about it? And if they did, what would happen? Every Tom, Dick or Harriet would want to change their past, or visit their dead ancestors, or both. The consequences could be disastrous.'

'I suppose so.'

'You suppose so? People who would have died might live, and vice versa. People like us could cease to exist in a heartbeat.'

'Wow! This is something you've actually thought about?'

'Well, someone has to. If time travel is ever found to be scientifically possible, then you can bet some idiot will want to do it.'

He looked into her eyes and thought he saw a hint of amusement there. Had she just called him an idiot? As if reading his mind, she smiled and said, 'I'm not suggesting you're an idiot, James. Far from it, but there's no guarantee that whoever discovered it would have the integrity to act responsibly. Unless they're a woman, of course.'

'Of course,' he replied with a grin.

Alone in her bed that night, Alice thought that James seemed too good to be true. Surely, no one could be as nice as he appeared to be, as well as being good at almost everything and handsome to boot. If he had faults, then she wanted to find out what they were.

On the other side of the wall, in the Taylors' guest room, James couldn't stop thinking about Alice. Her red hair and hazel eyes, the sound of her voice and her dry sense of humour, her crooked little smile and her infectious laugh. How had he not noticed before? He liked everything about her and, although he couldn't be sure, she seemed to like him. He thought about her ambition to be an astronomer and couldn't help wondering whether she could succeed in a profession that was almost entirely male-dominated.

One afternoon, James and Freddie were discussing a forthcoming physics assignment, in which they had been tasked with measuring the speed of light and sound. As Alice entered the room, she heard James say, '… and light travels faster than sound.'

'Is that why Freddie appears bright until you hear him speak?' she asked. Even her brother had to laugh.

13

St Annes-on-the-Sea, Lancashire
April 1917

James' last full day in St Annes was also Alice's twentieth birthday. Thankfully, Irene let it slip a few days earlier, giving him the chance to buy a card. When he handed it to Alice, he plucked up the courage to ask if she would like to go for a walk.

'That would be lovely,' she said with a smile, 'but why don't we go into town instead? I could show you the sights.'

'I'd love to, but I'll need your father's permission.'

'He's not here, but he would insist that my mother came along as chaperone, listening to our every word.'

'What are you saying?'

'I'll speak to her. It won't be a problem.'

Later that morning, they caught a tram into Blackpool and made a beeline for the amusement park and its wooden roller coaster. James bought ice creams on Victoria Pier, and they headed into the town on foot.

Alice proved to be a great tour guide, giving him a potted history of the town's growth since the arrival of the railway, when it became the most popular holiday resort in the country.

'Things have changed a bit, what with the war and everything,' she said, 'But eight million people used to come here every year. Did you know that the Lancashire cotton mills all have different shutdown weeks, so there was a steady stream of visitors right throughout the summer? And it's the only town in Britain with three piers.'

'I didn't know that.'

They arrived at Blackpool Tower in time to see the circus, before taking the lift to the top. Standing on the viewing platform, James could see a storm brewing on the horizon. Alice began to shiver, so he took off his coat and draped it round her shoulders.

'Thank you,' she said, 'but you'll catch your death up here without a coat on.'

'I'm fine,' he lied. 'I don't really feel the cold that much.'

'Well, thank you anyway,' she said with a smile.

Alice looked out to sea, watching the menacing cumulonimbus clouds building on the horizon, but James sensed that something else was troubling her.

'What is it?' he asked.

'I hope you don't mind me asking, but Freddie said you had a fight with your father, and he threw you out?'

'So?' he snapped, instantly regretting the rudeness of his response.

'I'm sorry, it's really none of my business,' she stammered. 'I didn't mean to …'

'No, it's me that should be sorry. That was uncalled for.' He blushed and looked down at his shoes, hoping he hadn't offended her. 'It wasn't really what you would call a fight,' he explained. 'He was drunk and started throwing his weight around. I'm not proud of what I said to him, but all I did was push him away. He fell over.'

'Was he hurt?'

'Only his pride. You have to understand that my father's an important man who employs a lot of people. He's used to getting his own way and when I refused to do what he wanted, he threatened to stop paying my school fees.'

'That seems a bit harsh. Doesn't he want what's best for you?'

'That's just it. He thinks he knows what's best, and what he says goes.' James shivered involuntarily.

'You are cold!' said Alice. 'Come on, let's go back down.'

They entered the lift and were separated as it filled with people. Alice caught sight of his sad expression in its mirrored walls and had an almost overwhelming urge to give him a hug. On the ground floor, she asked, 'Are you alright?'

'I'm fine,' he said. 'How about a cup of tea?'

'That would be lovely, thank you.'

In a tearoom on the Promenade, they ordered a pot of tea and some scones before finding a quiet corner.

'Do you think your father would take you out of school?' asked Alice.

'Not really,' he replied, 'but to be honest, I'm more worried about my mother. When I left, I didn't really think about her. She's had such a difficult time recently.'

'Because of your father?'

'Partly, but did Freddie tell you that my brother died last year at the Somme?'

'No, I'm so sorry,' she said, putting her hand on his. 'How old was he?'

'Same age as me. We were twins.'

Alice frowned and looked at him curiously. 'Then, why wasn't he still at school?'

'He lied about his age to join the army. My father could've stopped him. He never even asked my mother what she thought, and she still hasn't forgiven him.'

'That must have been very hard on all of you,' she said. 'I've been very lucky so far. I don't know anyone who's died, although one of my friends lost her father, and another one an older brother.'

'When we got the news about Alfie, it was the worst day of my life. We'd already lost my Uncle Mike a few weeks earlier. He and my mother were very close.'

'Poor woman. Do you think my father's right, that the war will be over by Christmas?'

'I hope so,' said James. 'I don't know what the Germans were thinking, picking a fight with America. It's bound to swing things in our favour. Whatever happens, I just feel as if Alfie died for nothing.'

'What do you mean?'

'I mean that the whole damn thing could have been avoided.'

'I'm so annoyed,' said Alice. 'Did we really go to war because of some treaty that was written before any of us were born?'

'It would seem so,' said James, 'but maybe the treaty was just an excuse. From what I've read, Germany was becoming a threat. They were building a huge navy, and threatening Russia and France. When they invaded Belgium, I think they expected us to stay out of it.'

'Perhaps we should have done,' said Alice. 'I would have thought we were too powerful for them to risk attacking us by sea.'

'You may be right, but I suppose we'll never know now, will we?' They drank their tea in silence, lost in their own thoughts, until James said, 'What am I thinking of? It's your birthday and I'm leaving tomorrow. Why are we wasting time talking about the war?'

'Because it matters,' said Alice. 'If we lose this war, life will never be the same again.'

'I know, sorry,' he replied. 'It's just something I prefer not to think about.'

'Come on then,' said Alice. 'Let's get out of here.'

The sky was dark as they walked back along the seafront in the direction of St Annes. 'What would you like to do next?' asked James.

'I don't mind,' she replied. 'I'm perfectly happy just walking and talking.'

'Fine, but I think we should change the subject.'

'Alright,' she replied, 'but before we do, can I just ask why you didn't join up along with your brother?'

James hesitated, wondering whether to tell her the truth. In the end, he said, 'I didn't agree with him. I thought he wasn't old enough, and I didn't want to risk my parents losing both of their sons.' The truth, that he believed killing to be wrong under any circumstances, might not have been to Alice's liking. Someone who was not prepared to do their duty was widely regarded as a coward.

'I see. I thought perhaps you were one of those conscientious objectors,' she said.

'No,' he lied, but instantly felt ashamed for doing so.

'So, what will you do if you're conscripted?'

'I don't know. It's something I'd rather not think about. I'm hoping the war will be over before that happens.'

'I hope you're right, but if it turns out that your father is serious, and you do have to leave school, what then?'

It was a question he had hoped to avoid. 'I suppose I'd have to get a job.' He neglected to mention that, as he was only six months shy of his eighteenth birthday, the chances of being called up for active service were high.

'I'm going back to Manchester soon,' said Alice. 'There might be jobs there.' She looked away, hoping that she hadn't seemed too keen. 'I mean, with so many men away fighting, you should be able to find something.'

'Let's hope it won't come to that. Thank you for listening to me, Alice. You're very easy to talk to. I just hope I haven't spoilt your birthday.'

'Not at all. I just wish I could say something to make you feel better.'

'You don't have to say anything. Just being here with you is enough.' Raindrops began to spatter the pavement as he moved closer and looked deep into her twinkling eyes. For the first time, he noticed the subtle mix of brown, green and gold flecks that gave them their hazel appearance. Alice smiled invitingly back at him, and they kissed for the first time. James wanted the moment to last forever, but the rain was getting heavier, and they were forced to move, shrieking with laughter as they held hands and ran towards a seafront shelter. Once inside, James gently parted the tangled, wet hair obscuring her face. His heart melted as she looked up at him, but he was painfully aware that he was leaving tomorrow and might never see her again.

As if reading his thoughts, Alice said, 'I'm going to miss you, James. Will you write to me every day?'

'I'll do my best,' he replied weakly. He was a terrible letter writer. Changing the subject, he said, 'By the way, what did you say to your mother this morning?'

'I just said that you were a very nice, polite young man who was going to invent time travel and become famous. I told her I would like to get to know you better, but you were leaving tomorrow, so it was now or never.'

'What did she say?'

'That she trusted me and was sure you would behave like a perfect gentleman, because if you didn't, my father would break your legs!'

James raised an eyebrow, unsure whether she was serious. 'Charming! And have I? Behaved myself, I mean.'

'Unfortunately, yes.' She smiled mischievously. 'The world is changing, James, and I don't think my parents are that bothered about outdated traditions. I think they like you.'

James laughed. 'That's a relief. Well, Egglescombe's only an hour from Manchester. We could meet up there once you're back at university.'

The end of the holiday came all too soon. With the boys' luggage packed into the boot of the Rover and Alice's parents upstairs, an unsuspecting Freddie saw James share a long-drawn-out kiss with his sister.

'What are you doing?' he asked indignantly.

'Just saying goodbye,' said James.

They laughed when he said, 'Well, I hope you're not thinking of saying goodbye to my mother like that!'

14

Egglescombe, Lancashire
April 1917

Mr Taylor turned off the main road onto a long tree-lined avenue. The boys fell silent as the car made its way through an arboreal honour guard of hundred-year-old Californian giant redwoods. James loved this place and often came here to study or simply to think. At the top of the drive, the huge mansion house came into view. Built in the sixteenth century on the site of a former monastery, it was now home to more than two hundred boarders.

With the holiday over, James and Freddie bade farewell to Mr Taylor and walked through the large double doors into the entrance hall, where Mr Lucas was waiting for them. Rather formally, he said, 'Welcome back, Taylor. Driscoll, come with me.'

'Yes, sir.' James followed him to his office and stood with his hands clasped behind his back.

'Sit down, Driscoll. I'm sorry to have to tell you that the principal has received a letter from your father informing us he is removing you from the school.'

Although he had discussed the possibility with Alice, James had not really taken the threat seriously. Now, the enormity of the situation hit him like a ton of bricks. 'I didn't think he would go through with it, sir,' he mumbled.

'I get the impression there is more to this than meets the eye. Is there anything I can do?'

'I'm afraid not, sir. My father and I had a difference of opinion and I'm not sure he will ever see things from my point of view.'

'Well, I'll be sorry to see you go. I've been lucky enough to teach some very talented science students in my time, but you're as good as any of them. Your project on Einstein was most enlightening. I must admit that you probably have a better understanding of his theories than I do.'

'Thank you, sir.'

'I have no doubt that you'll succeed at whatever you put your mind to, James. I've arranged for you to sleep here tonight but you will have to leave first thing in the morning. What are you going to do?'

‘I have no idea. I suppose I’ll have to look for employment. I hear there are plenty of jobs in Manchester.’

‘I would hate to see you waste your undoubted talent in some mundane occupation. If you do end up in Manchester, why don’t you contact my brother? He works at the university and might be able to open some doors for you.’ Mr Lucas scribbled on a sheet of paper and handed it to James.

‘Thank you, sir, that’s very kind of you.’

The following morning, he said goodbye to his friends and took a taxi to Egglescombe Halt Station. On the Manchester-bound train, he watched disconsolately as the countryside rolled by. James wondered whether his father expected him to return home with his tail between his legs. He already missed his mother, and he was going to miss his friends, but the ache he felt inside was for a girl he had known for little more than a week.

On the horizon, the world’s oldest industrial city appeared in silhouette. If there were jobs there, James might be able to see Alice more often. He was understandably nervous. After all, he had no idea what tomorrow might bring, nor even where he would spend the night. If there was no end to the war, he would probably be called up in six months’ time. The prospect did not scare him, but he could not think of any scenario that would persuade him to end another man’s life. He thought about Alfie and everything that had happened since his death. Was it really less than a year ago?

It was almost one o’clock when he left the train at London Road Station and dropped his cases off at the left luggage office. Alice had suggested the Wilmslow Road in Rusholme, not far from her lodgings, as a likely place to find work. He arrived by tram onto a wide, busy street in the middle of the afternoon. Starting at one end, he went from door to door, checking the windows for job vacancies, but there was little that interested him. At the first public house he came to, people were starting to leave.

‘We’re closing, son,’ said a woman behind the bar.

‘I was just wondering if you’re taking on staff?’

‘Nah, we can manage. Why don’t you try the Wilmslow? One of their barmen left last week.’

‘Thanks, I will. Where is it?’

‘About a couple of hundred yards up on the other side of the road. You’d better hurry, we’re all shutting now till half past six.’

James looked at his watch. It was twenty-five to three. He ran up the street, cursing his own stupidity for not arriving before the pubs closed. He reached the Wilmslow as a woman was bolting the large front doors.

'Excuse me, are there any jobs going?'

'We're closed,' she said without even looking at him. 'Come back later.'

For the rest of the afternoon, he wandered from shop to shop. He didn't have the skills to be a cobbler or a tailor, and he certainly didn't have the stomach to be a butcher. He had sheared a lot of sheep on his uncle Mike's farm, but he could never be around when they were slaughtered. The general dealers, bakers, sweet shops and estate agents were all well-staffed by women, doing work that was done by men before the war. James realised that he could have planned this a little better.

It was nearly five, and rain had started to fall when he passed the junction with Brighton Grove. The name seemed familiar. Reaching into his pocket, he pulled out a folded sheet of paper, on which was written "Professor Lucas, Oakwood House, Brighton Grove, Rusholme." He walked through a gated entrance onto a beautiful, tree-lined avenue where he found Oakwood House, an imposing Victorian property with an impressive portico. There was no one at home, so he sheltered under the canopy until the rain stopped.

Back on Wilmslow Road, he went from pub to pub, trying to avoid the seedier establishments. It was the same story at the first five he visited. All had a plentiful supply of part-time barmaids and didn't need any more. At the sixth, the landlord had taken someone on a few days earlier. Now, he was back at the Wilmslow. When he went in, he introduced himself to the woman behind the bar.

'Good evening.'

The woman looked him up and down and said in a soft Irish accent, 'Howya, what can I get you?'

'Nothing to drink, thank you. I'm looking for a job. Are you the landlady?'

'No, but if I was, I'd give you one.'

'Really? You don't know anything about me.'

'Oh, I t'ink I've seen enough.' She held out her hand and said, 'I'm Sarah.'

Taking it, he replied, 'James.'

She held on just long enough to make him feel uncomfortable. Gazing into his eyes, she said, 'Pleased to meet you, James.'

He blushed and looked away. Sarah was attractive, but she was much, much older than him. 'Is the landlord here?'

'I'll just give him a shout… Roy!'

A few minutes later a rather red-faced man in his sixties appeared from the cellar. 'What do you want? I'm up to me kneeballs down there.'

'This young man is here for a job. Do you want me to show him the ropes?'

'No, I do not!' Shaking hands with James, he said, 'Roy 'arris. Don't listen to a word she says, lad. She's a great one for the insinuendos, is our Sarah.'

James bit his lip to avoid laughing at the mangled nouns.

'Now, tell me, how come you're not away fighting for your country?'

'I'm only seventeen, sir.'

'Pull the other bell, it's got legs on.'

'Sorry?'

'You look older, son.'

'I'll say he does,' murmured Sarah.

'Have you ever worked behind a bar?'

'No, sir, but I'm a quick learner and I'm not afraid of hard work.'

'You'd better not be. You can 'ave a week's trial. Two pounds a week, and you deal with the deliveries while you're 'ere.'

'Do you have any accommodation?'

'You don't want much, do you lad? Still, you might be as well hung as a sheep or a lamb, I suppose.'

James saw Sarah cover her mouth with her hand and turn her head away. He couldn't recall the correct phrase, but he knew it wasn't what Roy had just said. 'So, is that a yes then?' he asked.

'Aye, if you pay for it. The room's ten bob a week. I can take it out of your wages.'

'Thank you, sir. When can I start?'

'How's about now? There's barrels need shifting.'

James had arrived with nothing more than an overnight bag, so the following day he returned to the station to collect his luggage. His room was larger than he'd expected, so there was plenty of room for his books, and he was able to continue studying physics as a hobby.

Pubs could only open for a few hours a day, so he had plenty of time to go running in the local park each morning, usually returning before Roy or Sarah got up. By the time the pub opened at noon, the bar and cellar were always spotless. A week's trial turned into a permanent job.

With time on his hands, he wrote to Alice to let her know that he had left school, which she already knew, courtesy of a phone call from Freddie. James told her about his new job and gave her the address. He asked whether it was far from her hall of residence. He complained that, with nowhere to conduct experiments and no money for equipment, he had no choice other than to be a theoretical physicist, like his hero, Einstein.

When his letter arrived, Alice had mixed emotions. She knew how much he had wanted to finish his studies, and yet she couldn't help being thrilled that when she returned, he was going to be living close by. She wrote back to say that she was looking forward to seeing him again. By her reckoning, the Wilmslow was only a twenty-minute walk from her rooms in Ashburne Hall. As he read her reply, James was surprised at how much he already missed her.

Charlottenburg, Berlin

After the tragic death of his friend, Max went into the kitchen, where he threw up in the sink. By the time Moritz returned, he was sitting on a sofa in the living room, but he still looked as white as a sheet.

'Are you alright?' asked Moritz.

'What do you think?' he replied.

Moritz handed him a fresh cup of coffee and said, 'I'm sorry you had to see all of that, but I couldn't have done it on my own.'

'I know.'

For several minutes the two men sat and stared into the flickering fire, lost in their own thoughts. Eventually the silence was broken by Moritz. 'He was talking about sending a message, wasn't he?'

Max nodded. 'What did you know of Albert's condition?' he asked.

'I called in to see him a few days ago. I was shocked to see how much weight he'd lost. He'd been having stomach pains for some time and was diagnosed with Gilbert's syndrome, a relatively harmless liver condition. He should not have become quite so ill. He had been too embarrassed to admit that he was suffering from an intense itching, which he thought was due to bed bugs. It might have suggested to his physician that the abdominal pain and jaundice were signs of gallstones, which could have been removed.'

'And that was the problem?'

'One of them, although I didn't know it at the time. I told him that if it was cancer, there was very little I could do other than to control the pain. The only way to find out was to operate.'

'How did he take the news?'

'Very well, as a matter of fact. He said that "If this is the end, then I will die happy in the knowledge that relativity will be my legacy."'

'That sounds like Albert.'

'When I told him I might have been able to help him if I'd only seen him earlier, he said "Perhaps you can." Obviously, I didn't know what he meant at first.'

'I cannot help him unless I go to his apartment.'

'I know. Will you be coming back?' asked Moritz.

'Only if I fail,' he said.

Moritz was puzzled. 'How will I know if you've been successful?'

'You won't, but you'll know if I fail. If I come back, this could end very badly for us. We need a plan in case we have to dispose of his body. In the meantime, I need you to write down what killed him in terms a layman can understand.'

Moritz took a single sheet of paper and wrote a few lines on it, before placing it in an envelope and handing it to Max. 'His apartment is only about a mile or so from here. Do you want me to find you a taxi?'

'No, the walk will clear my head. Do you have his keys?'

'Yes, and I almost forgot. He wrote you a letter.'

At the door, Max stopped to put on his coat. 'Wish me luck.'

Moritz shook him by the hand. 'Good luck, Max. I think you're going to need it.'

Wilmersdorf, Berlin

It was late when he let himself into the apartment on Wittelsbacherstrasse. Taking off his coat, he threw it over a chair, causing the letters from Moritz and Einstein to slip from his inside pocket and fall onto the wooden floor. He picked them up and placed them on the hall table while he took his bag into the guest room at the other end of the hall. Curiosity soon got the better of him and he picked up Einstein's letter, staring at the envelope which bore his name. There were two sheets of paper inside, the first of which read:

> My dear Max,
>
> If you are reading this then my worst fears have been realised, but do not mourn my passing until all hope is gone. My fate now lies in the lap of the gods, or should I say one god in particular? I trust that Moritz has determined the cause of my demise, so that you can warn me in time. You will find everything you need in my desk drawer. Thank you for your loyalty and friendship.
>
> Auf wiedersehen,
>
> Albert

Max understood that the god in question was Hermes. He wiped a tear from his eye and placed the letter on the table. He badly needed sleep if he was to play his part in the forthcoming drama, so he left the second sheet until the morning. Lying in bed, he regretted having drunk so much of Moritz's coffee. His thoughts drifted to the man he had known for more than ten years, a man he had always been in awe of, even though it was Max rather than Einstein who had won the Nobel Prize.

Dawn was breaking when he finally abandoned all hope of sleep. Surrendering to the inevitable, he wandered into the kitchen and cursed, realising that he had forgotten to borrow any more coffee from Moritz. On the day America declared war on Germany, the nation was still in the grip of what had become known as the Turnip Winter. Without basics such as bread, milk and eggs, people went hungry or made do with substitutes. Unless, like Moritz, you had contacts, luxuries such as coffee were a thing of the past. People made turnip coffee, but it tasted even worse than it sounded.

Max stood by the window and lit a cigarette, staring at the rain that fell steadily on the Berlin rooftops. When he went back into the hall, he was trembling at the thought of what he was about to do. The second sheet from Einstein's letter was headed "To whom it may concern" and was a note absolving Moritz and Max of any blame in the event that he should die in bizarre circumstances. Max wasn't sure it would do them any good if they were discovered, but he appreciated his friend's concern. He picked up the autopsy report. Moritz had certainly been concise, but he failed to mention death from lack of oxygen in the blood.

Patient: Albert Einstein

Date: 6 Apr 1917.   Time of death: 15:35

Cause of Death:
Peritonitis caused by perforated peptic ulcer;
Sepsis resulting from cholecystitis caused by gallstones.

Max knew the task that lay ahead, but nerves took over as he entered Einstein's darkened study and switched on the light. Apart from an assortment of files and papers that covered the desk, the room looked the same as on his previous visit. Sitting down at the desk, he took some paper from a drawer and wrote down the message he wanted to send, using Einstein's codebook. He checked and re-checked the message until he was ready to turn his attention to Hermes. It had not moved since his last visit. Slowly, methodically, he followed the procedure that Einstein had taught him. He knew it would take several hours to complete, and that one mistake would spell disaster. How he wished he'd remembered to ask Moritz for more of that delicious coffee.

December 1916

Four months before Einstein's death, on the day when he introduced the Wilmersdorf Hermes to Max and Moritz, they had discussed its potential for good or evil. After Moritz left, Einstein taught Max how to send messages and showed him a codebook that he had devised.

'The message that we sent to this morning was very simple, because I was expecting to receive a number and nothing else. To be useful, most messages would be much longer.'

'You seem to have thought of everything, Albert,' said Max.

'Now, are you ready to watch the next message arrive?' Max nodded nervously. Einstein flicked the switch and a blue glow lit up the darkened room.

15

Timeline Three

Wilmersdorf, Berlin
December 1916

'Quickly, pass me a pencil!' Einstein sat back in his armchair and started to record the sequence of colours appearing in front of him. 'We're going to be here for some time Max. Why don't you make yourself comfortable?'

It was dark by the time the last light beam faded away. Max had taken over from Einstein while he used his codebook to decode the message. When he had finished, he sat and stared at what was written on the paper.

**START VON LAUE DATE SEVEN
FOUR SEVENTEEN MK NOT GILBERTS
EINSTEIN DEATH APRIL PERITONITIS
SEPSIS CHOLECYSTITIS URGENT
CONTACT HZ PERFORATED PEPTIC
ULCER GALLSTONES END**

'This message came from you!' said Einstein.

'What does it say?'

'The doctor who told me I have Gilbert's syndrome was wrong.' Einstein began absent-mindedly scratching himself as he spoke. 'From your message, it seems I have an ulcer and gallstones, and I'll die in April!'

'*Mein Gott!* Is there anything you can do?'

'Well, now I know what's wrong with me, I might have a fighting chance.'

With Moritz on his way back to France, Einstein followed his own instructions to "CONTACT HZ". Heinrich Zangger was a professor of forensic medicine in Zurich. Einstein had spent half his adult life there and the two men were good friends. In fact, Zangger was the go-between whenever he needed to talk to his estranged wife Mileva about their children. He had even taken in Hans, Einstein's son, when the boy's mother became ill. Although he did not have the skills required to operate on Einstein, he was able to make the necessary arrangements for surgery to be performed at a private clinic in Switzerland. Following the operation, the surgeon expressed his astonishment at the accuracy of Zangger's diagnosis, and at Einstein's prescience in seeking treatment for a condition that could have been life-threatening, had it been left for another couple of months.

Rusholme, Manchester
April 1917

James found his new life in the city strange at first. The regulars reminded him of the men who worked for his father, the sort of men he had never mixed with before. He found them to be friendly, funny and more interested in who he was than where he came from.

Bill was something of a fixture at one end of the bar, so much so that the old man had his own stool. James often chatted with him when the pub wasn't too busy.

'Have you seen owt o' t'ghost yet, young 'un?'

'Ghost?'

'Aye, wanderin' about after dark. They reckon that's why the last barman did a runner.'

'I don't believe in ghosts, Bill,' he laughed, 'but I'll watch out for it.'

Among the many Wilmslow regulars, James couldn't help but notice a middle-aged man who came in two or three times a week, always wearing a suit and bowler hat. Sporting pince-nez spectacles and a large moustache, he would buy a pint and spend his evenings in a darkened corner, where he nursed a drink, smoked his pipe and read the *Manchester Evening News*. Bill said the man had followed the same routine, on and off, for the past couple of months, but he never spoke to anyone other than to buy a drink.

On his first evening off, James headed back to Brighton Grove. This time, when he knocked on the door, a dog barked. He heard shouting and a door slam, before the front door was opened by a tall, thin man wearing high-waisted trousers and a woollen cardigan. James could see a family resemblance.

‘Can I help you?’ The accent was very familiar.

‘My name’s James Driscoll. Your brother was my science teacher at Egglescombe. He suggested I look you up. Sorry, if you’re busy, I can come back another time.’

‘Not at all, I’ve been expecting you. Please, do come in.’ He led the way into a large living room, where a fire was burning in the grate. ‘Can I get you something to drink, James? I’ve just made a pot of tea.’

‘That would be nice. Thank you, Professor.’

‘Call me Paul, please.’ He disappeared into the kitchen, only to return in pursuit of his dog. It had shot past him when he’d opened the door and now had James pinned to the wall, trying to fend off its attempts to lick him.

‘Dalton, get down!’ Lucas had named the dog after John Dalton, the famous British chemist who hailed from the same part of Cumberland as the professor. The golden retriever did as it was told, crouching on its stomach with its tail wagging. ‘Sorry, James. I’ve only just got the mutt. He belonged to Mrs Higgins next door, but she couldn’t manage him.’

‘How old is he?’

‘Just a few months. He was an unwanted Christmas present.’

‘He’s certainly a handful.’

‘I know, he goes daft whenever anyone comes to the house.’

Once order was restored, the professor returned with the tea. He passed James a cup and offered him a biscuit.

‘Charles has told me a lot about you,’ he said. ‘I was sorry to hear of your loss. My brother’s not one for false praise, but he thinks you’d have no trouble passing the Higher School Certificate, even though you’re only halfway through the course.’

‘Perhaps,’ said James. ‘I’m good at remembering facts, which often seems to be all that’s required. To be honest, that’s why I found a lot of the course quite boring, Professor, … sorry, Paul.’

‘Well, Charles has no doubt that you’re going to make a name for yourself as a physicist one day.’

James blushed at the compliment. ‘I don’t know about that, sir, but it’s a fascinating subject and I’m keen to learn.’

‘Would you be interested in completing your studies if that could be arranged?’

'I want that more than anything,' he replied, surprised by the question. 'How would that be possible? I have no money, so I can't afford the fees.'

'There might be a way. Let me ask around and I'll let you know. Where are you staying?'

'The Wilmslow. I'm working there.'

'I know it. It's one of the nicer pubs in Rusholme.'

James spent the rest of the evening chatting with the professor about university life and how it had changed during the war. He didn't think he would ever get used to calling him Paul. It was quite late when he got back to the pub, and he walked into his room to find Sarah on her knees, wearing only a nightdress. He had never seen a woman reveal so much flesh before, and his face turned the colour of beetroot.

'What do you think you're doing?' he asked angrily, trying not to look.

'Oh, howya James, I was just looking for my earring,' she said coyly.

'And what makes you think it's in here?' His embarrassment was clear, which seemed to amuse her.

'Ah well, you see, the last barman and I had a bit of a t'ing going on and this was his room.'

'Even so, you could have asked. If I find it, I'll let you know.'

'Whatever you say, James,' she purred, running her hand up his arm as she left the room. Since his arrival, she had seemed determined to embarrass him, either through a constant stream of double entendres, or by deliberately squeezing past him as though there was not enough room behind the bar. James was not used to a woman being so forward and her ability to make him blush was unnerving. Could she really have designs on someone less than half her age, or did she just enjoy making him squirm?

When Alice arrived in Manchester for the summer term, James met her at London Road Station, and from their first embrace, it was as though they'd never been apart. On the tram journey down the Wilmslow Road, he noticed Sarah loitering in a shop doorway. As he watched, a man walked up to her, put an arm round her back and kissed her. James would have thought little of it, but for the fact that she took a brown envelope from inside her coat and handed it to him.

The man's face was turned away from James, but the envelope was pocketed a little too quickly, arousing his suspicions. What were they up to?

In Rusholme, James carried Alice's case the short distance to her hall of residence. There, much to his dismay, he learnt that gentleman callers were not allowed. As women were also barred from entering public houses, they would have to content themselves with early morning runs in Platt Fields Park and furtive meetings in his room, whenever he was able to smuggle her in by the side entrance.

James' attitude to work impressed Roy so much that he was happy to leave him in charge, while he took Sarah to a licensed victuallers' event. At the end of a typically busy Saturday night in May, James locked up and went to bed. Now that he was alone in the old building, he was much more aware of its creaky floorboards and rattling shutters. His thoughts turned to the ghost stories that were a regular topic of conversation among Bill and his mates. James had dismissed them as a poor attempt to unsettle him, but now he wasn't so sure. He pulled the covers up to his neck, told himself not to be so daft and drifted off to sleep.

Sometime later, he woke, sensing an eerie presence in the room. He heard a floorboard creak but, although now wide awake, he was too scared to move. Then the covers started to rise up, and before he could react, it was in the bed with him. He caught a sudden whiff of alcohol and perfume and, as something cold touched his leg, he leapt from the bed with a yell. His hands flailed desperately, searching for the light switch. When he found it, the dim glow revealed a nude Sarah looking up at him, an expression of sheer lust on her face. James was in a state of total shock, which turned to acute embarrassment as it dawned on him that he too was completely naked.

'What are you doing here?' she slurred.

'You're in my room! I thought you were a…' he stammered, covering himself with his hands as he decided not to say the word ghost.

'What? Come back to bed, love. I'm cold.'

He was suddenly angry. 'You're drunk, and you're old enough to be my mother. Now get out of my room!' He hadn't intended to be quite so blunt, but there was no taking it back.

Her voice took on a harder edge. 'You're a feckin' eejit. You don't know what you're missing,' she sneered, before gathering up her clothes and walking rather unsteadily out of the room.

Locking the door behind her, James sat on the edge of the bed and tried to make sense of what had just happened. With Alice sleeping less than half a mile away, he felt a sudden twinge of guilt, even though he had done nothing wrong.

The next morning, he tried to apologise to Sarah for his rudeness, explaining that she had taken him by surprise.

'I have absolutely no idea what you're talking about,' she said. 'You must have been dreaming, love.' The thought had crossed his mind, but the fact was that from then on, the flirting stopped, and she barely spoke to him.

He was too embarrassed to tell Alice, or indeed anyone else about his nocturnal encounter, so he tried to put it from his mind.

One evening, James was collecting glasses when he saw Sarah sitting in a corner booth with a man who had his back to him. He was holding her hand, and they seemed like more than friends. Later, he caught sight of him as he left, but he kept his head down, so his face wasn't visible. However, James could have sworn he was wearing a clerical collar. Was there more to Sarah Maguire than met the eye?

He was curious, so the following evening, he asked Bill, 'When did Sarah start working here?'

'Must have been about a year ago,' he replied. 'She certainly brightened the place up.'

'Has she had many men friends?'

'Why, d'you fancy your chances, lad?'

James blushed. 'No, she's far too old for me and besides, I have a girlfriend.'

The old man was quiet for a few moments, before saying, 'There is someone she sees occasionally. Funny thing, though…'

'He's a priest?' ventured James.

'That's right, how did you know?'

'He was in last night. I was wondering if it might be her brother.'

'I doubt it, somehow,' said Bill. 'I saw them kissing last week.'

James raised an eyebrow. 'What sort of priest goes round kissing barmaids?'

'Dunno, lad. Maybe it was his day off.'

His curiosity piqued, James probed a little deeper when the pub shut, and Roy handed him a shandy.

'Do you know why Frank Collins left, Roy?'

'That's a good question. I 'ad a feeling he were in some sort of bother, but he wouldn't talk about it. Takings were down, and Sarah reckoned he 'ad 'is fingers in the till.'

'Really, I thought the two of them were romantically involved?'

'Good God, no, they couldn't stand the sight of each other. Whatever gave you that idea?'

'Just something somebody said.'

'No, you've misconscrewed, Jim.' Roy had an uncanny ability to make everyday words and phrases sound ridiculous, yet still recognisable. 'When I asked 'im about it, he said it weren't 'im. Reckoned he were a scrapecoat.'

'Pardon?'

'A scrapecoat. You know, blamed for summat that wasn't 'is fault.'

A scapegoat! 'Ah, I see.'

'Any roads, one minute he were 'ere and the next he were gone. Never even packed a bag, and not a word to anyone. No more money went missing, so I suppose it must 'ave been 'im.'

When Paul Lucas called in to see James that weekend, they strolled across to the park and sat watching the ducks on the boating lake.

'I had a word with one of my colleagues. He's had the sort of career I think you might be interested in, and he'd be happy to meet you for a cup of coffee sometime, if you so wish. He's very experienced, so he can give you some sound advice about career options.'

'That's very kind of him, but I think my options are limited until I earn enough money to pay for my education. I certainly can't afford university fees on what Roy's paying me, and I wouldn't want to waste his time.'

'Just meet him and listen to what he has to say. What have you got to lose?'

'Nothing, I suppose. What's his name?'

'Rutherford.'

James' jaw almost hit the floor. 'Rutherford? Ernest Rutherford, the Nobel Prize winner?'

Paul smiled. 'The very same.'

‘I don’t know what to say, Professor. Thank you, of course I’d like to meet him.’

On a rainy morning less than a week later, James arrived at the university’s Physics Laboratory, just off Oxford Road. He sat in the reception area, scarcely able to believe that he was about to meet a world-famous scientist. Sir Ernest Rutherford FRS was a tall, stocky New Zealander, with a booming voice that heralded his arrival long before he entered the room.

When he did, he shook James’ hand warmly, saying, ‘Welcome to my world, Mr Driscoll.’

‘Thank you, Professor,’ he replied. ‘This is such an honour for me.’

Rutherford regarded him with staring blue eyes and replied, ‘Yes, I suppose it must be.’

James smiled. *Not a modest man, then,* he thought.

They went into a small meeting room and sat down at a table, where someone had placed two cups of coffee. Rutherford lit his pipe and drew on it, and James, feeling the need to fill the silence, said, ‘So, this is where you discovered the nucleus?’

‘That, and a few other things,’ said Rutherford. ‘We live in exciting times, Mr Driscoll. This department is at the forefront of nuclear physics, and we’re also heavily involved in war work.’

‘What sort of work?’ asked James curiously.

‘That will have to remain secret, I’m afraid. Much of what we’re doing here is covered by the Official Secrets Act, but I can tell you that we’ve saved a great many lives.’

‘I can imagine,’ said James.

‘You can? Well, imagination is a good place to start, but when Edison said, “Genius is one percent inspiration and ninety-nine percent perspiration,” he pretty much summed up what goes on here.’

In fact, as they spoke, Rutherford was only weeks away from splitting the atom. Had he not been constrained by the Official Secrets Act, he might have told James about his ground-breaking study of sound waves and their potential use in submarine detection. In fact, the basement of the building they were in was now a large concrete water tank, used for all manner of underwater experiments.

'Let's get down to business, shall we?' said Rutherford. 'How old are you, Mr Driscoll?'

'Eighteen in October, sir.'

'Really? You look older. Now, tell me about your father.'

James paused, a little surprised by the request. 'Erm, he owns a cotton mill in Welbeck. It was very successful before the war, but my father's something of a Luddite.'

'That's a strange thing to say about a mill owner.'

James laughed. 'I don't mean that he'd smash his own machines. He refused to invest in modern machinery because it would require fewer people. He couldn't stand the thought of his workers losing their jobs.'

'That's a little short-sighted, but understandable. So, how did the two of you fall out?'

'I'm the last of the Driscolls, you see. My father wanted me to become an engineer and take over the business one day. I'm afraid I've disappointed him.'

'So why do you want to be a physicist?'

James thought that if he told such an eminent man the real reason, he would think he had lost his mind. Instead, he said, 'I think it's the most exciting subject imaginable, sir. There is so much we don't yet know. Scientific experiment is the way in which we can begin to understand the way the world works.'

'That's a very good answer. You remind me of a young man who used to be a student here. His name was Tom Royds, and his parents worked in a cotton mill. He was like you in many ways, and he became an accomplished physicist. In fact, we published several papers together.'

'If his parents worked in a mill, how could he afford the fees?'

'He won a scholarship. Does that sound like something that would interest you?'

James felt a tingle of excitement at the thought. Until that moment, he had no idea that such a thing was even possible. 'I don't know, sir,' he said. 'What would it entail?'

'You would need to pass an examination in physics, chemistry and maths, as well as attending an interview. There is stiff competition for places, but if you were successful, the scholarship would give you an income of one hundred pounds a year for three years.'

‘Would I qualify? My family is wealthy. I would hate to think I was depriving someone worse off than me of the chance. And wouldn’t I need my parents’ permission?’

‘Yes, you would.’ Rutherford saw James’ shoulders sag at the news. He obviously thought that his father would deny him the opportunity. ‘Look,’ he said, ‘it’s an unusual situation, I’ll admit. It would not normally be open to someone from your background, but the admissions tutor agreed with me that these are unprecedented times. I think we’d be looking for the best candidate, not the most disadvantaged. Perhaps, if I was to speak to your parents?’

‘I think you’d be wasting your breath, sir, but you’re welcome to try.’

‘So, you would be interested if I could talk them round?’

Manchester University, or to give it its full title, the Victoria University of Manchester, was a cradle of modern science, the home of Nobel Prize winners. How could he not be interested?

‘Most definitely, sir, thank you.’

‘Very well, then. If your father’s amenable, you’ll hear from the registrar in due course.’

Later, when he met Alice for lunch, James was in high spirits as he regaled her with the details of his first meeting with a bona fide celebrity.

‘Did you mention time travel?’ she asked.

‘No, I think it might have been a very short meeting if I had.’

‘Wise decision,’ she said. ‘It does sound rather far-fetched.’

‘Perhaps. Anyway, it’s something of a moot point. My father won’t give his permission. He’s much too stubborn.’

‘You never know, he may surprise you.’

16

Wilmersdorf, Berlin
May 1917

Einstein was well enough to return home by the new year, but did not fully recover, mainly due to poor diet. The message had warned him when he would die, but as the proverb promised, April showers brought forth May flowers and he was still alive. Had the operation saved his life? The most recent weekend had been particularly difficult, and he had taken to his bed, feeling curiously lethargic. Monday was spent in dressing gown and slippers, with only a bowl of watery soup to sustain him. A concerned colleague had called in the evening, but his knocking was ignored.

Now, the knocking started again, but this time it was more persistent. Einstein rarely received visitors, other than the occasional student who was struggling with a problem. Today, he opened the door to his cousin Elsa.

'They tell me you've been unwell, Albertle.' It was the name she had called him by since childhood. Kissing him on the cheek, she walked past him into the kitchen, tut-tutting at the mess. 'You must be one of the untidiest men I have ever met. You're looking very thin. Have you been eating properly?' She opened a cupboard door and inspected the contents. 'There's nothing here! What have you been living on?'

'*Beruhige dich!* I'll eat when I'm hungry, but there's a war on you know.' He was right, of course, but he was wasting his breath telling Elsa to calm down. War meant shortages, particularly in the cities. Basic items such as bread and milk were in scarce supply and priority was naturally given to industrial workers and pregnant women. Berliners were becoming seriously malnourished, and Einstein found it difficult to look at the queues of people, holding cards for rations that did not exist, or the gaunt faces of children waiting in line outside the soup kitchens that had sprung up all over Berlin. It was no surprise to anyone that there were no elephants left in Berlin Zoo.

Evidence of abject poverty could be seen everywhere, even in wealthy middle-class suburbs like Wilmersdorf, where much of the parkland was given over to the production of fruit and vegetables. Elsa took a turnip and a small loaf of black bread from her bag.

'I had to queue for over an hour for this, so you're going to sit down and eat something.' Einstein knew there was no point in arguing and, when he thought about it, realised that he hadn't eaten in more than twenty-four hours. He smiled weakly, watching her try to produce something appetising from the meagre rations.

Later, while they ate, Elsa told him she had reached a decision. 'There's an empty apartment in my block in Schöneberg,' she said. 'I'm going to arrange for you to move there so I can keep an eye on you. You need looking after, Albertle.' He did not have the strength to argue. Although he and Elsa were first cousins, they'd had an affair five years earlier. Since then, his marriage to Mileva had broken down and she had taken his two sons back to Zurich. He had to admit that he liked the idea of being waited on hand and foot while he regained his strength.

By the end of the month, Einstein left Wilmersdorf for Haberlandstrasse in Schöneberg, where Elsa moved him into a fourth-floor apartment. There she fussed over him like a mother hen as she nursed him back to health. She went to great lengths to make sure he had eggs, butter and bread in his diet. She even found his favourite cigars. He often thought that he would not have survived without her.

Rusholme, Manchester
June 1917

After seeing Sarah hand an envelope to the man in the street, James couldn't get her out of his head. What was in that envelope? If she had lied about Frank, then she had not been looking for an earring, so why had she been in his room? Why had Frank Collins left without his things, and what was she doing, kissing a priest? He decided to look for some answers the next time she went out. He only had a couple of days to wait. Since his arrival, Sarah often disappeared for hours on end when she wasn't working. James knew that Roy kept a skeleton key on a hook in the downstairs pantry. When he saw her walk down Wilmslow Road and disappear out of sight, he retrieved the key and took his chance. Once inside, he saw that the room was a similar size to his own and sparsely furnished. There was a King James Bible on top of a chest of drawers, and a pad of foolscap paper lay on the dressing table. With the sun streaming in through the window, James could see shadows on the top sheet of the pad, caused by the impressions left by whatever had been written on the sheet above. It reminded him of an old story by Arthur Conan Doyle, in which Sherlock Holmes told Watson that a message written in pencil usually left markings on the sheet below. On an impulse, he grabbed the pad and ran back to his own room. Taking a soft-tipped pencil from the desk drawer, he pressed it onto the paper and rubbed it across the sheet. When he was done, the markings became clearer, and he sat looking at rows of numbers. What use did Sarah have for a sheet full of numbers?

Suddenly, he heard her voice downstairs. Leaping from the chair, he ripped off the top sheet and hurried back to her room with the pad. Returning it to the dressing table, he ran onto the landing, shut the door as quietly as he could and locked it, slipping the key into his trouser pocket. As he stood there with his back to the staircase, he could hear her footsteps behind him. He did the only thing he could think of and knocked loudly on the door.

'What do you want?' she asked sharply, as she reached the top of the stairs. She didn't seem too happy to see him.

'Oh, there you are. I was just going to ask if you wanted a cup of tea.'

'You've never offered me a cup of tea before. Why now?'

Thinking on his feet, he said, 'Call it a peace offering if you like.'

'Hmm, well, I don't need anything from you. Go away.'

'Suit yourself,' he said, retreating to his own room and breathing a huge sigh of relief. Locking the door, he sat at the desk and carefully copied the numbers onto a separate sheet, hiding the original inside a textbook. The numbers ranged from one to 371, and they were all separated by full stops. He noticed that two of the numbers appeared to have been crossed out. What could that mean? That evening, he went for a walk in Platt Fields Park with Alice. They sat on a bench by the lake, and he showed her the sheet.

'What do you make of this?' he asked.

'What is it?'

'I'm not sure, but it looks like some sort of code. I think it might be important.'

'How exciting! Let me see.' Alice studied the sheet for a few minutes, then glanced up at James. 'I could be wrong, but I think this is a book cipher.'

'A what?'

'A book cipher. It's one of the simplest ways of sending a secret message.'

'So, it should be easy to decode, then?'

'Not necessarily. The problem is, if you don't know which book was used, it's impossible to crack. If I'm right, then the total number of numbers should be divisible by three.'

James took the sheet and started to count. 'Sixty-nine numbers, you're right. Why a multiple of three?'

'In a book cipher, the first number is the page, the second the line and the third the word. We did it in history. Benedict Arnold used a cipher like this to send messages to the British during the American War of Independence.'

'And I thought I needed the help of a mathematician! Okay, well, there was a bible in the room where I found this.'

'That must be it, then. If you can get your hands on a copy, you can decode the message. It has to be the same edition though, or it won't work.'

'You're a genius!' he cried, taking her head in his hands and kissing her full on the lips.

'You noticed,' she laughed, putting her arms around him and pulling him closer.

Back at the Wilmslow, he waited for Sarah to go out again and watched her board a tram from his bedroom window. He had taken the precaution of having another skeleton key cut, so when he was back in her room, he examined the bible. Thankfully, it was a recent edition of a popular version. He took the coded sheet to the City Library on Oxford Road, where he found the same edition in the Religious Studies section. Sitting at a desk, he started to convert the numbers into words. The first word on the thirty-fourth line of page 143 was 'then.' He wrote it down. The fifth word on the twenty-sixth line of page sixty-four was 'fruit.' It didn't take him long to realise that the resulting passage was complete gibberish.

It was the wrong book.

At the weekend, James went for a walk with Alice and gave her the bad news.

'You're sure you used the same edition?'

‘Yes, exactly the same, just like you said.’

‘Well, if she’s up to no good, then no matter what book she used, she’d want to keep it close.’

‘I’ll have another look in her room, but I need to be careful. The first time I went in there, she almost caught me.’

‘Hmm, you need a lookout. Does she go out at the same time every day?’

‘Not every day, but I’ve noticed that she always goes out on a Wednesday afternoon.’

‘Right, then. Next Wednesday, I’ll be in your room, waiting for her to go out. When she does, I’ll keep watch at the window while you look for the book. What do you think?’

‘It’s worth a try.’

‘Good, that’s settled. Now, have you heard from the university yet?’

‘No, and I don’t think I will. Father will never give his permission.’

‘Do you think it would help if I spoke to him?’

The look on James’ face was a mixture of astonishment and amusement.

‘What have I said?’ asked Alice.

‘My father? The man who believes that a woman’s place is in the home, where she doesn’t have to worry about things that she hasn’t got the brains to understand.’

Alice bristled with indignation. ‘Oh, really? What sort of things?’

‘Business, money, making decisions, that sort of thing. In his opinion, women are too emotional and impressionable to be rational.’

‘He’s a dinosaur!’

‘Like many men of his generation, I’m afraid, but as you said, the world is changing.’

‘Not quickly enough for my liking.’ Alice looked around and saw a large Catholic church looming ahead of them. Realising where they were, she said, ‘Come with me, I want to show you something.’

Intrigued, James followed as she took the next turning on the right. They were in Nelson Street, where she stopped outside an innocuous-looking red-brick house.

‘Why are we here?’ asked James, nonplussed.

'Because this is where Emmeline Pankhurst used to live. You're living less than a mile from the place where she held her first meeting.'

'Is this your way of telling me that you're a suffragette?'

'Would it matter if I was?'

'Not really. I don't know enough about them to have an opinion.'

'Well, perhaps you should get one. You do know that women are not allowed to vote?'

'Of course, but neither are men, unless they own property.'

'I know. Do you think that's right?'

'No, but …'

'No buts. Unless your father stands in your way, you're going to go to university. You'll get a degree and a well-paid job. You'll buy property and get the vote. Women don't have those opportunities.'

'That's not entirely true. You're at university for a start.'

'Yes, but I shouldn't be here. I was offered a place at Cambridge, but I had to choose Manchester instead.' The anger in her voice was unmistakeable.

'Why? Cambridge is one of the best universities in the world.'

'That may be so, and I could have studied there, but they wouldn't have given me a degree.'

James couldn't hide his surprise. 'Because you're a woman?'

'Yes.'

'That's ridiculous.'

'I'm glad you think so.'

'Don't worry, I'm not my father, Alice. As far as I'm concerned, you're the equal of any man. If you want to stand up for your rights by chaining yourself to railings, I won't try to stop you. Just don't go jumping in front of any horses!' Four years earlier, Emily Davison had made worldwide headlines when she was killed after stepping in front of the King's horse during the Epsom Derby.

Alice put her arms round James' neck and kissed him. As they walked arm in arm down Oxford Road, she said, 'If it was just peaceful protest, I might be tempted to join them, but I don't think they're going to achieve their aims through violence. Putting lives at risk doesn't seem to me to be the best way of getting what they want.'

The Pankhursts had orchestrated a reign of terror that included arson and the planting of bombs in churches and on trains. They even sent letter bombs to the home of the then-Chancellor, David Lloyd

George. They suspended their campaign when war broke out, but by then, four people had been killed and many more injured.

'Maybe they thought it was the only way to make the government take them seriously,' said James.

'That's not an excuse,' said Alice.

As they walked back towards the Wilmslow, James said, 'I'll tell you something. The first time I walked along this road, when I was looking for work, almost every shop was staffed by women. As far as I could tell, they were doing just as good a job as men, and they were far more polite. With so many men away, the country would be on its knees right now if it wasn't for women.'

'Do you really think so?' said Alice. 'You should become a politician.'

'I didn't realise you thought so little of me,' quipped James.

She laughed. 'Seriously though, I don't think many men share your view. You watch, when the war is over, women will be expected to go back to being housewives who rely on their husbands for everything.'

'Surely not,' he replied, but he couldn't help thinking that she was probably right.

The following Wednesday afternoon, Sarah went out as usual. James and Alice were in the room next door and heard her leave. Alice sat on a chair next to the window and watched from behind the net curtains as she entered a shop on Wilmslow Road. James leapt into action, entering her room and starting a methodical search. He checked in, under and behind the chest of drawers, under the bed and in the wardrobe, where several shoeboxes were stacked underneath a rail full of dresses. Before he could look any closer, he heard Alice's fist banging on the wall between the two rooms. It was her signal that Sarah was on her way back.

'Well?' said Alice when he returned.

'Nothing,' he replied.

'So where did you look?'

'All the obvious places.'

'You mean all the places that she definitely wouldn't have hidden it?'

James paused. The look on Alice's face said, 'You're an idiot.'

'I, erm, I was going to keep looking. She's usually out for a lot longer.'

'Right. So, we've wasted the afternoon, then?'

'Not really,' he said, putting his arms around her waist and breathing in the heady scent of her perfume as he pulled her closer. 'I can't think of anywhere else I'd rather be right now.'

'Well, I've an assignment I should be working on,' she replied, as she ran her fingers through his hair. They kissed in a long, passionate embrace that continued as they fell onto the bed.

'Maybe I can help you,' said James. 'What's the assignment about?'

'What assignment?'

A week later, they tried again. This time, James kept watch while Alice searched the room. Unsurprisingly, the shoeboxes contained shoes. She walked over to a chest of drawers and opened the top drawer. It was stuffed with several pairs of rather voluminous knickers. She lifted them up and put her hand underneath, carefully feeling around the bottom of the drawer. At the back was what felt like a book. She lifted it out and looked at the cover. It was a first edition copy of John Buchan's latest spy novel, *Greenmantle*. Putting it back where she had found it, she checked that nothing looked out of place, and went back to James' room, having locked Sarah's door.

'Any luck?' he asked.

'You did say you checked the chest of drawers, didn't you?' she said.

'Yes. Well, sort of. I didn't want to rummage about in her underthings, if you know what I mean.'

'No, and I'm sure she wouldn't want you to.'

'You don't know Sarah,' he said under his breath.

'Pardon?'

'Nothing. So, you didn't find anything, then?' he asked.

'Yes, I did, by rummaging about in her underthings.'

'Oh!' His face coloured. 'Sorry.'

Alice smiled at his obvious embarrassment. She was excited by her find. 'Answer me this,' she said. 'If it isn't the book we're looking for, why would she hide it in her knicker drawer?'

'Good point,' he replied. 'Come on, then, Sherlock. We've got a code to break.'

On their way into town, James heard the word Greenmantle for the first time. Modern novels were not kept in the university library, but they found what they were looking for in a bookshop on Oxford Road. On campus, they found a quiet corner in the refectory and started converting numbers into words as before.

When they had finished, James' hands were shaking as he read out Sarah's message. 'It says "Munitions factory with ten thousand shells. Fifty-three whistled, twenty-eight minutes, fifteen seconds north. Two succeeded, eighteen minutes, thirty-nine seconds west."'

A couple of words were undoubtedly wrong, but Alice had been right, it was a book cipher. Sixty-nine numbers had created a message twenty-three words long. The words whistled and succeeded appeared where James would have expected to see the word degrees, but in both cases the number in the code had a line through it. Alice had been reading up on book ciphers and explained that the word degrees must have been missing from the text of Buchan's novel. In that event, the convention was to put a line through the number, signifying that it referred to a letter rather than a word.

James checked the seventh line on page one. 'The third letter on that line is d. Fifty-three d, twenty-eight minutes.' The same was true of the fourth letter on the nineteenth line of the same page. Two d, eighteen minutes. The cipher was surprisingly simple if you knew which book had been used as the key. If not, it was pretty much unbreakable. Sarah's mistake had been leaving the book where he, or rather Alice, could find it.

Grudgingly, James had to admire the audacity of using a novel about a female spy to send messages. For more than a year, the German command had been bombing key targets from Zeppelin airships, without much success. However, in recent weeks they had started using long-range Gotha bombers, and casualties were mounting. The information hidden in the message would have been like gold dust to an enemy targeting Trafford Park, one of the largest industrial parks in the world, and home to the huge Westinghouse engineering works. There was also the Ford Motor Company and a plethora of smaller factories, all turned over to the production of military vehicles, munitions and chemicals to aid the war effort.

17

Manchester University
June 1917

There was no doubt about it. Sarah was a spy, and James was going to have to do something. Alice had a tutorial to get to, so he kissed her goodbye and sprinted the short distance to the Schunck Building on Burlington Street, where Paul Lucas had an office in the School of Chemistry. He would know what to do.

'Hello, James, this is a surprise. What can I do for you?'

'I don't know where to start, Professor.'

'How about the beginning?'

He told him about the envelope, Sarah's alleged relationship with Frank Collins, and her lost earring. He explained why he had gone into her room, and how he had found the indented writing. Once he had seen the cipher and Buchan's novel, Paul sat back in his chair and puffed out his cheeks. 'You have been busy! I think you need to take this to the police right now.'

Within the hour, James was standing at the front desk of the Town Hall police station, his heart pounding in his chest. The desk sergeant kept him waiting for twenty minutes, and he almost lost his nerve. He was about to leave when the officer spoke in a gruff Geordie accent. 'What do you want?'

'I'd like to report a crime, officer.'

'Name?'

'James Driscoll.'

'Address?'

James was becoming irritated that the man hadn't even looked him in the eye. 'The Wilmslow Public House, Rusholme.'

The sergeant looked up. 'Have you reported this to your local station, Mr Driscoll?' he asked impatiently.

'No.'

'Well, can I suggest that you do so?'

'I thought it was too important for a local station.'

'What's so important that you had to come all the way here?'

James looked around at the people sitting in the reception area. 'It's a rather sensitive matter. Is there a room where I can make a statement?'

‘I’m afraid we don’t have anyone available right now. You can wait, but you could be here for hours.’

‘Forget it. Can I make a note of your name?’

‘Sergeant Clayton, why?’

‘For the newspapers, Sergeant. When this story is front-page news, I want to make sure everyone knows just how helpful you were.’

Timewasters were a great source of annoyance to Sergeant Clayton, who gave James a disparaging look. ‘Run along now, laddie,’ he said dismissively.

On the following Tuesday, a uniformed policeman walked into the Wilmslow. Showing his warrant card, he said, ‘PC Turner.’

James was on his own, while Sarah was somewhere in the back.

‘I can’t talk to you here!’ hissed James, looking around furtively.

The constable was confused. ‘Why not?’

‘I just can’t,’ he replied, unsure whether Sarah was within earshot.

‘We can always do this down at the station if you’d prefer. I simply want to know if you’ve seen Frank Collins.’

‘The man who used to work here?’ It was James’ turn to be confused.

‘That’s right, sir. He’s been reported missing. Do you have any information regarding his whereabouts?’

‘No, officer. He left before I started.’

‘There now, that wasn’t so difficult, was it, sir?’

‘I thought you were here for something else,’ said James as Sarah appeared next to him.

‘And what might that be?’

‘Nothing. This lady might be able to help you.’

James started collecting glasses. In a darkened corner of the bar, the customer in the suit and bowler hat handed him an empty pint glass but would not let go.

‘Same again, sir?’ asked James, looking him in the eye.

The man spoke quietly in a lilting Welsh accent. ‘What made you so jumpy in front of that policeman, lad?’

‘You wouldn’t believe me if I told you.’

‘Try me,’ the man said, leaning closer and showing him a warrant card that read DCI Hughes, Special Branch.

James' first thought was that he was in trouble, and he began to stutter. 'I… I'll come back when I get my break.'

'Take your time, lad,' said Hughes, who smiled as he relaxed his grip on the glass. 'Another one in there, if you don't mind.'

As James poured him another beer, he relaxed as he realised that the detective was hardly likely to be there for him. When he took his break half an hour later, Hughes was still sipping at his pint. 'Why did you think that policeman was here?' he asked once more.

James looked over his shoulder. In a whisper, he said, 'I can't really tell you here. It's to do with someone who works here, and she's less than ten yards away right now.'

'Can you come into the station tomorrow morning?'

'I was there last week. Your Sergeant Clayton didn't want to know.'

'Did he not? Well, I do. I'm not here for the good of my health, you know.'

The next day, James returned to the station. This time, he asked for DCI Hughes by name, and was shown into an interview room. Ten minutes later, Hughes arrived, followed by a red-faced Sergeant Clayton, who put two cups of tea down on the table and avoided eye contact with James as he left the room. The man had obviously been on the receiving end of a severe dressing-down from his superior.

'Thanks for coming in, lad,' said Hughes. 'Now then, what can you tell me about Sarah Maguire?'

'You know her name?'

'Let's just say I've been keeping tabs on Miss Maguire for some time. Now, what do you know?'

James handed over the sheet and told the detective everything he knew about the cipher, and his suspicions about Sarah.

'And you cracked this code all by yourself?'

'Yes, sir.' That wasn't strictly true, but something told him to keep Alice's name out of it.

'Very good. Now, what can you tell me about Frank Collins?'

'Only what I've been told. He didn't get on with Sarah, although she claimed to have had a relationship with him. That's all I know.'

'His family have reported him missing. Do you have any idea where he might have gone?'

'No, sorry. Do you think something may have happened to him?'

‘I’m afraid it’s too early to say,’ said Hughes, rising from his chair and bringing the interview to a close. ‘Thank you, sir, your information could be most helpful to our investigation.’

‘Why have you been watching her, inspector?’

‘There’s a lot I’m unable to tell you, Mr Driscoll, but it’s vital you say nothing to alarm her. If you could go back and act as if nothing has happened, we might just be able to set a little trap for her.’

James wasn’t at all sure that he could act normally around Sarah, so he decided to keep well out of her way.

Rusholme, Manchester

When a letter arrived from the university, inviting James to an interview in late July, he wondered how Rutherford had gained his father’s permission. He was excited at the possibility of studying at such a prestigious institution, and grateful to have something to take his mind off the fact that Alice had gone home for the summer. He had never been in love before and when they were apart, it felt as if a part of him was missing.

Much of his spare time was spent in the City Library, preparing for the forthcoming examination. Topics such as the general properties of matter and the behaviour of elements were simply a matter of revision. Algebra, geometry and trigonometry came easily to him, and his understanding of mechanics, angles and forces was particularly strong. What he hoped would give him the edge on the day was his detailed knowledge of the latest research into radiation, relativity and his favourite subject, crystallography. He had the feeling that, if time travel was ever discovered, crystals would play a part.

On the day of the interview, he arrived at the Science Department, smartly dressed in a new suit and tie. He was early, but after meeting the other candidates, many of them as poor as church mice, he wondered whether his affluent attire had been such a good idea. He didn’t want to alienate the interview panel from the start. After a two-hour exam that covered maths, physics and chemistry, lunch was provided in the university refectory. In the afternoon, when he walked nervously into the interview room, he was pleased to see

Rutherford, sitting between two rather stern-looking gentlemen, in his capacity as Langworthy Professor of Physics.

The great man looked him in the eye and said loudly, 'Ah yes, Mr Driscoll. Professor Lucas tells me that you understand the theory of relativity. Perhaps you could explain it to me one day.'

'I'm afraid that Professor Lucas was exaggerating, sir,' he replied. 'But I'm fairly confident that $e = mc^2$.'

The comment broke the ice, and they all smiled. James gave what he felt was an assured performance, despite being a little unnerved by the oldest member of the panel, who seemed determined to challenge everything he said.

'There are many who claim Professor Einstein's theory is nothing more than an unproven hypothesis,' said the man, 'based on conjecture rather than scientific fact. How would you respond to that?'

James thought for a moment before replying. 'It's a fair point, sir, but I think proof will be forthcoming and in years to come, it will be seen as the most important scientific advance since the days of Newton.'

When the interview was over, he called Alice from a phone box in the city centre. She wanted to know chapter and verse on the questions and the way he had answered them. She made encouraging noises, but only time would tell whether the interview panel were sufficiently impressed to offer him a scholarship.

The following week, when he had two days off, he made the three-hour journey to St Annes. Arriving at the railway station, he was reminded of his first visit on a wet and windy day, only four months earlier. This time, he was greeted by glorious sunshine and a beautiful girl running along the platform to fling her arms around him.

'I've missed you,' he said, kissing her on the lips, much to the disgust of an elderly lady, who was so shocked by such a public display of vulgarity that she hit him with her handbag. Alice laughed hysterically, that infectious laugh that he had grown to love so much.

As they walked along the seafront, she wanted to know more about his interview.

'It went pretty well,' he said, 'But I can't help thinking that there's going to be someone better qualified than I.'

'You're too modest for your own good, James,' she said. 'What was it that Roy said to you the other week?'

'Not to hide my light under a shovel.'

She burst out laughing. 'How could I forget?'

Two days with Alice was very precious but leaving her was torture. James mentioned that he was thinking of looking for a job in St Annes so that they could be together for the rest of the summer, but she wouldn't hear of it.

'You need to hang on to the job you've got for now, just in case the university are daft enough to give your place to someone else.'

'I suppose so,' he said gloomily. 'I just don't want to leave you.'

'Nor I you,' she said, as she wrapped her arms around his broad back. 'Juliet was right, wasn't she?'

'Juliet who?'

'Shakespeare's Juliet. Parting is such sweet sorrow.'

'I haven't read much Shakespeare,' he confessed. 'What's sweet about it?'

'He's talking about the anticipation of meeting again. It's not as if we're parting forever.'

On the journey back to Manchester, the weather took a turn for the worse, matching James' mood. By the time he was back in his room above the pub, his misery was complete. The way that Alice lit up every room she walked into was extraordinary, and this room felt empty without her.

One day in August, at an hour so early that even James was asleep, the house was disturbed by the hammering of fists on the front door, followed shortly afterwards by the sound of several pairs of boots running up the stairs. James opened his door just enough to see through the crack. There was a policeman on the landing. From Sarah's room, he heard the words '... treason. You are not obliged to say anything unless you wish to do so, but whatever you say will be taken down in…' As he was speaking, a shot rang out and the officer collapsed on the landing, mortally wounded. James shut his door quietly and sat down on the edge of his bed, shocked at what he'd just witnessed. There was a lot of shouting outside his room, followed by two more shots.

A voice cried out, 'All clear! Somebody call an ambulance!'

Shortly after that, there was a knock on his door. 'Who is it?' he asked.

'Police! Identify yourself!'

'James Driscoll, I live here. What's happening?'

'There's been an incident. Just stay where you are until we tell you to come out.'

When he was eventually allowed out of the room, there was a lone policeman guarding the scene. The landing was clear, save for a blood stain on the carpet.

'What's going on?' he asked.

'Your neighbour shot a policeman,' he answered.

'Is he alright?'

'No, he's dead, and so's she.'

Sarah's demise was the pub's main topic of conversation for the next week, but life slowly returned to normal, or as normal as life could be in wartime Rusholme. Late one evening, just before closing time, Paul Lucas called in.

'I'll have a pint,' he said, 'and one for yourself, James.'

They sat down at a table and Roy joined them.

'Evening, prof,' he said. 'I had a long chat with Gareth 'ughes yesterday.'

Lucas turned to James and explained. 'Roy was on the force with DCI Hughes, many years ago.'

'That's right, I were 'is sergeant when 'e were pounding the beat. He was still wet between the ears in them days.'

James knew that Roy meant wet behind the ears, but he smiled politely and nodded.

'Did he have anything to say about your barmaid?' asked Lucas.

'He certainly did.' Taking a copy of the *Manchester Evening News* from under his arm, he tossed it onto the table, saying, 'Have a read of this.'

Turning back to James, he said, 'You've really put the shit among the pigeons, lad.' James glanced at Lucas, who almost choked on his beer. Roy was oblivious to the mirth his latest malapropism had caused. 'Thanks to our Jim 'ere, Sarah and 'er 'ole network of spies were wiped out in one foul swoop.' More stifled laughter.

The front-page headline read, "Cop Killer Sinéad McKenna Shot and Killed." Underneath, the sub-heading read, "German spy ring exposed by local barman."

'Who's Sinéad McKenna?' asked James.

'That was Sarah's real name,' said Roy. 'The police had so much evidence against 'er, she didn't 'ave a case to stand on.' Lucas buried his face in his handkerchief and pretended to have a coughing fit.

The article revealed that she was the sister of Martin McKenna, a separatist republican rebel who was killed during the Easter uprising in 1916, along with James Connolly, Patrick Pearse, Tom Clarke and others. She had vowed revenge and offered her services to a German agent she met in Dublin. Sinéad was one of a number of spies who had gathered intelligence on the movement of ships, troops and munitions in north-west England for more than six months. Their handler, believed to be a man posing as a Catholic priest, had not yet been caught.

At Roy's insistence, James read aloud, 'It says "His network was exposed when coded messages were sent to a Gothenburg address, known to belong to an enemy agent."' He blushed as he read the next sentence. '"The code was broken by James Driscoll, a young barman at the Wilmslow Public House in Rusholme, who alerted the police."'

'You may have saved a great many lives, James,' said Lucas.

'Aye,' said Roy, 'and left me without a barmaid. We're going to be running round like eggless chickens in 'ere, son!'

Forest of Bowland, Lancashire
August 1917

Winter had set up camp on the banks of the River Hodder, not far from the village of Whitewell. He grieved for the loss of the woman he had hoped to spend the rest of his life with, a hope that was dashed through sheer bad luck. It was Sinéad's misfortune to have ended up in the same place as James Driscoll, a young man who was smart enough to have realised what she was up to. Smarter than Frank Collins, who had walked into the trap she had set for him, and who was now at the bottom of the Garside reservoir.

Winter's feelings were too raw at the moment, but he swore that Driscoll would feel his wrath. He and his nearest and dearest would suffer a terrible fate at Winter's hands, no matter how long it took.

Rusholme, Manchester

James read the grim news from Belgium, which brought back painful memories of the Somme, only a year earlier. Thousands of British troops were dying every day at Passchendaele, near Ypres, with no certainty that any real progress was being made. With conscription a real possibility, he wondered what his future might hold, should he be lucky enough to win a place at the university. By early September he had heard nothing, but he was looking forward to Alice returning for her final year.

One evening, Paul Lucas came to see him. 'Come and have a chat when you finish serving,' he said.

The last customer left at a quarter to ten, and James took his shandy over to the professor's table.

'I have some news for you. You should be getting a letter from the university about your application. They would like to offer you the scholarship …'

James' face broke into the widest smile. 'No! That's fantastic, thanks for letting me know.'

'Sorry James, I hadn't finished. They would like to offer you the scholarship, but they want to discuss it with you first. Someone noticed that you'll be eighteen by the time the course starts. You may well forfeit your place if you volunteer or are conscripted.'

His heart sank. Although he was thrilled to have been selected for a scholarship, it now seemed as though the war might rob him of his chance. Alice's father had been wrong, there was no sign of the conflict being over quickly. Tomorrow, James would make an appointment to see the admissions officer, but with little hope of success.

When everyone had left and the pub was locked up for the night, James retired to his room, put on his pyjamas, and sat in an armchair to read the final chapter of *Greenmantle*. When he was done, he closed the book and turned over the events of a long and eventful summer in his mind. He had fallen in love with a girl who he thought felt the same way about him. With her help, he had uncovered a nest of spies but, while he had no pity for Sarah, he couldn't help feeling a little guilty about the death of an innocent policeman. His future was uncertain, but he would never allow his father to dictate it. If anything, George had forced him to stand on his own two feet. Placing the book on the desk, he turned towards the bed and felt something sharp underfoot. Bending down, he picked up a woman's earring.

18

Manchester University
September 1917

When James arrived for his meeting with Rutherford, he was met by Mr Fiddes, the university's registrar. He took James into a meeting room, where Rutherford was sitting in an armchair, smoking his pipe. Fiddes was the first to speak.

'Are you aware of anything that would prevent you from being called up, on or after your eighteenth birthday?' The registrar's face was expressionless as he waited for the answer that would seal James' fate.

'No, sir.'

'Then I'm afraid we are unable to offer you a place at this university.'

James' heart sank. 'Thank you for letting me know,' he said, as he rose to leave.

'Hold on a moment.' Sir Ernest Rutherford's voice stopped James in his tracks, and he slowly sat back down again. 'Mr Driscoll, have you heard of Henry Moseley?

'As in Moseley's law? The formula for the atomic number?'

'Precisely. I knew Henry well. He was a brilliant young research assistant at this university before the war. Right now, he should be preparing to receive the Nobel Prize for his work on x-ray spectroscopy.'

James was surprised at the comment. 'I thought there was no prize for physics this year.'

'That's right, and do you know why? The panel decided not to award it. You see, Henry enlisted in the British Army. He was shot and killed at Gallipoli two years ago. This country lost one of its greatest scientific minds to a sniper's bullet that day.'

James was shocked. 'I had no idea,' he said. The Gallipoli campaign lasted eleven months and had been an unmitigated disaster for the Allies, who had been forced to withdraw after losing more than 140,000 men.

'After Henry died,' said Rutherford, 'the government banned our scientists from fighting for their country. Winning that scholarship was no mean feat, James. In my opinion, you have the potential to become one of this nation's most important young physicists, and you cannot be allowed to fight.'

James' chest swelled at the compliment. 'It's good of you to say so, sir.'

'I know you want to do your bit, James, but your country needs you here, where you can do the greatest good, not lying dead in a ditch somewhere that you can't even pronounce!'

James thought better of saying that he was a conscientious objector, for whom conscription would be a disaster. 'Very well, sir. What do you propose?'

'With your permission, I should like to request your exemption from conscription. Are you in agreement, Mr Fiddes?'

The registrar smiled and nodded.

'Then leave it with me. I'll be in touch.'

James' euphoria at this turn of events was plain to see. 'Thank you, sir,' he said quietly. 'Before you go, could I have a word in private, please?'

'If you make it quick. We'll have to walk and talk, I'm afraid.'

'Thank you, sir.' When they were alone, he continued. 'I was just wondering how you managed to change my father's mind?'

'I asked him if he was a patriot. I told him you were a remarkable young man, and this country needed you for the vital war work that lies ahead. I made it clear that we would only offer you a scholarship if you were the best man for the job.'

'Thank you,' said James, overwhelmed by such fulsome praise. 'What was his response?'

'He said that he wouldn't stand in your way, but he refused to pay for your education. He said that if your country needed you, it could bloody well pay for you, or words to that effect.'

'That sounds like Father,' said James with a rueful grin.

'No matter. He signed a letter of permission, there and then. I trust you're not going to let us down.'

'I won't sir, you have my word.'

With his place and finances secure, James told Roy he was leaving the Wilmslow. 'I'm sorry to be leaving you short-staffed, Roy,' he said.

'It's just another hurdle I'll 'ave to carry, son,' he replied.

'I suppose so.' James was going to miss Roy.

'You off to war, lad?'

'No. My country needs scientists, so I'm off to university.'

'Well, good luck to you, Jim. Mek your parents proud.'

'I don't think anything I do would make my father proud, Roy.'

'Don't you believe it, lad.' It was a throwaway remark, but the way he said it made James think that he was speaking from experience. The hug that followed was unexpected.

When Paul Lucas called in that evening, he shook him warmly by the hand. 'Well done, James. You have no idea how many people wanted that scholarship.' James' frown was not quite the reaction he had expected. 'You don't seem that happy about it.'

'I couldn't be happier, Professor, but I was just thinking about the people who didn't get it. Are they going to be called up to fight? Are their mothers going to be mourning them in a few months' time?'

'I don't really know what to say to that, other than to make sure you don't waste the opportunity you've been given. That really would be a tragedy.' Before leaving, Paul spoke with Roy for a while, and they called James over to join the chat.

'Roy tells me you're looking for somewhere to live. How would you like to rent my spare room in return for some gardening duties? There's only me and the dog now, so it would be good to have the company.'

James couldn't believe his luck. The Professor's home was only a ten-minute walk from Ashburne Hall. If Paul was agreeable, he would have a place to spend time with Alice at last, without having to sneak about. 'That's very kind of you, Professor.'

That weekend, he moved into Oakwood House and renewed his acquaintance with Dalton. Where James went, Dalton followed, and when Alice returned for her final year, the three of them became a familiar sight on their morning park runs.

James had never been fitter, and it wasn't long before he became the lynchpin of the university cross-country team. He was looking forward to playing for their cricket team in the Spring, but as fate would have it, almost three years would pass before he played the sport again.

James excelled at science and impressed everyone with his ability to pick up new and complex ideas. In addition to the taught syllabus, he was invited to take part in a project to examine the feasibility of sending secret signals, using sound waves that were outside the normal range of human hearing.

He also spent long hours in the library, looking for anything and everything to do with Albert Einstein. He found a tutor to help improve his German, so that he could read the latest publications, rather than having to wait for translations. He was particularly interested in one of Einstein's latest papers, in which he suggested that the process by which atoms emitted radiation in a spontaneous manner could be stimulated. It was a theory that James could test, in his quest to turn science fiction into scientific fact.

At Rutherford's suggestion, he also studied the legendary scientist, Nikola Tesla. He was the man responsible for designing the alternating current electricity supply system, as well as a series of revolutionary turbines, motors, and lamps. He had built an experimental wireless transmission station near New York, and proposed a World Wireless System to transmit text, voice and images around the globe. In 1892, he delivered a lecture to the Royal Institution during which, James was amazed to learn, he demonstrated the production of an incredibly bright light, the likes of which had never been seen before. There was no mention of the possible applications of such an unusual phenomenon. The article described Tesla as a "young but distinguished electrician", which to James was tantamount to saying that Einstein was 'not bad at physics.'

Rusholme, Manchester
December 1917

Having Alice living nearby was both a blessing and a curse for James. He was able to see her every day, but as his feelings for her grew stronger, so did the temptation to neglect his studies and spend more time with her. Fortunately, Alice was a little more conscientious than James and always put work ahead of pleasure, so much so that he began to wonder whether she felt as committed to their relationship as he did.

One morning, a couple of weeks before Christmas, James woke with a burning desire to show her how much she meant to him. He boarded an early train and was in St Annes by lunchtime. At Len Taylor's bank, he gave his name to the woman at the counter and asked if he could speak to the manager.

'Do you have an appointment, Mr Driscoll?' she asked. 'Mr Taylor is very busy today.'

'No, sorry,' he replied, 'but I do have a request that I think he should know about.'

'Can I ask the nature of the request?'

James thought for a moment. 'Can you just tell him that it has to do with a proposal?'

The woman disappeared into a back room. On her return, she showed him into an empty office, where he waited on tenterhooks for Alice's father to appear. Five minutes later, although it seemed much longer to James, the door opened and in walked Len Taylor.

'Good afternoon, Mr Driscoll,' he said in a very business-like manner, which made James even more nervous. 'I understand that you have a proposal for me, is that right?' His face gave nothing away.

'Not for you exactly, Mr Taylor,' replied James.

'Well, you can give me the details in a minute, but I have to remind you that there's a war on.' He sat back in his chair and steepled his fingers. 'As I'm sure you're aware, this is a difficult time to be making important decisions. I would need to be convinced that you have given this careful thought and weighed up the pros and cons before doing anything you might regret.'

'I most certainly have,' said James. 'I hope you'll understand when you hear what I have to say.'

'Come on then, out with it. What makes you think this proposal is sensible?'

'Because I love her, Mr Taylor.'

Len burst out laughing. 'I think you could have asked my permission in a slightly less cryptic way, James.'

'Is that a yes, then, sir?'

'I suppose it is, son, but I should warn you that Alice is hardly likely to be the sort of wife who stays at home while you go out to work.'

'I'm very glad to hear it,' said James.

'In that case, welcome to the family,' said his prospective father-in-law as they shook hands. 'Always assuming that she says yes, of course!'

James returned to Manchester in high spirits. That weekend, he bought a ring from a King Street jeweller, hoping it would be to her liking. On the Sunday morning, he brought it with him when they went for a run, accompanied as ever by Dalton. They stopped for a rest at a bench in a secluded part of the park, and he went down on one knee, as if to tie a shoelace. Alice's eyes widened in surprise as he produced a small box from his pocket. Dalton thought James wanted to play and leapt on him, knocking him to the ground. It wasn't quite what he'd planned. Alice was in hysterics as he lay on his back with Dalton licking his face, but he managed to blurt out, 'Will you marry me?'

'Who are you asking, me or the dog?' she laughed. Once he had recovered his composure, he got to his feet and sat down on the bench next to Alice. She couldn't look him in the eye. 'Ask me again,' she said.

'Alice Taylor, will you marry me?'

Taking his face in her hands, she looked deep into his cornflower blue eyes. 'Yes, of course I will. I love you, James, even though you smell like a dog! I'd like nothing more than to spend the rest of my life with you.'

They kissed, and James felt like the luckiest man in the world. 'Alice Driscoll,' he said. 'I like the sound of that.'

19

St Annes-on-the-Sea, Lancashire
December 1917

James and Alice spent a wonderful Christmas with her family, and she gave them the good news. Had it not been for the war and the grief it had caused, life for James would have been perfect. The Taylors made him feel part of their family, and the warm, happy household reminded him of childhood Christmases with Alfie. Every year, there had been a huge tree in the hallway of Allerton Manor, and the big house would be decked out in colourful streamers and lanterns. His father was fun back then, and family Christmases were special.

James wanted to tell his mother that he was getting married, but he didn't want Alice to suffer the humiliation of being snubbed by his father, so he decided to leave her in St Annes. On the day after Boxing Day, he made the journey to Kirk Allerton, where he checked into The Fleece for the night. After making sure his father wasn't at home, he surprised his mother with chocolates and flowers.

'Your father will think I have a secret admirer!' she said.

'Good. It might keep him on his toes.'

'Oh James, I've missed you so much. Are you still getting the headaches?'

'Yes, but they're not as bad as they once were. Why do you ask?'

'Haven't you guessed?' she asked.

'Guessed what?' It wasn't like his mother to be cryptic.

'It suddenly dawned on me. When you and Alfie were little, you often knew when the other was in pain.'

'Yes, I think it's a twin thing. I remember one time…' James' voice tailed off as he realised what his mother was saying. 'They started when Alfie was killed, didn't they?'

'I think so,' she said with a pained expression on her face. He put his arms around her, and they cried. Casting his mind back to the previous summer, James recalled reading Alfie's last letter, never suspecting that his brother was already dead.

'I do have some better news for you, Mother. I've met a girl. Her name's Alice and I think you'll like her. I've asked her to marry me.'

Ellen's eyes lit up and she clasped her hands together. 'That's wonderful news, James! What's she like? Does she come from money?'

'Does that matter?' he asked sharply.

'Not to me, but I imagine it might to your father.'

'That's his problem, then. He doesn't control my life anymore, Mother.'

'No, I suppose not, but I wish you two could resolve your differences.'

'So do I. I tell you what, why don't you come and meet Alice in Manchester in a few weeks' time?'

'I'd love to. I'll let you know when I'm coming, and I'll tell your father I'm going shopping.'

On his return to Rusholme, Paul Lucas was waiting to welcome him. 'Did you have a good Christmas, James?'

'Yes thanks, Paul. It was wonderful. What about you?'

'Very quiet, apart from the burglary.'

'Burglary! When?'

'Someone broke in here on Boxing Day, while I was out walking the dog.'

'Was anything taken?'

'That's the strange thing. As far as I can tell, absolutely nothing. You might want to check your room though.'

A quick look around revealed that, as far as James could tell, nothing was missing. 'You're right. Maybe you disturbed them?'

'I imagine so. The cheeky so-and-so made themselves a cup of tea and left half of it on the kitchen table. Dalton was agitated when we got back. Dashed annoying though. Oh, and by the way, there's a letter for you in the hall.'

The crumpled envelope and its contents were in a sorry state and looked as if they had been dried out after being dropped in the rain or snow. Thankfully, the letter was still legible. It was from Alice, telling him that she loved him and would arrive on New Year's Eve on the 5:15 train. He missed her more each day and couldn't wait for her return.

At London Road Station, he waited impatiently on the platform with butterflies in his stomach. When the train arrived, it was more than half full. He craned his neck, trying to spot her among the throng, but when the other passengers had left, he began to wonder whether she had missed it. He was about to look for a telephone box when he heard raised voices coming from the rear of the train. A guard came running past him, blowing his whistle, and James instinctively began to walk towards the commotion. As he reached the last carriage, the guard arrived with a policeman in tow. 'Make way there please, sir.'

He moved aside and held the door open for the two men. He could see that the carriage wasn't empty. Lying on the floor was the body of a woman, red hair lying in a tangled mess on the floor.

'ALICE!' he cried.

James stood at the door of the carriage, sheer horror etched upon his face. The compartment was enclosed, with eight seats and an external door on either side. When the train was in motion, it was inaccessible to anyone on board. There was an emergency cord, but it had not been pulled.

'I'm sorry sir, you can't come in here,' said the police officer. 'Please stay on the platform.'

'But I'm her fiancé. Is she alive?' he asked, dreading the answer.

The officer examined her and said, 'There's a faint pulse. Someone call an ambulance, now!' While the guard ran off to make the call, he started lifting Alice's arms up in the air, then crossing them over her chest.

'What are you doing?'

'I'm trying to help her breathe until the ambulance arrives. Can you tell me her name, sir?'

'Alice Taylor, and I'm James Driscoll. What's happened to her?'

'I would say she's been violently attacked by person or persons unknown.'

A sudden thought crossed James' mind. 'Where's her bag?'

'There doesn't appear to be one, sir.'

James looked at her hand and saw that her engagement ring was missing. 'They've taken her ring.'

'They?'

'Whoever did this.'

The officer lifted her hand and examined the torn skin on her ring finger. 'It's been ripped off with some force. This looks like a robbery.' A small crowd of curious bystanders had assembled by the time the ambulance arrived. James noticed them for the first time, total strangers casting accusatory looks in his direction. He saw a priest walking hurriedly away from the throng, and thought it strange that he was leaving, just when he might be needed. When Alice was placed in the back of the ambulance, James tried to climb in beside her.

'I'm sorry sir, you need to come with me,' said the policeman.

'You don't think I had anything to do with this, do you?'

'That's not for me to say, sir.'

At the police station, James found himself sitting in front of two policemen, in the same room where he had spoken to DCI Hughes a year earlier. He did his best to answer their questions.

'How long have you known Miss Taylor?'

'Erm, about nine months.'

'Were you with her on the train?'

James wondered where this was going. 'No, I was there to meet her.'

'Had the two of you argued recently?'

'No, never.' James' voice rose as he fought to hold back the tears. 'We're engaged to be married.'

'Can anyone corroborate your story?'

'Yes, Professor Lucas, my landlord. And it's not a story.'

'Good, because we will check. Now, can you think of anyone who might have wanted to hurt Alice?'

'No one. Everybody likes her. Now, can I go and see how she is?'

When he was finally allowed to leave, he was surprised to see Paul Lucas waiting for him. 'How did you know I was here?'

'A policeman called to ask questions about you and Alice.'

'Well, thanks for coming. I need to get to the hospital to see how she is.'

'I'll come with you.'

When they arrived at the Royal Infirmary, visiting time was over, but they were able to speak to the matron. 'She's still unconscious,' she said, 'but she has suffered severe head trauma. There are signs of strangulation, which may have caused damage to her brain function. If and when she wakes, we may have a better idea of her chances of recovery.'

'If and when?' echoed a distraught James.

The matron ignored his outburst. 'She also appears to have some broken bones, which will heal, but we are very concerned about her. The next forty-eight hours are going to be crucial, so her next of kin will have to be informed.'

'I'll do that,' said James.

'Very well. Let them know that visiting is from two to three and seven to eight. It's strictly limited to two people.'

'Thank you, matron,' said the professor. 'Come on, James, let's go,' he said, taking him by the arm.

They returned to Oakwood House, where James placed a call to the Taylors and told them what had happened. At midnight, neither he nor Paul were in the mood to celebrate the arrival of a new year.

In the morning, the Taylors drove down from St Annes and were already at the hospital when James arrived shortly before two. There was no change in Alice's condition, but her parents were allowed to sit with her, leaving James to pace the corridor. After half an hour, Len Taylor left her bedside so that James could spend some time with her.

When visiting time was over, James passed on a message from Paul. 'You're very welcome to stay with us while you're here,' he said. 'We're only a mile down the road in Rusholme.'

'That's very kind of you both,' said Len, 'but we want to be close at hand in case anything happens. We're going to check in to a hotel just round the corner.'

For several days, James was at the hospital for every visiting time, waiting impatiently for his turn to see Alice, who was still unconscious. Then, one morning, when he returned from his morning run, Paul was waiting for him.

'Alice's parents have just arrived,' he whispered. 'They're in the living room.'

James' blood ran cold as he opened the door, hardly daring to breathe. 'What's happened?' he asked. 'Is she…?'

Seeing the look on his face, Irene said, 'Oh, good God no, James! We came to tell you that she's awake!'

James sank into an armchair, which sagged under his weight, creating the impression that it was just as relieved as him. 'What more do you know?'

'We'll find out more at two o'clock,' she said.

While James had a bath and dressed himself, the Taylors drank tea and chatted to Paul. Later, they caught a tram to the hospital, where all three of them were shown into a visitors' room.

Eventually, a consultant popped his head round the door. 'Good afternoon,' he said cheerfully. 'I'm delighted to say that Alice is awake, but she does seem to be having a few problems with her memory. That's not unusual in cases like this, so I'm hopeful that it's only temporary.'

'She's talking, then?' asked Len.

'Yes, but her speech is slurred. There's also some sign of paralysis on her right side. We won't know for a while whether that's likely to be permanent.'

'She's alive, that's what counts,' said Irene. 'Can we see her?'

'I don't see why not, but please try not to upset her. She's a little confused at the moment.'

The Taylors filed into the ward, with James bringing up the rear. Alice was propped up on pillows and looked uncertainly at them as they approached. Her parents stood on opposite sides of the bed and Len took hold of her limp right hand.

'Daddy?' It was an effort for her to speak.

'We're here, darling,' he said. 'How are you feeling?'

'Not very good,' she slurred. 'I feel sick.'

'Who did this to you?' asked James.

'I don't know! I can't remember,' she said, bursting into tears.

'There's plenty of time for all that,' said her father. 'All that matters is that you get well.' Kissing her gently on the forehead, he said, 'We'll leave you to get some rest, darling.'

When they were outside the ward, Irene hugged James and said, 'You'll have to be patient with her.'

'I will be. I'll be here every day.'

'No, James,' she said firmly. 'I don't think that's such a good idea. You need to concentrate on your studies. Let us worry about Alice.'

James was taken aback by her words. He turned and walked away, rubbing the back of his neck as he tried to think of something to say. When he returned, his eyes were glistening. 'I want what's best for Alice, of course. I just thought that if I was there, it might help.'

'I think she just needs some peace and quiet to help her get better,' said Irene.

'Alright, whatever you say,' he said with a heavy heart, 'but would you let me know if you change your mind?'

'Of course,' said Len. 'Why don't you pop in at the weekend and spend some time with her.'

Back at Oakwood House, he updated Paul on Alice's condition.

'I'm sure everything's going to be alright, James,' he said unconvincingly. 'Oh, by the way, there's a parcel in the dining room for you.'

James assumed it would be from his mother, but when he checked the postmark, it had come from Preston. He didn't know anyone in the Lancashire town so, curiosity getting the better of him, he ripped it open. His cry of 'Oh God, no!' brought Paul rushing from the kitchen.

He found James, flicking through the pages of a book and scribbling furiously on a piece of paper.

'What is it?' he asked anxiously.

'That's Alice's engagement ring!' he cried, adding, 'and this is my book.' He held up a copy of John Buchan's *Greenmantle*. 'Look,' he said, opening the book to reveal his name on the inside cover. 'This is all my fault!'

'I don't understand,' said Paul. 'If this was the man who attacked Alice, how did he know which train she was going to be on?'

James hadn't thought of that. 'I don't know, unless…'

'Unless what?'

'Her letter. It was in a bit of a state when you gave it to me. What if he steamed it open?'

'I suppose,' said Paul. 'If he had to boil a kettle, that would explain the cup of tea.'

'The man who did this was Sarah's spymaster,' said James.

'What makes you say that?'

'Because the ring was wrapped up in this.' He handed Paul a crumpled piece of paper, on which was written six numbers, separated by full stops. Underneath them, James had written YOUR NEXT.

20

Rusholme, Manchester
January 1918

'Your thief's grammar leaves a lot to be desired,' said Paul, 'but the message is clear. You have to take this to the police, James. They may be able to find out who's responsible.'

'I already know who it was. I just don't know his name. The fact is that Alice is in hospital because of me. If I hadn't meddled in things that don't concern me, she would still be absolutely fine.'

'You can't think like that. You're not to blame, and your actions may have saved countless lives. Come on, I'll take you down to the station.'

When DCI Hughes examined the parcel and its contents, he was less than encouraging. 'Well, at least we have a motive for the attack on Miss Taylor.'

'Revenge?'

'That's right, and if you're now a target, you might just be our best chance of catching him.'

'What makes you say that?'

'Well, not to put too fine a point on it, Alice is unable to identify her attacker. We've not got a lot to go on, so unless he makes good on his threat to harm you, there's not a lot we can do.'

'So, what do you want me to do?'

'Just carry on as normal. We'll be watching your back, but if you see or hear anything out of the ordinary, let me know.'

By the end of January, Alice was well enough to be moved to Blackpool Victoria Hospital, where she was admitted to a general medical ward. She had started to get some movement back in her right arm and leg, and her strength was slowly returning, although she still had no memory of what had happened to her. James visited every Saturday, making the three-hour journey by train and staying overnight with the Taylors. His studies suffered as a result, but he never missed a weekend. He would sit by her bed, holding her hand and talking about nothing in particular. Every Sunday evening, when he returned to Manchester, he felt more alone than ever. During the week, he worked longer hours in order to keep up with the syllabus, but his mind was elsewhere. There was a noticeable decline in the quality of his work, which was soon brought to Rutherford's attention. James was summoned to see him.

'You don't seem yourself, Mr Driscoll. Is everything alright?'

'Yes, sir,' said James, who didn't want to make excuses. 'I've just had trouble sleeping recently.'

'Get yourself to a doctor if you can't sleep, man!'

'Yes, sir.'

One day in March, Alice was found unconscious on a bathroom floor. No one saw her fall and she couldn't remember what happened. She was bruised but otherwise unhurt.

'How did this happen, doctor?' asked a concerned Irene.

'We're not sure, but it's likely that she simply lost her balance,' he replied. 'We'll keep an eye on her for a few days, but as long as it doesn't happen again, she should be well enough to go home at the weekend.'

When James took the train to St Annes to spend Easter with the Taylors, he thought about the events of the past twelve months. A year ago, he had never heard of Alice Taylor. This wonderful, funny girl was now the most precious thing in his life, and yet because someone blamed him for Sarah's death, he had almost lost her. When he walked into the living room, he had no idea that she had been discharged from hospital, and was lying on the couch, covered by a blanket.

'Hello, James,' she said.

'Alice! What are you doing here?' he asked. Although he was thrilled to see her, he thought she looked very frail.

'I live here!' she replied. 'What are you doing here?'

'Sorry, I thought you were still in hospital.' He leant down and kissed her. 'Can you remember anything about your accident yet?'

'Not a thing, apart from it being Christmas. Then I woke up in hospital.'

Easter was a time when the whole family went to church, and this year was no exception. On the Saturday evening, the Taylor family took their pews for the Easter Vigil. The church was packed, so James sat in the row in front. He turned to smile at Alice, who smiled back as he took her hand. The smile faded as she began to tremble, and James realised that she was looking past him. He turned back to see a priest stepping onto the altar. 'Alice? What is it?' he whispered.

'I don't know. I can't quite ...'

'Take your time,' he said softly.

'It sounds unlikely, I know, but I think I might have been attacked by a priest.'

'A priest?' James recalled the scene at London Road Station. 'When I saw you on the train, there was a priest in the crowd. I thought it was odd that he just walked away.'

Alice began to cry, and her father put a protective arm around her shoulder. He raised his other hand to warn James not to say any more.

When they returned home, James said, 'I'm sorry if I made you cry, Alice. Just say if you don't want to do it, but I think it might help you to remember if the police were to show you some photographs.'

'I don't remember his face at all,' she said. 'I don't think I want to remember.'

Kirk Allerton, Yorkshire
April 1918

After Easter, the trip to Kirk Allerton was a last-minute decision. Paul Lucas had passed on a message from James' mother, telling him that George had gone to Wales to visit his mother, who was unwell. At St Annes railway station, James bought a copy of the local paper to read on the journey home. He was shocked to learn, in an account by an injured soldier who was invalided home from the Western front, that the Germans had launched a massive offensive from the Hindenburg Line. They had quickly recaptured the ground lost at such a high cost at the Somme. The report suggested that their objective was to break through enemy lines and take the channel ports, destroying the Allied supply routes before the arrival of US troops. If the newspaper was to be believed, the outcome of the war was in serious doubt, despite America's intervention.

Had Alfie and so many others died in vain? It was a deeply depressing thought, and one that James tried to put from his mind when he stepped from the train at Kirk Allerton Station. He forced a smile when he saw his mother on the platform, waiting to take him for lunch at The Fleece.

She wasted no time in telling him about his grandmother, saying, 'You should really be there, James. She's in her eighties now, and she's not at all well.'

James hadn't seen Nana Driscoll since the summer of 1913, the last time the whole family went on holiday together. They stayed at the seafront townhouse that George's mother had run as bed and breakfast accommodation after his father's death.

'I'll go and see her when he's not there,' he said. 'Alice has started to remember details of the attack, and the doctors seem confident that she'll make a full recovery.'

'That's wonderful news. I say a prayer for her every time I go to church, you know.' She became quiet, and a troubled look spread across her face. 'There's something else I need to talk to you about,' she said.

James frowned. 'What is it, Mother? Are you alright?'

'I'm fine. No, it's something that I don't want to come as a surprise. Your father's not sure how much longer he can keep the mill going. Business is very bad now that exports have dried up.'

'The war won't last for ever, Mother. He needs to cut his costs to the bone and try to ride out the storm.'

'Well, you know your father. He refuses to get rid of any more staff.'

'I know, that's why he wouldn't invest in new machines, because it meant he'd need fewer men.'

'That's a good thing, isn't it? I know you two have had your differences, but your father's a good man at heart. He's very loyal to his workers.'

'Maybe so, but when the war is over, he's going to find his costs are too high and he won't be able to make a profit anymore. Then everyone will be out of work.'

The Lake District, Westmorland

In the early hours of the following day, Winter drew on a cigarette, a smug expression on his face as he stared into the flames from his campfire, deep within a wooded area near the village of Windermere. Earlier that evening, he had used a wireless telephone transmitter to send his latest coded message. So confident had he been of his own invulnerability that he hadn't bothered to leave the area. He would not have been so smug if he had known that more than a dozen policemen were converging on his lair, guided by the smoke from the fire.

Three listening stations in the north of England had picked up his signal, and its source had been triangulated by Room 40, the Admiralty's signals interception and codebreaking unit. The same unit had decoded the Zimmermann Telegram a year earlier. From that secret communication between the German Empire and Mexico, Britain proved that Germany was plotting against the United States, resulting in their entry into the war.

Six officers were within thirty yards of their prey when one of them cursed after tripping over a tree root in the darkness. It took Winter a matter of seconds to grab his bag, fire up his old Triumph motorcycle and speed away down the track, with policemen only feet away. Whistles sounded and they ran back to their vehicles. In the nearest village, a sergeant stopped and called headquarters to let them know their quarry was heading south at speed, in the direction of Manchester. By the time the message reached DCI Hughes, there were too many routes into the city and too little time to set up roadblocks. He had to admit that his prey had eluded him, at least for the time being.

Rusholme, Manchester

The morning sun shone brightly, casting long shadows across Platt Fields Park. Winter sat on a bench by the lake, smoking a cigarette. He saw the man's dog first, as it raced across the grass, happily fetching a stick that its master had thrown. In the distance, the man leant into the biting wind, buttoned up his coat and thrust his hands deep into his pockets. As he drew closer, Winter turned his head away.

'Good morning,' said the man as he walked past.

Winter turned his head to look at him, causing him to stop dead in his tracks, open-mouthed. 'How good to see you again, Professor Lucas. I see you've lost the beard and moustache, and your eyesight's improved!'

Lucas' blood ran cold, and for a moment he could not speak. It was almost four years since he'd done a deal with the Devil in the Victoria Hotel, and he never expected to see him again. He managed to pull himself together sufficiently to stammer, 'How do you know my name?'

'I know a lot more about you than you might think, Professor.'

What in hell's name do you want?'

'That's no way to talk to an old friend now, is it?' said Winter. 'I thought we might discuss a matter that could be to our mutual benefit.'

'Please, just leave me alone. I don't want any more to do with you.'

'At least listen to what I have to say. You know a man called Driscoll, I believe?'

'Never heard of him,' said Lucas, unconvincingly.

Winter stood up and moved threateningly towards him, until they were inches from each other. 'Don't lie to me now, or this could end very badly for you,' he hissed.

Dalton began to emit a low growl, causing Winter to reach into his inside pocket.

'Down, boy,' said Lucas.

'Where is Driscoll now?'

'I've already told you, I don't know anyone by that name.'

'Ah, but you do, Professor. Now, if you do as you're told, you will never see me again. If not, the police will be informed that an employee of Manchester University has been selling state secrets.'

'State secrets! What are you talking about? You said it would help the war effort.'

'That's right, Professor. The German war effort, to be exact.'

Lucas' knees buckled and he slumped onto the bench.

Winter looked down at him and smiled. 'This is what you're going to do.'

All was still in Brighton Grove, save for the occasional hooting of an owl somewhere in the trees. At the rear of Oakwood House, someone was hiding in the bushes. Shortly after eleven, the landing light was extinguished, leaving the house in darkness. Winter moved silently through the garden, before lifting a plant pot and picking up a key. He unlocked the back door, turned the handle and entered the kitchen, where he stood motionless until his eyes became accustomed to the dark. He checked the downstairs rooms, before climbing the stairs to the first floor. All but one of the bedroom doors were open. Pulling out a Luger, he moved to the closed door, gently turned the handle and went inside. The bedroom was dark, but he could just make out a shape under the covers. Raising the gun, he fired three shots at close range.

He approached the bed and pulled back the covers, revealing a bolster where James' body should have been.

'I'm a police officer,' shouted Hughes. 'Put down the gun!'

Startled, Winter spun round and fired in the direction of the voice. At the same moment, a bullet to his left shoulder slammed him into the bedroom wall, knocking the gun from his grasp. Hughes rose from a crouched position in the far corner of the room, grunting with the pain from a wound to his right thigh. On the far side of the room, Winter was grappling with DC Hackett and desperately trying to reach his gun. Hughes limped across to help but was knocked to the floor when Hackett was pushed into him. Winter grabbed the gun and ran out onto the landing, straight into a punch that lifted him off his feet and dumped him on his back in the doorway. Blood spurted from a nose that would never be the same shape again. A figure appeared above him and a foot was planted on his wrist, while the gun was prised from his grasp.

'You're a big man when it comes to young girls, aren't you, Winter?' snarled James. 'Not quite so brave now, though.' He was full of righteous fury as he pointed the gun at Winter, and Hughes thought he was about to pull the trigger.

'Driscoll, stop!' he shouted.

James looked at the detective and shrugged, before handing him the gun.

'You're a dead man, Driscoll,' said Winter, spitting out blood as he spoke. 'When you killed my woman, you signed your own death warrant.'

'Your woman? You mean the woman who jumped into bed with me at the first opportunity?'

'When did that happen?' asked Hackett, showing an unhealthy interest in James' private life and regarding him with envious eyes. The DC was a middle-aged, married man who should have known better. Hughes gave him a disapproving glance.

'You don't have to answer that, Mr Driscoll,' he said.

'You're a liar,' snarled Winter. 'She wouldn't look twice at a brat like you,' he added, but he knew that wasn't true, and the thought of the two of them together filled him with rage. He wasn't to know that James had rebuffed Sinéad's advances.

'I don't think you believe that,' said James with a smile, 'and I didn't kill anyone.'

'As good as.' Winter's voice was full of menace as he added, 'You've no idea who you're dealing with.'

'Oh, I think I do,' sneered James. 'A pathetic little lowlife who gets his thrills from hurting defenceless women.' He bent down and delivered another heavy blow to Winter's bloodied face, before being dragged away by Hackett.

Hughes said, 'That never happened, Mr Driscoll. The prisoner suffered an unfortunate injury while resisting arrest, isn't that right, Hackett?'

'Yes, sir. That's some right hook you've got there, Mr Driscoll. Have you ever done any boxing?'

'No, sir. What's going to happen to him now?'

'Well,' said Hughes, 'You can add two counts of attempted murder to a charge of treason. We're no longer executing spies, more's the pity, or he'd definitely end up dangling from a rope.' Turning to Hackett, he said, 'Cuff him and take him away.'

Five hours earlier

On his return from Kirk Allerton, James had been heading for the exit at London Road Station when he saw DCI Hughes waving at him. The detective shook his hand and said, 'We've received new information from the Irish police. The spy we've been chasing for several months matches the description of a man by the name of Kevin Winter. I believe him to be the same man who attacked Miss Taylor.'

'So, he's Irish?' said James.

'We don't know yet, but I had a call this afternoon from Professor Lucas, who told us that he's going to be in Brighton Grove tonight, looking for you.'

James was puzzled. 'What's the professor got to do with this?'

'Again, I don't know, but we're going to be there in your place. I've arranged for someone to escort you to a hotel for the night.'

'No thank you,' protested James. 'I'm going home, Inspector. I've got a score to settle with that swine.'

'So have we, Mr Driscoll, but if you go anywhere near Brighton Grove tonight, your life will be in danger. Professor Lucas has

already been taken to a place of safety. Let me take care of this, and I'll let you know when the coast is clear.'

Reluctantly, James agreed to go along with the detective's plan, but later, sitting alone in a dismal hotel room, he started to wonder whether Hughes was telling the truth. How could Paul have known that this Winter would be there tonight? Had there been a message? A warning? Had he been threatened? Something didn't add up.

He lay on the bed and closed his eyes, but all he could see was the image of Alice, lying on the floor of the carriage. He became more and more restless at the thought of missing this opportunity to confront the man who had put her there.

When he could stand it no longer, he muttered, 'Sod this,' grabbed his coat and left the hotel.

21

Rusholme, Manchester
April 1918

On his morning run the following day, James felt a huge sense of relief that Winter was behind bars, where he could not reach him or his family. It only remained for him to discover how Paul had become involved in this sorry affair, but he was nowhere to be seen. It was midday before he made an appearance, accompanied by DCI Hughes, who was now on crutches.

'I wanted to speak to the two of you together,' said Hughes. 'DC Hackett's taken your dog for a walk so that we can get to the bottom of this.'

'I'm as in the dark as you, Inspector,' replied James. He glanced at Paul, who seemed thoroughly miserable.

'Professor Lucas,' said Hughes, 'I have to ask you, how do you know the man who came here last night?'

'I saw him in the park yesterday,' said Paul evasively. 'He wanted to know about James, but I told him I didn't know anyone called Driscoll.'

'So, what made you think he was going to come here?'

Paul hesitated, then slowly put his head in his hands. 'Inspector, I've done something incredibly stupid.'

'I'm listening.'

'It's a long story. I'm not quite sure where to begin.'

'Just tell me what made you contact the police yesterday. How do you know Kevin Winter?' James had been wondering the same thing.

Paul took a deep breath and cast his mind back to the worst time of his life. 'It all began a few years ago when my wife became ill with TB. I loved Mary very much, and I would have done anything to make her better. Anything.' Tears welled up in his eyes and he struggled to speak.

'Take your time, Professor,' said Hughes.

He swallowed hard and continued, jaw clenched. 'She was in a hospital near Bolton, and her treatment took all of our savings. I got a second job, working in a pub, but I still had to take out loans against the house. Then, one day, she died.' He did not bother to wipe away the tears that flowed freely down his cheeks and dripped from his jawline, staining his shirt.

'I'm sorry, Professor,' said the detective.

'The bank gave me a deadline to repay the loans, and there was nothing left. The house my parents worked so hard for was going to be taken from me. I was desperate.'

'So, what did you do?'

'There was some loose talk in the pub, and I'd had a bit too much to drink.' Lucas paused, remembering the night when he became a criminal. 'Not long before the war started, I let it slip that Professor Weizmann was developing a new process that could be vital if we did end up in a war. Before I knew it, I was approached by someone who said there were people who would pay a lot of money for that information. I should have just walked away, but I didn't. I told him he could have it for four thousand pounds. A few days later, I met a man in the Victoria Hotel.'

'In Manchester?'

'Yes. It was the day that war broke out. I remember, I was so nervous when I arrived at the hotel, I thought I was going to be sick. As instructed, I carried a green bag. I was worried that someone might recognise me, so I wore a disguise. I stood there in the foyer, just waiting. I realise now that I must have looked ridiculous. I might as well have carried a sign saying, "I'm up to no good." Then he turned up.'

'Winter?' asked James.

'Yes.'

'What did he say?' asked Hughes.

'Act naturally. Pretend we're friends. I asked him if he had the money, and he said he had a thousand pounds and a gun. It was a case of take it or leave it.'

'What did you do?'

'I said I'd leave it.' Lucas sighed a sigh full of regret. 'I wish I had, now.'

'But you'd have lost your house,' said James.

'I know. Anyway, we settled on two and a half, and that was that. I only found out yesterday that he sold it to the Germans.'

Hughes regarded him with a mixture of anger and pity. 'Didn't you think it odd that a total stranger was offering you so much money?'

‘I did wonder, if I’m honest, but I acted with the best of intentions.’

‘Yes, well, hell is paved with good intentions, Professor.’

‘Anyway, he turned up yesterday morning and told me that, unless I cooperated, he was going to tell the police what I did.’

‘And you told him where Mr Driscoll would be?’

Lucas’ face reddened. ‘Yes. He told me where to leave a key, and to make sure I wasn’t home last night. I realised he was planning to do him harm, so I called you. I knew the truth would probably come out, but I couldn’t let him get away with it.’

James could no longer hold his tongue. He glared at Lucas and said, ‘Professor, you’re telling us you betrayed your country!’

‘Not knowingly, James. I honestly thought I was doing something that would help us win the war.’

‘Nevertheless,’ said Hughes, ‘you’ve stolen state secrets and sold them to a foreign power.’

‘They weren’t state secrets when I took them!’

‘We’ll have to let the courts decide about that, Professor, but I rather think you’re going to prison.’ Leaning on his crutches, Hughes continued. ‘Paul Lucas, you are under arrest. You are not obliged to say anything unless you wish to do so, but whatever you say will be taken down in writing and may be given in evidence.’

More than a week had passed since Paul’s arrest. Sitting in the kitchen of Oakwood House, James finished off the last of his mother’s fruit scones and sifted through the morning post. He had been wondering where he was going to live, now that his landlord was incarcerated. The answer arrived in the form of a letter from the professor. He sipped his tea and began to read.

> Dear James,
>
> I must apologise for my actions, of which I’m deeply ashamed. I have of course written to the university to tender my resignation. It will not be easy to live with the fact that my selfishness may have cost thousands of British lives. I have already found out the hard way what they do to traitors in prison.

I don't know whether I have the strength to get through this but, in any event, I'll not be home for some time. I can only hope that the man who put me here spends the rest of his miserable life in prison. If he ever gets out, please keep well away from him. He seems to have some very powerful friends.

Please feel free to live in the house for as long as you want. When Alice is better, it would make a nice first home for the pair of you. Would you take care of Dalton for me?

Yours sincerely,

Paul

James was no longer angry with the professor. When all was said and done, he was a decent man who had found himself in an impossible situation. His warning was troubling. Could Winter still get to him, or his family, or, heaven forbid, Alice, from prison? Although he had seen her just a few days earlier, he desperately wanted to be with her, to keep her safe from that madman's clutches.

With Lucas in prison, Dalton was not going to get the attention he needed. James rang the Taylors to ask whether they would look after him until Alice was better. They jumped at the chance, and Len Taylor even drove to Rusholme to save James from having to cope with the dog on the train. Dalton was beside himself with joy when he was reunited with Alice, and it was all James could do to stop him from jumping all over her. 'Someone's missed you,' he laughed. It felt so good for the three of them to be together again.

As Alice's health improved, James started to relax and was able to concentrate more on his coursework. He was already familiar with electricity, magnetism, thermodynamics and classical mechanics. In crystallography, he studied the arrangement of atoms in crystals. It was a branch of physics that had earned von Laue the Nobel Prize in 1914, and the father and son Braggs the same honour a year later. With Rutherford's permission, he recreated their experiments in the laboratory, but always from behind a lead-lined shield. Prolonged exposure to x-rays had killed Clarence Dally, Edison's long-serving assistant, in 1904. If only James had had access to a magdalite crystal, he might have made the same mental leap as Einstein, eighteen months earlier.

Towards the end of the academic year, James attended Manchester Assizes as a character witness for Paul. The charge of stealing state secrets had been dropped because, as he correctly surmised, they were not state secrets when he sold them to Winter. Nevertheless, he was found guilty of the offences of simple larceny and corruptly taking a reward. He was sentenced to five years' penal servitude.

The Taylors had been so welcoming from the moment James met them, and he was elated when they invited him to spend the summer with them, enabling him to stay close to Alice. Living with the Taylors improved his diet, despite rationing. The family were well-liked by their local butcher and greengrocer, who knew about Alice's mishap and often gave them preferential treatment. When supplemented with the vegetables grown in her own garden, Irene Taylor was able to ensure that her family was well fed. For several weeks, the weather was warm and sunny. Alice had started to walk short distances unaided, always with James by her side. It was just a matter of time before she was back to normal. Dalton loved everything about this new arrangement, from runs along the beach with James to being spoilt by Irene, who had clearly fallen in love with the dog.

One evening in early August, Len Taylor came home from work in an uncharacteristically sombre mood.

'Is everything alright, love?' asked Irene.

'I'm sorry,' he replied. 'We had some bad news at work today. One of our young cashiers, Colin, was killed in France.'

'Oh no, I know his mother!' exclaimed Irene.

'You don't mean Colin Reid, do you?' said Alice.

'Yes, did you know him?' asked Len.

'He was in my class at school,' she said. 'That's so sad.'

Reid had been conscripted two years earlier and ended up in the 51st (Highland) Division. He had been in the thick of the action at the Second Battle of the Marne and was killed as Allied troops successfully defended German attempts to cross the River Marne near Reims. It was a turning point in the war, but one that came too late for Colin. Germany had lost a third of a million men in regaining lost ground and no longer had sufficient reserves to replace them. Once the Allies mounted a counterattack, the German stormtroopers were in full retreat. However, what few realised was that the casualties of war were beginning to be exceeded on both sides by losses from an influenza epidemic that was now raging across Europe.

22

St Annes-on-the-Sea, Lancashire
August 1918

The weather on the west coast became changeable, as it often did in late summer. One wet afternoon, Alice told her father that she was ready to help the police with their enquiries. 'I keep seeing his face now,' she said. 'I think I might be able to identify him.'

'Are you sure?' he asked. 'It could be very upsetting for you.'

'I'm sure. That man needs to pay for what he did. If he ends up being released and doing the same to someone else, I couldn't live with myself.'

Alice's eyewitness testimony would be the final link in a chain of otherwise circumstantial evidence. The stolen ring and the book, sent to James. The message, using the same book cipher as Sinéad McKenna. And the motive, that James was the cause of McKenna's death. With a positive identification from his victim, Winter could be facing a third charge of attempted murder, espionage and possibly even treason, a crime that still carried the death penalty.

DCI Hughes travelled up to St Annes to show Alice a file containing photographs of known criminals. After admiring the sea view from the Taylors' living room, he sat at the parlour table and opened the file. 'Take your time now, Miss Taylor,' he said gently. 'There's no rush.'

James watched closely as she leafed through the images. Once or twice, she lingered over a particular photograph before moving on. When she came to her attacker, her brow furrowed noticeably, and she started to shake. Pointing to the man in the photograph, she stammered, 'That's him.'

'Are you sure, Miss?'

'Yes, quite sure. He was dressed in priest's robes, but I can see his face. He spoke to me.'

'Can you remember what he said?'

'No, sorry, but I do remember that he had a northern accent. He seemed perfectly nice, until ...' Alice struggled to get the words out. 'I just remember him standing up. I thought he was getting ready to leave the train. I don't remember anything after that.' She stood up to walk away from the table, but stopped and said, 'I feel dizzy.' Her body went rigid, and she started to fall, but James jumped to his feet and caught her. He managed to drop to the floor first, so that she landed on top of him, saving her from more serious injury. A few minutes later, she came to and asked, 'What happened?'

'You fainted,' said DCI Hughes. 'I'm sorry if that photograph upset you, Miss Taylor. You have been a great help.'

'I'm just relieved that you know who did this,' said Alice. Turning to her father, she said, 'I still feel very dizzy.'

Taking hold of her hand, he said, 'We're going to get the doctor to have another look at you, darling.'

'What happens now, detective?' asked James.

'We'll present our evidence to the Director of Public Prosecutions and see what he says. I would imagine that, at the very least, Winter will get a longer sentence and lose any chance of parole.'

The following day, as James paced back and forth around the living room, an elderly man on a bicycle stopped at the garden gate and removed his cycle clips. Len Taylor recognised him as one of the local GPs. Once inside, he examined Alice and diagnosed a bad case of vertigo. He prescribed a blue pill to be taken at bedtime and a black draught to be taken each morning. No one was quite sure what it was, but it smelt awful.

Armley Gaol, Leeds
October 1918

As the Great War came to an end, the British penal system was still seen as a means of punishment rather than rehabilitation. Although the days of the treadwheel and the crank were gone, replaced by the sewing of mailbags for the General Post Office, brutal warders, floggings and solitary confinement were still commonplace. Food was of poor quality, and barely adequate to sustain a grown man. Winter was forty-six years old when he entered the system for the first time. He still had more than four thousand pounds in the bank, and a lot more waiting for him in America, but it wasn't much use to him now.

Following his arrest, Winter had been remanded to Armley to await trial. A man who was used to sleeping rough might have been expected to adapt well to life in prison, but he loved the outdoors. In

Armley he couldn't even see it. He went from sleeping under the stars in the fresh air, to a room with one small, barred window, high up on the wall. There was a chamber pot, but no ventilation.

At first, he prowled around his cell like a caged animal, his mood fluctuating between anger and despair. Despair at his predicament and anger towards the British nation in general and James Driscoll in particular. Sinéad had been murdered, and Driscoll was as guilty as the man who pulled the trigger. Winter's thirst for revenge was what kept him going when things were looking particularly bleak.

While on remand, he wrote two letters. The first informed Nico Varese that he was likely to be in prison for a very long time. The other, to his sister-in-law Ailbhe, told her that the Tullybay cottage was hers for as long as she needed it.

On the eve of his trial, he was allowed his first visitor in three months. He sat on the other side of a table from Nico Varese, who had risked an Atlantic crossing to see his friend.

'What 'appened to your *shnazole, mio amico*?'

Six months after it had been broken, Winter's once aquiline nose was no longer symmetrical. 'Driscoll,' he said with a grimace. 'He caught me with a sucker punch.'

'Wow! 'e must be pretty tough to catch you off guard like that.'

'Nah, I didn't even know he was there.' The truth was that Winter didn't care about the shape of his nose. In prison, it only added to the air of menace that surrounded him. As an outward sign that he had lost a fight, he wasn't quite sure why that should be, but other prisoners avoided him.

'You gonna be okay? If you get a long sentence, 'ow you gonna stick it?' It was a question that Winter had asked himself many times.

'One day at a time, Nico, one day at a time.'

Looking around, his friend said in a low voice, 'We could bust you out of 'ere, you know.'

Winter laughed. 'And get yourself killed in the process?' He knew that his friend was serious, but it wasn't the most sensible idea. 'Thanks, but no thanks. Now, how's Edith?'

Varese looked away for a split second. When he looked Winter in the eye, his face wore a fixed smile. '*Bene,*' he said. If they hadn't been such close friends, Winter might not have noticed.

'Why the hesitation?'

'No reason. That English broad got in touch with 'er, you know. Took a real shine to 'er, by all accounts. Said she's gonna be a star.'

'I hope she's right.' Winter was surprised and delighted that Ellen Terry had kept her promise. Nico could have said a lot more. He could have told him that he had fallen in love with Edith, and they were now living together, but he was afraid of his friend's reaction.

'When you get back, would you give Edith this letter from me?' said Winter. 'Ask her to keep in touch, will you?'

'*Nessun problema*. Whaddya want me to do about Driscoll?'

'Nothing for now. You could kill him of course, but then his suffering would be over. I want him to wake up every day, thinking it could be his last.'

Nico could sense the rage behind his friend's words. 'Just let me know when you're ready,' he said quietly. 'I'll bring a couple of the boys with me next time.'

'Thanks Nico, you're a good friend.'

'You take care of yourself. Good luck tomorrow.'

The following morning, Winter sat on the side of the hard, plank bed and rubbed his left shoulder. It was a permanent, painful reminder that James Driscoll had put him there, but the pain only fuelled his desire for revenge. That afternoon, he appeared at Leeds Assizes, where he was defended by Sir Clifford Anstruther QC, one of the country's leading defence lawyers. Before the trial, the Director of Public Prosecutions decided that, due to his German heritage, Winter should be charged with espionage rather than treason. There was also the small matter of the attempted murders of Alice Taylor, James Driscoll and DCI Hughes.

Curiosity got the better of James, and on the day of the verdict he sat in the public gallery, looking down at Winter. The two men stared at each other with pure hatred in their eyes, and the tension in the packed courtroom was palpable. James had no intention of being the first to break eye contact, but Winter did something he would never forget. With James looking directly at him, he slowly turned his head to the right until he was looking at someone to James' left. He followed Winter's gaze and saw a man of Latin appearance who was also looking at him. The man raised his right hand and slowly ran a finger across his throat. An involuntary shiver ran down James' spine and he returned his gaze to Winter, who smiled, mouthing the words, 'You're next.'

With Alice's testimony, the evidence against Winter was overwhelming, and it took the jury less than two hours to find him guilty. The verdict, when it came, was roundly applauded. Afterwards, the judge pronounced sentence. 'Kevin Winter, you have been found guilty of the offence of espionage under the Official Secrets Act of 1911, and being convicted thereof, it is my judgement that you shall be kept in penal servitude for a term of not less than seven years. You have also been found guilty of three counts of attempted murder under Section 14 of the Offences against the Person Act of 1861, and of a threat to kill under Section 16 of said Act. Being convicted thereof, it is my judgement that you shall be kept in penal servitude for a term of not less than ten years. Terms to be served concurrently. Take him down.'

In St Annes-on-the-Sea, Alice's health continued to improve, but her vertigo remained. When James returned to Rusholme for the new university year, he was determined to find a breakthrough in his search for the key to time travel. The focus of his research was to try heating crystals to a high temperature, but he learnt nothing new.

Oakwood House was the perfect place for him to work, but he hated being alone in the big, empty house. He would spend every weekend with the Taylors until the end of term, apart from a trip to see his mother in Kirk Allerton when his father was away.

The tide had finally turned in Europe. Sustained attacks from Allied forces, bolstered by a huge influx of fresh troops from the USA, had the Germans in full retreat. When the Allies broke through the Hindenburg Line at the end of September, it was the beginning of the end for Germany and the Central Powers. The Spring Offensive had been one last, desperate throw of the dice by a nation brought to its knees by the Allied blockade.

One Monday in November, James was walking back to Rusholme from the Manchester campus when he heard something that he hadn't heard for more than four years. Bells rang out across the city and throughout the land, signalling the end of the war. The armistice of the eleventh of November was the final act in a conflict that had seen more than forty million deaths.

23

St Annes-on-the-Sea, Lancashire
December 1918

Less than a week before Christmas, James and Alice walked along the seafront together, with Dalton trotting happily beside them. It was a crisp, clear morning and James was feeling more optimistic than he had in a long time. The war was over, and Alice was almost back to her old self. The only outward sign of her ordeal was a slight limp. Now they could start making plans again. They would get married, live in Oakwood House, and have lots of children. Alice loved the house, so he was going to ask the professor whether he was interested in selling it to them.

They arrived at one of their favourite places, an octagonal pavilion in the Promenade Gardens. It was empty, and James decided the time was right.

'Let's get married,' he said.

'What's the hurry?' she asked. 'I'd rather not have to limp down the aisle on my wedding day.' It wasn't the response he had hoped for.

'I don't care if you limp, hop, skip or jump,' he said. 'I'll carry you down the aisle if I have to. Can we at least set a date and see how you are?'

She had tears in her eyes as she looked up at him, saying, 'I'll think about it.' He held her tightly and was about to reply when he felt her go rigid, becoming a dead weight in his arms. He knew straight away that she'd fainted again, so he laid her gently down on the floor. Had he squeezed too hard? When he looked at her face, he could see that this was much worse than before. Her lips had started to turn blue, and she was having convulsions, her arms jerking involuntarily. In a complete panic, he ran to the door of the pavilion and yelled at the top of his voice, 'Help me, someone!'

His cries were heard by an elderly couple who were walking past. While her husband went to ring for an ambulance, the old woman said, 'I think she should be on her side, dear.' James rolled Alice over and covered her with his coat to keep her warm. When the ambulance arrived, he thanked the couple for their help.

'Is there anything else we can do?' asked the man.

'Yes, if you wouldn't mind. Could you take the dog back home and let Alice's parents know what's happened?' He pointed back the way they had come and said, 'It's a house called Holmleigh, about half a mile along the promenade.'

'Leave that to us, lad. We'll be praying for her.'

There was very little traffic on the roads, and in less than fifteen minutes, they arrived at Blackpool Victoria Hospital. James followed the ambulancemen as they carried their patient into the casualty department and moved her onto a trolley. Her convulsions had stopped, and colour was returning to her face. By the time she was seen by the casualty officer, she was awake and seemed perfectly fine.

'Why was she brought here?' he asked.

Somewhat taken aback, James almost said, 'Because it's a hospital,' but thought better of it. 'She collapsed,' he said. 'It's happened before, but this time she started shaking violently. I thought she was going to die.'

The casualty officer raised an eyebrow and sighed. 'I see,' he said. His demeanour was that of someone who found patients a bit of a nuisance. 'Where are her parents?'

'They should be here soon,' said James.

'Do they have funds?'

James was surprised by the question. Coming from a wealthy family, paying for healthcare was something that had never concerned him. 'Her parents have money, if that's what you mean,' he said. 'Her father's a bank manager.'

The man's attitude softened somewhat. 'That should be fine, then,' he said, 'but they will need to sign some forms when they get here.' He scribbled a note and handed it to James. It read "Medical: refer physicians." 'Someone will be along presently,' he added.

They were still waiting to be seen when the Taylors arrived. 'Sorry we've been so long,' said Len. 'We went to Lytham Cottage Hospital, but it was full. They sent us here. What happened?'

James described Alice's collapse and her subsequent 'examination.'

'Right, leave this to me,' said Irene and off she went in search of a more senior clinician. Before long, she returned with a doctor who clearly wasn't enjoying the earbashing she was dishing out.

'My daughter's been very ill and now she's collapsed,' she shouted. 'Why is this not being taken seriously?'

'We're very busy, ma'am.'

'So, why is the place virtually empty? Lindsay Parkinson is a personal friend of mine. Don't make me trouble him with this.' Parkinson was the newly elected MP for Blackpool and a powerful figure in the community.

The doctor knew when he was beaten. He listened carefully as James described the attack of a year earlier and Alice's subsequent symptoms. 'Thank you, Mr….?

'Driscoll. What's wrong with her, doctor?'

Speaking directly to Alice, he said, 'I rather think that your injuries may have left you suffering from epilepsy, Miss Taylor. We'll need to keep you in hospital and carry out some neurological tests.'

'Can it be cured, doctor?' asked Alice.

'It's difficult to say. Some patients have to live with it, while others have been known to make a full recovery. It very much depends on the severity of the original injury.' He took the Taylors to one side and warned them that a great many patients had died from the condition. 'She will need constant care and attention,' he said.

'She will certainly get that, doctor,' said Len. 'Not least from that young man over there.'

Alice was admitted to an eight-bedded ward and was visited every day by James and her family. As the days passed, her parents asked whether she could come home for Christmas.

'I'm afraid not,' said her doctor. 'We have to be thorough with these tests. It's more likely to be the new year.'

On Christmas Day, James sat next to Freddie in the back of Len Taylor's Rover for the short journey to the hospital. They brought with them bags of unopened presents, not wanting Alice to miss out on any part of a Taylor family Christmas. The only empty bed was the one between Alice and the entrance. Once the nurses had finished their morning routine, visitors were allowed in. It was a special day, one that none of them would forget. Alice had tasked her father with a clandestine visit to a Church Street jeweller, and he furtively passed her a small, expertly wrapped package.

When James gave her an expensive handbag to match her favourite coat, she kissed him and whispered, 'That question you asked me? The answer's yes.'

'Are you sure?'

'Yes, I've had plenty of time to think.' With a cheeky grin, she added, 'Life's too short to wait for the perfect moment.' She handed him her gift, adding, 'Happy Christmas, James.'

With glistening eyes, he said in a low voice, 'You've already given me the best Christmas present I could ever imagine. I love you so much.'

He removed the wrapping paper from his present, a beautiful silver Mappin wristlet watch.

'This is what our soldiers wear,' she said. 'I thought you'd like the luminous display.'

'Whatever will they think of next?' asked her father.

'Soldiers have to be able to tell the time at night,' said James. 'The radium emits gamma rays which react with the zinc sulphide phosphor in the paint.'

'That's interesting,' said Freddie, with little enthusiasm. Everyone burst out laughing.

James sat down next to Alice. 'I've read about them, but I've never seen one before,' he said, kissing her tenderly on the cheek. 'It's wonderful. Thank you so much.'

All too soon, it was time to leave. Alice's mother placed a biscuit tin on the bedside table. 'There's some Christmas cake and a few other treats in there. Don't eat them all at once.'

'You're talking to me, not Freddie!' she laughed.

'Shut up, Stringbean!' he shouted, but he too was laughing.

'I'll make my own way back,' said James, as the Taylors said their goodbyes. When they had gone, the ward was silent, save for the intermittent coughing of an old woman in the far corner. James sat on a chair next to the bed and checked the time on his new watch. It was almost eight o'clock. He held Alice's hand and looked adoringly into her eyes. 'I love you, Alice Taylor.'

'I love you too,' she replied. 'I can't wait to marry you, James.'

On New Year's Day, James visited the hospital alone, so that he and Alice could plan their wedding. They had already decided on a church service in the spring.

'Your mother's booked the Catholic Church in St Annes for Saturday, the twenty-sixth of April. The reception's at the Imperial Hydro Hotel. '

'That's perfect,' said Alice. 'We need to think about a guest list.'

‘That won’t take me long,’ said James, rather forlornly. ‘Obviously my mother will be there, and her dad, Grandad Evan, will come down from Scotland. Then there’s Nana Driscoll, if she’s well enough, but I doubt that my father will come. Paul Lucas is in prison. Other than that, I’ll just have a few close friends from school.’

‘It would be nice to meet your mother before we get married but, as long as you’re there, I don’t really care,’ said Alice. ‘Have you thought about a best man?’

‘I would have asked Alfie.’ James was silent for a while and Alice gently squeezed his hand.

‘You two were very close, weren’t you?’

‘Yes, he was my best friend,’ he said. ‘Would you mind if I asked Freddie?’

‘On one condition,’ she said. ‘No jokes at my expense.’

‘It’s a deal,’ he laughed. He bent over and laid his head down next to hers, happier than he had been in a long time. He had not intended to fall asleep. A noise in the corridor woke him, and he heard a man’s voice saying, ‘Hang on a mo’, I’ll just check in ‘ere.’ The door opened slightly, and he heard the man say, a little too loudly, ‘There’s a spare bed by the door. She weighs a ton, let’s just leave ‘er there.’

‘I’ve never known this place be so busy,’ gasped his colleague. ‘It’s completely full. There’s nowhere else to put her.’

‘It’ll be reet. We’ll just tell someone where she is before we go.’

James opened one eye and peered at the uniformed men on the other side of Alice’s bed. They didn’t notice him. When they had transferred their obese patient to the empty bed, they left and all became quiet again.

He checked his watch. Ten past nine. The walk back to St Annes was only six or seven miles. If he ran, he could do it in under an hour. He kissed Alice lightly on the forehead and left.

24

St Annes-on-the-Sea, Lancashire
January 1919

The next day, the Taylors set off to visit Irene's elderly parents in Harrogate, leaving James to visit Alice on his own again. When he arrived at the ward, there was a "DO NOT ENTER" sign on the door. He went to find a nurse, completely unprepared for what she had to say. 'Some of the patients have become seriously ill. The whole ward is in isolation.'

'I don't understand. Everything seemed fine yesterday.'

'If you've been visiting regularly, there is a chance that you've been infected.'

'I feel fine. Now, can I see my fiancée?'

'Only if you wear a gown and mask.'

Several beds were empty, including the one next to Alice. From the blue tinge to her skin James could tell that something was seriously wrong. She had seemed perfectly well the night before, but now she was shivering uncontrollably, her hair was matted and she was drenched in sweat. Taking her hand, he said, 'Alice, can you hear me? How are you feeling?'

She opened her eyes and forced a smile through gritted teeth. 'Terrible.' She struggled to speak. 'I've got a pounding headache and a really sore throat.'

'Don't talk, and don't worry. I'm going to make them give you something to make you feel better.'

When he found the nurse again, James said, 'I want to see her doctor.'

'He's very busy at the moment. You'll have to wait.'

'Just fetch him. I want to know if this has anything to do with the woman who was brought in on Sunday.' He could see from the nurse's reaction that she had no idea what he was talking about.

'What woman?'

'Two men in uniform put a woman in the bed next to Alice last night. Now the bed's empty.'

'I don't know anything about that. I was on early shifts last week. If you wait here, I'll see what I can find out.' She disappeared along the corridor. Whatever she said to the doctor had the desired effect. He returned with her in a matter of minutes.

'I'm Dr Sutton. What seems to be the problem?'

'Good morning, Doctor. I'm James Driscoll, Miss Taylor's fiancé.'

'Mr Driscoll, are Miss Taylor's parents with you?'

'No, they're away visiting family today.'

'Well, I'm afraid she is very seriously ill. We're about to move her to an isolation ward.'

'I don't have a number for them. I don't understand, she was right as rain yesterday. I asked the nurse whether this has anything to do with the woman who was put in the bed next to her?'

'At the moment, all I can tell you is that the woman you're referring to passed away during the night. It's too early to say, but it is likely that she passed it on to Miss Taylor.'

'Passed what on?'

'Influenza.'

'But you can treat influenza, surely? How bad can it be?'

'Very bad, I'm afraid. It's a new strain they're calling Spanish flu. We don't know nearly enough about it. We can treat the symptoms with aspirin, but people are still dying in larger and larger numbers.'

'Yes, but Alice is young and strong. Surely you would expect her to fight it off?'

'She's not as strong as she looks. One of the odd things about this virus is that young people seem to be particularly susceptible to it.'

'I have to contact her parents,' said James. 'Do you have any information on her next of kin?'

'No, I'm sorry. Why don't you see if the police can track them down?'

It was raining steadily as James ran the mile to the police station in under five minutes. The desk sergeant lifted his eyes from a newspaper to check what was causing a puddle on his clean floor. 'Can I help you, sonny?'

Still breathing heavily, he gasped, 'I have to contact someone urgently in Harrogate.'

'Have you tried the telephone?'

'I don't have their number. My fiancée's critically ill in The Vic and her parents are away visiting relatives. Is there any way I can get a message to them?'

The sergeant's manner changed. 'Let me have their details and I'll see what I can do. What's your full name?'

'James Henry Driscoll.'

'Full name of fiancée?'

James had to think for a moment. 'Alice Weatherall Taylor.'

'Address?'

'Holmleigh, North Promenade, St Annes. I'm staying with her parents.'

'Name of fiancée's father?'

'Len Taylor.'

'What's the address in Harrogate?'

'I have no idea. They're visiting his wife's parents.'

'And you have no idea what their name is?'

'I'm afraid not.'

'It's not much to go on then, is it, sir?' The sergeant thought for a moment before saying, 'Hmm, I wonder. My wife's middle name was her mother's maiden name. It's a lot more common than you might think nowadays. I'll get in touch with West Riding Constabulary and see how many Weatheralls there are in the Harrogate area. In the meantime, see what you can do with this.' He handed James a mop and bucket and pointed to the wet floor. 'We don't want someone doing themselves a mischief.' Twenty minutes later, he returned. 'A stroke of luck, lad. They were in the Harrogate telephone directory. I've just spoken to Mr Taylor at his father-in-law's house. They're heading back now.'

'I can't thank you enough, sergeant.'

'Think nothing of it. I hope she'll be alright. Here, you can borrow this umbrella. Wouldn't want you catching your death ..., sorry, bad choice of words. Mind how you go, lad.'

It was getting dark when the family was ushered into a waiting room, to find James pacing the floor. Irene Taylor hugged him, and he shook hands with Len and Freddie. 'Thank you for letting us know, James,' said Len.

'Have you seen her?' asked Irene.

'Not since this morning. She was complaining of a headache and sore throat, and they were giving her aspirin.'

'What's brought this on?' asked Irene with tears in her eyes. 'She seemed fine a couple of days ago.'

'From what I've been told, Spanish flu is a new virus and it's very difficult to treat,' said James.

'Why's it called Spanish flu?' asked Freddie.

'According to the doctor, it's because Spain was the only country reporting it. Something to do with wartime censorship. He said they really have no idea where it came from, but a lot of soldiers brought it back with them.'

At a little after eight o'clock, the doctor entered the room. They all looked at him, hoping for good news, but he avoided eye contact. He looked down at the floor as he said, 'I'm so sorry. Your daughter died about ten minutes ago.' Irene Taylor screamed and collapsed into her husband's arms.

Freddie shouted, 'No! Don't say that!'

James was rooted to the spot, unable to take in what they had just been told.

Len Taylor looked at the doctor with tears in his eyes and asked, 'How could this happen?'

'I'm afraid we're in the grip of an epidemic, Mr Taylor. It could be years before we have a vaccine to fight it, and until we do, anyone could get it. If it's any consolation, Alice would not have been in pain. Her lungs filled with fluid and she suffocated.'

'Thank you for telling us, doctor,' said Len. 'That can't have been easy.'

'Unfortunately, I'm having to do it more and more often. Does anyone have any questions before I go?'

'Yes, doctor.' It was James. 'Could this have been avoided?'

'No, I'm sorry.' The doctor looked at him compassionately as he added, 'If you're asking whether the staff here did their jobs properly, then yes they did, every one of them.'

'No, that's not what I meant. I'm sorry if you thought I was looking for someone to blame.'

'We have no way of knowing who's going to catch the virus. I wish we had a crystal ball to tell us in advance. Then we could keep them safe until the danger's passed, but we can't. All we can do is try to make our patients comfortable and hope for the best.'

'Thank you, doctor. Can I see her?'

'Only from a distance, I'm afraid. The risk of infection is just too great.'

So it was that James stood in a corridor with Alice's distraught family, peering at her body through a window. She looked so peaceful, as if she were only sleeping. He felt a horrible, gnawing pain inside, and seeing the Taylors like this just made it worse. Quietly, he made his excuses and left. Once outside the hospital, he set off at a run in the direction of the beach. When he got there, he sat on a soaking wet bench and cried bitterly, remembering the times they had held hands and walked along the seafront together. He wished that he'd told her more often that he loved her. For the second time in his short life, he had lost the thing that was most precious to him. It spelt the end of all his hopes and dreams. Unless ... His objective, the discovery of time travel, was an obsession. Now, he had to succeed. His own life felt utterly pointless without Alfie and Alice, so he resolved to redouble his efforts and do whatever he could to bring them back.

On the day of Alice's funeral, Our Lady Star of the Sea Church was packed with family and friends. James looked around the church where he was to have married Alice. He would not allow himself to grieve while there was a chance that he could save her from her fate. However, he did become deeply upset at the effect her death had on her family. After the service, Mrs Taylor had to be helped from the church by her husband. The heavens opened as Len, Freddie and James helped to carry the coffin to the graveside. Later, when everyone else had left, James sheltered beneath the portico with the Taylors, and Freddie began to cry.

'I used to make fun of her all the time,' he sobbed, 'but I never told her I loved her.'

'Brothers and sisters rarely do, but she knew, believe me,' said James. 'She only ever had nice things to say about you when you weren't there. It was obvious she loved you very much.'

25

Manchester, Lancashire
January 1919

On his way back to Rusholme, James visited Paul Lucas in Strangeways Prison. The professor was shocked to learn of Alice's death. 'I'm so sorry, James, I wish there was something I could do or say. She was such a lovely, sweet girl. I thought the two of you were made for each other.'

'We were. I thought we'd be together forever, but it wasn't to be.'

'How are you coping? I know what it's like to lose the one you love. The pain will always be there, but time is a great healer.'

'I know, but it's so hard, Paul. First Alfie and now Alice. I would give anything to have them back.'

'And I Mary, but we can't turn the clock back, sadly.'

'So people keep telling me,' said James, who desperately wanted to change the subject. 'Oh, by the way, I wanted to ask your permission to make some changes to Oakwood House. I spend far too long travelling to and from the university. Would you mind if I turn the basement into a laboratory?'

'I don't see why not. It's just wasted space at the moment. I tell you what, Roy Harris has a brother in the building trade. I'm told he's very good. Why don't you ask him for a quote, and I'll split the cost with you? How does that sound?'

'If you're sure. Oh, and one last thing. I wanted to ask about Dalton. Would you mind if he stays with the Taylors in St Annes? They would love to have him.'

'If they're going to look after him properly, I've no objection. I will miss him, though.'

'I'm sorry, Paul, but you can be sure he'll get all the love and attention he deserves in St Annes. I spoke to Mr Taylor yesterday, and I understand that their son Freddie now takes him for daily walks along the beach. If you knew Freddie, you'd know how unlikely that sounds.'

With Alice and Dalton gone, James' world was crumbling around him. The only thing that kept him going was the thought that the past might not be set in stone. He clung to the hope that a solution would present itself, but whenever he stopped working, the silence and solitude of Oakwood House was oppressive, and a constant reminder of what he'd lost. Whenever James had been feeling low because of Alfie, Alice had helped him to cope. Now, those feelings were doubled. If anything, losing Alice was worse. Alfie had died fighting for something he believed in, whereas Alice was the unfortunate victim of a senseless act of violence. The tears he felt inside were never far from the surface, but he had to deal with his grief and loneliness on his own.

James found that hard work took his mind off his troubles, and a daily dose of Extract Cannabis, the headache tablets given to him by his mother, helped to dull the pain. If he kept himself busy seven days a week, he could stay on top of the university syllabus and have plenty of spare time to pore over scientific journals and papers, searching for inspiration. After weeks of study, it was clear that, from an academic point of view, time travel was not taken seriously. He failed to find anything of interest, apart from a couple of articles by Nikola Tesla that contradicted Einstein's Theory of Relativity. In one, he claimed that the electrical impulses from his wireless transmission tower at Wardenclyffe would travel faster than the speed of light, and in the other, that he had intercepted superluminary cosmic rays from the Sun. James thought that if someone of Tesla's stature was making such statements, they must surely have some merit. Sadly, he found himself engaged in a wild-goose chase. If there was any truth to Tesla's claims, it eluded him.

In February, a turning point of sorts came from an unlikely source. James had run out of Extract Cannabis tablets, and it was a few weeks before he got round to buying more from his local pharmacy. In the meantime, he took aspirin whenever he had a headache. He didn't put two and two together at the time, but he started having vivid dreams when he stopped taking cannabis. With his waking hours dominated by thoughts of Alice and time travel, it was no surprise that they featured prominently in his nightmares. In one, he dreamt that he and Alice were being chased while searching for something, though he knew not what. The faster he tried to run, the heavier his legs became, and the slower his progress. Alice shouted, 'Here it is!' and threw something in his direction. He was too slow to catch it, but as it flew past, he could see that it was the crystal that Harry Milburn used to keep on his desk. It landed with a splash in a river, where it disappeared from view. He dived in after it, and as in so many of his dreams, began to drown. When he woke, he was drenched in sweat, and Alice's words were ringing in his ears. He lay there for a while, trying to separate dream from reality.

James would not have described himself as being given to irrational thoughts, but thus far, logic had failed him in his quest. He suspected that, had Alice been there, she would have told him not to ignore his dreams. He closed his eyes and allowed his mind to wander. If the dreams were a sign, what did they mean, and if crystals were the answer, what was the question? Could they really possess properties that made time travel possible? He decided to start again from scratch, making no assumptions and taking nothing for granted.

Late one evening, he arrived home to find a note on the mat, asking him to call DCI Hughes. The following day, his call was put through to the detective's office.

'I just wanted to offer my condolences,' said Hughes. 'Alice was a lovely girl.'

'Thank you, Inspector. When are you going to charge Winter with her murder?'

'I'm afraid that won't be possible.'

'Why ever not? You know as well as I that she was only in that hospital because of him.'

'That's true, but unfortunately it would be difficult to argue that he was the direct cause of her death. She was well on the road to recovery when she caught the flu. Not only that, but there's a time limit. Her death occurred more than a year and a day after the attack. I'm sorry.'

The news plunged James into a new pit of despair, and he took to his bed. He had no idea that two days had passed when he was disturbed by a persistent knocking on the front door. By the time he opened it, a stocky, dungaree-clad figure was disappearing down the driveway.

'Can I help you?' he shouted after him.

The man turned and smiled. ''Arry 'Arris,' he said cheerfully.

'Pardon?' James had no idea what the man had just said.

'I'm Roy's brother, 'Arry 'Arris. You wanted a quote.'

'Oh, Harry Harris,' said James.

'That's what I said.'

‘Sorry, do come in.’ He took him down to the cellar and told him what he wanted. The builder went through a well-worn routine, alternately tutting, sighing and shaking his head. When he gave his verdict, James pretended to be shocked, even though it was less than he’d expected.

It was all a game that ended with them agreeing a price for the job. They went outside, and James asked how long it would take. The builder pursed his lips, scratched his head and said, ‘This is not your average building job, lad. It’s a big job. For all intensive purposes, you’re looking at seven, eight, … ten weeks.’

Intensive purposes? Weird and wonderful turns of phrase clearly ran in the Harris family.

‘Fine,’ said James. ‘When can you start?’

‘I’ll see you on Saturday,’ replied Harris. As he walked away, he passed an attractive young woman and turned to watch admiringly as she walked up the drive.

James saw her smiling at him and said, ‘Can I help you, miss?’

‘You don’t recognise me, do you?’ she replied.

He didn’t, but the broad Lancashire accent gave her away. ‘Molly?’

‘Yes! ’Ave I changed that much?’

‘You have a bit, yes.’ James had only met Alfie’s girlfriend once, more than five years ago, when she was sixteen. ‘Mind, it’s years since I last saw you.’ She was still staring at him, but now she had tears in her eyes. ‘Are you alright?’ he asked.

She placed a cool hand on his cheek and smiled a sad smile. ‘I’m sorry, you’re the spitting image of your brother. It’s almost as if ’e’s still alive.’

‘It must be hard for you. Please, come in.’ He showed her into the living room and said, ‘Make yourself at home.’

‘Are you alright, James?’ she asked. ‘You look tired.’

‘I’m fine. I’ve just had trouble sleeping recently. I’m going to make a pot of tea, and then I’ll throw some clothes on while it’s brewing.’

‘Take your time,’ she said.

‘Now, what can I do for you?’ asked James when he returned.

‘I’m ’ere to ask for your ’elp.’

‘Tell me more.’

‘I’m going to France to look for Tommy’s body. I asked Stan Grimes to go wi’ me, but ’e said ’e couldn’t face going back there. I thought you might like to come.’

‘I see.’ James knew that the only way of getting to France was by boat, a journey that he couldn’t face. ‘Well, I’d love to,’ he lied, ‘but I’ve just arranged to have some work done on the house. I’m afraid I’m far too busy at the moment.’

Molly’s face fell. ‘Then I’ll ’ave to ask me dad to take me. He won’t want to, though, ’e’s always busy in the shop. Please come wi’ me.’ Tears filled her eyes, and James’ heart melted at the sight. ‘Alright, let me think about it,’ he said, ‘but I certainly can’t go until the summer at the earliest.’

‘Oh, thank you!’ she cried, in a way that made James realise she had taken his reply to be a promise. She hugged him and couldn’t help noticing that he flinched. ‘I suppose a few more months won’t make any difference. Mind, you’ll ’ave to gerra passport.’

‘I haven’t said I’m going yet,’ he protested. To change the subject, he said, ‘Why don’t I make you some lunch?’

April 1919

Ellen Driscoll had been trying to contact James all day. When he eventually answered the phone, something in his voice told her that all was not well.

‘What’s wrong, James? You don’t sound very happy.’

‘Happy? Do you know what day it is?’ he asked forlornly.

‘It’s Saturday. Why?’

‘It’s not just any Saturday, Mother. It’s my wedding day.’

‘James, I’m so sorry, I completely forgot.’

‘What do you want, Mother?’

‘Forgive me, I won’t keep you. Your father’s had a letter from the Imperial War Graves Commission. Alfie’s been buried in France.’

‘They’re not bringing his body home?’

‘No. Apparently, it would be an impossible task to repatriate hundreds of thousands of bodies. He will have a headstone, and we can choose the inscription. Your father and I are going to go there at Easter. Do you want to come?’

‘I would have said yes, but I’ve already arranged to go in the summer and look for Tommy Bradshaw’s body. I can visit Alfie’s grave then.' After his meeting with Molly, James had discovered that mercifully, from August, it would be possible to fly to France.

In May, Sir Ernest Rutherford announced that he was leaving Manchester after twelve years to become Director of the prestigious Cavendish Laboratory at the University of Cambridge. His replacement as Langworthy Professor of Physics was his friend, Lawrence Bragg. The Australian became the youngest ever Nobel laureate in 1915 when, at the age of only twenty-five, he and his father William received the award "For their services in the analysis of crystal structure by means of X-rays." He and Rutherford met in Manchester shortly before the end of the academic year. Sir Ernest mentioned several names as outstanding students, including James. 'Mr Driscoll is an interesting character,' he said. 'Some of his work is quite brilliant, and he has a particular interest in crystallography. You'll like him, but he's had a difficult time recently. He lost his fiancée to Spanish flu at Christmas, and his brother was killed at the Somme.' Bragg's own brother had died at Gallipoli.

26

Northern France
August 1919

James and Molly stayed in adjoining rooms, in a small but comfortable *chambre d'hotes* in the Pas-de-Calais, near the place where Stan had last seen Alfie and Tom alive. He looked out at the barren landscape, scarcely able to believe that in the last five years, countless men had lost their lives fighting over what appeared to be a worthless piece of land. Over breakfast, Molly was still talking about the previous day's journey.

'That were the scariest thing I've ever done in me life! And the most exciting.'

'It was my first flight as well, you know.'

'Why didn't you just book a ferry? It would 'ave bin much cheaper.'

'Don't worry about that. The flights are my treat.' James wasn't about to admit that he still had a fear of water. The service from Hounslow to Le Bourget had launched less than a week earlier, and in his opinion the two-and-a-half-hour flight was far preferable to bobbing up and down on the English Channel for hours on end.

'I'm not sure how we get to the battlefield from here,' said Molly.

'It's not that far, according to Stan's map. There's somewhere I'd like to take you first, though.' James hadn't told Molly about Alfie's grave. 'As it's such a lovely day, I thought we could walk.'

It took them twenty minutes to reach the Serre Road Cemetery on the Rue de Mailly Maillet. Facing them were row upon row of gleaming white headstones, all the same size and shape. James' mother had given him directions to help him find the plot where Alfie was buried. They walked among the gravestones and James said, 'A lot of these men were friends of Alfie and Tommy.'

'Such a terrible waste,' said Molly. 'Wouldn't you think…' her voice tailed off. 'James!'

He walked over to where Molly was weeping silently, her whole body shaking with the shock of her discovery. Seeing her reaction, he began to cry, and instinctively put a protective arm around her shoulder, as they gazed down at his brother's final resting place. A bunch of dead flowers were propped against the carved headstone, left there by James' parents. Underneath a regimental crest, there was an inscription.

2396 PRIVATE

A.G.DRISCOLL

EAST LANCASHIRE REGIMENT

1ST JULY 1916 AGE 19

A cross was engraved above the epitaph chosen by his father. It read "He did his duty." No fuss, as usual.

'They got his age wrong,' said Molly.

'I know,' said James. 'He lied when he joined up.'

'You knew 'e was 'ere, didn't you?'

'Yes, sorry, would you rather have known in advance?'

'Yes, at least I could've brought some fresh flowers.'

'We'll get some, don't worry.' When they left the cemetery, they continued down the road until they came to a junction. All around them was a desolate wasteland.

'Is this it?' asked Molly, dubiously.

'If the map's accurate, yes, but it's just a sea of mud.'

In the distance, Molly saw a group of uniformed men. 'Let's ask those soldiers if they know anything.'

'Wait here,' said James. When he returned, he was crestfallen. 'They're British troops who stayed behind to help clear the battlefields of unexploded shells. They said bodies are being found every day, often by local farmers who've returned to plough the land.'

'Can they identify them?'

'If they're wearing dog tags, yes. If they find Tommy, you'll be contacted by the War Graves Commission.'

'D'you think there's any chance they'll find 'im?'

'All we can do is hope and pray.'

What neither of them could know was that, while bodies would continue to be unearthed in northern France for years to come, the remains of more than seventy thousand British and Commonwealth soldiers would never be found.

That night, James lay awake, listening to Molly crying on the other side of the bedroom wall. When he could stand it no longer, he got up and tiptoed along the corridor, before tapping lightly on her door. She let him into her room, and they hugged each other silently. They lay down on the bed and fell asleep in each other's arms. In the morning, he woke to find Molly staring at him.

Tearfully, she said, 'Sorry, James, but you're so like him. You have the same eyes.'

'We had the same everything,' he said dolefully. 'Identical twins usually do.'

'Don't make fun of me, please,' she said. It was easy for her to pretend that it was Alfie lying next to her and not his brother. She began to stroke his hair and kissed him lightly on the lips, but when she started to pull him closer, he tensed up.

'I'm sorry Molly, you're lovely and I'm flattered, but it doesn't feel right to be doing this here, so soon after Alice's death. I hope you understand.'

'Not really,' she said despondently. 'It were seven months ago, James.'

'I know, but it seems like yesterday,' He knew she was right, but he still couldn't accept the fact that Alice wasn't coming back, or shake the feeling that moving on with his life would be a betrayal and an admission of failure.

Manchester University
November 1919

James walked into Bragg's office to see a newspaper, strategically placed on the professor's desk. The headlines almost jumped off the page.

NEWTONIAN IDEAS

"OVER-THROWN."

NEW THEORY OF THE UNIVERSE.

The article that followed described the most remarkable astronomical event since the discovery of Neptune, more than seventy years earlier. The Astronomer Royal confirmed that "definite and conclusive results" were found that, during a total solar eclipse on May 29 last, the deflection of light from those stars in the same part of the sky as the Sun was in close accord with that predicted by Einstein, and twice the amount predicted by Newton's Law of Gravitation.

'Well, well, Mr Driscoll. Einstein was right.'

'I never doubted it. Maybe now they'll give him the Nobel Prize.'

'I suspect the reason he hasn't already has more to do with race than merit.'

It was not the first time James had heard of the reluctance of the Nobel committee to honour Jewish scientists. Some even referred disparagingly to 'Jewish physics' as an inferior branch of science.

When Rutherford left Manchester, James could not have wished for a better replacement than Lawrence Bragg. James had read his book, "X-rays and Crystal Structure" more than once. The study of crystallography was still in its infancy, and James hoped that it might be the key to making time travel a reality. Not only was Bragg one of the world's leading experts on the subject, but he was only ten years older than James. They bonded immediately, partly due to a shared love of science, but also because they had both lost a brother in the war.

Their mutual respect grew when James came to Bragg's rescue early in his first term. He was not yet confident in charge of a class and found it difficult to handle the first-year students. Many of them were former soldiers with a low opinion of anyone who hadn't fought in the war. When James found out what was going on, he cornered some of the ringleaders, telling them that Bragg had won the Military Cross for his groundbreaking work in locating enemy guns using sound. 'People like him did their bit to keep people like you safe. Have a little respect.'

'And what about you, big man?' one of them ventured. 'What did you do during the war?'

'It's classified. If I told you, I'd have to kill you.'

No one was brave enough to pursue the matter.

Bragg looked out of the rain-spattered window at the black clouds overhead. 'Does it ever stop raining in Manchester?'

'Yes, sir. It's famous for its year-round sunshine.'

Bragg laughed as he sat down. 'Have you thought about your final-year dissertation yet, James?' It was the first time he had addressed him by his first name.

'As a matter of fact, I've had something in mind for some time, sir.'

'Something related to crystallography?'

'Yes, sir. You may think me mad, but I have a theory that there might be a link between crystals and time travel.'

Bragg raised an eyebrow. 'Well, I wasn't expecting that! Tell me how you came to that conclusion.'

'It was something in relativity. That an infinite amount of energy would be required to accelerate a particle to the speed of light.'

'Yes, that's why time travel is widely assumed to be impossible.'

'Ah, but is it? What if the particle in question did not have to accelerate, because it was already travelling faster than the speed of light?'

'Do you have any evidence to suggest that such a thing might be possible?'

'Not yet, sir, no.'

The way he said it left Bragg in no doubt that he expected to find evidence in the fullness of time. 'It's an interesting hypothesis, but I'm not sure how it could be anything more than that.'

'Correct me if I'm wrong, sir, but I need to find empirical evidence of the existence of phenomena that cannot be explained. What if I write to all the leading physics departments?'

'That sounds like a good place to start, but I think you'll need a back-up plan in case nothing comes of ...' Bragg became silent.

'Sir?'

He held up his hand, left his seat and paced around the room, deep in thought, while James waited patiently for him to speak. 'I wonder.'

'What is it, sir?'

'It may be nothing, but you've reminded me of something I heard at a symposium earlier this year. Apparently, a student of von Laue in Frankfurt made an unusual observation. According to her account, she saw the results of her experiment before it was initiated.'

'What was the experiment, sir?'

'Firing x-rays into crystals to observe the patterns produced. Of course, it was dismissed as a figment of her imagination.'

James was stunned. 'That's exactly the sort of thing I'm hoping to find! What did von Laue say about it?'

'He wasn't there, I'm afraid. Too soon after the war. Why don't you write to him? He's at the University of Berlin now.'

'I'll do that, thank you.'

'Whatever the outcome, I think you've found a fascinating title for your dissertation. "A theoretical discourse on the role of faster-than-light particles in creating the conditions necessary for time travel." What do you think?'

'That sounds great! I'll give it some serious consideration and let you know, sir.' The more he thought about Bragg's suggestion, the more excited he became. He kept returning to the idea that a crystal might be the key. The x-ray story could have been apocryphal, but if not, what possible explanation could there be? If the effects of an experiment appeared before it began, the only explanation that made any sense to James was that the particles had somehow travelled back in time.

He knew enough about von Laue's x-ray experiments to know they would have been repeated hundreds of times. The crystal and the photographic plates were the only variables in the equation. There was a good chance that the crystal was the cause of any anomaly. He had to find out whether the story was true and, if so, which crystal was responsible. He wrote to Professor von Laue the very next day.

Haberlandstrasse, Berlin

The newlywed Einsteins were preparing for a trip to Switzerland when the phone rang. Elsa answered with a formal 'Einstein residence.'

'Hello, Elsa, it's Max. Is Albert there?'

'You've only just caught us,' she said, signalling to Albert that the call was for him. 'We're about to leave for Switzerland, Max.'

'Oh, sorry. I'll be brief.'

Taking the handset from his wife, Einstein said, 'Hello Max, what can I do for you?'

'Albert, I've had a rather troubling letter from England. It's from a young scientist called Driscoll, who's studying under Professor Bragg in Manchester. Bragg suggested that he write to me to find out more about the Frankfurt experiment. The one that led to Hermes.'

'How do they know about that?'

'I don't know. Word gets around, I suppose. He wants to know whether I have considered the possibility that the crystal used in the experiment has special properties.'

Einstein raised an eyebrow. This was not good news. 'You said his name was Driscoll? How old is he?'

'I have no idea, but he's an undergraduate, so I suppose no more than twenty-one.'

'I have a feeling that this won't be the last we hear of Herr Driscoll.'

'Then what should I do about his letter?'

Einstein thought for a few moments, before making a decision. 'Ignore it for now. If he writes again, tell him there is no truth to the story.'

'Okay. Have a good trip.'

'We won't be there long, Max. I'm afraid my mother's dying, so we're bringing her back to Berlin. Elsa will look after her for the time she has left.'

'I'm so sorry, Albert. Let me know if there's anything I can do.'

'I will. Talk to you soon, Max.'

After her husband's death in 1902, Pauline Einstein lived with her sister Fanny, Elsa's mother. She fell ill with cancer during the war and was moved to a sanatorium in Lucerne in 1918. It was obvious that she was dying when Albert and Elsa brought her to Haberlandstrasse. She spent the last three months of her life there.

27

West Prussia
May 1920

Shafts of sunlight arrowed through the trees, transforming the forest floor into a rich mosaic of light and shade. Rudi Krämer breathed deeply, savouring the familiar, earthy smells and listening to the sound of birdsong. He couldn't remember the last time he'd heard birds singing. A few paces in front of him was his older brother Gerd, and to their left and right, battle-hardened marines waited for the signal.

They were in the heart of Waldfrieden, a thousand-acre estate in West Prussia that was mainly forest. This was Rudi's first mission, and he trembled with excitement at the thought of what might lie ahead. They were close now. Close to the house where communist revolutionaries might be ready and willing to fight to the death. Their objective was to locate and seize a hidden weapons cache. Suddenly they were moving again, and the trees gave way to a clearing, revealing a large, palatial house with two towers. The marines encircled it and the Krämer brothers found themselves at the rear of the property, weapons raised in readiness.

From the front, they heard their commander shout, 'You are surrounded, lay down your weapons and come out with your hands above your head!' There was no reply. The order was repeated, again with no response. Then the loud thud of the front door being kicked open, followed by the sound of jackboots on wooden floors. They waited for anyone who might try to escape through the back door, but no one did. They could hear their fellow marines moving from room to room and shouting, '*Klar*!' at regular intervals. When the search was complete, the men were called to the front of the house, where they stood to attention. 'Form yourselves into groups of six men. I want you to fan out and search the estate. You know what to do, but be careful, they're armed and dangerous. This might be a trap.'

It was eighteen months since the war had ended in the total capitulation of German forces. The country had been starved into submission by the Allied blockade, which was only lifted after the signing of the Treaty of Versailles in July 1919. The treaty imposed reparations the country could ill afford, acceptance that the war was Germany's fault and removal of the country's military capability. There was a widespread belief that the socialists had stabbed the nation in the back to seize power. Nationalists opposed democracy and wanted a return to an authoritarian, autocratic state.

Against this backdrop, unofficial paramilitary groups known as Freikorps had sprung up everywhere. One such unit of six thousand men was commanded by Captain Hermann Ehrhardt, a diehard monarchist. The Ehrhardt Brigade became famous as it fought against communism throughout Germany, funded but not controlled by the government. Communist uprisings in Berlin and Munich were swiftly and violently put down by the Ehrhardt Brigade and others.

Having dealt with the threat from the far left, Ehrhardt pursued his own nationalist agenda. He believed that the socialists had betrayed the country. Many shared his view and, in March 1920, nationalist opposition to the government led to an attempted coup by the military. Twelve thousand Freikorps soldiers occupied Berlin and installed Wolfgang Kapp as chancellor. The government fled to Stuttgart and called for a general strike, supported by the unions. Twelve million workers went on strike and Berlin was soon without water, gas or electricity. No newspapers were printed and, without civil servants, the Kapp administration was unable to govern. The coup collapsed after only four days, forcing Erhardt to seek refuge in Bavaria. There he found an ally in Ernst Pöhner, Munich's Chief of Police. Pöhner was a committed nationalist and anti-Communist, and he embezzled money to help Ehrhardt set up the Bavarian Wood Products Company, a front for a new terrorist organisation. It was called Organisation Consul, and its aim was to wage war against Social Democrats, Jews and left-wing radicals. When its men needed to lie low, Pöhner could be relied upon to falsify passports to aid their escape.

Rudi Krämer had joined up in the last days of the war. Robbed of the chance of seeing any action, the Ehrhardt Brigade and Organisation Consul gave him a way of following in Gerd's footsteps. His entire life had been spent in his brother's shadow, but that was going to change. Rudi's mind was made up when he read an OC notice that proclaimed, "Only those men who have determination, who obey unconditionally and who are without scruples will be accepted. This is a secret organisation." Gerd was furious when he found out that Rudi had joined the OC. It meant that he was going to have to watch his little brother's back.

'Come with me,' he snapped, leading the way to a group of men, some of whom were already known to Rudi. Peter Brandt, Franz Schneider and Günter Teufel were his brother's childhood friends, growing up in Wittenberge before the war.

'You know Peter, Franz and Günter,' said Gerd. 'And this is Klaus Müller.'

Rudi came face to face with one of the largest and scariest men he had ever met. Holding out his hand, he stammered, 'Rudi Krämer.'

Müller looked him up and down, stubbed out a cigarette and cast a sideways glance at Gerd. 'Don't get in the way!' he growled. When the order came to move, it was clear that Müller was the natural leader of the group. He strode deeper into the forest, barking orders to keep up and stay alert. The path ahead started to slope downwards, and Rudi could hear the faint chatter of children at play. Through the trees, the men caught their first glimpse of a lake, from where the sound of laughter and splashing could be heard. Müller signalled to them to halt. A man's voice called out. 'Jochen, watch Ivan for me.'

'Yes, Papa,' came the reply. Rudi saw a man striding up the path towards them. He was wearing a bathing suit and towelling his hair dry as he walked.

'Captain Paasche?' It was Müller's voice.

The man removed the towel from his head, revealing a handsome face and sharply chiselled jaw. Hans Paasche was thirty-nine years old, a decorated naval officer who had seen first-hand the horrors of war and became a committed pacifist. His wife had died from Spanish flu a year earlier, leaving him to bring up four young children alone. By 1920, he was one of the most influential political journalists in Germany, campaigning against violence, militarism and nationalism. He was much admired by Albert Einstein, who was particularly drawn to his idea of establishing a League of Nations to work for and maintain peace throughout the world.

Paasche faced the armed men in front of him, but if he was scared, he didn't show it. 'I am Hans Paasche. I don't know who you are, but what are you doing coming here with guns?' He turned and pointed towards the lake. 'My children are ...' The words died in his throat as Müller shot him in the back, killing him instantly. The sudden violence of it rooted Rudi to the spot. It was his first experience of death, and he felt sick to his stomach. He walked further down the path, trying hard not to throw up for fear of losing face in front of the others. The children's laughter was replaced by the sound of a young girl screaming. Rudi could see her standing next to her three brothers, all looking at him with terror in their eyes. The eldest couldn't have been more than ten years old.

'You okay, Rudi?' said Gerd.

He wasn't okay by any means, but he couldn't show it. '*Ja,*' he said, 'what should we do about the children?'

'Leave them. Come on, let's get out of here.'

Haberlandstrasse, Berlin
June 1920

The atmosphere was somewhat strained at the Einsteins' dining table. Albert had forgotten the anniversary of his marriage to Elsa, as he would frequently do in the years before he employed a secretary. He was not an overly romantic man and had more important things on his mind that Wednesday morning. His friend Hans Paasche had been murdered, and he was awaiting a call from Bernhard Weiss, the Deputy Chief of Kripo, the Berlin Criminal Police. Einstein knew him as a fellow member of the German Democratic Party, and both were well aware of the threats made against Paasche.

Weiss was also the fifth and newest member of the Hermes Alliance, after Max, Moritz and Elsa. Einstein trusted them all implicitly to keep his secret. When the telephone rang, it gave him a welcome excuse to leave the table. 'What have you found out, Bernhard?' he asked.

'Not a great deal, I'm afraid. A lot of rumours. We know that more than fifty armed men were seen in the area on the day Paasche was killed. There was mention of a group calling themselves Organisation Consul. Someone made a phone call to local police, warning of armed revolutionaries and a hidden weapons cache on Paasche's land, but no evidence of it was ever found.'

'A weapons cache, hidden by a sworn pacifist? Who would believe it?'

'I know. You might want to think about your own safety, Albert. Paasche was a well-known Jew, and a pacifist. He told me last year that he was on a murder list. He went into hiding for several weeks, but it didn't stop him from speaking out against nationalism.'

Einstein looked at Elsa and wondered just how safe they were. 'Hans used to say that in the face of evil, it is those that look on and do nothing that make the world a dangerous place.'

'Talk like that gets people killed, Albert.'

'What would you have me do, Bernhard? Remain silent? Live my life like a fugitive? That is what these criminals want.'

'Just be careful, Albert. You have many enemies in Berlin.'

'Thank you, Bernhard. Let me know if you hear anything else.'

Einstein replaced the handset in its cradle and returned to the dining room. He looked out of the window at the gathering storm clouds. The idea that his own name might be on a murder list was terrifying. The thought that people might wish him dead for wanting peace, or simply for being a well-known Jew, was difficult to comprehend.

His thoughts turned to Hermes, sitting forlornly at one end of his study for the past three years. He'd been tempted to use it on a number of occasions, but the world was changing so fast, he was worried he might do more harm than good. Now he would put it to good use. He might not be able to change the political landscape with a message, but he could save his friend's life. Even without a detailed account of the events in the forest, he could warn Hans about the plot to kill him. That should give him time to escape death and prevent his children from being orphaned. He might even be able to save Ellen Paasche from the Spanish flu that took her life in 1918. With advance warning, perhaps Hans could protect his wife from the disease.

Einstein called out, 'I have work to do,' before retiring to his study. It was the last Elsa would see of him for several days. He began to think about the contents of the message. All being well, he would receive it on the third of December 1916. He first encountered Paasche at a meeting of the German League for Human Rights in February 1917, so delivering the message would not be a problem. Although Paasche was a friend, he might not believe it possible to predict the future, so proof was needed. Einstein turned to his diaries, in which he kept all manner of seemingly useless facts and figures. He soon found what he was looking for in a list of deaths during March 1917. He picked two, one of whom was Ferdinand von Zeppelin, the aircraft manufacturer, and set to work turning the information into binary codes. It was a laborious and time-consuming task, but by the early hours of the following day, he was ready to send the message. He was exhausted, and he knew that one mistake would render the message meaningless, so he quite wisely decided to go to bed.

In the morning, after several cups of strong coffee, he returned to the library and fired up what he now referred to as the Schöneberg Hermes. Sending the message would take most of the day. Precise details of the deaths of three people would surely be enough to convince the most sceptical of men. He was confident Paasche would take whatever steps were necessary to prevent his own assassination and his wife's untimely death.

Einstein fired the first infrared beam into the magdalite crystal, anticipating a bright blue light. There was only the faintest pale blue glow. He tried again. The same result. He stared aghast at the equipment, unsure where the problem lay. Everything was as it should be, but the crystal no longer showed any signs of life.

It had not been used since Max warned Einstein of his potentially fatal condition, more than three years ago. He decided to call him.

'Max, it's Albert. The crystal is no longer fluorescing. Why would that be?'

Max was used to his friend coming straight to the point. 'Has it been kept in the dark all this time?'

'Yes, apart from the day it was brought here from Wilmersdorf.'

'Then that may be the problem. Prolonged exposure to light can destroy any fluorescent properties a crystal may have. What were you doing with it?'

'Did you hear about Hans Paasche?' asked Einstein, the emotion evident in his voice.

'Yes, a terrible business. In front of his children as well.'

'I was going to warn him. Do you have any more magdalite?'

'No, I'm sorry. I could return to the caves and collect some more samples if that would help.'

'It won't help poor Hans, I'm afraid. Replacing the crystal means resetting the device. Any future messages can only be sent back to the date when Hermes is reactivated. Nevertheless, if you're free this weekend, I could come with you.'

The Ofnet Caves, Bavaria

When Max returned to Bavaria, this time with Einstein for company, he recalled the day a decade earlier that ultimately saved his friend's life. In July of 1910, back when he was plain Max Laue, he and his young bride Magdalena had spent part of their honeymoon in the pretty town of Nördlingen. At the time, Max was a promising young crystallographer at the University of Munich. His interest in Nördlingen stemmed from its unique location inside a huge crater, believed to be the remains of an extinct volcano. He'd been curious about the way the town's buildings shimmered in the sunshine. They were built from local rock that contained what appeared to be glass or crystal.

Intrigued, he'd persuaded Magdalena to accompany him to the crater's edge, where he could study the geology of the area in more detail. On a memorable afternoon, they stumbled across a hidden but seemingly unremarkable cave. Max still remembered the thrill he felt when a piercing shaft of sunlight illuminated the dull brown rock, transforming it into a visual cacophony of colour. Flaming reds, verdant greens, electric blues, vivid oranges, intense purples and vibrant yellows had created an unforgettable patchwork tapestry of iridescence. He had taken as many samples as he could carry in his haversack and, when the honeymoon was over, examined them under ultraviolet light in the university laboratory. He had identified all but one by their colour, lustre, hardness and density, leaving a hitherto unknown crystal that he named magdalite, after his wife. He would later discover that Nördlingen's buildings were built from suevite, a rock in which the carbon had been transformed into millions of tiny diamonds by the impact of an asteroid.

Ten years on from his earlier trip, the landscape looked little different to Max. In fact, the only thing to have changed was his name, the term von being added when his father was raised to the ranks of hereditary nobility in 1913. He parked the car well away from other sightseers, of whom there were few, due to the rain that was now falling steadily.

'Put on your hat and glasses, Albert. And keep your head down if anyone comes near.' Einstein was just too recognisable to risk being discovered.

Laden down with empty bags and a couple of lamps, the pair made their way towards the hidden cave. It took Max some time to find the entrance but, once inside, it seemed untouched from ten years earlier.

'I don't think I can squeeze through that gap,' protested Einstein.

'You don't have to. I'll pass the bags out as I fill them, and you can carry them back to the car.'

'What should I say if someone challenges me?'

'Just tell them you work for the Federal Geological Service, but try not to be recognised.'

'Easier said than done,' replied Einstein.

Max smiled. 'I'll be as fast as I can,' he said. In fact, it took him less than two hours to fill twelve bags with rocks. Eight of them were already safely concealed under a blanket in his Audi. He handed the last four bags and the lamps through the gap and took Einstein's hand, following them into the daylight.

'Don't look now, but there's someone coming.'

'Right, let's get this lot into the car and get out of here.' They moved off at a brisk pace, prompting their rather overweight and breathless pursuer to give up the chase. When they reached the car, they could see the man scratching his head, unable to see the cave entrance and obviously wondering what they had been doing. Hopefully, the cave would remain their secret for several more years.

'How did you know which rocks to take?' asked Einstein.

'I didn't. I just took as much as I thought we could carry. I'll go through them when we get back. It shouldn't take too long to identify them in the lab.'

28

Manchester University
July 1920

Whitworth Hall was packed for James' graduation ceremony. He waited in line for his name to be called and looked out at the audience. His mother was sitting in the third row, but there was no sign of George. He had hoped that his father's pride in his achievements might have brought about a reconciliation of sorts. It was more than three years since they had fallen out, and he had begun to doubt whether the damage could ever be repaired. He was lost in his own thoughts when he heard the announcer say, 'James Driscoll, Physics.' Ellen beamed with pride when her son strode onto the stage to accept his certificate from Sir Henry Miers, the university's Vice-Chancellor. Sir Henry, a distinguished crystallographer in his own right and a Fellow of the Royal Society, paused to have a few words with James and wish him well.

Lawrence Bragg sat amongst the begowned professoriate that formed the backdrop to the ceremony. Although he was now one of them, his youth made him feel like an outsider. Looking around, he thought it fitting that the collective term for professors was a pomposity. He smiled at James as he left the stage and wondered just how much his young prodigy could achieve in his chosen field. His dissertation had been a revelation, posing theoretical questions and identifying areas for further study that Bragg himself had not considered. He was looking forward to the next academic year, when James would return as a postgraduate student.

Outside, in the quadrangle, James hugged his mother. They posed together for the obligatory photographs before finding a seat away from the crowds.

'I thought I might have seen Father today,' said James forlornly.

'I don't know whether he would have come, but he had to go to Aberystwyth. Nana Driscoll's been taken ill.'

'Please say it's not the flu.' The Spanish flu epidemic was over, but James could not get it out of his head.

'They don't know yet. She's taken to her bed with a cold and a high temperature. Her doctor wants to make sure it's nothing serious, so he's arranged for some tests. Your father's gone to look after her for a while.'

'I'll keep my fingers crossed, then. Let me know when he comes home, and I'll pay her a visit.' James saw the pained expression on his mother's face and hugged her again.

'I wish you two would settle your differences. It breaks my heart to have this bad feeling between you.'

'I don't know what more I can do, Mother. He asked me to leave. Surely it's up to him to ask me to come back?'

'You know what he's like, James. It's stubborn pride, that's all.'

'Well, all I can do is wait for him to come round to the idea that I'm not going to be an engineer.'

As they were preparing to leave, James noticed Professor Bragg standing nearby, trying to catch his attention. He took Ellen by the arm and led her towards Bragg, saying, 'Mother, there's someone I'd like you to meet.'

Before James could introduce him, his mother extended a hand and said, 'I'm James' mother. Were you two on the same course together?'

Bragg smiled as he shook her hand, realising that she had mistaken him for a student. 'Sadly not,' he said. 'My name's Lawrence Bragg. It's a pleasure to meet you, Mrs Driscoll. James and I are friends.'

'How nice, he never talks about his friends.'

They chatted for a while, before Bragg turned to James. 'I was just wondering whether you had any plans for next year?' he asked. 'The university's launching a research doctorate programme, and I thought you might be interested.'

'Most definitely,' he replied. 'Can we discuss it later?

'By all means,' he said. 'I'm free at six, you know where I'll be.'

'Yes, thank you Professor,' said James. 'I'll see you later.'

Bragg said goodbye to Ellen and went to join a group of older people. When he had gone, Ellen was puzzled. 'Why did you call him Professor? He can't be much older than you, James.'

'Because he's not a student, Mother. You've been talking to the man who won the Nobel Prize for Physics five years ago.'

'Well, I never! What must he think of me?'

'He probably thinks what a lucky woman you are to have a genius for a son!'

James had been contemplating his future and seriously considered looking for a full-time job when he finished university. The opportunity to continue his studies in Manchester was a dream come true. Lawrence Bragg was aware of his financial situation and had already made sure that the funds for a PhD scholarship would be available, should he want it. When he offered it to James, he gladly accepted but, while it solved his financial worries for the time being, he was far from happy. If it hadn't been for Winter, he and Alice would have been married for more than a year by now. They might even have started a family. Instead, he was alone, and he missed her so much, it hurt.

Over the previous couple of years, James had become something of an expert in particle physics. He studied the chemistry of various compounds and examined the behaviour of crystals when subjected to high temperatures. The properties of faster-than-light particles were of particular interest, but there were no textbooks or scientific papers to help him, other than the early works of Einstein. In truth, he had made little progress, but he only had to think of Alice to find the motivation he needed to carry on.

For the first time in almost three years, he felt like playing cricket again. One of his old schoolfriends was a regular for Rochdale Cricket Club, and James was invited along for a trial. They couldn't believe their luck when they saw what he could do with bat and ball, and he soon found himself playing cricket throughout the summer. In fact, he scored so many runs that year that the county selectors invited him to Old Trafford for a trial at the start of the following season.

Armley Gaol, Leeds
December 1920

The room was large and bare, save for a row of wooden tables and chairs running down each side. Half a dozen prisoners sat at tables, well apart from each other and watched over by prison warders. When the visitors filed in, Varese followed a woman who was holding her daughter's hand a little too tightly.

'Mummy, you're hurting me,' complained the little girl.

'Will you stop your complaining, Agnes? Now, where's your dad?'

'Daddy!' yelled Agnes, trying to break free and dragging her mother towards the far end of the room.

Varese looked around the room and caught sight of Winter, half-hidden by the stocky frame of a powerfully built warder. '*Ciao*, Kevin!' he shouted, smiling broadly as he approached his friend with outstretched hand.

'No touching!' barked the warder.

Still smiling, Varese replied with a friendly, '*A fanabla!*' before sitting down at Winter's table. Thankfully, the warder knew no Italian and had no idea he was being insulted.

'Nico, it's good to see you, my friend. You got my letter then?'

'*Si.* I thought you could do with cheering up.'

Winter leant forward and spoke in a whisper so that the warder couldn't hear him. 'This place is designed to grind you down, but it won't get the better of me.'

Nico studied his friend closely. He couldn't help thinking that this was not the Kevin of old. 'You look tired, *mio amico*. You sure they're looking after you properly in here?'

'It's not exactly the Savoy, but I get by. Now, what's been happening in the Garden State?'

'Business is booming. They banned alcohol, so we started smuggling it. They can't figure out why they can't catch us, but we got cops on the payroll. It's beautiful.'

'So, you're a bootlegger now?'

'Nah, not me. I've got men doin' the dirty work while I get myself some sun down in Miami! D'you remember that job you did for us in 'fourteen?'

'How could I forget?' It had been Winter's biggest pay day.

'Well, that's what I've bin doin' for the last five years.'

'Tell me more.'

'Sure. The Germans were runnin' out of raw materials because of the British blockade. They got round the problem by sendin' merchant subs to the States. They brought gems, dyes 'n' stuff in exchange for rubber, nickel, tin 'n' so on. Until the US declared war on Germany, nobody could stop them.'

Winter was intrigued. 'Where did you come in?'

'What nobody knew was that we already had three subs doin' the same thing for us in Florida. They'd bring us gems 'n' drugs, 'n' we'd send them acetone. We made huge quantities in our own distillery 'n' shipped it to the coast. We own a big stretch of the shoreline, and we have a coastguard who turns a blind eye, so the subs could come ’n’ go with no one bein’ any the wiser. We made a fortune. Sweet, huh?’

Winter laughed. ‘So, what happened when the war was over?’

‘We kept goin,’ but prohibition meant shuttin’ down the distillery. Now they’re sendin’ us booze. Whichever way you look at it, we made a small fortune from your little recipe.’

‘Yeah, well, I wish I could’ve been part of it.’

‘Don’t worry, when you get outta here, you got a nice little bank account waitin’ for you in the States.’

‘That’s not what I meant,’ said Winter. He had plenty of money stashed away. ‘I just wanted Germany to win the war.’

‘It was never gonna ’appen once America joined in. Now then, you said in your letter you need a favour. What can I do for you, my friend?’

‘I can’t stand the fact that he’s out there, living his life without a care in the world, while I’m in here.’

‘Who, Driscoll?’

‘Yes, Driscoll!’ There was venom in the way that Winter spat out the name. ‘I’m gonna make him rue the day he ever crossed me. This is what I want you to do.’

Aberystwyth, Wales
January 1921

From the top of Constitution Hill, George Driscoll looked out across Cardigan Bay. The picturesque town of Aberystwyth lay below him. To the north, the Snowdonian peaks were partially obscured by clouds, but still a wonderful sight. In his youth, he could have walked to the top of this hill, but now he was thankful for the funicular railway that took the effort out of the journey. This was one of his favourite places, far removed from the hustle and bustle of everyday life.

His mother Rhiannon had died at the age of seventy-two, two weeks before Christmas, with George at her bedside. She had lived in the shadow of her husband, Henry, until his death in 1895. Henry had known that he didn’t have long to live and handed control of the mill to his only son. If he was honest, he didn’t think his son had it in him to make a success of the family business. George cared more about the men who worked there than he did about profit and loss.

No matter, there was no one else. Henry died nine months later and was buried in the family plot in Kirk Allerton.

The large seafront property in Aberystwyth had been Rhiannon's idea. With the help of her sister Glynis and niece Olwen, she had built a thriving bed and breakfast business. Her health had been up and down since the summer, but in November, she caught the measles. In the end, she succumbed to pneumonia, known as the 'friend of the aged' because of the quick and relatively painless death that often followed.

On her deathbed, she made George promise to make things right with James. She reminded him that he'd had just as difficult a relationship with his father, yet they eventually reconciled, and both regretted the wasted years. George was her executor and after she died, he had met with her solicitor, Illtyd Price. Price was a solemn, humourless man whose funereal expression was more suited to an undertaker than a solicitor, in George's opinion. He was not surprised to learn that two of Mr Price's brothers worked for the company that buried his mother. According to Rhiannon, who it seemed knew everyone in the town, no one in the family drank. George couldn't help but think that parties in the Price household must have been a right barrel of laughs.

The contents of Rhiannon's will had come as a complete shock to George, who assumed that he would be the main beneficiary. He was planning to use his inheritance to shore up the business, but everything went to James, apart from a sizeable donation to the Imperial Cancer Research Fund. George's parents had invested their money wisely over the years, and their legacy was going to make James a very wealthy man in his own right. Wealthier than his father. The initial sense of indignation that George felt at his mother's decision came from the realisation that he no longer had any hold over his son. However, the more he thought about it, there was still a chance that, if they could resolve their differences, James might be prepared to invest some of his fortune in the mill.

George was almost ready to go home. He wanted to give James the news face to face, so he rang Ellen and asked her to invite him to Allerton Manor. She was overjoyed at the thought that they might finally be able to put their differences behind them. That evening, she called her son.

'Hello, Mother, is everything alright?' he asked. 'You don't usually call on a Monday.'

‘Yes, right as rain, but your father’s asked if you can be here on Thursday.’

‘He wants to see me? Are you sure?’

‘Yes, can you come?’

‘Of course. I have a meeting with my tutor on Wednesday afternoon, but I’ll get an evening train. I should be with you by eight.

‘Okay, see you then.’

29

Kirk Allerton, Yorkshire
January 1921

James was woken in the early hours of Thursday morning by a loud knocking. By the time he started down the wide staircase, his mother had already opened the front door to Eric Jenkins, the village bobby.

'Sorry to trouble you at this hour, Mrs Driscoll.'

Ellen was alarmed. The police didn't usually turn up in the middle of the night. 'Sergeant, what is it?'

'May I come in, ma'am?

'What's wrong?' she asked, her voice faltering. 'Is it George?'

'Please, ma'am, if I could just come in for a moment.'

'Yes, of course. Would you like a cup of tea, Eric?'

'No, thank you. Hello, sir,' he said as James arrived at his mother's side.

'Sergeant. Why are you here?'

'I'm afraid there's been a terrible accident.'

'Is George alright?' cried Ellen.

'I'm sorry to have to tell you that there was a train crash in Wales yesterday. Your husband did not survive.'

She let out a strangled cry and fell weeping into James' arms. As he held her, he could hear himself saying, 'What happened?'

'It's too early to say, sir, but we know that two trains collided somewhere between Aberystwyth and Welshpool in Wales.'

'And my father was definitely on one of them?'

'Yes, sir. He was conscious when he was pulled from the wreckage. He told them his name, but I'm afraid he died before reaching hospital.'

When Jenkins had gone, James sat with his heartbroken mother for what seemed like hours. He felt a deep sense of unease that his father's death might have had something to do with Kevin Winter, but for now his mother needed him. When dawn broke over Allerton Manor, he gave her one of her sleeping draughts and carried her up to bed.

He stood in George's study and looked out over the rolling fields to the fells beyond. He could not bring himself to sit in his father's chair. Despite their differences, James had loved him and wanted to patch things up between them. Now he would have to live with the guilt of not having done so. He burst out crying, overcome by a crushing sense of loss and despair. It seemed as if tragedy was following him around. Was this a punishment for attempting to meddle with God's plan? Was it arrogant to think that this was all about him, rather than his loved ones? Of course it was, he decided. Nana Driscoll had been old. His father was simply in the wrong place at the wrong time, as were Alfie and Alice. On the other hand, what were the chances of four unrelated deaths within four years? He felt as though he was losing his mind.

He must have fallen asleep. When he woke, he was unsure where he was at first. His head was on a desk, and he was sitting in a plush leather executive chair, although he had no recollection of having sat down. It was the middle of the afternoon. Had last night really happened? He began to cry again at the realisation that any chance of reconciliation had been snatched away from him.

His thoughts turned to his fruitless attempts to use science to turn back time and save the lives of those he loved. Although he was no closer to a solution, he would make it his business to find out what caused the crash, so that one day he might be able to prevent it or at least stop his father from getting on a doomed train. The responsibility felt overwhelming.

Was he mad? Something deep inside kept telling him that time travel was possible if only he could find the key. He longed to see Alfie again, and Alice, and his father. His nana's life had reached its natural conclusion, but he resolved to spend more time with her, should he ever succeed in his quest. He had work to do.

George's funeral was attended by many of his workers, all keen to show their affection and respect for the man who had kept them in jobs and improved their working conditions, while other mills were exploiting their workforces. It was a very public expression of the high regard in which George was held, and it made a huge impression on James. He vowed to do whatever he could to protect the futures of those loyal men and their families.

Following the accident, the newspapers reported that twenty-one people had died, including Lord Herbert Vane-Tempest, a director of the railway, and the driver and fireman on one of the trains. Like many of the casualties, George had been in one of the front carriages. Many more people were badly injured. The public inquiry concluded that the cause was a series of misunderstandings and slack working practices by the staff at Abermule station, resulting in the misuse of an electrical tablet system, designed to prevent more than one train from entering a single line stretch of track. The system had worked effectively throughout Britain for many years, but on this occasion the wrong tablet was given to one of the drivers. His failure to spot the mistake cost him his life. James was relieved that foul play had been ruled out. His fears about Winter were unfounded, at least for now.

March 1921

Following weeks of discussion with bankers, mill owners and assorted businessmen, it was clear that the mill could not carry on as it was. James told his mother that the only option was to sell the business for a knockdown price. 'I've found a buyer who will take the mill off our hands and leave us debt-free.'

'Your father would turn in his grave if he could hear you.'

'We have no choice, Mother. Since the war, imported cotton has become so cheap that it's selling for less than it costs us to make it. Father refused to invest in modern machinery to avoid cutting jobs. Now, only the mills that did invest can compete with Japanese imports, and even they're struggling. I tried to warn him this would happen, but he wouldn't listen. It's not our fault that the world has changed.'

'But all those men will be out of work. They have mouths to feed. What will they do?'

The future of the millworkers and their families had been uppermost in James' mind. 'Blackett and Muir are one of the largest companies in the north. They've agreed to keep the entire workforce on for at least a year. We'll not find a better deal in the circumstances.'

'Can't we just keep going until business picks up?'

'Business isn't going to pick up, Mother. If we keep going, we'll be bankrupt, and all those men will lose their jobs. We'll have to sell the Manor. Is that what you want?'

'I just want everything to go back to the way it was,' she cried, running from the room.

The next morning, James waited for his mother to come downstairs before leaving for the mill. He had not meant to upset her and wanted to clear the air, particularly as it was her forty-ninth birthday. He had bought her an exquisite jewellery box that, when opened, played a Chopin Nocturne as a ballerina spun round in front of a mirror. When she finally appeared, her mood had not improved. James decided to wait until later in the day to give her the present.

'I'm sorry about last night, Mother. If there was any other solution, I'd have found it.'

'There's nothing more to be said then,' she answered tersely.

'No, but I still need your signature on the sale documents.'

Ellen signed the papers grudgingly and left the room without saying another word.

On his way to work, James felt as though the weight of the world was on his shoulders. When he arrived at the mill, his father's secretary was waiting for him.

'Good morning, sir. Can you call a Mr Price on this number?'

'Who is he?' asked James.

'A solicitor from Aberystwyth,' she replied. 'Shall I get him for you?' Five minutes later, Illtyd Price came on the line.

'Mr Driscoll, I was sorry to hear about your father,' said the Welshman. 'He was a good man, so he was. Now then, are you sitting down?'

'Why do you ask?' replied James.

'I wanted to give you advance warning of the contents of your grandmother's will. Her estate was to have been shared equally between you and your brother. Following his death, you're the main beneficiary.'

Nana Driscoll had always joked that when she died, she was going to leave everything to the local dog shelter. 'She left me the house?' he asked.

'Not only the house,' said Mr Price. 'There was also a large sum of money and various other effects. If you're able to meet me, I have a cheque here for a little over thirty-four thousand pounds.' There was silence on the other end of the line. 'Mr Driscoll?'

'Thirty-four thousand? That's a fortune!'

'It's a tidy sum, and no mistake,' agreed Price. 'You're a very wealthy man, Mr Driscoll.'

James couldn't think of anything to say. 'Mr Price, I'll have to call you back.' He sat in stunned silence, unable to comprehend the news. He was still sitting there when Charlie Earnshaw knocked on his door an hour later.

'You had summat important you wanted to say to the men, Mr Driscoll?'

James looked up at him. 'It can wait, Charlie. Have a seat.'

The mill foreman sat down with a puzzled look on his face. 'Summat up, sir?'

'No, not at all. How long have you worked here, Charlie?'

'Forty-two-year, man and boy.'

'Pretty much your whole life, then?'

'Aye, since I were a lad.'

James could hear the pride in the foreman's voice. 'So, you'll be well aware that we're going through a difficult time right now?'

'I don't like the way this is eading, sir.'

'Relax, Charlie. I've had an idea, but I want your opinion before I take it any further.'

Driving home late that evening, James felt positive for the first time in years. He couldn't wait to tell his mother about the sudden upturn in his fortunes, and his plans for the mill. Things would be very different from now on. A strong wind blew across the valley as he drove up the long drive, to find the manor house in total darkness. He wondered whether there had been another power cut. Getting out of the car, a gust of wind caught the door and almost pulled it from his grasp. Had the wind brought down one of the power lines?

The front door was unlocked, and he went inside, struggling to close it against the wind. He tried the switch, and the huge atrium slowly filled with light. He was about to shout for his mother when a slight movement made him look up. There, slowly spinning, silently swinging, swollen-faced, with bulging eyes staring sightlessly down at him, was his mother's body. The rope around her broken neck was tied to the heavy wooden balustrade on the landing. James stared in horror, unable to comprehend the nightmarish vision above him.

As he slumped onto the cold marble floor, the thought that this was his fault wouldn't go away. He should have seen this coming. He should never have left her alone, not even for a second. The

Driscoll curse had struck again, and now he was all alone in the world.

30

Kirk Allerton, Yorkshire
March 1921

Following his mother's death, when the doctor, police and undertakers had all left, James sat in George's study for hours, drinking his whisky, trying to erase the image of his dead mother from his mind. Trying to come to terms with the loss of his entire family and the girl he had loved, all within the space of five short years. With tragedy heaped upon tragedy, he was no longer convinced that he could stop any of this from happening.

He had been mad to think that he might be able to turn back time. He was a scientist, not a magician, and if he couldn't bring back Alice, or Alfie, or his parents, what was the point of anything anymore?

At his lowest ebb, he sat with his father's handgun, playing with the contents of a box of bullets, thinking how easy it would be to make all of this go away, and to be with Alice once more.

Evan Jackson, Ellen's father, arrived from Scotland on the day before her funeral. James hadn't seen him in more than ten years. Evan spent the evening drinking George's whisky and telling stories about Ellen that James had never heard before. 'She was always headstrong,' he said. 'Got herself into some right old scrapes when she was young.'

'Really?'

'Aye, did she ever tell you how she met your father?'

'No,' said James, eager to know more.

'We were visiting my sister, Gwyneth,' he said. 'She used to live in the village, you know. It was the day of the Queen's Jubilee. 1887, I think it was. Ellen was only fifteen at the time. Little minx set fire to the beacon up on Allerton Edge, an hour early. George saw her do it and helped her get away.'

'I've heard that story before, but I had no idea that Mother was the culprit!'

'Aye. George once told me that, despite her age, that was when he fell in love with her.' Evan became quiet and stared into his glass. 'Funny how things turn out.'

Ellen's funeral was a much smaller affair than her husband's. The cause of death had not been made public and at the wake, James endured a wave of sympathy from well-meaning friends and relatives, one of whom was his great-aunt.

'Hello James,' she said. 'I'm Glynis Powell, your grandma's sister.'

'I remember you. Thank you for coming,' he replied politely.

'I'm sorry to talk business at a time like this, but I may not get another chance.'

James was relieved that the conversation was not about the loss of his mother. 'That's quite alright, Glynis. What do you want to talk about?'

'I have a proposition for you,' said the elderly woman. 'Rhiannon became too ill to keep the bed and breakfast going, but if you are agreeable, my daughter Olwen and I would like to open it up again. She would do most of the work, and we could pay you rent.'

'I haven't made any decisions yet,' he said. 'Why don't you give it a try and just pay me whatever you think is a fair rent for the time being? If I decide to sell, I'll give you plenty of notice. We can always draw up an agreement if you think you need one.'

Looking back, James only had a vague recollection of the weeks that followed. He never left the house, surviving on his father's whisky and whatever he could find in the kitchen. Rubbish covered the work surfaces and began to spill onto the floor. Eventually there were unread newspapers and assorted bottles everywhere. The papers provided a warm home for a nest of mice that had taken up residence of late. Empty whisky bottles were piled up under an old Belfast sink, while rows of unopened milk bottles had accumulated by the back door.

In the midst of this squalor sat James, hungover, haggard and with hair down over his shoulders. Wallowing in self-pity, he had lost all track of time. The loud knock on the front door barely registered in his befuddled brain. Whoever it was would come back if it was important. His mother's unopened present sat in the middle of the table, alongside two empty bottles of Extract Cannabis and a half-empty bottle of whisky. It was the last of his father's supply. A sharp knock on the windowpane made him look round. It was Professor Bragg. What did he want? If he ignored him, perhaps he would just go away. The next thing he knew, Bragg was standing in front of him with a bottle of milk in each hand.

'You left your door unlocked.'

James had no idea when the door had last been locked. 'Come in, why don't you?'

'I was worried about you, with good cause, it seems.' Placing the bottles in the sink, he added, 'There are another six bottles of milk on your doorstep. How long have they been there?'

'Dunno,' slurred James. He had no idea that, with no reply to his repeated knocking, the milkman had stopped delivering ten days ago.

'You're covered in bruises, James. Have you been in a fight?'

'I fell,' he replied. The details were hazy and he had lost all track of time, but three days earlier, while high on a mixture of alcohol and cannabis, he had fallen down the stairs.

'You need to see a doctor,' said Bragg.

'Don't you worry about me, sir.'

'Well, someone has to. I was sorry to read about your father in the paper, but that was months ago. What's happened to make you like this?'

'Oh, nothing. Apart from my mother killing herself.'

'What?' Bragg was so shocked that he was lost for words. 'When?' he spluttered.

'I dunno. Erm, on her birthday. March the eleventh. A lovely surprise, finding your mother hanging in the hallway.' James chewed on his bottom lip in a vain attempt to stop from crying. When the tears came, he did not wipe them away. He was too mentally and physically drained to care, even though Driscolls were not meant to cry. Bragg moved behind him and placed his hands on his shoulders.

'You poor man. I'm so sorry. Sit there and I'll get you some coffee. Then I'll tidy up in here a bit, and we can decide whether you're up to coming back to Manchester with me.'

'You don't have to do this,' he protested, but he didn't try to stop him.

'I can't leave you like this,' said Bragg. 'Good God, man, you smell like a distillery!'

The milk was off, but with a couple of mugs of strong black coffee inside him, James' started to feel a little more human. 'Thank you, Lawrence.'

'Think nothing of it. Go and get cleaned up and we'll talk.'

Two hours later, he was almost presentable. Almost, because he had done no washing or ironing since his mother's death. Bragg persuaded him to come with him to his hall of residence, less than a mile up the Wilmslow Road from Oakwood House.

'I'll take you to Rusholme for some clean clothes and arrange for your laundry to be taken care of.'

With several suitcases full of dirty washing in the back of Bragg's car, they set off. In Brighton Grove, he waited as James opened the front door of a chilly Oakwood House. He filled an empty suitcase with clean clothes, gathered up the pile of mail that had accumulated on the mat and returned to the car. Bragg's rooms in Hulme Hall were warm in comparison, and James soon settled into one of the visitor rooms. Having unpacked and made himself a cup of tea, he turned his attention to the post, which included a large brown envelope, bearing a Liverpool postmark.

He took out his penknife and slit open one end. Reaching inside, he pulled out a book. Its brown cloth cover was attractively decorated with an art nouveau design, and bore the inscription *The Mysterious Affair at Styles*, above the name Agatha Christie. Although he was an avid reader, James had never heard of the author. He checked the envelope to see if there was a note, then picked up the book by the cover and held it over the bed so that the pages fell open. A piece of paper dropped out, but it turned out to be a receipt for seven shillings and sixpence from Openshaw of Liverpool, Purveyor of Fine Books. He breathed a sigh of relief, realising there was no message. Who would have taken the trouble to send him a book without leaving any clue as to their identity? Perhaps it was intended for the professor, or could it have come from Winter? Was it another message?

Later that evening, he examined the book again and started to read the opening chapters. It told the story of Emily Inglethorp, the owner of a country manor who was murdered by poisoning. James thought it a first-rate detective story, and he was particularly taken with the main character, a detective by the name of Hercule Poirot. He would have been even more impressed had he known it was Mrs Christie's first novel.

In the early hours of Monday morning, James was unsure whether he was awake or dreaming. Before he was fully conscious, he found himself sitting bolt upright in bed. 'No! It can't be!' He knew now why there was no message in the book. The book was the message! A woman, the owner of a country manor, murdered by poisoning. Emily Inglethorp was his mother! She hadn't hung herself at all. Somehow, Winter had got to her.

He tried and failed to go back to sleep. If he was right, Winter had an accomplice on the outside. Could it have been the man from the trial? If so, how had he managed to poison his mother and make it look like suicide?

He wondered what the police would make of his theory. Would they take it seriously? These and many other questions went round and round in his head until he thought it might explode. He got up at first light, donned a vest and shorts, and went for a run. As was often the case, he could see things more clearly when he was running. Despondency turned to anger and a determination to see Winter pay for what he had done. He would call DCI Hughes later that morning and tell him his mother was murdered. He would know what to do.

Hughes arrived at police headquarters in the early afternoon. He didn't like late shifts, mainly because there was more chance of being kept back to deal with problems at the end of the shift. The previous night was a case in point. The sighting, pursuit and arrest of a wanted criminal had kept him busy until well after midnight, and he had slept until late morning. On late shifts, the pattern always seemed to be work, sleep and repeat. He was not in the best of moods when he entered his office to find several messages on his desk. One of them was from James Driscoll, who wanted to speak to him urgently and would call at three o'clock.

Right on time, the operator connected the call. 'Manchester Police,' said Hughes.

James recognised the accent immediately. 'DCI Hughes. It's James Driscoll.'

'I'm a little busy at the moment, Mr Driscoll, what can I do for you?'

'I'll come straight to the point. I believe my mother was poisoned on the orders of Kevin Winter.'

'I thought your mother hanged herself?'

'So did I, Inspector, but I have new evidence. Another book.'

'In that case, I'll see you here this evening at six. Good day to you.'

When James arrived, he was seen by Hughes and a DC by the name of Tony Phillips. The young officer seemed to take an instant dislike to James. 'Right, let's see this book,' said Hughes. James handed it to him. 'And the message?'

'There was no message, Inspector, just the book.'

'Then I don't understand, where's your evidence?' Hughes was struggling to see the connection.

'The book is about a woman who was poisoned, Inspector.'

'Seems rather tenuous to me, sir,' ventured Phillips. 'A book is pushed through your letterbox, and you decide that your mother was murdered?'

'If you knew Winter like I do,' said James, 'you'd know that's precisely the sort of thing he would do.'

'Even so, you haven't given us much to go on.'

'Have you kept the envelope?' asked Hughes.

'Yes,' said James, pushing it across the table.

'Alright, I tell you what I'm going to do. I'll ask our fingerprint department whether they can take any prints from it or the book. We'll need your prints to exclude them from our search. I'll also make some enquiries about Mr Winter. If we find anything to corroborate your theory, we'll have to apply for an exhumation. That means your mother's body would have to be examined for signs of poisoning.'

'Thank you, Inspector. That's not something I really want to think about, but if that's what it takes. Oh, and you already have my fingerprints, from when my fiancée was attacked.'

'Ah yes, I was forgetting. Forgive me. Goodbye, Mr Driscoll.' Outside, he turned to Phillips and said, 'Well, what do you think?'

Tony Phillips was an ambitious young detective who was determined to make a name for himself, no matter what it took. He had already made his mind up. 'I think the whole thing is very suspicious, sir,' he said. 'That man stands to inherit his father's fortune, and his entire family dies in separate incidents? Then he points the finger at someone who's already locked up. If it were up to me, I'd be looking a lot closer at James Driscoll.'

'He's always seemed to me to be a thoroughly decent young chap, but perhaps you can look at him with fresh eyes. Let me know what you find.'

'Yes, sir.'

It was all the encouragement that Phillips needed. He didn't believe in coincidences, and four deaths connected to one person was about as big a coincidence as he could imagine. A young man like James Driscoll might be prepared to do almost anything to become the sole heir to his father's fortune. As far as Phillips was concerned, James was guilty, and this could be the case to earn him a swift promotion. He just needed enough evidence to bring him in, and once he did he was sure he would crack under the pressure.

He began by looking at the facts surrounding the four deaths. The manner of Ellen Driscoll's death would not have been difficult to arrange. All James had to do was overpower her, put a noose around her neck and push her off a balcony. Not difficult at all. George Driscoll's death, on the other hand, would have required a lot of careful planning, but that was by no means impossible for a man with a university education and a cool head. Phillips had been brought up in poverty in one of the poorest parts of Manchester, and he hated rich kids. If James Driscoll, Esquire had killed his father, then he was also guilty of the murders of twenty train passengers and crew.

Then there was Alice Taylor. James had been present at London Road Station on the day of her attack and was also the last person to visit her before her death. His motive for wanting her dead was unclear, but it could just have been a lovers' tiff or, who knows, perhaps he just liked killing. His brother's death was a different matter. No court in the land would convict James of Alfie's murder during a battle in a faraway land, no matter how many people he had killed at home. Nevertheless, on the balance of probabilities, the young detective was satisfied that he had enough to warrant bringing him in for questioning.

31

Rusholme, Manchester
April 1921

Lawrence Bragg was just leaving Hulme Hall on his bicycle when a Black Maria passed him, travelling in the other direction. James had just spoken to Bragg and was eating breakfast in the refectory, when he saw the detective and a burly constable being directed to his table. Hoping for some positive news, he cast a welcoming smile in Phillips' direction, but it wasn't returned.

'Good morning, detective,' he said. 'Do you have any news for me?'

'I do,' said Phillips, a thin smile forming as he said the words he had practised on his way to the hall of residence. 'James Driscoll, I'm arresting you on suspicion of the murders of Ellen Driscoll, George Driscoll and Alice Taylor.' He proceeded to read James his rights, in front of several astonished students.

Incredulous, James said, 'Have you taken leave of your senses?' He was handcuffed and escorted unceremoniously to the waiting vehicle. At the station, he was frogmarched to a cell, where he was informed that someone would be along later. In fact, although he was given food and water, Phillips left him to stew until the following morning. The detective wanted him at his most vulnerable when he was interviewed. Meanwhile, he made a call to a local newspaper. Phillips knew how these things went, so he had waited until it was Hughes' day off before making the arrest. He didn't want his superior taking any of the credit for his actions.

Armley Gaol, Leeds

Winter knew from newspaper reports that George Driscoll, Lord of the Manor of Kirk Allerton, had died in January. He had been surprised at Nico's willingness to sacrifice so many innocent people, just to kill one man. Somehow, it didn't seem like his style. He had also read about the death of Mrs Driscoll. She was thought to have taken her own life in a fit of depression, and her body was found by her son. Winter could only imagine the devastating effect their deaths must have had on the young man. How he wished he could have been a fly on the wall when Driscoll made his gruesome discovery. All being well, the Agatha Christie novel had been sent to him before Nico returned to America. It was Winter's idea, sent in the knowledge that Driscoll was smart enough to figure out its meaning. As agreed, Nico had not made contact after the woman's death, just in case the police made the connection.

Winter picked up a discarded copy of the *Leeds Mercury*. His heart sank when he read the latest headline. "Murder at the Manor – Arrest Made." His immediate thought was that something had gone badly wrong with Nico's plan. When he read that the person arrested was the victim's son, he punched the air in delight and laughed out loud. The sense of euphoria he felt made him forget where he was for a moment.

'Now you know how it feels,' he said out loud. He wondered what the chances were of Driscoll being sent to Armley. It seemed highly unlikely, but it was nice to fantasise about what he would do if ever got his hands on him again.

Manchester, Lancashire

DCI Hughes entered his terraced house, close to Ardwick Green Park, having walked his dog to the paper shop and back. He made himself a cup of tea, cut a large slice of cake, and settled into his favourite armchair to read the paper. His day off was about to be ruined by the same front page that Winter had found so entertaining.

'What the bloody hell …?' he spluttered, as tea and cake exploded from his mouth. He marched into the hallway and grabbed the telephone handset from its stand. By the time he was put through to Tony Phillips, he had calmed down, but only slightly.

'Is there something you've forgotten to tell me, Phillips?'

A little unnerved by the tone of his boss's voice, Phillips said, 'If you're talking about James Driscoll, I was going to tell you when you got back.'

'In that case, answer me this,' said Hughes, trying to control his temper. 'Do you think you might have exceeded your authority by arresting someone behind my back?'

'That was never my intention, sir,' lied Phillips. 'I thought we had enough evidence to bring him in.'

'Well, I sincerely hope you have, because otherwise you're going to be on desk duties for a very long time! Tell me what you've got.'

Phillips gave Hughes his version of the chain of events. It was a version that portrayed James as a man who had been prepared to kill to avoid an unhappy marriage and murder both of his parents to get his hands on their money.

'I know you're relatively new here, Phillips, but have you read any of the evidence in this case?' asked Hughes. 'When I asked you to look more deeply into James Driscoll, I was hoping for something new. Something that might have been missed. It was a chance for you to show what you could do.'

'If you allow me to interview the suspect, I think I can do that, sir,' said Phillips.

'He's not a suspect!' shouted Hughes. 'Miss Taylor named her attacker. She had plenty of opportunity to point the finger at Driscoll, but she didn't. In fact, I don't think I've ever seen a couple as much in love as they were.'

Phillips was beginning to realise that he might have jumped the gun.

'What's more,' said Hughes, 'there are at least a dozen witnesses who said that Mr Driscoll was more than a hundred miles away at the time of the train crash.'

'But, sir, …,' said Phillips.

'I haven't finished! A pathologist calculated Mrs Driscoll's time of death as mid-afternoon. Witnesses confirmed that Driscoll was in Welbeck at the time, and that's not all. I found out that his father's mill was in financial difficulties. His mother was in the process of selling the business for a song on the day she died.'

'Yes, but sir, I think he may have employed a hitman.' Phillips was making this up as he went along, in a desperate attempt to justify the arrest.

'Show me a shred of evidence to support that theory.'

Phillips shrugged. 'I was going to force it out of him when I interviewed him, sir.'

'That's enough!' shouted Hughes. Referring to the unfailingly incompetent, fictional policemen who had featured in a number of Mack Sennett comedies, he said, 'Good God, man, you've turned this force into the Keystone Cops. When you came here, I was told you were ambitious, and I thought that was a good thing, but you've let it cloud your judgement. So, this is what you're going to do.

You're going to release Mr Driscoll, and you're going to apologise to him for any distress this has caused, and then you're going to go home until I decide what to do with you, do you understand?'

'Yes, sir,' mumbled Phillips dejectedly as he replaced the receiver.

Hughes arrived shortly after lunch. Angry to have lost his day off because of Phillips' rash behaviour, he was desperate for some good news to brighten his day. It came in the form of a report that had been left on his desk. The Fingerprint Department confirmed that prints taken from Driscoll's envelope had been matched to an American man. He was known to the US Bureau of Investigation and his name, Domenico Varese, was familiar to Hughes.

He opened his notebook and soon found the entry. Winter had been visited by someone called Nico Varese on the thirteenth of December. The Bureau of Investigation reported that Varese was a member of one of the largest crime families on the east coast of America. It didn't take Hughes long to find out that he arrived in Liverpool on the RMS *Celtic,* two days before his meeting with Winter. He left on the same ship four days after Ellen Driscoll's death. Further enquiries in the United States established that many years earlier, a young hoodlum by the name of Kevin Winter had been arrested in New York. He was known to have links with the Vareses, but after being bailed he simply disappeared.

Shaken by his ordeal, James returned to Hulme Hall to continue his slow recovery. It was hard to remain optimistic when he was feeling so depressed about life in general. In that frame of mind, it seemed ridiculous to think that he might be able to break through the invisible barrier that was preventing him from changing the past. *I've read too many science-fiction books*, he thought. He couldn't forgive himself for not making his peace with his father while he had the chance, or for upsetting his mother in the days leading up to her death. When he did go for a run, he avoided Platt Fields Park, the scene of his proposal to Alice.

However, he did find cricket therapeutic. His love of the game was rekindled when he saw, pinned to a notice board in his room, the letter from Lancashire Cricket Club inviting him to Old Trafford for a trial. Although he wasn't at his best, he did enough to be selected for the county's second eleven. He would have played more regularly, but he was unavailable for most of the midweek matches. He had already missed too much of the summer term and felt indebted to Lawrence Bragg, who had gone out of his way to help him. Instead, he resumed playing for Rochdale, but it soon became apparent that something was wrong. At the crease, he often seemed distracted and would lose his wicket playing silly shots. He was no longer the fearless, swashbuckling batsman of the previous summer.

Based on DCI Hughes' evidence, Manchester's Chief Constable had ordered the exhumation of Ellen Driscoll's body. When the results of the pathologist's toxicology tests came back, they confirmed that she had indeed been poisoned. Varese must have killed her before putting a noose around her neck and pushing her off the balcony to make it seem as if she had taken her own life. James' hunch had been right, but unfortunately, there was nothing to prove conclusively that Winter had played any part in her death. It was yet another blow.

By the end of May, James had become bored with life at Hulme Hall and decided to return to Oakwood House. Lawrence Bragg had persuaded the university to overlook his recent absences, given the exceptional circumstances. James was aware that he had been given more leeway than would normally have been afforded to a PhD student, and he didn't want to let Bragg down. For the remainder of the Summer Term, he did his best to justify his tutor's faith in him, working hard and demonstrating an encyclopaedic knowledge of the structure and characteristics of a wide range of crystals. His diligence persuaded Bragg to allow him to continue his research into faster-than-light particles, on condition that he turn his undergraduate dissertation into a serious academic paper, worthy of submission to one of the leading scientific periodicals.

James agreed, but over the course of the following academic year, he struggled to make any significant progress. He did have the occasional flash of inspiration, however, most notably when researching crystal formation. He came across a 1905 paper, written by a geologist named Daniel Barringer, who claimed to have proof that a giant crater in Arizona was "due to the collision with the earth of an extra-terrestrial body, possibly a small asteroid." It occurred to James that the composition of rocks coming from outer space could be completely different to those on earth. Perhaps space rocks already contained faster-than-light particles, or a metamorphosis occurred when an asteroid hit the Earth. It was a theory worth investigating.

32

Liguria, Italy
April 1922

In the hills above Rapallo, Richard Keller brought beer and wine to his guests. He was careful not to spill anything on the maps that already covered most of the table. Keller was a staunch supporter of Kaiser Wilhelm, even in exile. Now in his seventies, he had spent his life at sea and wanted to spend his retirement somewhere warm with a view of the ocean. He was angry at the humiliation that had been heaped upon his king and country. Had he been younger, he would have fought alongside these men. Tomorrow, he would take them to the boat, but from there it was up to them.

'*Danke, mein Herr*,' said Rudi Krämer.

'*Du bist willkommen*,' he replied before going inside and leaving them to their plans.

Rudi looked around the table at his comrades in arms. It was almost two years since he witnessed Klaus Müller's cold-blooded execution of the traitor Paasche, but he was not yet a killer himself. After all this time, he still found it difficult to make eye contact with Müller.

'You okay, Rudi?' asked Gerd, looking closely at his brother.

'*Ja*, just impatient for tomorrow.'

'All you've got to do is handle the boat,' said Müller. 'You know how to do that, right?'

'Of course.' This was only Rudi's fourth mission and Müller still considered him a liability.

'How many men have you killed now, Klaus?' Everyone stared at Gerd, surprised at the temerity of the question. He was the only one who could have asked it without incurring the towering Bavarian's wrath.

Müller shrugged. 'You mean since the war? Maybe fifty or so.'

'Anyone we might have heard of?' asked Franz Schneider, emboldened by his friend's nerve.

Müller fixed him with a hard stare that made him regret his impertinence. Then, uncharacteristically, he cracked a smile before taking a large swig of ale. 'You should have heard of all of them.

The politicians and the pacifists. The Jews and the traitors to the cause.'

'I remember when you killed Gareis,' said Gerd. Karl Gareis had been chairman of the USPD, the Independent Social Democratic Party of Germany. He constantly spoke out against violence as a means of political conflict and was earmarked for assassination by Organisation Consul. In June of the previous year, he was shot in the head outside his house in Munich.

'What about Erzberger?' asked Rudi.

'That was Tillessen and Schulz,' said Peter Brandt. Matthias Erzberger was the Weimar Republic's Finance Minister. As the man who signed the armistice in November 1918, he was at the top of the OC's murder list. His assassins shot him while he was out walking in the Black Forest the previous August.

'They made the mistake of talking to the wrong people,' said Gerd. 'They were nearly caught.'

'They would have been if it hadn't been for Pöhner,' said Günter Teufel.

'Who?' asked Rudi.

'Ernst Pöhner. He used to be Munich's Chief of Police, and he's a friend of the OC. He helped them escape to Hungary. Gave them money and false passports. Others too.'

'You should all learn a lesson from that,' barked Müller. 'Don't say nothing to nobody. Stay in the shadows, like me.'

'You have to,' laughed Gerd. 'Anyone who saw you would remember you!'

'That's true,' he roared, a big, booming laugh that put them all at ease.

'Is it true that Einstein's on the list?' asked Schneider.

'Why wouldn't he be?' asked Teufel. 'He's a famous Jewish pacifist. A prime target.'

'I suppose so,' replied Schneider. 'He's very popular, though.'

'Who was the guy with the moustache in Munich?' asked Rudi. 'Who killed him?'

'Hitler? Also me,' nodded Müller. 'They said he was a war hero, but he squealed like a pig when I stuck him. Called himself the Führer. What a joke!' Adolf Hitler had been leader of the NSDAP, the up-and-coming National Socialist Workers' Party. Due to his popularity, he was seen as a threat by Organisation Consul. In November 1921, he was speaking at a party meeting in the

Hofbräuhaus am Platzl in Munich, when violence erupted between his thugs and their Social Democrat and Communist opponents. In the confusion, Müller and Teufel got close enough to Hitler to strike the killer blow, before disappearing into the night.

'If tomorrow goes as planned, the government will be kaput. We'll be national heroes,' said Gerd.

'Who is this Rathenau?' asked Rudi. Everyone looked at him, surprised that he hadn't heard of their latest target.

'Don't you read the papers?' asked Gerd. 'He's the Foreign Minister, Rudi. The man who negotiated the Treaty of Rapallo with Soviet Russia. It's due to be signed tomorrow.'

'He's also one of the richest men in Germany,' said Brandt.

'Not after tomorrow,' said Teufel. 'There's a song about him, you know. How did it go, now? "Shoot down Walther Rathenau, the God-damned Jewish pig!" I think that was it.'

'It's no *"Lila Lied,"* is it?' said Gerd, referring to the popular cabaret song.

'No, but at least it's patriotic!' fired back Teufel. 'That song would have been banned if it wasn't for this depraved government.' The Weimar administration had abolished censorship and introduced basic democratic rights for lesbians and gay men. "*Das Lila Lied*," the Lavender Song, had become something of an anthem for the gay community.

Walther Rathenau was an extremely wealthy Jewish businessman and politician. In 1915, he succeeded his father Emil as head of AEG, the largest electrical manufacturing company in Germany. In the early days of the war, he was put in charge of the KRA, the War Ministry's Raw Materials Department, tasked with obtaining essential raw materials that were threatened by the Allied blockade. He was instrumental in establishing secret submarine trade routes with the United States before its entry into the war in 1917. When the war ended, he was one of the founders, along with his close friend Einstein, of the DDP, the German Democratic Party. He became Minister for Reconstruction in the Weimar government and was promoted to Foreign Minister in January 1922. His first act was to negotiate the Treaty of Rapallo with Russia. Rathenau's determination that Germany should fulfil its obligations under the Treaty of Versailles infuriated Organisation Consul.

At Rathenau's last dinner party in his palatial Grunewald villa, he drank port and smoked cigars on the terrace with Einstein. It became clear that he was concerned for his own safety. 'I represent a people who do not accept me,' he said. 'They listen to my enemies, who tell them I am part of some Jewish-Communist conspiracy.'

'That's why I advised you not to take the job,' said Einstein. 'It's a poisoned chalice. You and I have very different ideas of how a Jew should behave in Germany.'

'I've always believed that the way to overcome antisemitism is through assimilation. I still do.'

'You're an idealist, Walther. You cannot overcome such prejudice by becoming more German than the Germans. We should strive for the day when we have a patch of land to call our own. A place where we are not considered aliens. Until then, we must preserve our identity and our dignity.'

'In the meantime, our names are on a murder list, my friend.'

'Are we at the top of the list?' asked Einstein with a wry smile.

'I rather think that I am. The Treaty of Versailles did not make me popular.'

'But I'm not even an active member of the party, Walther. Why would I be on such a list?'

'You're a public figure and a Jew who talks of peace. Our enemies don't want peace, Albert. They think it is their patriotic duty to shoot pacifists!'

'You should stop now. Give it up. Go to Switzerland and count your money.' Einstein knew that he was wasting his breath.

'If I don't see this through, then who will? I have to do this. But you should be careful. I would not want the same fate to befall you.'

'Would you have me stay silent, Walther? If the world is a dangerous place to live, it's not because of evil people, but people who do nothing about it.'

'A noble sentiment, Albert, but one that may very well get you killed.'

'I'll bear that in mind. Now let's go back inside and play for your guests.' Einstein made light of his friend's warning, but he would soon learn that he had every right to be worried.

David Lloyd George, the British Prime Minister, called for a symposium to discuss the rebuilding of Germany and negotiate a new relationship between Europe and Russia. The Genoa Economic and Financial Conference was to be held at the Palazzo di San Giorgio over six weeks in April and May. The OC team travelled separately from their Konstanz hideout to Keller's home, arriving at the beginning of April. Their mission was ordered by Hermann Ehrhardt, the head of the OC. From Rapallo, a fast boat would take them to the harbour in front of the palace in Genoa. Once there, they would assassinate Rathenau as he arrived at the conference.

With thirty-four nations represented, there was such a heavy security presence in Genoa that Müller was forced to abandon the attack and wait for another opportunity. It came with word of a secret meeting between Germany and Russia in Santa Margherita Ligure. Confirmation of time and place had come through earlier in the day from OC's highly placed Weimar contact. Richard Keller quickly reconnoitred the hotel and its grounds. Schneider and Teufel went into Rapallo to buy maps of the area, giving Müller and the others several hours to put together a plan.

Gerd Krämer checked his watch. 'It's getting late, and we have to be up before dawn. You all know your jobs, so try to get some sleep and I'll wake you at four.'

Early the next morning, while Peter Brandt remained onshore with their getaway vehicle, the others set off in a motorboat, with Rudi Krämer at the controls. He covered the first mile of the crossing in less than five minutes. When they were half a mile from their destination, he cut the boat's engine. With four men rowing, the rest of the journey took them another twenty minutes, and they made a silent approach to the shore in complete darkness. They landed at the eastern end of Santa Margherita Ligure, one hundred yards south of the Imperiale Palace Hotel. It was half past five in the morning, and all was still. Leaving Rudi with the boat, the others went ashore and made their way up the winding steps towards the hotel. Out of sight of the entrance, they fanned out, concealing themselves in the bushes and shrubbery to await Rathenau's arrival.

The sun was high in the sky when Georgi Chicherin, the Russian Foreign Minister, arrived by car. Flanked by four bodyguards, he walked straight into the hotel to await his German counterpart. Fifteen minutes later, Rathenau's black limousine pulled up alongside the porticoed entrance. Two bodyguards emerged from the vehicle, one of them opening the car door for Rathenau to step out. As soon as he had one foot on the ground, machine gun fire erupted from all sides, killing the German bodyguards instantly. Rathenau tried to get back into the vehicle but was dragged out by Schneider and forced to his knees.

Müller pulled out a pistol and stood over him. 'You have been found guilty of crimes against the Fatherland,' he snarled. 'Do you have anything to say for yourself?'

Rathenau, though terrified, looked his executioner in the eye and said, 'You have no authority here. I'm going to ...'

At that moment two of the Russian guards, fearing that their man might be the target, came running out of the hotel. Müller turned and shot the first man to appear but as he fell, the second Russian fired from a crouching position, hitting Müller in the chest and knocking him off his feet. Schneider placed his gun to the back of Rathenau's head and pulled the trigger, a split second before he too was hit in the head by a bullet from the Russian, who continued to fire. He shot Müller again and turned to face Krämer, who killed him with a burst of machine gun fire.

A quick check on Müller and Schneider confirmed that both were beyond help. Rathenau was already dead. 'Let's go,' shouted Teufel, and the two men ran back down the steps towards the boat.

'Rudi, start the engine!' shouted Gerd as they ran for their lives.

'Where are the others?'

'They died as heroes,' said his brother. 'Schneider killed the Jew.'

Rudi appealed to his brother. 'We have to take their bodies home.'

'Don't be a fool. The place is crawling with guards, and the police will be there any minute. If we stay, we die. They wouldn't want that. Now get moving!'

Ten minutes later, the boat was back in the same cove it had left several hours earlier. Brandt led them to a car, and they were well on their way to Florence before the Italian police knew what had happened. This part of the journey was well planned, until the men arrived at Firenze Santa Maria Novella Station. From there, they split up and took separate trains to Germany via Switzerland or Austria.

Two weeks later, when the four men met again in a Munich hotel, they received a personal visit from Ehrhardt.

'The government is collapsing,' he began. 'When it is dead and buried, your names will go down in history. Müller and Schneider are martyrs to a noble cause, one that we must continue to fight for. We cannot let the Communists and the Jews destroy our great nation.' Ehrhardt turned to Günter Teufel. 'You are the leader of this squad now, Teufel. Take them off to the Tyrol. Have a holiday. Enjoy yourselves, you've earned it.' Handing him a bag, he said, 'You know what to do with this.'

When he had gone, Teufel opened the bag. It contained four fake passports and a large sum of money, courtesy of Pöhner. Raising his glass, he said, '*Zum Sieg und abwesenden Freunden*.'

'To victory and absent friends!'

33

Schöneberg, Berlin
April 1922

The Einsteins returned from a two-week lecture tour of Paris to the news of Rathenau's assassination. Elsa noticed a dramatic change in her husband in the days that followed. Having cancelled all his public speeches and presentations, he became withdrawn and distracted. He spent hours alone in the library, or sitting in an armchair staring out of the window. At dinner one evening, Elsa voiced her concern. 'What's troubling you, *mein Liebste*?'

After a long pause, he replied. 'I'm thinking that Berlin is not safe for us right now.'

'Surely you're not thinking of leaving?'

'If they can kill Walther, what makes you think they can't kill me? Anti-Semitism is rife here now. Do you want to be a widow?'

'Of course not, Albertle, but this is our home. All our friends are here.'

'I'm sure our friends will understand. I know you dislike change, but we have to face facts, Else. I attract too much publicity here. I upset a lot of people.' He could see that he had worried her.

'Where would we go?' she asked.

'I don't know yet. I've had a great many offers that would suit me very well. I was even asked if I wanted to give up physics and become an engineer in Kiel.'

'What did you say?'

'Well, I must admit that a normal life has its attractions, not to mention the scenery and the sailing.'

'I can't see you working in a factory for the rest of your life.'

He smiled. She knew him too well. 'No, that's why I turned it down.'

'So, what will you do?'

'Nothing until I've spoken to Weiss at Walther's funeral.'

'You should stay away. It's too dangerous.'

'I have to go, Else. He was my friend.'

Hermann Ehrhardt had underestimated the esteem in which Walther Rathenau was held by the German public. His belief that Rathenau's murder would bring down the government was mistaken. The left did not rise up against the Weimar Republic. There was no civil war. For the time being at least, there would be no regime change. When Rathenau's coffin arrived in Berlin, his body lay in state in the Reichstag. On the day of his funeral, millions of Germans took to the streets to protest against terrorism and mourn the loss of a great statesman.

Einstein was in the crowd but left when Weiss warned him that it was unsafe. Later, in his apartment, Weiss told him what he knew. 'The men who did this were very well informed. They must have had help from within the government.'

'Do you have any idea who they were, Bernhard?' asked Einstein.

'Not yet. I spoke to the Chief of Police in Munich, not that he would have told me if he had known.'

'Why do you say that?'

'Munich is very different to Berlin. We have intelligence sources there, but they're not inside the police. I once asked the last police chief whether there were any groups of right-wing assassins in the city. You know what he said? "Yes, but too few of them." That's what we're up against.'

'Could you speak to the police in Italy?'

Weiss shook his head. 'I have no contacts there. The fact is, unless someone talks, we may never find out.'

Einstein puffed on his pipe and gazed out of the window. 'He told me this would happen, you know. I asked him not to take the job and he said "If not me, then who else?"'

'He was a brave man, Albert, but look where it got him.'

'I know. He told me his name was on a death list. Mine too. I'm thinking of leaving Germany, Bernhard.'

'You should get away, at least until things settle down a little. Berlin is a dangerous place for us Jews right now.'

'Then why haven't you left?'

'And let the lunatics take over the asylum? It's my job to defend the republic.'

Einstein scowled and muttered, 'If not you, then who else?'

The Einsteins spent most of the following year away from Berlin. Three months on the Baltic coast was followed by a five-and-a-half-month tour of the Far East, Palestine and Spain. They made a huge amount of money from a lecture tour of Japan. Judging by their reception, Albert was now a celebrity on a global scale. In November, he was awarded the 1921 Nobel Prize for Physics, for "his services to theoretical physics, and especially for his discovery of the law of the photoelectric effect." No mention of relativity, but it cemented his growing reputation as the smartest man on the planet.

Thankfully, neither his lecture fees nor the Nobel prize money were paid in marks. Due to raging inflation, the cost of a loaf of bread, which was one mark in 1920, rose to 700 marks by the end of 1922, and a billion marks a year later.

In March of 1923, Einstein returned to Germany feeling refreshed, after three months of solitude at sea.

He had only been home for a couple of days when the phone rang.

'Albert, it's Max. Welcome back, and congratulations on your award. It's long overdue.'

'Thank you, Max. How have you been, my friend?'

'Fine, fine. Have you read the latest issue of *Annalen der Physik?'*

'Not yet, why?'

'There's a paper by Professor Bragg and a Mr Driscoll. Do you remember the letter I told you about a while back?'

Einstein was alarmed. 'Yes, I told you to ignore it.'

'I did, but that clearly didn't stop him. "On the existence of faster-than-light particles." You should read it.'

'What exactly is your concern, Max?'

'Sending information to the past. They've figured it out, Albert, and now they've announced it to the world. The cat is out of the bag, and now everyone will be looking for crystals with faster-than-light particles.'

'*Verdammt!'* exclaimed Einstein. He was silent for several seconds, before adding, 'We have to do something. If we don't, the world may never be safe again.'

'There's only one thing you can do, Albert,' said Max.

'I know. What do we know of this Driscoll?'

'He was a student of Bragg's in Manchester. From what I can tell, it's his paper and he used Bragg's name to give it some credibility.'

'Manchester? That's the younger Bragg, isn't it? Lawrence, the son?'

'Yes. I believe his father William is at the university in London.'

'I met Lawrence once in Amsterdam,' said Einstein. 'I'll contact him.'

Lawrence Bragg could hardly have been happier. Admittedly, Manchester could not compare with Cambridge, but here in the garden of his new Didsbury home, life was good. He was a keen gardener, and on the first weekend of the Easter break, he was hard at work when his young wife called to him.

'Telephone, darling.'

'Who is it?' he asked, reluctant to break off from his spring planting.

'Someone called Einstein, dear,' she replied, knowing the effect the name would have on her husband.

Bragg dropped what he was doing and practically sprinted into the house, tearing off his gardening gloves as he ran. 'Hello?' he said, rather breathlessly.

The voice on the other end of the line was warm and softly spoken. In clipped tones, Elsa Einstein said, 'Professor Bragg. It's good to speak with you.'

'Frau Einstein,' he replied, trying to hide his disappointment. 'To what do I owe this honour?'

'Albert would have spoken to you himself, but his English is poor. He wants to ask you about a student of yours by the name of Driscoll. You wrote a paper together.'

'That's not strictly true, ma'am. It was Mr Driscoll's paper. I merely edited it for publication.'

'I see. Do you think it would be possible for me to speak with him?'

'That will be difficult, ma'am. James had some sort of breakdown. He's been in a hospital in Manchester for several months.'

The stress of working long hours while deeply depressed, and with no tangible outcome, had taken its toll on James' health. He hadn't been eating or sleeping properly for some time and had lost the motivation to go running regularly, which affected his mood and his fitness. He had missed several tutorials with Bragg, who had failed to recognise the warning signs until it was too late.

'I'm very sorry to hear that,' said Elsa.

'It's a sad story, I'm afraid. After his breakdown, he asked me to publish his paper, so that someone like your husband might complete his work.'

'That's very sad. I will pass this news on to Albert. Herr Driscoll sounds like a most interesting character. Is there anything else you can tell me about him?'

Bragg thought for a moment. 'Erm, I tell you what. The local newspaper printed a short biography of him last year, before he became ill. I could get it copied and sent to you if that would be of interest?'

'Indeed. That's very kind of you.'

When Bragg's letter arrived, he had included a photostatted copy of one of the sports pages from an old *Manchester Guardian,* containing a piece about a promising young cricketer by the name of James Driscoll. It revealed that, in addition to his academic achievements, James had made a couple of appearances for the Lancashire 2nd Eleven and scored a lot of runs for Rochdale Cricket Club in the Central Lancashire League.

'I'm not quite sure how this is going to help, Albertle.'

Unable to read a word, Einstein's eyes were drawn to an illustrated entry in one corner of the page. The words *John Wisden's Cricketers' Almanack for 1922* stood out. 'What is this?' he asked.

'It appears to be an advertisement,' said Elsa, 'for a book containing the details of every game of cricket played in 1921.'

Einstein's face lit up. '*Exzellent!* We must obtain a copy.'

Seeing a London address at the bottom of the advert, Elsa said, 'Leave it to me.'

'*Danke, meine Liebste*. Now,' he announced, 'I have work to do,' and with that he retired to his study.

Several weeks later, the peace and quiet of Haberlandstrasse was shattered by the sound of a fist hammering on the Einsteins' front door. Elsa opened it to find Bernhard Weiss standing there, looking rather flushed.

'Is Albert at home?' he asked.

'He is. Can I get you anything, Bernhard? You look as though you've been running.'

'Tea would be nice, thank you. I have some news for him.'

Elsa showed him into the library, where Einstein was seated at a desk, carefully and systematically recording numbers on a sheet of squared paper. He showed the palm of his hand to block any interruption. When he was done, he turned to Weiss. 'Apologies, Bernhard. It's so easy to lose track of these damned numbers. What can I do for you?'

Weiss knew what the numbers represented. 'If that's a message you're composing, then I'm here in the nick of time,' he said.

'Why do you say that?' asked Einstein curiously.

'I wanted you to hear this first-hand, Albert' he replied. 'Walther's murder. There's been a breakthrough!'

'What do you mean?'

'We have the man who piloted the boat used in the attack.'

'*Oh mein Wort!* How did you find him?'

'Mainly through chance and some good police work. One of my officers overheard a conversation in a bar about a meeting in Berlin. A meeting to be attended by some of the "stars of the Munich outfit." It turned out to be a recruitment meeting for Organisation Consul. Some of my men posed as new recruits, and the men from Munich spoke of their exploits, including their sojourn in Italy. They said that the men killed at the Imperiale Palace were martyrs.'

Anger flashed in Einstein's eyes. 'Martyrs? Barbarians more like. If anyone's a martyr, it's Walther!'

'No matter. When the meeting was over, we rounded them all up and took them in for questioning. Our Bavarian contacts managed to put some names to faces. The youngest is one Rudi Krämer. His older brother is also a member of the gang.'

'How did you get him to talk?'

'Bluff. We told him that his brother had been identified and would be hanged for murder, but that he could do a deal to save him.'

'Did he tell you anything useful?' The triumphant look on Weiss' face gave him his answer.

'We have names, Albert! The men who carried out the attack, including Müller and Schneider, the so-called martyrs.'

'We need more than their names, Bernhard.'

'We have more, my friend! Krämer gave up the location of an OC safe house in Rosenheim. They were there, on and off, from the autumn of 1920 until just before Walther's murder. When will you receive your message?'

'With any luck, June 1920!'

'Why do you say with any luck?'

Einstein looked at the floor. Sombrely, he said, 'The last message failed to arrive, and Paasche remains dead as a result. This is an unreliable device, Bernhard. All I can do is to hope for the best.'

'Fingers crossed then. If it does get through, give me the details of their camp and we'll hit them when they least expect it.'

'You know what this means? This is going to be the longest message I've ever had to send. It'll probably take an entire day to send it!'

'Can I help?'

'Thank you, but no. There's less chance of a mistake if only one person does it.'

When Einstein was ready to send the message he paused, recalling the events surrounding the death of his friend Hans Paasche.

June 1920

The failed attempt to prevent Paasche's murder weighed heavily on Einstein's mind. He knew that the Hermes device was too fragile, and the process of sending a message too prone to errors, but for now it was all that there was.

His recent trip to Bavaria with Max had yielded quite a variety of rock crystals. It had taken Max several days to classify them all, but the previous evening, he had turned up with a small box containing two new magdalite crystals.

'Don't let them see daylight this time,' he had said.

'Don't worry, I won't make the same mistake twice,' Einstein had replied.

Einstein closed the drapes and switched on a small table lamp by the door. With a new crystal in place, Hermes was ready to go. Once activated, it should begin to receive any message sent from the future. Walking across the room, he took hold of a lever on the side of the table and pulled it to his right.

34

Timeline Four

Schöneberg, Berlin
June 1920

A blue glow lit up the room. Carefully and methodically, Einstein recorded the blue light as a zero and waited for the next colour. In 1917, the brief message from Max had taken more than five hours to send. Since then, Einstein had improved the code considerably, so that now, a similar message would only take as long. As messages included a number to indicate their length, he was able to estimate that this one would take up to eighteen hours to arrive. He was going to have to find a way of speeding things up if he wanted to send messages of any length in the future. He had wisely installed a commode chair in a corner of the room, but he really hoped he wouldn't have to use it. Thankfully, Max arrived in the early afternoon. Because one mistake would render a message meaningless, Max was the only other person he trusted to accurately record messages as they arrived. Working in two-hour shifts, they diligently observed the seemingly endless display of red and blue lights in groups of six. In the middle of the night, Einstein recorded a group of six consecutive red lights, signalling the end of the message. He quickly deciphered what had been received during his latest shift, then called out to Max, who was doing the same for earlier segments of the message.

'Are you ready, Max?'

'Yes, but there's a lot here. You sent this message on the thirty-first of March 1923. You're going to have to arrange a visit to Manchester on your return from America next June.'

'I'm not going to America next year!'

'Apparently you are, arriving back in Liverpool on the eighth of June. There is a man you have to meet when you get there.' Max told him about James Driscoll and his paper on the possibility of crystals containing faster-than-light particles.

'*Mein Gott!* I've never heard of this Driscoll, who is he?'

'If you recall, he's the student from England who wrote to me last year. You're going to learn English so that you can speak with him.

His home address is in the message, and he will be there on the day you land.'

'Is there anything that proves I have information from the future?'

'Yes, details of a sporting event to be held on the same day.'

'Very good. Let's hope that Herr Driscoll can be made to see sense, because the future of humanity may depend on it.'

'There's something else.' Max read out the details of Walther Rathenau's promotion to Foreign Minister and subsequent assassination by OC in April 1922.

Einstein let out an anguished cry. 'No! Not Walther!'

'I'm sorry, Albert. It doesn't say who OC is.'

'It's not a person. Organisation Consul used to be called Marine Brigade Ehrhardt. They're the same people who killed Hans Paasche.' Referring to the *Kapp Putsch*, an attempt to overthrow the government in Berlin three months earlier, he added, 'They were banned after the failed coup, but all they did was change their name. I have to warn Walther.'

'You might be able to do better than that. Bernhard Weiss has given you the names of the assassins and the location of their hideout in Bavaria. They'll be there from August. If you tell him where they're going to be, he can stop them before they get to Walther.'

'That might stop a handful of individuals, but nationalism is spreading like a disease. I fear that others will rise up to take their place.'

'You may be right, but at least it gives Walther a chance. To quote an old proverb, "forewarned is forearmed," Albert.'

By the following morning, Einstein had settled on a plan of action. He would compose a letter to Lawrence Bragg at Manchester University, mentioning the possibility of a visit at some future date. Elsa would translate the letter into English for him. She would attempt to teach him the language, so that he could speak to James Driscoll without the need for an interpreter. Walther and Bernhard would be invited to Haberlandstrasse, where he would warn them about the horrendous events of April 1922.

The following weekend saw the second meeting of the Hermes Alliance within a month. Even before Einstein told Rathenau about his murder, he noticed that he kept rubbing the back of his head.

'Are you alright, Walther?' he asked.

'It's just a headache, Albert,' he replied. 'Why do you ask?'

'There's something I have to tell you.'

Rathenau was visibly shaken by the news of his impending demise. There was an uncomfortable silence in the room, only broken when he spoke. 'How?'

'A bullet to the back of the head.'

Instinctively, he put his hand to the very spot that he'd been rubbing before. Looking at Einstein, he said, 'Perhaps this is an indication that I'm doing something right.'

'That's as may be,' said Einstein, 'but is democracy a cause worth dying for?'

'Maybe not, but it's a cause worth living for.'

'Enough of this living and dying!' interrupted Weiss. 'Nobody's dead yet, and I'm going to do my utmost to keep it that way.'

'What can you do, Bernhard? There are extremists everywhere.'

'I know that, Albert, but I want to send them a message. They have to know that murderers will be hunted down and killed.'

'Eliminating a few terrorists will not make the problem go away,' said Rathenau. 'We need to understand these people. Why they feel alienated and angry enough to kill. Only then can we begin to win their hearts and minds.'

'You may be right, but that won't happen overnight, if at all,' said Einstein. 'In the meantime, you'll be dead in less than two years' time.'

'No, he won't,' said Weiss. 'I have a friend in the Reich Criminal Police Office who will help find the people responsible for this.'

'Will he? No crime has been committed yet. How will you convince him the threat is real?'

'I'm the head of the National Crime Investigation Agency. If I tell him we have evidence of threats to the Weimar leadership, he will have to act.'

'What about the security police in Munich?' asked Rathenau.

'They cannot be trusted. Bavaria's a law unto itself. We have to do this without their knowledge.'

'You think they would try to stop you?'

'I'm not prepared to take the risk. I'm also going to talk to the Berlin security police about increasing your protection.'

Manchester University
October 1920

When he returned to the university following the summer recess, Lawrence Bragg was surprised to find a letter from Einstein in his pigeon-hole. The possibility of a future visit from the great man was the most exciting news he'd received in a long time, and he wasted no time in telling the Vice-Chancellor.

Sir Henry Miers was equally enthusiastic. 'Do you realise what this could do for the profile of the university?' he asked. 'For him to come here, even before he visits Oxford or Cambridge, would be such a feather in our cap. We might even be able to persuade him to give the Adamson Lecture. It could turn us into one of the leading scientific institutions in Europe, if not the world!'

'Let's not get ahead of ourselves, Sir Henry. Are you going to send him an invitation?'

'I'll need to take it to Council first. Once I have their approval I will write to Professor Einstein.'

Bragg replied to Einstein's letter, apologising for the delay in responding and thanking him for his warm wishes. He informed him that he could expect a letter from Sir Henry in due course.

Haberlandstrasse, Berlin

The receipt of Bragg's letter prompted Einstein to contact Bernhard Weiss, who he had not heard from in some time.

'Hello, Albert.'

'Bernhard. What's the news from Bavaria?'

'We have a house under surveillance in Rosenheim. People come and go, and it takes time to identify them, but we are close. Unfortunately, none of the OC leadership ever go there. I thought we might catch Ehrhardt or von Killinger, but they're too clever to be linked with the death squads in any way.'

'So, when will you make your move?'

'Soon, I hope. The main man appears to be a Klaus Müller, one of the men to be killed in the Italy attack. When he's there, a lot of the others appear. It's just a matter of time.'

They did not have long to wait. Weiss' intelligence gathering revealed that the best time for an attack was early on a Sunday morning, when the occupants of the Rosenheim safe house would still be drunk, or at least hungover from their weekend of carousing. The last weekend of October saw the arrival, among others, of Klaus Müller and several of his death squad. On the Saturday, they headed east into the foothills of the Bavarian Alps, where Müller took charge of their training, observed at a safe distance by two members of the Reich Police. When they returned, their evening was spent in a marketplace tavern in Rosenheim. A total of nine terrorists returned to their lair before midnight.

Save for the sound of snoring, all was quiet in the safe house as eight men of the Reich Criminal Police rowed silently up the River Inn in folding kayaks. It was an hour before dawn, and they came ashore less than fifty yards from their target, before moving stealthily into position. They knew the men slept in three rooms on the upper floor. They had practised for this moment many times and did not expect to meet much in the way of resistance. Their aim was to kill everyone inside apart from Müller. It was hoped that his capture and interrogation would provide valuable information.

On the agreed signal, windows were smashed and grenades tossed inside. The explosions were followed by gunfire from the police and screaming from the men inside. Four officers smashed open the front door, but they had not counted on Müller, who was asleep at the kitchen table. By the time the first men came through the door, he was wide awake and crouched, gun in hand. Two men fell dead, cut down by Müller's bullets, before he was killed with a shot to the head. They had lost their intelligence source.

The scene in the bedrooms was one of utter carnage. Günter Teufel was the sole survivor of the barrage of grenades and bullets that had rained in through the windows, but he was mortally wounded by a severed femoral artery. He died before anyone could reach him. As quickly as they arrived, the assault team returned to their kayaks and rowed off into the night. A mile to the south, a powerful motorboat was waiting to take them over the border into Austria, where a plane was fuelled and ready to fly them to Berlin.

The annihilation of Müller's death squad, and the increased security placed around Walther Rathenau in Italy, gave the Foreign Minister a much better chance of avoiding death at the hands of the OC. Klaus Müller's death, however, was not without consequences. Karl Gareis still died in Munich, albeit with a different hand on the trigger, but Adolf Hitler avoided his fate. Müller and Teufel's replacements were less efficient than their predecessors. During the Hofbräuhaus brawl of November 1921, Hitler's bodyguards managed to hold off his attackers long enough for him to flee the scene. In time, the repercussions would be felt throughout the world.

It was something that Einstein had not even considered in his eagerness to save his friend. There was a moral dimension to tinkering with history. What if, in the alternate future that unfolded, saving one man adversely affected millions?

February 1921

Confirmation of Einstein's American trip came in the form of a telegram from Chaim Weizmann, President of the World Zionist Organisation. Weizmann persuaded the British government to support the creation of a Jewish homeland in Palestine and one day, he would become the first president of Israel. For now, he was a chemistry professor at Manchester University, the very man whose fermentation process was stolen by Paul Lucas before the war.

Einstein wanted to lend his support to the development of a Hebrew University in Jerusalem, but he also needed an excuse to visit Manchester. After some feigned reluctance, he accepted Weizmann's invitation. Four days later, Sir Henry Miers sent him a formal invitation to deliver a lecture in Manchester on a convenient date. Things were starting to fall into place. Einstein immediately wrote back to accept, adding that a date could not be settled until his forthcoming trip to America was finalised.

Kirk Allerton, Yorkshire
March 1921

James was in George's study, poring over the latest mill accounts. They did not make good reading. When the phone rang, he lunged for the receiver, hoping it had not woken his mother.

'Hello.'

'James, it's Professor Bragg.'

'Good morning, Professor. What can I do for you at such an early hour?'

'I was wondering if you'd heard the news. Albert Einstein is coming here to give a lecture!'

'To England?'

‘To Manchester! It’s in all the papers.’

James was astonished. ‘What ..., why? When?’

Bragg laughed. ‘I don’t know the details, but he’s stopping off here to talk about relativity on his return from America.’

‘But he doesn’t speak English!’

‘We have interpreters for that sort of thing. Would you like me to see if I can get you an invitation?’ There was silence on the other end of the line. ‘James?’

He was so surprised that it took him a few moments to gather his thoughts. ‘Yes! Sorry, yes please, Professor. Thank you.’

‘Leave it with me. When can we expect to see you back in class?’

‘Soon. I just have a few problems to sort out at the mill first.’

‘Okay. I’ll look forward to your return. Good day, James.’

‘Goodbye, Professor.’ He wandered into the kitchen in a daze. Picking up a copy of the previous day’s *Manchester Evening News*, he scanned it for news of Einstein. There, on page 5, under “Items of Interest from Far and Near,” and just above news of the election of a secretary to the Rochdale Infirmary, he found it. “During his visit to England in the near future, Professor Einstein has consented to give a lecture at the Manchester University. Date and hour are yet to be fixed, but the subject almost chooses itself. It will be Relativity.”

If James could only speak to him and share his thoughts on the subject of time travel, he felt sure the great man could provide some answers. In the meantime, he had the unenviable task of trying to save the family business. George’s loyalty to his workers, commendable though it was, had brought the mill to its knees. If he didn’t do something, the Driscoll family faced financial ruin. Two days later, his mother’s death drove all thoughts of Einstein’s visit from his head and sent James on a downward spiral.

New York City
April 1921

The Einsteins’ tour of the eastern United States commenced in New York, where Albert gave a series of lectures. Three weeks later, they left for Washington, where they met President Harding. Visits to Chicago and Boston followed, before they finally arrived in the small, peaceful township of Princeton. For Einstein, it was the highlight of the trip, and he gave a week-long series of lectures there. He was also introduced to Louis Bamberger and his sister Carrie Bamberger Fuld who, along with her husband Felix, owned the famous Bamberger's department store in Newark, New Jersey. It was the beginning of a lifelong friendship that would eventually see the Einsteins settle in Princeton when they left Europe. By the end of May, there was no doubt that Albert was a worldwide celebrity. His lectures were delivered to packed audiences, and wherever they went, adoring crowds lined the parade routes. His fame was something he felt a little uncomfortable with, so he was relieved when he and Elsa were able to settle into their stateroom for the return journey to Europe on the RMS *Celtic*.

35

Kirk Allerton, Yorkshire
April 1921

Alighting from the footplate of the Bullnose Morris, Lawrence Bragg's first thought was that he had stepped into the pages of a Jane Austen novel. Allerton Manor was an imposing sight in the spring sunshine. Bragg had the strangest feeling that he had been there before, even though he had never been within ten miles of the place. Perhaps he had seen it in the pages of a magazine. The splendour of his surroundings was incongruous, given the purpose of his visit. He had not seen or heard from James Driscoll since the phone call about Einstein's visit, more than a month earlier. James had said there were problems at the mill, but he was disappointed that he had not been in touch. Their friendship was the reason for Bragg's visit, but he had no idea that yet another tragedy had befallen his young protégé.

He lifted the brass knocker on the large front door and let it fall. The echoing sound of metal upon metal failed to elicit a response, so he knocked twice more. With no answer, he wandered round to the rear of the house, where there was another entrance. He peered through a window and saw what appeared to be a bearded old man, hunched over a large table. When he rapped on the windowpane the man did not get up, but turned to look at him. He gasped when he realised it was James.

He picked up two bottles of milk from the doorstep and opened the door to the kitchen. Stepping inside, he was met by a repulsive smell, a combination of stale alcohol, sour milk and body odour. Something had clearly gone very wrong in James' life since they last spoke. 'What's happened?' he asked.

James looked up at him, struggling to form his words. 'My mother,' he slurred. 'She killed herself.' His upper body began to shake as he wept silently.

Bragg walked round the table and placed his hands on James' heaving shoulders. He wrinkled his nose at the sickly, sweet smell emanating from the young man, the result of several weeks of heavy drinking.

‘I’m so sorry, James. You sit there and I’ll get you some coffee. I’ll tidy up in here a bit, and then we can decide whether you’re up to coming back to Manchester with me.’

Three hours later, they left Kirk Allerton behind. Rusholme, Agatha Christie and DCI Hughes awaited.

Rusholme, Manchester
June 1921

Due in no small part to Lawrence Bragg’s efforts, James had been slowly rebuilding his life. He had stopped drinking, started to eat properly and taken up running again. He spent several weeks reviewing everything he had ever read about time travel in the works of Einstein and others, in the forlorn hope that he had missed something.

At the end of the summer term, he returned to Allerton Manor, which was in need of some serious attention. With Alfie dead, James had inherited the whole of his parents’ estate and the title Lord of the Manor. By early June, a small army of gardeners, cleaners, painters and decorators were hard at work, restoring the Manor to its former glory.

On the day before Einstein’s lecture at Manchester University, James left Allerton Manor by the back door. He walked slowly through the walled garden, the smell of the roses, magnolias and rhododendrons redolent of summers long ago, when his grandparents spent most of their time in this idyllic place. The low buzzing of the bees told him that this promised to be a perfect summer’s day. He picked two roses, one red and one white, before opening a gate at the far end of the garden and taking the footpath that led to the village.

Ten minutes later he was standing by his parents’ graves in the cemetery at Holy Trinity Church. He stood there for a long time, oblivious to the limousine that passed by the front of the church on its way to the Manor. Eyes glistening and emotions raw, he bent to place a flower at the head of each grave, before turning and walking quickly away.

When he reached the village green, a cricket match was in full swing. The teams were a mixture of old and young men, all dressed in white. In times gone by, James would have been there, opening the bowling or hitting boundaries, the nearest thing to an all-rounder that the village could muster on a weekday. Today he had a train to catch, but he had time to watch a little cricket first. He wandered round the boundary towards the pavilion, or to be more precise, a large shed that had been given a fresh coat of white paint. Outside, some of his former teammates were sitting on a bench, so he said hello and sat down. The smell of pipe tobacco drifted across from the only other spectator, a somewhat scruffy, short, squat man who stood with his back to the game and seemed more interested in the ducks on the neighbouring pond. From the back there was something vaguely familiar about him, but James could not think where he had seen him before.

The cricketers watched as the limousine returned from the Manor and stopped outside the post office.

'Ey up, tha dunt see many cars like that round these parts,' said Ted Pickersgill, the village blacksmith. 'That'll be for you, is it Jim?'

They saw the driver, a tall, thin man in a grey uniform and peaked cap, get out and walk across to speak to the man with the pipe, who half-turned to reply. Ted looked at James, who had let out a gasp and sat there, mouth open in astonishment.

'Careful tha dunt catch any flies there, lad. Someone tha knows?'

'I …, erm, no. It can't be,' was all he could say as he stood up and walked towards the pair.

'Excuse me.'

The shorter man turned to face him, and James saw that he was not mistaken. It was a face he knew well, if only from photographs.

'I don't mean to be rude, but you look a lot like Albert Einstein.'

The man smiled. 'People often say that, young man, but Herr Einstein is much better looking than me.'

'Sorry, my mistake,' said James, suddenly embarrassed. 'You're speaking English, of course you're not him, but you're the spit and image. You could be his twin.' Einstein's lack of English was common knowledge, but it was curious that this man's accent was distinctly German. James was intrigued. 'Do you mind my asking what brings you to Kirk Allerton?'

'I am looking for a man who goes by the name of James Driscoll. Would you happen to know where I can find him?'

'You're speaking to him!'

The man leaned in towards James and murmured conspiratorially, 'In that case, you were right the first time. Call me Albert.'

James took an involuntary step backwards and stood there, dumbfounded. Was this a dream? Had he spent so long studying Einstein that he was now appearing to him in his sleep?

'Perhaps we could sit down and I'll explain,' said Einstein. James followed his lead and sat down on the grass, while the driver returned to the limousine and leaned against the door, smoking a cigarette and watching the cricket. He soon decided to move his pride and joy to a safer distance when Ted Pickersgill launched a mighty six in his direction.

James pinched himself. He wasn't dreaming, but there was something surreal about this whole encounter. 'This is a joke,' he said. 'You're just someone who looks like Einstein. One of my so-called friends has put you up to this to make a fool of me, because they know he's a hero of mine, right?'

'This is not a joke …'

'But Einstein cannot speak English. Everyone knows that.' This man's English was almost perfect.

'Suppose that he found the time to learn?' the man replied. 'I am afraid that much stranger than fiction is truth, Mr Driscoll. I am here because you are going to publish a paper that will change the world, and not for the better.'

'I don't understand,' said James. 'A paper I haven't written yet? That makes no sense. How could you possibly know what I'm going to do tomorrow, never mind in two years' time?'

'You study physics, Mr Driscoll. How could someone possibly know what is going to happen in advance?'

James thought for a few moments, a puzzled look on his face that slowly turned to incredulity. The answer was obvious. 'Are you saying you're a time traveller?'

'Not exactly, but close. Some years ago, I discovered a way to send information back in time.'

'A telegraph to the past?'

'So you've read my work?'

James had to pinch himself before he could accept that he was actually having this conversation. 'Yes, but you concluded that time travel was impossible.'

'No, I did not, but I have many times been misquoted. My discovery has already allowed me to save a number of lives, including my own, Herr Driscoll.'

'Please, call me James.'

'If I can prove to you that it is possible to learn what the future holds, James, will you accept that my name is Albert Einstein, and that I am here to ask for your help?'

James' head was reeling. 'I … I don't know. How can you prove it?'

Einstein waved an arm in the direction of the village green. 'I believe you follow this game.'

'Cricket?'

'Yes. If I could accurately predict the score in a game of cricket, would you accept that I had knowledge of the future before it happened?'

'You're going to tell me what the score of this game will be?' This was becoming more surreal by the minute.

'Not this game, no. Before I came here, I did some research that you may find interesting. There is a game today between the teams of Middlesex and Yorkshire in London, am I right?'

'Yes, at Lords.'

'And Yorkshire is your, how do you say in English, your preferred team?'

'My favourite team, yes.'

'If I was to tell you that Yorkshire will score 221 runs and Herr Kilner will score fifty-two, would that surprise you?'

Roy Kilner was one of James' favourite cricketers. 'I would say that was impossible to predict.'

'Not only that, but Middlesex will then score ninety runs by the end of the day, and will lose two wickets, both to Mr Kilner.'

'I don't mean to be rude, but how does a German know so much about cricket? I didn't think you played the game?'

'Oh, we don't, but I read what Herr Wisden had to say about it next year.'

James had several editions of Wisden's Cricketer's Almanack on his bookshelf at home. 'You're talking about next year as if it's in the past.'

'For the man who sent this message, it is,' replied Einstein. 'He couldn't speak English at all, but I found the time to learn. Now, I must confess that I do not share your fascination with such a strange sport. I am told that some men spend a lifetime trying to acquaint themselves with the rules of cricket, while others amuse themselves with somewhat simpler subjects, like relativity.'

James had to laugh. 'I aim to do both, Professor. Now then, if you're right about the cricket in every detail, I would have to admit that you've somehow found a way to look into the future. Do you mind me asking how?'

'The story is long. Locked inside some crystals, there are faster-than-light particles. I found a way of setting them free and observing them as they travelled back in time. I called my invention Hermes, after the Messenger of the Gods.'

Einstein had done what James could not. 'Unbelievable!' he exclaimed.

'You don't believe me?'

'No. I mean, yes, of course I believe you! You said that you came here to ask for my help. What do you mean?'

'I have to ask that your paper, you do not publish. If my invention was to fall into the wrong hands, what might be the result? In the war, if the German army had known every move of the British before it happened, we would not here be sitting.'

'But what if another scientist were to make the same discovery? What would you do?'

Einstein took his time before replying. 'It is something I have thought much about. There are perhaps three possibilities. I can try to persuade them not to reveal what they know, as I am doing with you today. Or, through my work, I can try to mislead those that get too close. Only a small number of people know what I have told you. I call them the Hermes Alliance. They do everything in their power to protect my secret.'

'You said there were three things?'

'Ah yes, the third is more challenging and would take time and money.'

'What is it?'

'To control the world's supply of crystals with faster-than-light properties.'

James was dubious. 'That doesn't sound feasible.'

'Perhaps, but I have one of the world's finest crystallographers working on it.'

'Professor von Laue?'

'Yes, but he could do with some help. Will you join us in Berlin, James?'

He sat and thought for a while. 'On one condition. My family and my future wife have all died within the last five years, but their deaths were preventable. If you could send a message back in time, I might be able to save them.'

'It's a very dangerous thing, to meddle with the past. It could have many unintended consequences.'

'I understand, but those are my terms. Help me, and I will come and work with Professor von Laue in Berlin.'

Einstein was about to explain that messages could only be sent back as far as 1920, when a high-pitched whistle sounded from the direction of Allerton Station.

'Damn it, I've missed my train!' cursed James.

'Can I offer you a lift somewhere?' asked Einstein.

'That depends. Do we have a deal?'

'Yes, we do, but I must warn you that it has not always worked. I tried to save someone's life once, but the crystal lost its phosphorescence. Because of that failure, it is now only possible to send messages to the year 1920.'

'No earlier?'

'No, only to the last time Hermes was activated. You could not save anyone who died before June 1920. Sorry.'

James was devastated, and he found it difficult to speak at first. On the one hand, Hermes could not save Alice or Alfie. On the other, Einstein had shown him that the past was not fixed, and in so doing, raised his hopes of saving his parents. The very fact of Hermes' existence told him that the boundaries of science had not yet been reached, which was all the motivation he needed to continue with his research.

Once he was in control of his emotions, he said, 'That's better than nothing I suppose.'

'You must act with extreme caution, James. If I help you, you must promise to use the information most carefully. Only change that which must be changed, or you could make matters worse.'

'I'll bear that in mind. Now, I must get to Manchester. I have an invitation to attend your lecture tomorrow.'

'Oh, I would not bother. It will be in German.'

'Why not English? You speak it rather well.'

‘When I talk of relativity, nobody understands what I am saying, whatever language I say it in. If I speak in German, my audience has not to confront their failings.’

‘Very considerate of you,’ laughed James. ‘But if you cannot communicate your ideas, what good is that?’

‘People do not seem to mind. I think speaking in a foreign tongue is for them more mysterious.’ With a mischievous grin, he added, ‘Also, I can listen to what they say about me.’

When the county cricket scores appeared in the following day’s newspaper, Einstein’s prediction was correct in every detail. James attended the lecture in the university’s Whitworth Hall. Despite being in German, it was well received by a packed audience. Having been assured that James would follow as soon as the mill’s troubles had been addressed, the Einsteins left Manchester. En route to Germany, they met the Prime Minister, David Lloyd George in London, and the physicist Frederick Lindemann in Oxford, before setting sail for Hamburg.

Harry Milburn, James’ old school friend, had just completed a business degree at Leeds University. James met him in a public house in Headingley to outline his vision for a new company. The Welbeck mill was to be sold to Blackett and Muir. Using a large chunk of his inheritance, James would build a new factory in Welbeck, fill it with modern machinery and employ as many of George’s workers as possible. The engineer in him had seen the potential for automation in the garment industry. Welbeck Ready-to-Wear would take woven fabric from British cotton mills and manufacture large quantities of good quality coats, suits, shirts and dresses in standard sizes. They would sell them at affordable prices in established high street clothing stores throughout Yorkshire and Lancashire. Harry was excited by the challenge and accepted James’ offer to be the company’s first Managing Director.

With Harry on board, they held a meeting with Charlie Earnshaw and senior staff, explaining that the company had to move with the times or die. There was some resistance at first but, with Charlie’s enthusiastic support, they managed to talk the men round. Harry was impressed by Charlie and made him Factory Manager. A new management team was appointed, many of them from within the existing workforce.

Within two weeks, James was satisfied that he had done everything in his power to guarantee the future prosperity of his father's business and its workers. He was ready to embark on the greatest adventure of his life, but could he really bring his parents back from the dead?

36

Hendon, Middlesex
June 1921

The train slowed as it passed Hendon Aerodrome on the outskirts of London. Looking to the east, James had a great view of Alexandra Palace, perched high upon a hill. To the south, he could see the blackened dome of St Paul's looming out of a yellow haze in the distance. His journey was taking him into one of the most polluted cities on earth. Had he arrived a few months earlier, the sulphurous fumes from thousands of coal fires and factory chimneys would have mingled with the cold winter air to produce a smog that obscured the view completely. He had spent the last three hours documenting what needed to go into a message warning him of the fate awaiting his parents. It was vital that he provide precise details of the Abermule train crash, together with something to prove to his father that the future really was predictable. There was also the small matter of preventing Winter's American ally from poisoning his mother. When he was satisfied that he had thought of everything, he sat back to admire the view.

At St Pancras, he took the Piccadilly Line to Kensington, where he checked in to a comfortable hotel on Queens Gate. After a memorable afternoon wandering the corridors of the South Kensington museums, he returned to his hotel for a meal and an early night. He was a lot more relaxed about his trip to Berlin, now that he knew there was an alternative to sea travel. He slept well and, armed with his passport, arrived at Croydon Airport early the next morning. He was one of only four passengers on this, his third flight, but he would never tire of the thrill he felt on take-off and landing. After a night in Amsterdam, he took an afternoon flight to Hamburg.

Berlin, Germany

James arrived in Berlin by train. A taxi took him to Haberlandstrasse, where his knock was answered by Einstein. Standing just behind him was an elegantly dressed man with a receding hairline and a large moustache.

'We've been expecting you,' he said. Gesturing towards the other man, he continued, 'May I introduce you to my good friend, Professor Max von Laue? Max, this is Doctor James Driscoll.'

Max offered his hand and said, 'Pleased to meet you, Doctor.'

James shook his hand. He was still plain Mister, but manners stopped him from correcting Einstein in front of his friend. 'I'm honoured to meet you, sir.

'Are you up for a little tour of Berlin, James?' asked Einstein.

'Yes, of course,' he replied, despite being tired after his long journey. They headed north, with von Laue at the wheel of his Audi. Even though there was little in the way of traffic, he never drove anywhere slowly, and they were soon tearing through the Tiergarten at breakneck speed.

Seated next to James in the back of the vehicle, Einstein pleaded, 'Slow down, Max. Give the boy a chance to see the city.'

'I'm sorry, force of habit,' he replied, slowing down to a slightly more sedate pace. He took a right turn onto Charlottenburger Chaussee, a wide, tree-lined boulevard that took them into the heart of the city. Just as the Brandenburg Gate came into view, von Laue turned left and sped north. The setting sun glinted on a bronze statue, perched high on a stone column ahead of them. 'Victoria,' said Einstein. 'The Roman goddess of victory. Rather inappropriate, wouldn't you say?' James nodded, taking no pleasure from a German defeat that had cost so many lives on both sides.

Von Laue turned right at the statue, giving James a great view of the Reichstag building and its impressive cupola. Another right turn and they were speeding along the rear of the Reichstag towards the Brandenburg Gate. Topped by a horse-drawn chariot, it reminded James of a photograph he had seen of the Acropolis in Athens. They drove through the gate and were back on the tree-lined boulevard, leading out of the city past the enormous copper-domed Berlin Cathedral.

The church receded behind them and James asked, 'Where are we going?'

'To the hospital,' said Einstein. 'I want you to meet Moritz, the surgeon who performed my autopsy and saved my life.'

'You make that sound like the most natural thing in the world!'

Five minutes later, they arrived at the Berlin-Friedrichshain Hospital. Heads turned as the three men walked in through the main entrance. In the Surgical Department, Einstein stopped when he reached a door marked *Direktor*.

Moritz Katzenstein was discussing a patient with one of his staff nurses when there was a knock at the door. '*Komm herein!*' Einstein entered the room, followed by von Laue and James.

'*Danke, Oberschwester*,' said Moritz. The staff nurse rose to leave, smiling broadly at their famous visitor. When she saw James her smile disappeared, and her mouth dropped open. '*Mein Gott!*' she exclaimed. James raised an eyebrow, confused.

'You look as though you've seen a ghost, *meine Liebste*,' said an intrigued Einstein.

'I'm sorry, Professor. Your friend reminds me very much of someone who was once a patient here.'

'Well, it seems you have a German doppelganger, James.' With a twinkle in his eye, he added, 'Did your father ever spend time in Berlin?'

James smiled, appreciating the joke. 'He went to America once,' he said, 'but other than that, I don't think he ever left Britain.' Turning to the nurse, who was still staring at him, he said, 'I'm afraid you're mistaken, ma'am.'

'*Bitte*,' said the nurse, moving closer to James and gently lifting his chin. 'Please accept my apologies. The likeness is uncanny, but he died last year.'

'Who did?'

'I never knew his name, but he had a scar under his chin.'

James froze, open-mouthed, as the nurse's words hung in the air.

'Are you alright, James?' asked Einstein.

'I ..., I had a brother with a scar under his chin,' he stammered. 'We were twins.'

'What happened to him?' asked Moritz.

'He was killed at the Somme and buried in France.'

Moritz and the nurse exchanged a knowing look. 'The Unknown Soldier!'

The nurse nodded. '*Ja, Herr Direktor!*'

'Who's the unknown soldier?' asked James.

'*Herr Driscoll*,' said Moritz. 'I think you'd better sit down.'

Moritz took a set of keys from his pocket and unlocked a store cupboard in a corner of his office. He went inside and emerged a couple of minutes later with a neatly folded newspaper, the *Berliner*

Tageblatt. Beckoning James over, he opened it at page five. Above a photograph of a young man with his eyes closed, the headline read "*Wer ist dieser Soldat?*"

Moritz translated. 'It says "Who is this soldier?" Was this your brother?'

'Yes,' said a shocked James. 'His name was Alfie, but I don't understand. The War Office told us he was dead. His girlfriend received a letter, taken from his body. If it wasn't him, then who the hell was it? And if he survived the war, how did he end up here? Why didn't someone contact his family?'

'He never regained consciousness. We had no way of identifying him.'

'A friend of his saw him get shot. What happened to him after that?'

'He was very badly wounded on the battlefield. It was a very chaotic morning, and by the time he was brought into my field hospital, his uniform had been removed. There was nothing on his body to identify him. In the confusion, no one knew who he was.'

James was incredulous. 'You thought he was German?'

'Yes, but I would have treated him anyway. He had several bullet wounds, including one to the head. Luckily, I managed to relieve the pressure on his brain.'

'So, you saved his life?'

'I only did my job. On that day, thousands were dead or dying. We concentrated on the ones that had a chance. I lost count of how many. We just did what we could.'

'I'm very grateful. Thank you.'

'When your brother was stable and there was nothing more to be done for him, he was taken to Berlin on a hospital train. I had him admitted to a neurological rehabilitation ward in this hospital. Then, when the war was over, I discovered he was still here. No one came forward to claim him. That's when the press started a campaign to identify him.'

James looked at the newspaper again. 'Good God!' he exclaimed suddenly.

'What's the matter?' asked Einstein.

'The date!'

Moritz read aloud, '*Mittwoch,* September the third, 1919. Is it important?'

‘In the first week of September that year, I was in France with Alfie’s girlfriend, visiting his grave. He was here all the time, alive.’ James sat down on a chair and put his head in his hands.

Moritz looked at Einstein and von Laue, saying, ‘It’s such a shame we cannot turn back the clock.’

James looked up at the three men. With the nurse in the room, there was an awkward silence, before Moritz continued. ‘We never gave up hope that he might regain consciousness. He did open his eyes from time to time, but he was not aware of anything going on around him.’

‘He opened his eyes? So, he was coming out of the coma?’

‘Yes and no. He entered what we call a vegetative state, but he was unresponsive to the end. He died in October.’

James’ eyes filled with tears. ‘Did he die alone?’

‘He was never alone,’ said the staff nurse. ‘One of my nurses used to sit with him for hours, trying to bring him out of his coma.’

‘Can I speak with her?’

‘She’ll be here tomorrow,’ said Moritz. ‘I’ll ask her if she is happy to talk to you.’

‘Thank you, Doctor. Do you know where he’s buried?’

‘In a military cemetery, about five kilometres or so from here.’

‘Does he have a headstone?’

‘Yes, but of course it has no name, like so many of the graves there.’

The following morning, Einstein introduced James to his invention by repeating the book trick he had once played on Max, using a demonstration device to preserve the crystal in the Schöneberg Hermes. On first viewing, it looked a bit Heath Robinson to James, but the way in which Einstein had adapted von Laue’s x-ray experiments to transmit messages was astonishing.

‘Your message should arrive here on the ninth of June 1920. Do you have it with you?’

‘Yes, apart from my brother’s details. I wrote the rest of it while I was travelling.’

‘Don’t forget that I need to know where you were living then. The message must tell me to write you a letter. It will contain details of another cricket match. I had Elsa purchase this year’s copy of Wisden for just such an eventuality.’

'Excellent. There's also something in the message that no one else could possibly know.'

'Very good. In that case, I'll start coding it, while you record what we know about your brother.'

'Before you do,' said James, 'I want to know everything there is to know about this crystal. Its structure, properties, and so on.'

'Very well. Are you paying attention?'

'I'm all ears.' Einstein looked at his ears with a perplexed look on his face.

Early in the afternoon, Moritz paid a visit to Haberlandstrasse, accompanied by a middle-aged nurse. They waited in the library with Albert, while Elsa went to find James. When he walked into the room, the nurse gasped, even though she had been told there was a family likeness. Moritz spoke first. 'Nurse Kohler, I'd like you to meet James Driscoll. His brother Alfie was your patient.'

'*Guten Tag*,' she said, shyly. She had kind eyes and reminded James of his mother.

'Nice to meet you,' said James. 'What can you tell me about my brother?'

'I spent a lot of time with him,' she said. 'I held his hand and tried to wake him up, but towards the end he just faded away. I was there when he died.' She wiped away a tear. 'He had no pain.'

Turning to Moritz, she said, '*Er ist das Doppel seines Bruders*.'

'She says you are the double of your brother,' said Moritz.

'Yes, we were identical twins.' James smiled at the nurse and said, 'Did you attend his funeral?'

'Yes. Would you like to visit his grave?'

'I'd like that very much.' James wanted to feel close to Alfie. Later that day, in a corner of the *Neuer Garnisonfriedhof* cemetery, he stood with Nurse Kohler at a grave marked *Unbekannt*. Unknown.

'Are you alright?' he asked, noticing a single tear rolling down her cheek.

'Yes,' she said tenderly, taking hold of his hand. 'And you?'

James nodded, but he couldn't tell her what he was really thinking. He had mourned his brother at two gravesides, five hundred miles apart, and yet the past was no longer set in stone. With the help of Hermes, he was going to bring Alfie back.

37

Timeline Five

Rusholme, Manchester
June 1920

James had been having the strangest dream for days now. In it, Alfie was alive, but his parents were dead. It made no sense at all. Returning to Oakwood House after a run, he washed and dressed and was coming downstairs when the morning mail plopped onto the mat. He thumbed through it, hoping for a letter from the university informing him of his final grade. Instead, there was his weekly copy of *The English Mechanic and World of Science*, a letter from his mother, which he would read over breakfast, and a curious-looking envelope with a Berlin postmark. Of course! Professor von Laue had finally got round to replying to the letter he wrote last year. Perhaps he would have a plausible explanation for the seemingly impossible observations made by one of his students.

Impatiently, he ripped open the envelope and pulled out a smaller one, wrapped in a sheet of paper. Unfolding the sheet, his jaw dropped as he read what was typed upon it.

Haberlandstrasse 5
Schöneberg
Berlin
June 10, 1920

Sir:

Professor von Laue has informed me of your interest in x-ray crystallography. I have some expertise in that area and would be prepared to share it with you, but I must impress upon you the need for complete secrecy. I am sure you will understand when we meet and will find what I have to say most illuminating.

The answer to your query may be found in the result of a cricket match to be played in London. Middlesex 407, Hendren 183. Lancashire 182 and 188. If you need further evidence, I know that your brother was scarred while trying to save you from drowning in a river.

It is imperative that we speak. I have enclosed fifty English pounds in the hope that you will accept my invitation to Berlin before the end of the month. You will find many sailings to Hamburg from London and Hull. Please offer my warmest regards to Professor Bragg when you see him next.

Yours very truly

Albert Einstein

The letter was so obviously a fake, and a poor one at that. Whichever one of his so-called friends had sent this, it was no secret how Alfie had got his scar. As if the world's greatest scientist would write to him, a lowly undergraduate. And whoever heard of a German with an interest in cricket? Preposterous.

James turned his attention to the smaller envelope, which contained a single white fifty-pound note. It seemed real enough, but who would part with such a huge sum for the sake of a prank? He read the letter again. When he wrote to von Laue, he had asked whether the crystal used in the Frankfurt experiment had any special properties. If the answer lay in the result of a cricket match that had not yet been played, was this evidence of a telegraph to the past? Intrigued, he checked his Lancashire Cricket Club yearbook. The match was due to start the following day, so if this was someone's idea of a joke, it would be short-lived. He only had to wait for the score from Lord's to find out. On the other hand, if the prediction was correct, it would prove that Einstein's 'telegraph to the past' was more than a theory. If that was the case, could it bring back Alfie and Alice?

If this was from Einstein, how could he possibly know about Alfie's accident when they were children? It was never reported in any newspaper. Against his better judgement, James was starting to become excited, though he scolded himself for doing so. It was widely known that Einstein did not speak English, so he couldn't have typed the letter. Admittedly, someone could have translated his words for him.

The next day, he bought a copy of the *Manchester Evening News*. Turning to page three, he found a report on the day's play from Lord's. Middlesex batted first and scored 188 for three by the tea interval. Patsy Hendren was still there on seventy-eight not out. The hairs stood up on the back of James' neck. Monday's evening edition confirmed that Middlesex were all out for 407, with Hendren still at the crease, having scored 183 not out. Lancashire had scored 171 for eight by the time the paper went to print. There was no doubt about it. Whoever wrote that letter had seen into the future!

Getting to Berlin was not as simple as boarding a ferry in Hull. His fear of water made a journey by sea the last resort. Thankfully, there were daily flights from London to Amsterdam, from where he could catch a train to Germany.

Berlin, Germany

James arrived in the German capital eight days after receiving Einstein's letter and made his way to Haberlandstrasse by taxicab. Climbing the stairs to the fourth floor, he had an attack of the jitters. He had been in awe of this man for as long as he could remember, and it was hard to believe that he was really going to meet him. At the door of the apartment, he stood awhile, trying to overcome his nerves. His knock was answered by a rather plump woman who he took to be Einstein's wife, although he had never seen her picture.

She smiled at him and said in English, 'You must be James, we've been expecting you.'

'Thank you, Frau …?'

'Einstein, but please call me Elsa. Come in.' A servant took his bags, and he followed Elsa into a large room that was simply but elegantly furnished. The centrepiece was a gleaming black Bechstein grand piano. In his head, James could almost hear Alfie playing a Schubert piano sonata on his father's Steinway.

While his host went to organise refreshments, he paced around the room, wondering why it felt so familiar. The longer he waited, the more nervous he became. More nervous even than when he had met Ernest Rutherford. He was sweating profusely, so he opened the doors to the balcony that overlooked the street. He was holding onto the rail and breathing deeply when a voice behind him said, 'Don't do it!' Startled, he turned to find himself face to smiling face with a tall, smartly dressed, middle-aged man. He held out a hand and said, 'Moritz Katzenstein. I'm a friend of Professor Einstein. Welcome to Berlin.'

'Thank you,' said James. 'Is he here?'

'He is, but he wanted me to meet you first. He does not speak any English, but I can translate.'

'I speak a little German, sir,' said James, 'but just what I learnt at school, I'm afraid.'

'*Das ist gut. Sollen wir hineingehen?*' Moritz could see that James was struggling. 'Shall we go inside?'

They walked back into the lounge to find Einstein standing by the piano, puffing on a briar pipe. He had a somewhat dishevelled appearance, accentuated by ill-fitting trousers and an old cardigan.

James felt incredibly awkward as he walked towards his hero. 'Einstein. Sorry, I mean Albert. Oh bugger! Sir. It's such a pleasure to meet me. I mean you, sorry!' He couldn't stop apologising, and now he could feel his face turning red. 'Sorry!' He'd done it again. 'Erm, I'll start again.'

Moritz spoke in German to Einstein, who smiled and said something in return. 'He says you should relax, he's not that scary. Come and have a seat, Doctor Driscoll.'

'Thank you,' said an embarrassed James, shaking hands with Einstein, 'but I'm not a doctor, just plain Mister.'

'My mistake.' With Moritz translating, James gradually started to regain his composure and enjoy the conversation.

'Can you ask him what was so important that I had to come to Berlin straight away?'

Moritz picked up a pad from the top of the piano. It was full of copious, scrawled notes. Reading from it, he said, 'There are a number of reasons for bringing you here, but nothing I'm about to tell you is certain anymore. We know, from messages sent back from 1923, that your father will die in an accident on the twenty-sixth of January next year.'

James couldn't believe his ears. 'What sort of accident?'

'A train crash, but you can save him.'

He gulped. 'I hope you're right. I'm finding this very difficult to take in. Where is your proof?'

Moritz turned to the front page of the pad. It contained the original message, a lengthy series of zeroes and ones arranged in groups of six. 'These are binary numbers. They represent words or phrases that form a message, sent back from a date in the future. It's really quite ingenious. Would you like to see a demonstration tomorrow?'

'Yes, please. What else does it say?'

'Before I continue, you must promise never to reveal this secret. If you are going to save your father's life, you must do so without revealing that we know how to send messages back in time.'

'That might be difficult.'

'Maybe, but unless you agree, our discussion is over.'

James shrugged. 'In that case, I suppose I have no choice.'

'It's settled then. Your mother will also die, on her birthday, the eleventh of March next year. It was thought to be suicide but was later found to be murder.'

'Murder? Who would want to murder my mother?'

'Someone acting on the instructions of a Herr Winter.'

James gasped. His chest tightened and he felt sick. 'That monster! I've got to stop him.'

'I'm sure you will, with the help of the police. I have more details when you're ready, but for now, there is a third reason that is more pressing.'

'What could be more pressing than what you've already told me?'

'There is someone we'd like you to meet.'

'Professor von Laue?'

'No, although you will meet him tomorrow. James, have you heard of the Unknown Soldier?'

'Yes, in London.' James was aware of the plan to bury the remains of an unknown British soldier in Westminster Abbey, to honour the unidentified dead. 'What does that have to do with my visit?'

'I meant our unknown soldier, here in Berlin. He's still alive, in a hospital not far from here.'

'Why do you want me to meet him?'

'He's been in a coma since the Battle of the Somme.' Moritz paused. 'He has a curved scar under his chin.'

‘Alfie?’ James felt faint and he took an involuntary step sideways before dropping to his knees, where he remained, head bowed, overcome with emotion.

On the way to the hospital in Moritz’s battered Opel, he explained that, according to the message, the soldier did not come out of his coma and died in October, in four months’ time. ‘I was the surgeon who treated him on the battlefield. He was incredibly lucky to survive a bullet to the head. It went in and out of the left side, missing the most important parts of the brain.’

‘Is there any chance he could survive if he wakes up?’

‘Yes, but unless he does wake up, we have no way of knowing how much damage was done. He may never make a full recovery.’

‘Why couldn’t he be identified?’

‘There was a lot of confusion on that day. Thousands of soldiers needed urgent treatment. This man had no clothing by the time I saw him. His features were Aryan, as are yours. He was assumed to be a German soldier.’

At the hospital, Moritz led them to his office, where he donned a white coat, saying, ‘Wait here.’ The two men stood awkwardly for what seemed an age. James had so many questions for Einstein, yet for now he could only communicate by hand signals. At long last, Moritz returned with a nurse in tow. She took a sharp intake of breath when she saw James.

‘This is Nurse Kohler. She has been caring for our patient for the past two years. Would you like to meet him now?’

James nodded. Nervous anticipation left him almost speechless, but he managed to whisper, ‘Yes please.’

They took a paternoster lift to the second floor and entered a private room on the rehabilitation ward. Standing at the foot of the bed, Moritz asked, ‘Is it him?’

James walked forwards and stared down at the man’s face. He seemed so peaceful, as though he was only sleeping. Grasping his hand tightly, he murmured, ‘Hello, Alfie.’

Kirk Allerton, Yorkshire

George arrived home to find a yellow envelope on his desk, left there by one of the servants. Inside was a sheet of paper bearing the heading Post Office Telegraphs, its office of origin the *Deutsche Reichspost* in Berlin. Intrigued, he put on his glasses and read the handwritten message. “URGENT STOP ALFIE ALIVE IN COMA STOP FRIEDRICHSHAIN HOSPITAL BERLIN STOP ASK FOR DOCTOR UNGER STOP JAMES.”

His head began to swim, and he put a hand on the desk to steady himself. Alfie was alive! How was that possible? Why hadn’t anyone told them? Whose body was in that grave in France? And what the hell was James doing in Berlin? His hand was shaking violently as he reached for the whisky bottle. He sat down and took a large gulp of the golden liquid. His cheeks were wet from the tears streaming down his cheeks. He couldn’t let anyone see him like this, it simply wouldn’t do.

By the time dinner was served, he had recovered sufficiently to sit and pick at his food. He waited until the meal was over and the servants had left before joining Ellen in the drawing room. Had he been paying attention, he would have noticed her rubbing her neck. It had been troubling her for more than a week now, though her cannabis tablets certainly helped.

‘I had a telegram from Berlin today,’ said George.

‘Was it from James?’

‘What makes you say that? Have you been in touch with him behind my back?’

‘Yes, dear. He told me he was going to Berlin to see Professor Einstein.’

‘The scientist?’

‘I don’t know, dear, how many Professor Einsteins are there?’

George glared at her. ‘Anyway, he’s there. Here, read this.’ George handed the telegram to his wife and waited for the inevitable reaction. She got no further than the first line before the screaming started. George sat down next to her, holding her tightly until she calmed down.

‘My Alfie’s alive!’ she cried. ‘We have to go to him!’

38

Friedrichshain Hospital, Berlin
July 1920

The taxicab turned in through heavy, wrought iron gates, set in a grand brick archway emblazoned with the words *KRANKENHAUS IM FRIEDRICHSHAIN*. Ellen Driscoll had not slept for two nights, through a mixture of anticipation and the discomfort of twenty-four hours at sea. George had balked at the extra cost of flying, arguing that because of the flight times, the journey was no faster. His reputation for being careful with money was no secret, but Ellen suspected that on this occasion he was simply scared of flying. It was such a novel form of travel, and no one really knew how reliable aeroplanes were. She decided not to say anything and had to put up with unremitting sea sickness on the journey from Hull to Hamburg. She really didn't care. It was something she would have gladly accepted for a week, a month or even a year just to be reunited with her eldest son.

Doctor Unger was otherwise engaged when the Driscolls arrived, but he had left instructions for a ward sister to welcome them. She arrived with James, who had taken up residence in Alfie's room. He hugged Ellen before offering a handshake to his father. To his relief, George shook his hand warmly and said, 'I don't know how you found him, Son, but thank you.'

'It's a long story, Father. Shall we go and see him?'

'Aye, there's no point hanging around here.'

They followed the sister to the ward, where they were shown into a side room. 'The doctor would like to speak with you before you go in,' she said.

The tension was almost unbearable in the hot, stuffy room. Eventually, they were joined by a short, balding man wearing a white coat. '*Guten Tag*,' he said, ignoring James and addressing his parents. 'I am Doctor Unger.'

'When can I see my boy?' asked Ellen.

'Very soon,' the doctor replied. 'The nurses are just exercising his joints and moving him to prevent bedsores. I wanted you to know what to expect when you see him.'

'Does he look bad?' asked George.

'No, quite the opposite, but I don't want to get your hopes up. I have seen many patients with brain injuries. Very few of them make a full recovery after such a long time in a coma. When he opened his eyes last December, we thought for a while that he might start to improve.'

'What made him open his eyes?' asked James.

'The only thing we could think of was the Christmas music.'

'He loves music!' said Ellen excitedly. 'Would it help if we played to him?'

'It certainly wouldn't hurt. Play music, sing to him, talk about familiar things. Anything to stimulate his memory.'

A nurse knocked on the door to let them know that Alfie was ready to receive visitors.

'This is Nurse Kohler,' he said. 'She has spent a lot of time with your son. If I'm not available, then you should ask for her. Would you take them in now, nurse?'

James followed his parents into the room and stood at the foot of the bed. They moved to the other end, one on each side, looking down at the son they had mourned for the past four years. He looked so peaceful, lying there. Ellen cried softly as she reached across and hugged her first-born.

'The surgeon who saved his life still works here, in this hospital,' said James. 'Doctor Katzenstein. You can meet him later.'

George was euphoric, clasping and unclasping his fists, fighting to control his emotions. 'There doesn't seem to be a mark on him,' he said. 'I thought he was shot in the head?'

'He was,' she said. 'He had five wounds in total. Four in the, erm, how do you say *der Rumpf* in English?'

'The rump?' queried George. 'Are you saying he was running away?'

'I don't understand,' said the confused nurse. *'Der Rumpf? Der Torso?'*

'Ah, the torso,' said James who'd, like his father, had a brief but disturbing vision of a fleeing Alfie being shot four times in the backside.

'*Ja*, the torso. Four in the torso. We think he was already falling when he was hit by a fifth bullet. It must have gone through his helmet and entered his head above the hairline. Part of his skull was blown out at the back, which may have saved his life.'

George was puzzled. 'How?'

'It allowed the brain to swell without becoming crushed.'

'So, he's missing part of his head?'

'No,' she replied. 'It was still attached to the scalp, so when the swelling went down, we were able to reattach it.'

For the next couple of weeks, the Driscolls tried to follow Unger's advice to the letter. They took it in turns in their attempts to wake Alfie. George talked incessantly about the mill and the problems awaiting him on his return. James asked him about things they did together as children, and Ellen sang to him. There was a fleeting moment when he opened his eyes as she sang *Wind The Bobbin Up*, his favourite nursery rhyme as a baby. She was dismayed to see that there was no recognition in the cornflower blue eyes, but it was still lovely to see them again.

James spent much of his free time in Einstein's company. He had seen Hermes in action. With Elsa translating, he committed every detail of the message to memory. It contained two proofs from November 1920 and January 1921. The key to saving his parents' lives lay in convincing his father that he knew what was coming, but how? Only a few weeks ago, he had given his word that he would never reveal Hermes' existence to anyone. Try as he might, he couldn't think of a way of saving his father's life without breaking his promise. He wasn't sure that he could be trusted with such a huge secret, but he had to take the risk. He just needed to find the right time.

When George heard from his secretary that Aunt Glynis had been in touch to say his mother was ill and was asking for him, he decided to return to England. 'When I've been to see my mam, I'll check that the mill isn't going to rack and ruin. I'll be back as soon as I can.'

James had thought about going with him so that he could attend his graduation ceremony, but he didn't want to leave his mother on her own. 'We'll be fine here,' he said. 'You get yourself away.'

'Your mam won't leave Alfie to come with me. Will you keep an eye on her for me?'

James nodded. It was the first time that he could remember his father asking him for anything. In the past, it would have been an instruction.

'Thanks, Son. Before I go, just answer me one thing. How the hell did you find out he was here in Germany?'

It was now or never. 'There's something I have to tell you, Father. You will find it hard to believe, but I swear that it's true, and it could save your life.'

George looked at him as if he was mad. 'Right, well, you've got my attention. What is it?'

'Before I tell you, you have to promise me that you will never repeat this to another living soul.'

'Why the secrecy?' George was beginning to lose patience with his son.

'You'll understand once I've told you, but I'm breaking a promise by doing that. I need you to give me your word.'

'You have it. Come on, spit it out.'

'Read this,' said James, pulling Einstein's letter from his pocket. He waited impatiently as his father read it. When he had finished, he looked up at James and said, 'I don't understand. He wrote to you about a cricket match and asked you not to say anything? Why?'

'It was his way of telling me that he's invented a way of sending messages to the past. How else would he know the result of a cricket match before it had even been played? Every detail was correct.'

'You're joking! You can't seriously expect me to believe that. It's just not possible.'

'I promise you it is. It's how I found out that Alfie was still alive, and there's more.'

'What do you mean, more?'

'Things that are going to happen in the future, including a train crash in Wales that's going to kill a lot of people, including you.'

George was stunned. 'Prove it,' he exclaimed.

'I will,' replied James. 'In November, there is going to be an attack in Dublin. The papers will call it Bloody Sunday. Not only that, but in January, a British submarine will sink in the English Channel with the loss of all hands. When those events take place, will you accept that Einstein can see into the future?'

'And you're telling me all this …'

'To save your life. Don't get on that train, Father.'

'Alright, but I'll ask you again, why the secrecy?'

James breathed a sigh of relief and tried to answer his father's question. 'Imagine if Germany knew how to do this during the war. If they'd known about the Allied plans, they'd have won the war, even though they lost it the first time round. Do you see why it's so important to keep it secret? Men would kill for less.'

His father finally understood. 'My lips are sealed, Son,' he said.

After George went home, James and Ellen continued their efforts to bring Alfie out of his coma. The news from Wales was that Nana Driscoll was much improved, and her sister was going to look after her, so George returned to Berlin in late September. As he walked through the hospital, he noticed a piano in one of the common rooms. From the amount of dust that had gathered, it looked as if it hadn't been used in a while, but it gave him an idea. After a lot of pleading and a little bribery, he persuaded a nurse to have it brought into Alfie's room.

'Right then,' he said, 'I'm a bit rusty, but let's see if this makes any difference.'

He proceeded to play some of the pieces he had taught Alfie at an early age. The sound of Mozart and Bach filled the room. Disappointingly, there was no reaction from his eldest son.

When he began to play Grieg's *Piano Concerto in A Minor*, Ellen exclaimed, 'This is his favourite piece!' They all watched closely as George played the dramatic opening flourish. Nothing.

'Play it again,' said Ellen. Still nothing.

'And again,' she said with more urgency.

George sighed. He was starting to become irritated, but he played it once more, and this time, Alfie's eyes flickered and his fingers twitched.

'Did you see that?' asked James, wondering whether he had imagined it.

'Yes! Again,' she said, becoming more animated.

On the next play, almost imperceptibly at first, Alfie's eyes blinked and then opened. He started to become agitated, and it was clear that something extraordinary was happening.

George ran to the door, threw it open and yelled down the corridor, 'Get a doctor, sharpish! Hurry up, we need help in here!' The sound of running footsteps followed, and the nursing staff took charge.

'Find Doctor Unger!' shouted one of the nurses.

Alfie slowly regained full consciousness, but he was so weak that the doctors did not expect him to survive. However, now that he was awake, they were determined to do all they could to save him. No one could say whether he would make a long-term recovery. It would be a long and painful process, and he might never speak again. Every morning, a nurse made him use the parallel bars in his room, building up the strength in his arms and trying to make him put one foot in front of the other. Eventually, it was hoped that he would be able to do this for himself, but for now he was confined to a wheelchair.

Early in November, they received word from Wales that Nana Driscoll had taken a turn for the worse, and George prepared to go home again. 'She could be up and down like this for months, or even years,' he said to James.

'I know,' he replied. 'There was nothing about Nana in Einstein's message, but I don't think I want to know how much time she has left. Do you?'

'No,' said George, 'but she's old and frail, so I'm going to try to spend more time with her whenever I can.' To James' great surprise, and for the first time he could remember, George hugged him. It meant more to James than anything his father could have said, and felt like an apology for all of the bullying and criticism he had suffered when Alfie went off to war.

'I'll leave in the morning,' said George. 'Look after your mother for me, will you?'

39

Aberystwyth, Wales
November 1920

Several weeks later, George left Wales to deal with a few problems at the mill. He took a late train back to Aberystwyth and settled down to read his paper. A headline caught his eye. It read "BLOODY SUNDAY." Below it was a report from Ireland, where fourteen military and legal officers had been shot dead in Dublin. Later the same day, twelve people, including one of the players, were killed during a hurling match at Croke Park. Hundreds were wounded. Einstein's prediction had come to pass.

Berlin, Germany

Ellen was becoming more and more concerned about Alfie's mental state. When he slept, he often appeared to be in agony and would wake up shaking and sweating. She asked Doctor Unger whether this was normal.

'We have noticed that some injured soldiers have nightmares, almost as if they are reliving the events that caused their injuries.'

'Will he get better?'

'It's difficult to say. Every patient is different. I treated a soldier in the Great War who was badly injured by shrapnel. Mentally, he was fine, so we patched him up and sent him back to the front, where he wanted to be. I also know a man who fought in the Franco-Prussian war fifty years ago. He still suffers from what we call war neuroses, yet he had no physical injuries to speak of.'

Friedrichshain was a fine hospital. Ellen couldn't fault the staff or the facilities, but it was clear that Alfie's treatment was not their top priority. He would lie in bed for hours, waiting for therapists who would spend no more than half an hour at a time with him. She realised that his chances of a full recovery would be greater if he had specialist care around the clock. When she raised this with Doctor Unger, he agreed.

'Your son's recovery would certainly be faster if we had more resources,' he said. 'If you have the time and the money to arrange private care, I would advise you to do so.'

When the arrangements had been made and they were ready to leave Germany, Ellen decided that she could not face a repeat of the tortuous sea journey from Hamburg, particularly with Alfie in a wheelchair. Instead, it was decided that they would travel to Amsterdam by train and fly to London the following morning, where Ralph would be waiting to take them home in time for supper. At the airport in Schiphol-les-bains near Amsterdam, the airline's misgivings about taking a disabled passenger were put to rest when James picked Alfie up and carried him onto the plane over his shoulder.

Kirk Allerton, Yorkshire
December 1920

Alfie was delighted to find his room exactly the way he had left it five years earlier. In Manchester, he was examined by a specialist, who was amazed that he had survived his ordeal, but cautious about his prospects for a normal life. He told George and Ellen not to expect miracles. As Christmas loomed, Ellen spent every waking minute looking after Alfie. She stubbornly refused to accept his disability, subjecting him to a punishing schedule of physiotherapy and exercise, but he was unable to walk.

On Christmas Eve, James pushed him and his wheelchair down to The Fleece, where they enjoyed their first drink together. The previous day, he had broken his promise to Moritz for a second time by telling Alfie about Hermes. They had never kept any secrets from each other, and he wasn't about to start now. He was at the bar when George walked in unexpectedly, to be greeted by deferential nods from several of the locals. It was the first time the brothers had seen their father in a public house, although as a young man he had been a regular at The Fleece. The landlord handed George a pint and told James that his round was on the house. The brothers saw a very different side to George as he stood, beer in hand, regaling the room with stories of drunken escapades in years gone by.

'Tell 'em about Jubilee, Mr Driscoll,' shouted an old man in the corner.

George laughed. 'I'll tell you, but I'm not naming names!' He proceeded to tell a tale about Queen Victoria's Golden Jubilee in June 1887 when, in celebration, hundreds of beacons were to be lit on the highest peaks across the nation, at ten o'clock precisely. The lighting of each beacon was meant to be a signal to light the next one in line, so that within a short space of time, a bird's-eye view of Britain would have shown a shimmering necklace of fire adorning the nation to honour the monarch's fifty years on the throne.

Someone who would remain nameless, although James and Alfie were convinced it was George, had climbed to the top of Allerton Edge. From there, the beacons of Yorkshire, Lancashire and the Lake District were visible, including the one on Pendle Hill. The prankster crept up behind the beacon and set light to it an hour early, triggering a chain reaction throughout the north of England as beacon-lighters acted upon the signal. No one ever discovered the culprit, but whoever it was caused a mixture of disapproval and mirth throughout the land.

George bought drinks for everyone in the bar, before taking his sons into the snug, where they raised a glass to Nana Driscoll. She had died in Aberystwyth a week earlier, with her only son by her side. Thanks to James, George was there to care for his mother in the last weeks of her life.

Back at the manor, George spoke to James in private. 'Before I go, I want you to know how proud I am of you. I know how hard you worked to get where you are, and I'm sorry if I made things difficult for you.' James could hardly believe his ears. He guessed, correctly, that the death of his grandmother had given his father a different outlook on life.

'It's good of you to say so, Father,' he replied. 'That means a lot.'

They hugged for a second time and George coughed self-consciously. 'Now,' he said, 'I need to go to Wales to sort out Nana's estate. What should I know about this train crash?'

James told him that, according to the message, he was one of twenty-one people who had died in a train crash at Abermule in Wales on the twenty-sixth of January 1921. 'It was caused by the wrong tablet, Father.'

'The wrong tablet? What does that mean?'

'I have no idea, and I don't know which train is going to crash, so if you have to travel on that day, get Ralph to drive you.'

'Don't worry, I have no intention of being anywhere near a train on the twenty-sixth!'

The Driscolls had a wonderful Christmas and New Year, reminiscent of the ones they had enjoyed when the boys were young.

George seemed like a different man and together, the whole family would go for long walks, with James pushing Alfie's wheelchair. They would invariably end up in The Fleece, where they would get drunk and listen to George's stories. James discovered that his father had a great sense of humour, and he was delighted to observe the effect it had on his mother, who had never really seen this side of her husband before.

Their evenings were spent playing whist or cribbage and, for the first time, George showed interest in the progress of James' studies at Manchester University. On New Year's Day, Ralph drove George and James to see the laboratory in the basement of Oakwood House. On the journey, James found out for the first time that his father was a supporter of the Manchester City football team, although he had never been to a match.

'Why don't we go?' suggested James. 'They're playing Sunderland today, and it's only a mile or so from Rusholme.'

Ralph took them to the Hyde Road stadium in time for kick-off, and accepted the invitation to join them, as they stood with 35,000 other fans to watch City run out 3-1 winners. James couldn't help but feel sad that this was something father and son could have done together throughout his childhood years.

When George returned to Wales by train to deal with his mother's estate, he asked the guard whether there had ever been any accidents on the line.

'There was one in Shropshire a few years back,' he said. 'They put it down to the weather, and the design of the tablet instruments. It couldn't happen now.'

George's ears pricked up. 'Tablet instruments?'

'Yes. The tablets that prevent two trains being on the same stretch of single track at the same time. The driver cannot proceed until he has the tablet, you see. Only one driver can have it at any one time.'

'Ingenious,' said George.

In Allerton Manor, Ellen was taking down the last of the decorations from the Christmas tree when there was a knock at the door. The young woman standing on the doorstep looked vaguely familiar.

''Ello, Mrs Driscoll,' she said nervously.

'I'm sorry, do I know you?' she replied.

‘It’s Molly. Molly Bradshaw? Alfie and I were courting before ’e joined the Army.’

Ellen had met Molly once before and remembered thinking that she was common. Although she was a pleasant enough girl, Ellen had been sure that Alfie would tire of her and find someone more suitable. She had grown into a beautiful young woman but was still common.

‘Molly! Of course. How lovely to see you. What brings you here?’

‘I’ve only just found out that ’e’s alive.’

‘Oh, who told you?’ she asked curiously.

‘It were Alfie’s friend, Stan. ’E’s me next-door neighbour, you see. Alfie wrote ’im a letter.’ Since the news of Alfie’s death in 1916 and Molly’s visit to his grave three years later, she had resigned herself to the prospect of a life of spinsterhood. After all, there were so few eligible young men left alive in Lancashire. She had fainted on the morning that Stan showed her the letter. It ended with “If you should happen to see Molly Bradshaw, would you be so good as to give her my best wishes?”

‘Did Stan tell you what happened to my son?’ asked Ellen.

‘No, just that ’e were in a coma. Can I see ’im?’ she pleaded.

‘You’d better come in,’ she said, ‘but you should prepare yourself.’

‘Why? ’E’s alright, isn’t ’e?’ she asked, suddenly alarmed.

‘He was very badly injured, Molly. To be honest with you, we really don’t know how he survived.’

‘But ’e’s on the mend, surely?’

‘Molly,’ she said, as gently as she could, ‘he may never walk again, and he hasn’t spoken since he woke up. Are you sure you want to see him like that?’

‘I love ’im, Mrs Driscoll!’ she cried. ‘I don’t care what ’e looks like, I just want to tell ’im that.’

Ellen could see that there was no dissuading her. ‘Very well, then, come with me.’ She led the way to George’s study and knocked on the door before opening it. Alfie was sitting in a wheelchair, reading a book.

‘Someone to see you, Alfie,’ she said.

‘’Ello, Alfie, remember me?’ said Molly, her big, brown eyes filling with tears. He tried to stand, a broad smile on his face as he mouthed her name. When no sound came, she hurried across the room and threw her arms around him, scarcely able to believe he was back from the dead.

'I'll leave you two to get reacquainted,' said Ellen, closing the door softly.

'I thought you were dead,' said Molly, taking his head in her hands and kissing him firmly on the lips.

He took a piece of paper and a pencil from the desk and wrote "You're even more beautiful than I remember. You must be disappointed I'm not the man I once was."

'You'll do for me,' she sobbed, kissing him again. 'I've missed you so much, Alfie Driscoll!' Later, they sat together in the drawing room. The effect of Molly's visit on Alfie was clear for all to see, so at Ellen's suggestion, she rang her father and stayed overnight in the guest room.

In the morning, she was woken by the smell of coffee drifting up from the kitchen. Ellen was waiting for her when she came down.

'Alfie and I have had an idea,' she said. 'He needs a full-time carer and he tells me that you need a job. Would you be interested?'

Molly's heart missed a beat. 'Really?' she asked tearfully. 'You would do that for me?'

'I'd be doing it for Alfie. You've only been here for a matter of hours and the change in him is amazing. I want him out of that wheelchair by Easter. Do you think you can help him?'

'If it's 'umanly possible, I'll get 'im walkin' again!'

'Then we have a deal. If you don't mind me asking, how much did you get paid working for your father?'

'Nothing,' replied Molly ruefully.

'Oh. Well, I think we can do a little better than that!'

'Thank you, but I would do it for nothing,' she said.

Over the next few weeks, Molly rarely left Alfie's side and attended to his every need. Slowly but surely, he discovered what it was like to fall in love. As a teenager, he hadn't taken his friendship with Molly that seriously, but now his heart skipped a beat every time she entered the room.

His parents had avoided asking him about the war, to spare him any distress, but when Molly told him about the letters found on another man's body, he knew for sure that her brother was lying in the wrong grave in France. He found himself thinking back to their last night together on the eve of the Battle of the Somme.

Tommy Bradshaw had asked Alfie to do him a favour. Handing him a letter, he'd said, 'Would you see that this gets home if I don't?'

'Only if you'll do the same for me,' Alfie had replied, passing two letters to his friend and never considering the possibility that neither he nor Tommy would make it through the day. They had shaken hands and hugged each other. Now, he realised that his letters had been taken from Tommy's body and sent back to George and Molly. She was devastated when she read the note he had written to explain what happened, but in time she took comfort from the fact that Tommy's body was not lost in the mud like so many others.

By late January, George's mother's estate was finalised, to be split equally between James and Alfie. He was ready to leave Wales for good, and he thought about coming home a day early to avoid the twenty-sixth, but something was troubling him. If James was right, a lot of innocent people were going to die. He didn't know what, but he had to do something.

On the twenty-fifth of January, James was relieved to learn that George had summoned Ralph to bring him home from Wales. However, the following night, he returned to the manor alone, looking very upset. Ellen had already retired for the night, and James was in George's study. He knew instantly that it was bad news.

'What is it, Ralph? What's wrong?'

'It's Lord Driscoll, Sir. He's dead.'

'What do you mean, dead? How?'

Ralph tried to speak but broke down completely. James sat him down and poured him a large whisky. He was in shock himself, yet somehow managed to remain calm.

'Take your time and tell me what happened,' he said.

'I don't really understand it myself, Sir. His Lordship said that the trains were cancelled and asked me to drive down to fetch him home. We were on our way back this morning when a train passed us.'

'What made him think there were no trains running?'

'He said he'd spoken to one of the railway bosses. Hubert somebody, I think.'

'Herbert.' said James. 'Lord Herbert Vane-Tempest?'

'That's the feller. Do you know him?'

'No, but I've heard of him.'

'Anyway, your father was mad as hell. Said that he would have to stop it or die trying. We managed to catch up with the train before it left Newtown. His Lordship tried to stop it leaving. Reckoned it was going to crash. I dunno where he got that idea from, but he was adamant. He told me to give a lift to a woman and her two young kids and then he boarded the train.'

'So, it set off with him on board?' said James.

'Yes, Sir. It only went a mile or so before it hit a train coming in the opposite direction. I ran across the fields to see if I could help, but I couldn't find him, just a lot of dead bodies. It was terrible.'

Ralph's words gave James a glimmer of hope. 'If you couldn't find him, how do you know he was still on the train?'

'I don't, Sir, but one of the carriages was so crushed, it would've taken some time to get the people out. Do you think he might have jumped off at the last minute? That's what the driver did.'

'Until they've identified the bodies, I really have no idea, but to be honest, I doubt it. The driver will have seen what was about to happen, unlike his passengers. I just hope he didn't suffer.'

'From what I saw, I don't think he would have known much about it.'

'I hope you're right, but I still don't understand what made him get on that train. He was warned.'

Ralph was shocked. 'Warned? What do you mean?'

James realised that he had said too much. 'Erm, I mean he had a premonition. He told me he wasn't going to travel by train on the twenty-sixth, so what made him change his mind?'

'I suppose he was trying to save lives, Sir,' said Ralph. 'I'm sure if there had been any other way, he would have chosen it. That woman and her kids would probably be dead now if it wasn't for him. Your father died a hero, Master James. Sorry, I shouldn't call you that anymore. Doesn't this make you the new Lord of the Manor, Sir?'

'I haven't even thought about it,' said James, 'but no. Alfie is older than me. Just call me James?'

'Oh, I couldn't do that, Sir. Wouldn't be right.'

'Go home, Ralph. Have some time off and we'll talk again on Monday.'

'Thank you, Master James.'

The next morning, James broke the news to Ellen and Alfie. His mother was inconsolable and remained in her room for the rest of the day. The staff were sent home, so Molly spent the day fussing around Alfie and James, preparing their meals and sitting with Alfie as he grieved.

James was devastated that the chance to save his father had gone. Their relationship had improved significantly since Alfie had been saved, and James had been looking forward to helping him turn the mill's fortunes around. Now, he was worried for the future of the family business. He was going to have to spend a significant amount of time at the mill, trying to assess what condition his father had left the business in, so he took a leave of absence from the university. He didn't want to ask for Alfie's help, as he wanted him to concentrate on recovering his health and hopefully the power of speech.

Molly continued to work towards the same goal. She pushed Alfie to the limit, but he never complained and in early February, her diligence paid off. To everyone's surprise, he managed to walk a few steps with the aid of a walking stick, and on Valentine's Day, he took his first steps without it. In the weeks that followed, he concentrated on building up the strength in his legs until, with Molly by his side, he was able to walk as far as the village and back.

40

Manchester, Lancashire
March 1921

James had warned DCI Hughes that on Friday, the eleventh of March, there would be an attempt on his mother's life. He couldn't explain how he knew, but he was most insistent, and Hughes was keen to catch Varese and his American associates in the act. He agreed to keep a close eye on their movements.

On the morning of the eleventh, he opened his office door and shouted, 'Geordie, get in here!'

DS Reg Clayton, originally from Tyneside and known to all as Geordie, ambled along the corridor, pie in hand. 'Sir?'

'Have you heard from Phillips yet?'

'Er, no sir,' he mumbled through a mouthful of pastry. 'His wife called and said he's at home. He's not feeling too good.'

'What? He's meant to be watching the Yanks!'

'I know, sir, but he's a bit under the weather.'

'Give me strength! Where are they now, Sergeant?'

'As of last night, they were holed up in a hotel in Scarthwaite.' The village was only six miles from Kirk Allerton.

'I don't care about last night, where are they now?'

'Er, I'm not sure, sir.'

'So, what are you doing about it?'

'I sent young Hartley out there. I'm waiting for him to get in touch, sir.'

'Well, don't wait any longer. Call the hotel and find out if they're still there.'

'Will do, sir. I'm just making a brew, would you like …?'

'Forget the sodding brew!' He went back into his office, shouted, 'Do it now!' and slammed the door. His heart sank when Clayton returned ten minutes later.

'Sorry, sir. It seems that they checked out this morning. Is there anything I can do?'

'Yes, Geordie. When he gets in touch, tell Hartley to meet me at Allerton Manor. Oh, and if you should happen to find a real policeman round here, would you let me know?'

'There's no need to be like that, sir. I can't help it if …'

‘Get out!’ shouted Hughes. ‘Stick to making tea in future,’ he said, slamming the door for the second time. He had to warn James Driscoll.

Kirk Allerton, Yorkshire

Later the same morning, Alfie was in the top field, tending to the Driscoll’s flock of Lonk sheep. It had been such a long time since he had been able to help out on the estate, and he loved it here. The view across the valley, with the village nestled below, was a sight that had no equal, in his opinion. He felt lucky to live in such a beautiful place, far away from the horrors of war. Molly had changed so much from the innocent young girl he had known, and she was totally devoted to him. She would not rest until he was as healthy as his battered body and mind would allow. She kept telling him that if that meant he never spoke again, so be it, but she longed to hear his voice. Alfie could feel himself getting stronger by the day, but the war had left mental scars that would stay with him forever. He was just grateful for a second chance at life.

When he looked down on the village, Alfie noticed a man loitering in the lane near the Manor. The man remained motionless for several minutes, and something about him made Alfie suspicious. From his vantage point, he could see two more men talking at the far end of the lane. His mother was alone in the house, so he decided to head back down to the Manor. When he was about a hundred yards away, he heard a loud cry, followed by silence. Under the cover of trees, he quickly made his way to the rear of the house and opened the back door, removing his boots so that he made no sound. In the hallway, he stopped and listened. The man’s voice was low and menacing. Alfie heard him say, ‘Sit there and be quiet,’ in an accent that he couldn’t quite place, but it wasn’t English.

He tiptoed into George’s study and removed his father’s Remington Derringer pistol from the desk drawer. Loading it from a box of bullets, he slipped it into his waistband and moved stealthily towards the kitchen. From where he was standing, he could just see the terrified face of his mother looking pleadingly at the intruder. In front of her was a bowl of porridge from the pan on the stove.

‘Who are you and what do you want?’ she cried.

‘Eat up,’ he said.

'Do you want money? I can give you money!'

'Eat up or I'll shoot you.'

'If I eat that I'll die!'

'If I shoot you, you die, *donna sciocca!*'

To Alfie, he sounded Italian. He moved to get a better view of the table. On it was scattered the contents of a box of rat poison.

'Last chance,' said the man, cocking the pistol in his hand.

She was sobbing as she lifted the spoon to her lips.'

'STOP!' shouted Alfie, his gun aimed at the would-be assassin. The man spun round, a surprised expression on his face. He raised the pistol, and a single shot rang out.

Ellen looked up at her son, wide-eyed. 'You spoke!' There was no reply, and she saw that he was shaking violently. 'Are you hurt?' she cried.

He shook his head. It was the first gunshot he had heard since the Somme, and it unnerved him more than the sight of his victim, sprawled on the floor with blood oozing from a hole in his chest. Ellen put her arms around him, but he pulled free and motioned for her to follow him into the study. Try as he might, he couldn't speak again, so he quickly scribbled a note, which read "2 MORE MEN. RING POLICE. I'LL LOCK DOORS." When he returned, he closed the heavy drapes and made Ellen hide under the desk, while he took up a position from where he could see anyone who managed to get in through the locked door. Before long, they heard gunshots in the distance. They stayed where they were for what seemed like an eternity. Then there was the sound of breaking glass. They were in the house! Alfie's heart began beating so loudly that he felt sure someone would hear it. As the door handle turned, he prepared to fire again.

'Mrs Driscoll,' called out a voice in a decidedly Lancashire accent. 'It's Eric Jenkins. Are you in there?'

Alfie helped his mother out of her hiding place and unlocked the door. 'Put the gun down, sir,' said a voice from behind Sergeant Jenkins. He had forgotten that he was still holding the weapon. 'Don't shoot, he can't speak!' yelled James, who had arrived after the police.

Alfie handed the gun to Jenkins, who passed it to a man in an overcoat. Ellen ran to James and hugged him. 'I'm DCI Hughes,' said the man in the coat, leading them back to the kitchen, where the intruder's body lay untouched on the floor. 'We've been watching this man for some time. When I heard the gunshot, I thought we were too late. I'm sorry we couldn't get here any faster.'

'Who is he?' asked Ellen.

'His name is Nico Varese,' said DCI Hughes. 'He's part of a very powerful criminal gang in America.'

'What was he doing here?'

'It's all my fault, Mother,' said James, who had recognised Varese from Winter's trial. 'I helped to put a friend of his behind bars.'

'Are you alright?' she asked. 'We heard shots.'

'He had two accomplices with him. They shot a policeman in the lane, but you don't need to worry about them.'

Hughes turned to Sergeant Jenkins and said, 'Would you be good enough to go and see how he is?'

'Certainly, sir,' said Jenkins.

'Are there any more of them?' asked Ellen. 'Are we safe here?'

'Varese's friend will be behind bars for a very long time,' said Hughes. 'From what we know, this was a personal vendetta. I don't believe it will continue now that he's dead. His family may want revenge, but my report will say that all three were killed by the police, which will hopefully keep your name out of it.'

'Can I have a word, sir?' said Jenkins when he returned. He led Hughes outside and whispered in his ear. James watched through a window as Hughes shook his head and walked out into the lane. He found out later that a young PC by the name of Hartley was gunned down by one of Varese's men and died from loss of blood.

The policeman's death affected Hughes deeply. He blamed Clayton for failing to keep Varese under surveillance, and the hapless Geordie was soon transferred back to Tyneside. He blamed Winter for orchestrating this attack from behind bars and vowed to keep a very close eye on his visitors in future. Most of all, he blamed himself for putting a raw recruit's life at risk by allowing him to walk into an ambush. He should have known how dangerous these men were.

Armley Gaol, Leeds

The headline on the front page of the Leeds Mercury read "PC Killed in Yorkshire village." The article underneath described how police had shot and killed three men, foiling a plot to murder a prominent local woman, Mrs Ellen Driscoll, Lady of the Manor of Kirk Allerton. Sadly, a young police constable was shot and killed in the line of duty. The three men were believed to have entered the country several days before the attempt on Mrs Driscoll's life, which came only a matter of weeks after the death of her husband George in the Abermule train disaster.

Winter clung to the hope that Nico was not one of the three men involved, but deep down, he knew. It was not Nico's style to send other men to do his dirty work. No, Winter's vendetta against the Driscolls had only resulted in the death of his best friend. He had no idea how the police could possibly have known where Nico would be on that fateful day. Had they been watching his every move? The more he thought about it, the only thing that made any sense was that someone must have talked. The police must have been tipped off by the FBI when Nico and his soldiers sailed for Liverpool. Why else would they have been lying in wait in a place like Kirk Allerton?

Kirk Allerton, Yorkshire

Ellen had difficulty sleeping after the trauma of Varese's attempt on her life. She found it troubling that, had it not been for Alfie, she would now be dead. Molly returned from France to discover that Alfie had spoken his first word. She consulted his doctor, whose opinion was that his silence was a mental rather than physical affliction. With the doctor's help, she found a London speech therapist called Ron Stewart, who had successfully treated shell-shocked war veterans in the past. Ellen paid for Alfie's treatment and arranged for him to stay with Molly at a cousin's house in Bayswater. Several weeks into their stay, the treatment was beginning to work. Stewart was a patient, sympathetic man who gradually taught Alfie to speak again.

In July, as they walked in Hyde Park, Molly heard him speak a complete sentence for the first time.

'Molly,' he said slowly but clearly, 'would you do me the very great honour of becoming my wife?' She dissolved into tears of joy. Her soulmate, the man she thought she had lost forever, wanted to spend the rest of his life with her.

They married in Kirk Allerton in August. The service was held in Holy Trinity Church and was followed by a reception in a large marquee, in the grounds of the Manor. It was the proudest day of

Harold Bradshaw's life. He gave his daughter away and paid tribute to those who could not be there. He became emotional talking about Molly's brother Tommy, who had loved her from the day she was born, and Alfie's father George, who died a hero. Alfie insisted on making a short speech, in which he thanked James for finding him in Berlin and Ron Stewart for making the effort to attend the wedding.

'Without Ron,' he said, 'we might still have been here at midnight!'

Ellen's present to the happy couple was a house, or at least the plans for a house that she intended to have built on the estate, close to Allerton Manor. It was her way of ensuring that Alfie remained close by. As she watched them leave for a honeymoon in Scarborough, she reflected on the fact that, although her family had only been whole again for less than four months, their last Christmas together was a memory she would cherish for the rest of her life.

41

Kirk Allerton, Yorkshire
August 1921

With help from Harry Milburn, he persuaded his mother that moving into the garment industry was the way to safeguard the future of George's workforce. Welbeck Ready-To-Wear was now a joint venture between the Driscoll brothers, and Alfie was keen to play a role in the new business. He became the company's Financial Director, while Ellen came on board as its first chairperson.

James agreed to oversee the engineering side of the operation, but as Charlie Earnshaw was bringing some very good engineers with him from the Welbeck cotton mill, he had time to pursue his other goal, "to control the world's supply of crystals with faster-than-light properties." He could afford to purchase mineral rights anywhere in the world, if he could only locate a plentiful supply of faster-than-light crystals.

Einstein believed that Nördlingen was the location of a meteor strike. It stood to reason that there must be similar sites elsewhere, and James only needed one. If he had the crystals, he could control his own destiny by replicating or even improving on Einstein's design. His discoveries might even lead to time travel.

When James returned to his postgraduate studies in the autumn of 1921, Lawrence Bragg agreed that he needed to carry out fieldwork in support of his research. His search for faster-than-light crystals began when he spoke to Helen Watson, a professor at Leeds University. An eminent geologist and Fellow of the European Geological Society, with a lifelong interest in volcanos, she had recently published a paper on crater formation through impact from meteorites. James caught a train to Leeds and met her in the university's Great Hall.

'It's such a nice day. Why don't we walk and talk?' she suggested.

'Good idea,' said James. They strolled across Woodhouse Moor, its tree-lined paths carpeted with brown and gold autumn leaves.

'How can I be of assistance, Mr Driscoll?' she asked.

‘Please, call me James. I’m working on the structure of crystals. Specifically, crystals formed by meteor strikes. I’d like to carry out some fieldwork, but I’m not sure where to begin.’

‘Well, you won’t find much of interest here in Britain. You should go to Scandinavia.’

‘Why do you say that?’

‘I married a Swedish man and lived in Stockholm for many years, specialising in vulcanology. What I found interesting was that several craters did not appear to be volcanic at all. There were often ridge formations around the crater rim that strongly suggested an impact from some external force.’

‘Sweden it is then,’ he said.

Through Bragg’s contacts, he was able to spend the Spring Term at the University of Uppsala. The Swedish city was 150 miles by road or rail from the Siljan Ring which, at thirty-two miles in diameter, was the largest known impact crater in Europe. Professor Watson had identified several sites of interest, all located around the southern half of the ring.

There only remained the thorny issue of travel arrangements. There were no scheduled flights to or from Sweden, which was separated from mainland Europe by the Baltic Sea. James did not want to travel by boat, but the alternative was a logistical nightmare, an exhausting week-long drive through Germany, Poland, Russia and Finland. He was ready to throw in the towel and look for somewhere that was easier to get to, when he saw an advertisement in the London Times for the de Havilland Aeroplane Hire Service. After a phone call and a little negotiation, he agreed a price of four hundred pounds to charter a plane for two days. It was a huge amount of money to pay, but he was still unable to overcome his fear of water.

In January, James flew from London to Stockholm with an overnight stop in Copenhagen. From there, Uppsala was only a short train journey away. Each Monday morning, he caught a train to Rättvik on the eastern shore of Lake Siljan, staying in the same bed and breakfast hotel for the first three days of the week. From there, he either took a taxi east to Boda, or west to Mora. There were large deposits of crystalline rocks in both areas.

James worked tirelessly, collecting samples for further analysis. Every Friday was spent in the university laboratory, bombarding rock samples with ultraviolet light in the hope that the impact that created them, millions of years ago, had produced faster-than-light particles, as it had in Bavaria. During his time there, James found two previously undiscovered crystals, which he called driscolium and alicium. The latter, named after Alice, made him think of Elysium, the mythological dwelling place that virtuous people went to after death. He thought that was fitting.

At the end of the Spring Term, he returned to Rusholme with a large number of assorted rocks in his luggage. He was exhausted, but he refused to take a break. His work continued in the lab at Oakwood House, which he now owned. Paul Lucas had told him that he wanted to make a fresh start, away from academia and wagging tongues. He had been writing short stories to pass the time in prison, and thought he might enjoy writing spy novels, given his first-hand experience.

It was James who came up with the idea of swapping their respective properties in Rusholme and Aberystwyth. James' great-aunt Glynis was ready to retire, but Paul agreed to keep the property as a guest house, with Glynis' daughter Olwen remaining as manager. Paul would live on the top floor, in a street and a town where no one knew him. On his release in 1923, the income from the guest house would allow him to pursue a new, albeit poorly paid career, writing under an assumed name. It was an arrangement that suited everyone, especially Olwen, who found him mysterious and charming.

Armley Gaol, Leeds
June 1922

Winter was becoming more and more frustrated with life inside. Driscoll may have lost his parents, but he was still free to do whatever he wanted, with whoever he wanted, while Winter was cooped up in his cell. When he saw a headline in the newspaper that mentioned Driscoll by name, in relation to his performance in a local cricket match, he felt as if he was being taunted. Furious at his predicament, he decided that Driscoll needed a reminder that he was on borrowed time, so he wrote to Aunt Mitzi and asked her to do him a favour.

Two weeks later, James received a second parcel from Liverpool. This one contained a book that needed no explanation. It was a new bestseller, *If Winter Comes*, by ASM Hutchinson. The title left him in no doubt who it was from.

Grunewald, Berlin

On a warm, sunny, Saturday morning in Berlin, Walther Rathenau's chauffeur put the top down on the NAG-convertible, as he had done many times before. Rathenau climbed into the back and took the morning paper from his attaché case, before settling down for the short drive to the Foreign Office in Wilhelmstrasse. His driver made the usual left turn onto Konigsallee, where armed members of Organisation Consul lay in wait. Neither man noticed the open-top Mercedes until it was alongside them. It contained three men, all dressed in long leather coats and driving helmets. The driver, Ernst Werner Techow, was only twenty years old, the same age as Rudi Krämer at the time of Hans Paasche's murder. The two men in the rear seats, Erwin Kern and Hermann Fischer, were not much older, but they were trained killers.

Rathenau lifted his eyes from the newspaper and glanced to his left, straight down the barrel of a sub-machine gun. Before he could react, Kern opened fire, hitting him with a volley of bullets to the chest. As the Foreign Minister lay dying in a pool of blood, Fischer threw a hand grenade into the rear of the limousine, and Techow gunned the engine of the Mercedes, accelerating away with tyres squealing. In his rear-view mirror, he watched the grenade explode, tearing the vehicle apart. Thanks to Hermes, Rathenau had escaped death at the Imperiale Palace Hotel, only to die nine weeks later within a few hundred yards of his home.

Kirk Allerton, Yorkshire

When James read of his death, his first thought was unashamedly selfish. If Rathenau's killers could be caught and made to talk, Einstein might be able to repeat his earlier success and prevent his friend's death. If he could do that, there was nothing to stop him sending another warning about the train crash that was going to kill George.

Kern and Fischer died in a bloody shootout with police in July, but Techow was captured. When James read about it in the paper, he hoped that a confession would be forthcoming. To avoid suspicion, he sent Einstein a cryptic telegram, which read "CONDOLENCES ON THE DEATH OF YOUR FRIEND STOP LOOKING FORWARD TO SEEING GEORGE AGAIN STOP PLEASE CONFIRM INTENTIONS REGARDING MESSAGE STOP." Four days later, he received a reply that simply read "MESSAGE TO FOLLOW STOP." He heard nothing more for three weeks, so one evening he decided to call Berlin from the telephone he'd had installed in Oakwood House.

It was a rather sombre Einstein who came to the phone. 'My apologies for not contacting you,' he said. 'I'm afraid I was unable to save Walther or your father. The message did not reach its destination.'

'Why not?' asked James.

'The tube containing the crystal shattered.'

To James, it was the worst possible news. Even if Hermes was rebuilt, it would no longer be able to send messages back to a time before his father's death. Unless and until someone found a different way of changing the past, George and Alice were no more.

'Do you only have the one machine?' he asked.

'Yes, apart from the demonstration device, which was used too recently to be of any use. I was thinking of building a backup machine in case of emergencies, but I never got round to it.'

Well, it's too late now, Albert,' he said forlornly.

'I was going to ask you if you would be prepared to come to Berlin? I'm going to be travelling for several months, but I need an engineer to help me build a better Hermes.'

'That won't help me, though, will it? It won't bring my father back, or Alice.'

'No, it won't,' he admitted, 'but it might help others in the future.'

'Maybe, but I'm going to have to look for another way of changing the past. I heard that Nikola Tesla has some interesting theories.'

'And what if you should fail? What if there is no other way? What if ...'

James interrupted him, 'Life's full of what ifs, Albert. Wasn't it you who told me that you never fail until you stop trying?'

'It was,' he conceded, 'but if you should change your mind, you know where I am.'

James' put the phone down and screamed at the top of his voice. There were so many things he had wanted to tell his father, and he regretted ever having fallen out with him. Now, it seemed that his last chance of saving him had gone. Although he had made some important discoveries, his research had reached a point where he didn't know what to try next. He found himself repeating experiments that had always failed to produce any useful results. Was such repetition, as a nineteenth century writer had claimed, an indication of insanity?

He looked around the laboratory, feeling as he often did that the answer he was looking for was staring him in the face. Frustratingly, it refused to reveal itself. He picked up a glass-framed picture from his desk and stared at an image of Thomas Edison. Alongside it was a quote that read "I have not failed ten thousand times. I have not failed once. I have succeeded in proving that those ten thousand ways will not work. When I have eliminated the ways that will not work, I will find the way that will work." The picture had been a source of inspiration in the past, but no longer.

Because of his obsession with changing the past, James had never allowed himself to grieve for Alice. Now, after his latest failure, he was overwhelmed by pain and sorrow. In his troubled state, he sought solace in a bottle of whisky. It was his first drink in more than a year, and it was soon followed by a second. He started to think that perhaps Einstein was right. He could end up spending the rest of his life trying to achieve the impossible. When he had finished the bottle, he picked up the picture again. In a drunken rage, he threw it across the room, smashing the glass into a hundred pieces against the wall. He woke late the following morning, remembering little of the night before, but an empty bottle lay on the floor and his precious laboratory was wrecked. Almost nothing had survived intact.

When the Autumn Term began at Manchester University, Lawrence Bragg was not surprised that James' seemed downbeat after what must have been an unsuccessful trip to Sweden. He had no inkling of the distress that his latest setback had caused, but he could see that he had put on weight during the summer recess.

In their tutorials, he wanted to be supportive and asked whether everything was alright. James became tearful and was quick to change the subject. Bragg was aware that the death of his father and the attempt on his mother's life, following on from the loss of his fiancée, must have left him feeling extremely fragile, so he didn't pursue the matter.

Although James had repaired the damage done to his laboratory following his destructive rampage, he would lie awake at night, tormented by feelings of anger and worthlessness. He might be a rising star in the field of crystallography, but he took no pleasure from it. If he couldn't achieve the breakthrough he was searching for, his life was meaningless. As his frustration grew, he turned again to alcohol and cannabis tablets.

He went home for Christmas, but when Alfie asked to discuss some of the challenges facing the new business, he wasn't interested. He became irritable and argumentative, and eventually made an excuse to return to Rusholme early.

In the new year, James' attendance on campus became erratic. Bragg didn't make an issue of it at first, assuming that he simply felt more comfortable working in his own laboratory at Oakwood House. However, when James did make an appearance towards the end of term, he seemed distracted.

Bragg decided it was time to intervene. 'I want to know what you've been working on and what progress you've made,' he said.

'It's all in my head at the moment,' replied James evasively.

'Very well, but questions are being asked. I need you to document everything so we can discuss it properly the next time we meet.'

'Okay, I will,' he lied.

'This is not what I expected from you, James. You look terrible. Are you taking care of yourself?'

'I don't know what you mean,' he replied. 'I have a cold at the moment, and I've had a bit of trouble sleeping, but I'll be right as rain in a day or so.'

Bragg wasn't convinced. 'I'll take your word for it. Sort yourself out over Easter and come and see me at the start of next term.'

42

The Pennines, Lancashire
May 1923

The journey across the moors was not for the faint-hearted. On a sunny summer day, the views would have been spectacular, but in that morning's heavy rain and poor visibility, the steep, winding descent towards Manchester was hair-raising to say the least. A grim-faced Alfie drove his father's old Rolls-Royce as fast as he dared, but with a terrified Molly sitting next to him, he was rarely able to exceed thirty miles an hour.

Only two hours earlier, when Professor Bragg rang from the university, asking to speak to James, Molly had suggested that he try Oakwood House. She was surprised to learn that the number was unobtainable. The professor was deeply concerned at James' current state of mind. His behaviour and attendance had been erratic for some time, and he had not returned after Easter. Bragg had visited James' home three times in the last week. On each occasion, there was no answer, and the house was in darkness.

Alfie was ashamed to admit that he had not given his brother much thought in recent months. When they last met, they had argued about James' apparent lack of interest in the new business. There were several engineering issues that Alfie was sure his brother could have resolved, had he been there. When the subject was raised, James was uncharacteristically irritable and aggressive. They had parted on bad terms and hadn't spoken since. In the past, James would have let him know if he was going to be away for any length of time. Perhaps he was just being stubborn, but something didn't feel right.

The rain had turned to drizzle by the time they pulled into the driveway at Oakwood House. Alfie lifted the heavy brass knocker and struck the front door three times, while Molly went to check whether the rear door was unlocked. Alfie hammered on the door with his fist, but there was no answer. Molly's scream brought him running to the back of the house, where he found her rapping on the kitchen window.

'James!' she shouted. 'Are you alright?'

Alfie checked underneath a flowerpot by the back door. Thankfully, the spare key was still there. He unlocked the door, and they went inside. James was lying face down on the floor, unconscious, with an empty brandy bottle nearby.

'Jimmy, wake up!' shouted Alfie, getting down on his hands and knees next to him. There was a strong smell of alcohol.

'Turn 'im on 'is side, love,' said Molly. 'Shall I ring for an ambulance?'

'There's no phone, darling. Give me a minute to see if I can rouse him. He's breathing, at any rate.' With some difficulty, Alfie rolled James onto his side. His dressing gown fell open, leaving nothing to the imagination.

Molly gulped, but not from embarrassment. 'Alfie, just look at 'im!' The last time she had seen him, James was his usual, athletic self. Now, he looked several stones heavier. 'What's 'e bin doing to get in this state?'

'God knows. Can you get me a glass of water?'

Molly did as she was asked ''Ow are you gonna get 'im to drink it?'

'I'm not,' said Alfie, as he threw the water in his brother's bearded face.

James gasped and opened his eyes. They had a wild look that Alfie had never seen before. 'Warra yer doin'?' he snarled groggily.

'Take it easy,' said Alfie, putting his hand on James' shoulder. 'What in heaven's name has happened to you?'

'Why're yer 'ere?' he mumbled, pulling his arm away.

'Your professor called me. You haven't been seen on campus for over a month, and you didn't answer the door when he came to find you. He was worried.'

'I don't need anyone's help,' he said, slurring his words. 'Just leave me alone.'

'James, it's me, Molly. Please let us 'elp you.' Her calming voice seemed to bring him to his senses.

'I… I'm sorry, Molly. I don't need help. I'll be fine.'

'Have you looked in the mirror recently?' asked Alfie. 'You look like a tramp.' He held out a hand and helped him into a sitting position with his back against a kitchen cupboard.

'Cover yourself up, James,' said Molly as she averted her eyes. 'Your wotsits are on show.'

'Sorry,' he said, making a half-hearted attempt to rearrange his dressing gown. 'What day is it?'

'Monday, why?'

'What date?'

'Erm, the fourteenth.'

'It's Alice's birthday.' He struggled to his feet and leant against the cupboard. 'I want to light a candle for her.'

'Her birthday was last month,' said Alfie. 'It's the fourteenth of May, Jimmy.'

'May! What the hell happened to April?'

'I don't know. Sit down on this chair and talk to me.'

'I-I don't… I can't… '

'Just sit down, James,' said Molly, guiding him gently towards the chair. 'I'll make us a pot of tea.'

'There's no milk,' he said, sitting down on a chair that groaned under his weight.

'No matter, you can 'ave it black. You look as if you 'aven't slept in a week.'

'I have trouble sleeping. I'll be alright when I finish what I'm working on.'

'Which is?' asked Alfie.

'Just stuff. Stuff that Einstein said was impossible, but I never believed him.'

'Are you still trying to send messages back in time?'

James sighed. 'Yes, but further than Einstein could. If I can just crack this, there is no end to what I could achieve. I could save Alice, and Father. I could even stop you from spending years in a German hospital.'

The kettle began to whistle on the stove and Molly filled the teapot.

'Jimmy,' said Alfie, 'this obsession's going to kill you if you don't look after yourself.'

'I don't know what you mean. It's not an obsession; it's just my work.'

'And what happens if you're wrong and what you're trying to do is impossible? You're drinking again. You're not sleeping or getting any exercise. If you're in the lab all the time, you're not even getting any daylight. What are you eating?'

'I'll tell you what 'e's not eating,' said Molly, emerging from the larder with a wooden crate. 'You 'ave got milk, James. You must've 'ad a grocery delivery recently.'

'I don't remember.'

Rummaging in the crate, Molly said, 'There's milk, eggs, bread, butter, sugar, tea and chocolate. It 'asn't been touched, apart from the chocolate.'

'I like chocolate,' muttered James.

'So I can see,' said Alfie. 'Forgive me for saying so, Jimmy, but you're beginning to look a lot like Fatty Arbuckle.' Roscoe 'Fatty' Arbuckle was an American silent movie star who weighed almost twenty stones. 'And you stink.'

'If you say so.' This was not like James at all. 'He's a wonderful singer, you know. Caruso said so.'

'Who?'

'Arbuckle.'

'What's that got to do with anything? You're not listening to me, James. When was the last time you went for a run? You used to run every day, in all weathers. What's happened to make you like this?'

'Like what? I've been busy.'

Molly placed a steaming cup of tea in front of him. ''Ow many sugars?'

'Four, please.' Molly looked at Alfie and rolled her eyes.

'James, you're not well,' he said. 'Come back with us and we'll get Doctor McKenzie to have a look at you.'

'I have too much to do. I might come up at the weekend.'

'I don't believe you. Why did you disconnect your phone?'

'I needed peace and quiet. Too many distractions. Like now.'

'You'd still be unconscious on the floor if it wasn't for us, you ungrateful sod.' Alfie had never spoken to his brother like that before.

'I'd like you to leave now,' said James.

'We're not going anywhere. I'm going to find you some clean clothes.'

'I don't have any.'

'You must have something you can put on. What were you wearing yesterday?'

'This,' he replied, looking down at the grubby dressing gown.

'You didn't get dressed?'

'No point. I never see anyone from one day to the next. Besides, nothing fits me anymore.'

'Right. Molly's going to run you a bath and make you some breakfast. I'll nip down to Cromptons to get you some clothes. Get off your backside and pull yourself together. And have a shave!'

Cromptons were one of the largest clothing retailers in the north-west of England and one of the first to stock the Welbeck Ready-to-Wear range. Their store on Wilmslow Road was less than half a mile away. Having introduced himself to the manager, who knew him from a factory visit, Alfie picked two suits, shirts and assorted underwear. 'I don't know what size he is, Cyril,' he said. 'I would hazard a guess at six feet three and twenty stones.'

'No problem,' said Cyril. 'I'll give you everything in three different sizes. Bring back what doesn't fit.'

'Thanks, this should cover it,' said Alfie, handing over a twenty-pound note.

When he returned to Oakwood House, Molly was alone in the kitchen. ''E's 'ad a bath and summat to eat. 'E's up there now, 'aving a shave. I told 'im you'd bring 'im some new clothes when you got back.'

Alfie hugged her. 'Thanks. What am I going to do, Molly?'

'I 'ate to say it, but I think e needs to see a psychiatrist.'

James was locked in the bathroom when Alfie went upstairs. 'Jimmy, your clothes are on your bed,' he shouted from the landing. 'Find a size that fits and come down when you're ready. I need to talk to you.'

Back in the kitchen, Molly said, 'Don't be too 'ard on 'im, Alfie. 'E's not well.'

'I know. I wish I'd realised sooner.'

'It's not your fault.'

He decided to adopt a gentler tone when James came downstairs, looking tired but a little more presentable. 'I think you're having some sort of nervous breakdown, Jimmy. You've been working too hard and you're not taking care of yourself. You need some fresh air and exercise.'

'Stop fussing. I'll go for a walk this afternoon,' said James.

'No, you won't. You're coming back to Kirk Allerton with us. No arguments.'

James' eyes glazed over, and he grabbed Alfie by the throat, pushing him back against the wall and shouting, 'Don't tell me what to do!' He seemed barely conscious of what he was doing.

Molly screamed 'Stop it!' and grabbed his arm, but he pushed her away and she banged her head against the wall.

He looked shocked at what he'd done. 'I'm so sorry, Molly,' he said, releasing his grip and becoming compliant.

She hugged him tightly. 'You're scaring me, James. You can't go on like this.'

He looked into her eyes and his shoulders sagged. There were tears in his eyes as he said, 'Am I really going mad? I can't think straight anymore. I can't sleep, or if I do, I have terrible nightmares.'

'Come with us, Jimmy, please,' said Alfie. 'Just until you're feeling better. There's no harm in seeing Doctor McKenzie. He might be able to give you something to help you sleep.'

'Alright, but promise me you won't let them lock me away somewhere. I'm not a lunatic.'

'That's not going to happen, believe me.' Even as he said the words, Alfie wasn't sure if they were true. 'Let's get you back home. Mother's worried sick about you.'

43

Kirk Allerton, Yorkshire
May 1923

Doctor McKenzie was looking forward to a well-deserved retirement. At almost seventy years old, he didn't care much for new ideas and only had a limited understanding of mental illness. As the family physician for over thirty years, he knew James as an extremely fit and strong young man. When he visited Allerton Manor, he didn't recognise him at first. It was only when he spoke that he realised the bloated, shuffling shell of a man in front of him was James.

After spending twenty minutes with him, McKenzie spoke to his family, who were waiting anxiously in the drawing room. 'He's suffering from a severe bout of melancholia. It's not surprising when you think of the misfortune he's had to deal with.'

'Can you help him?' asked Ellen.

'I rather think he needs specialist psychiatric help. I'm particularly concerned about the delusions.'

'Delusions? What do you mean?'

'He tells me that he must go back to Manchester, so that he can go back in time and save his father. He seems absolutely convinced that he has some sort of special powers.' The doctor stressed the word powers, making it clear that he thought James was seriously disturbed.

'He's a scientist, doctor,' said Alfie. 'It's what he's been working on.'

'Well, he's clearly been working too hard, and it's resulted in a complete mental breakdown. In accordance with the Lunacy Act of 1890, serious mental cases are to be sent to an asylum immediately.'

'My boy's not a lunatic!' cried Ellen indignantly. 'He just needs a little rest and recuperation.'

'I'm sorry, Mrs Driscoll, the law is quite clear. I have no choice in the matter.'

'How long will he have to be there?' asked Alfie.

'It's difficult to say. Some patients recover in a matter of months. Others take years.' The vagueness of his answer made Alfie think that if James went into an asylum, he might never come out. 'It just depends on the seriousness of their condition when first diagnosed,' added McKenzie.

'We could look after him, doctor,' said Alfie. 'I'm sure he would be better off here than locked up somewhere.'

'I'm afraid that's not an option, Mr Driscoll. If he escaped and hurt someone, it's not your neck that would be on the block.'

'Does he have to go now?'

'No. It's getting late, and I can't do anything without a reception order. I'll speak to a magistrate in the morning and come back with the legal certification. Then he can be admitted to a hospital for the insane.'

The word insane was too much for Ellen, who began sobbing. Alfie had heard enough. He put a protective arm around his mother and gave the doctor a threatening stare. As politely as he could, he said, 'Thank you, doctor. We'll see you tomorrow.'

When McKenzie had gone, Molly was the first to speak. She hadn't said anything in the doctor's presence, for what she had to say would only have made matters worse. 'I'm sorry, Alfie, but 'e's talking utter rubbish. We do 'ave a choice.'

'What makes you say that?'

'I 'ad a friend at school whose mum was taken into the asylum in Burnley. I saw 'er a year or so back and she were very angry.'

'The mum?'

'No, my friend. She said the stigma of 'aving a lunatic for a mother were terrible. If they'd 'ad the money, she could've been treated in a private clinic without anyone knowing. She said it were one rule for the rich and another for the poor.'

'Poor woman,' said Ellen, who had become quite emotional at the sadness of the tale. 'What happened to her mother?'

'She died in there. She said she just gave up once they locked 'er away with all the idiots and imbeciles.'

'They're people, Molly!' said Alfie.

'I know that! They were 'er words, not mine.'

'That's so sad,' said Ellen, 'but if our money can help James, then so be it.'

'We don't have much time,' said Alfie. 'I don't know what to do.'

Molly had a sudden thought. 'What about Ron Stewart?'

'Ron's a speech therapist, Molly. He can't help us.'

‘I’m not so sure. When we were in London, I used to talk to ’im about your nightmares. ’E said ’e ’ad a roommate at college who might be able to ’elp. Some sort of ’ead doctor. ’E did a lot of work with men who were traumatised from the war.’

‘And you think he could help James?’

‘It’s worth a phone call at least.’

Alfie was pleased to be able to do something. Anything was better than doing nothing in the circumstances. ‘Right, well, I’ll ring Ron now.’

‘No need. ’E gave me the man’s card in case your nightmares got any worse.’

‘Have you got it with you?’

‘No, you ’ave. It should still be in that posh silver card case of yours. I tucked it in behind Ron’s card.’

Alfie hurried across to Allerton House and found the card case in his study. When he returned, he read from the card. ‘Dr Duncan Fraser FRCP. There are two Edinburgh numbers here. I’ll try ringing him from Father’s study.’

The operator connected him to the first number, which turned out to be the Royal Edinburgh Infirmary. A receptionist informed him that Doctor Fraser had left for the day. The second was answered by a man with a mellifluous, soothing voice.

‘Fraser,’ he said. The mention of Ron Stewart’s name broke the ice, and the two men had a long discussion about James’ mental state.

‘Can you help him?’ asked Alfie. ‘We can afford to pay.’

‘From what you’ve told me, it sounds as though your brother is suffering from depression. I have a private practice here in Edinburgh, and I work closely with a wonderful nursing home in Morningside. When could you bring him in?’

‘It has to be first thing tomorrow. The doctor’s going to have him certified once he has the order.’

‘Very well. I’ll make the necessary arrangements for his admission. Rest assured, he will not be certified.’

‘But what happens when the doctor turns up with a court order? Won’t the police start looking for him?’

‘Don’t you worry about that. You can tell him from me that under the 1862 Lunatics Act Amendment, your brother has been admitted voluntarily to a registered nursing home, for treatment of incipient and transitory mental disorder.’

'That sounds a lot better than insanity or lunacy.'

Fraser gave Alfie the address and said, 'I look forward to seeing you both tomorrow.'

Back in the living room, he gave Ellen the good news. Turning to his wife, he said, 'Molly, you never cease to amaze me! I think you may have just saved Jimmy's life!'

Armley Gaol, Leeds
September 1923

The visit from Ailbhe, Winter's sister-in-law, came out of the blue. He was almost halfway through his sentence, and his only visitor in the last two years had been his solicitor. As soon as he saw her face, he knew that it was bad news.

'What is it?' he asked. 'What's wrong?'

'Dieter's dead,' she replied, her voice cracking with emotion.

Her words were like a punch to the gut, leaving him struggling to speak. Ailbhe put her arm out to comfort him but was stopped by a warder.

'How?' he rasped. 'What happened?'

'He hung himself.'

Tears began to flow freely down her cheeks as she spoke, and Winter was close to tears himself. He wanted to give her a hug, but any form of physical contact was banned.

'Do you know why?' he asked.

'He's never been the same since the war,' replied Ailbhe. 'It messed with his mind. Barbed wire disease, they call it.'

'I don't know what to say. What will you do?'

'Feck knows. We have no money. Kathleen said she would get a job, but that's easier said than done.'

'How old is she now?'

'Fifteen, and Esther's twelve. I think it's the workhouse for us.'

In Ireland, the workhouse was a place where the poor could live and work in return for food. Conditions were deliberately harsh, as an incentive to leave and find somewhere better, but many had no choice. Ailbhe began to cry again, overcome by the hopelessness of her situation.

'That's not going to happen,' said Winter.

'Why not?'

'Because I'm going to help you.'

Back in his cell, Winter grieved for the brother he had grown up with, yet hardly knew. They had seen little of each other since he left for America as a teenager. He had no doubt that the British were to blame for Dieter's death, but he couldn't shake the feeling that he could have done more to help him, even from inside the prison walls. His only cause for comfort was the knowledge that he was keeping his promise to look after Dieter's family when he couldn't.

Three weeks later, Ailbhe received a letter from Winter's solicitor. Inside was a cheque for a thousand pounds, together with instructions to open an account at the Letterkenny branch of the Bank of Ireland. There was also a message from Winter. He told her that she should not think of the money as charity, because of his promise to Dieter. The money was of more use to her than it was to him, but she should make it last. He hoped that it would tide her over until she was able to get a job.

Ailbhe was overwhelmed by Winter's generosity. A thousand pounds was a fortune, perhaps five year's wages to an Irish worker. She wondered just how rich her brother-in-law was, and how he had earned his money. She made a promise to herself that, one day, she would find a way to repay him.

When the cheque cleared, she withdrew most of the money. Dieter had never trusted banks and had always kept their cash in an old wooden cigar box, hidden under a loose floorboard below their bed, and covered by a threadbare mat, on top of which stood a chamber pot. Ailbhe was sure that no one would want to look there.

Edinburgh, Scotland
November 1923

Duncan Fraser had studied psychiatry at University College London and was a follower of the pioneering Swiss psychologist, Carl Jung. He was particularly interested in ancient philosophical traditions and what they had to offer to the treatment of mental disorders.

Fraser advocated talk therapy as an alternative to the traditional approach of committing patients to a psychiatric hospital. Controversially, he used deep sleep therapy, a relatively new treatment involving an injection of barbiturates to render the patient unconscious for hours or days at a time. It would eventually be banned on the grounds of safety, after a number of patients died in their sleep, but in 1923 it was the most effective treatment available to those who could afford it. The aim was to reduce the patient's level of anxiety and agitation when he or she regained consciousness.

James' symptoms included sleep deprivation and feelings of anger, anxiety and guilt. He blamed himself for the loss of Alice and his father. More concerning to Fraser were his delusions. His obsession with time travel was a major concern. Fraser contacted Lawrence Bragg, who confirmed that his former student did indeed know Albert Einstein and had often shown flashes of genius. Perhaps he was not so delusional after all.

Fraser also used word association, hypnosis and dream analysis to more fully understand James' thoughts and feelings. He counselled him about his anger, helping him to find ways of controlling self-destructive behaviour. Alcohol was banned in the nursing home, and the staff helped James with his diet and exercise regimes. Every morning, he would go jogging with Fergus, the nursing home administrator and a former military man. They would jog round Blackford Hill, less than a mile away. Over many months, his level of fitness began to improve and the jog turned into a run, until one day he left Fergus in his wake and ran to the top of the hill, a climb of more than a hundred yards.

An unexpected benefit of Fraser's hypnosis therapy was that he cured James of his fear of water. For the first time in his life, he travelled by boat when they took the ferry across the Firth of Forth together.

Once he was satisfied that James' symptoms were under control, Fraser decided to contact his family. He let Alfie know that he was happy for James to go home, as long as he was not left on his own. He continued his convalescence at Allerton Manor under the watchful eye of his mother, but it would be another six months before he was well enough to return to university life.

In September, Ellen put her own life on hold and moved into Oakwood House with him, to make sure he didn't slip back into his old ways. On the first day of the Autumn Term, he was welcomed by Lawrence Bragg, who was now fully aware of James' illness and treatment. 'It's good to have you back,' he said. 'You've been sorely missed.'

'Thank you, Lawrence. The feeling's mutual.'

'I could really do with your help this year,' said Bragg. 'Crystallography is becoming such an important field of study, and our research programme is second to none. You could really make a name for yourself if you put your mind to it.'

'I'd like that, thank you. I'm feeling much better now, and I'm itching to get back to work.'

'I'm glad to hear it, but if you have any problems, please bring them straight to me.'

'I will, but you have my word. I won't let you down again.'

By the December of 1924, everyone had noticed that James was much more like his old self. He was eating properly, thanks to his mother, and sleeping better. As he became more disciplined about his working hours, Ellen agreed that he could return to Manchester alone after Christmas, as long as he agreed to her visiting every weekend.

44

Armley Gaol, Leeds
May 1925

British prisons changed significantly during Winter's years in Armley. There was a shift in emphasis from punishment towards reform, rehabilitation and even education of prisoners. Winter's diet improved, and heating was installed in his cell. He still sewed mailbags, and time passed slowly, but it gave him time to think. He read anything and everything he could lay his hands on, but his favourite works were by the great crime writers of the age. Someone told him that prison was a university of crime, and they were right. It was knowledge he would put to good use when the time came.

His first victim, the abusive priest, had deserved everything he got, as had his mother's lover, the pig farmer who for a time was the secret ingredient in Schmidt's pork pies. The same was true of his father's customers-turned-killers, even though it was unlikely that any one of them had dealt the fatal blow. They were guilty by association and paid the ultimate price. Winter had no qualms about their deaths, but he did feel bad about some of his earlier victims in turn-of-the-century New Jersey. It was clear that many of them had simply been hard-working men with families, struggling to make ends meet. Men like his own father.

With little else to occupy his mind in prison, he often thought of Edith Banks, although she would always be Maureen O'Neill to him. Other than Sinéad, Maureen was the only woman he had ever really cared about. Helping her was one of the few things he could look back on with pride. He'd kept in touch and received several letters from her over the years, telling him about the films she'd been in, the stars she'd met and the wonderful life she had in LA following her move there in 1920. In contrast, her latest scrawled and tear-stained letter was deeply troubling. Winter lay on his bunk and began to read.

Dearest Kevin,

This is such a hard letter to write, for I've not been truthful about my life here in my previous letters. My 'career' as an actress amounted to nothing more than a couple of minor roles. You wouldn't believe what a girl has to do to be successful here. I was once offered a leading role in a new movie, but then the producer forced himself on me. I tried to stop him, but he was too strong for me. When I threatened to go to the police, the role was given to someone else.

After that, I couldn't even get an audition. There was a rumour going around that I was a troublemaker, so I found myself penniless and pregnant with his bastard child. When it was born, I couldn't even look at it, so I gave it up for adoption. I live in a poor neighbourhood with no real hope of ever getting out. The only work I can get is in hotels or bars, but everyone takes advantage of you here. I find it hard to think about the future, only the past and what might have been.

I hope that prison hasn't been too much of an ordeal for you, and that you have not forgotten me. I will never forget the help you gave me all those years ago. I was very close to your friend Nico for a while, but he left suddenly, and I never saw him again. If you hear from him, please give him my love. There is more I could tell you, but I fear you would not forgive me.

Goodbye and good luck.

Maureen

She had never ended a letter with goodbye before, and what did she mean, he would not forgive her? He wrote back and asked his solicitor to enclose a cheque for two thousand pounds, made out to

Edith Banks and paid in US dollars. He knew it would leave him with very little in the bank, but his attitude to money had always been easy come, easy go. As far as he was concerned, if it helped Maureen to turn her life around, it was money well spent.

Coincidentally, he received a letter from Ellen Terry a few weeks later. Winter's conviction and sentence were headline news in 1918, so he was not surprised that she had tracked him down, but he was curious as to why. As he read her letter, the reason became clear.

> Dear Mr Winter,
>
> I am writing to you because when we met, it was clear that you cared deeply about Miss Edith Banks and had her best interests at heart. I wrote to her following our meeting at sea and found her to be a delightful and talented young woman. However, I recently received a very troubling letter from Edith, who I am sad to say has fallen on hard times after an alleged incident with the head of Newman Dean Studios. I am only too well aware of Mr Newman's reputation as a man who preys on young women and regards himself as above the law because of his wealth and power.
>
> Edith's letter was a cry for help from a woman at the end of her tether. I am worried that she may now feel there is only one way out. Although I am aware of your current predicament, I thought you might be able to use whatever influence you still have to help her in some way.
>
> Yours sincerely,
>
> Dame Ellen Terry, DBE

Her letter only deepened his fears for Maureen's state of mind. It also gave him what Maureen's letter had not – the name of the man responsible for her plight. One day, he would track Newman down and make him pay, but in the meantime, he could only hope that the cheque had made a difference. Days turned into weeks, but he heard nothing more from Maureen.

In August, a letter arrived from Thaddeus J White JD, an attorney with a Los Angeles law firm. It was brief and to the point.

> I am currently dealing with the estate of the late Miss Edith Banks, who passed away on July 10th, 1925. Please accept my condolences at this difficult time.

So, Ellen Terry had been right to be worried. If Maureen had taken her own life, Newman was a dead man walking. Winter balled his fists, furious that someone would use her and cast her aside like an unwanted toy. When his anger subsided, he continued to read.

> I was able to identify you from an item in the deceased's effects, viz. a letter dated July 5th, containing a cheque for $9,700.00, made out to the deceased. I can confirm that this amount was added to her estate, which will pass to your daughter Niamh in accordance with the terms of Miss Banks' will.

Winter stared blankly at the letter. He read the last sentence again and checked the name on the envelope, just to make sure it was really for him.

What the hell does it mean? he wondered. *Did Maureen have a daughter? My daughter? Why didn't she tell me? Was that what she meant when she said I would never forgive her?* He hadn't seen her since their Atlantic crossing in April 1915. If she had fallen pregnant then, the baby would have been born the following January.

Why had Nico never told him? Winter had no idea that for the first five years of Niamh's life, Nico had raised her as his own. He had wanted to be honest with his friend, but Edith asked him not to say anything. Her last letter was the first Winter knew of them being anything more than friends. Tragically, Varese's untimely death had been the start of the end for Edith. Without his support, she struggled for work, even though she was a talented actress.

Niamh would be about ten years old now, and Winter had so many questions for her. Did she know about him? Would she want to meet him? Had she been with Maureen when she died? He replied to the attorney's letter, asking for his daughter's contact details. A reply came several weeks later, informing him that she was in foster care, but that unfortunately the details were confidential. Nevertheless, she would be informed of her father's request. He waited in vain for her to contact him.

He was seven years into a ten-year sentence, with little prospect of parole, but the attorney's letter had changed everything. Winter was sure of one thing. He had to get out of this place. His first thought was to bribe one of the prison warders, but now he was short of funds, and there was no guarantee that anyone would help him once he had parted with his money.

He decided to write to Maurizio Varese, expressing his deep sorrow over the death of his eldest son, and asking whether he could provide details of the bank account that Nico had referred to. In late October, he received Moe's reply. He still referred to him as kid and thanked him for everything he had done for the family over the years, and for being a friend to Nico. His bookkeeper had been able to confirm that an account had been set up in Winter's name at the National State Bank of Newark, but in order to access it, he would have to visit the bank in person.

He started to observe prison routines, looking for any weaknesses that might make escape possible. The prison walls were very high, but if he could cause a distraction, there might be some way of getting over them. To do so, he would need a ladder, but unsurprisingly, the prison guards didn't leave such things lying around. To collect the materials needed to construct a makeshift rope ladder would take many months, and he wasn't prepared to wait. In any case, there were too many ways in which such a plan could go wrong.

He was beginning to think that Armley was escape-proof when, in November, he started chatting to his latest cellmate, an elderly and spectacularly unsuccessful petty thief from Durham, who went by the curious name of Chester Chicken.

'I come from a long line of poultry farmers,' he explained.

Chester had spent most of his adult life in prison, and joked that if his surname had been Starling or Sparrow, he might have been able to fly the coop. He told Winter that the closest he ever came to escaping was when he was rushed to Leeds City Hospital with a suspected heart attack. It turned out to be a false alarm, but he was handcuffed to a hospital bed and watched by a prison warder, before being returned to prison a week later.

'The only time that bugger wasn't watching me was when I went to the toilet,' said Chester.

Winter's ears pricked up. 'Did it have a window?' he asked.

'Now why would you be asking me that, lad? It did, as it happens, but I was in no fit state to do owt about it.'

'You didn't think of climbing out?'

'I did have a look, but where would I have gone at my age? Anyway, I was out of fettle at the time. I'd have either broken me neck or given meself a real heart attack. The ward was on the top floor!'

'That's a pity.'

It was obvious what Winter was thinking. Sensing the disappointment in his voice, Chester said, 'Mind you, if I'd been younger and fitter, I think I could have made it.'

'What makes you say that?'

'There was a drainpipe leading up to the roof. Don't ask me how I know, but there's a big metal fire escape on the other side of that building.'

45

Armley Gaol, Leeds
November 1925

Winter's knowledge of Leeds was limited to what he had read in a local history book in the prison library. The city began as one of many Yorkshire mill towns that prospered during the Industrial Revolution. It rose to prominence in the nineteenth century, due in large part to its great transport links to the ports of Liverpool and Hull, by canal and rail. That had given him an idea, but he would need outside help. He wrote to Ailbhe, asking her to request a prison visit. She was thrilled to receive his letter, having thought about him a lot in the two years since Dieter's death. His stories about life in America had made her realise just how boring her life had become. Her husband had been a good man, but he was so dull that her Irish friends had labelled him a 'dry shite.' She often wondered whether she had married the wrong brother.

A week later, she made the long journey from Tullybay, leaving her daughter Kathleen to look after her younger sister, Ellen.

'How are you bearing up, Kevin?' she asked when she saw him.

'I'm fine, Ailbhe, but things have changed. I have a daughter in America.' He told her about the letter from California.

'And you didn't know? That's grand, so.'

'It is, but I'm no good to her in here. I've got to get out, and I need your help.'

'Anything. Just name it.'

'I want you to go and see a man in Liverpool. He was a friend of my father. Mitzi can tell you where to find him. Now, don't write anything down, just listen.'

He told her his plan and her part in it. She owed him so much that she couldn't say no, even if she'd wanted to. When she left, she was trembling with anticipation. She was about to embark on the most exciting adventure of her hitherto humdrum life, and the stakes couldn't be higher. She would not let him down.

Winter chose a Friday night to put his plan into action. The hospitals were busier, so less attention would be paid to his admission. Not only that, but his plan would have more chance of success at the weekend, when the police were less vigilant. After lights out, he removed a knotted handkerchief from his pocket and poured its contents into a mug of water. Then he dropped to the floor and did a hundred press-ups, before drinking the salt water and waiting for it to take effect. It was almost eleven o'clock when he began to hammer on the cell door with the metal mug, eliciting several foul-mouthed complaints from neighbouring cells.

By the time a warder opened the door, Winter was curled up in a ball, drenched in sweat and holding his left arm. The salt water had made him throw up. 'Help me!' he moaned, hoping he sounded convincing.

'What's up, Winter?' asked the warder unsympathetically.

'Pains in my arm… and chest,' he mumbled with an agonised look on his face.

'Oh crap,' said the warder. Chicken had done a good job of describing his own symptoms because an hour later, Winter was in Leeds City Hospital, dressed in prison-issue pyjamas and handcuffed to a bed. An initial examination showed nothing untoward, but he was kept in overnight as a precaution.

In addition to Chicken's drainpipe idea, he had considered two alternative escape plans. The first involved Ailbhe posing as a nurse and somehow acquiring a key to unlock the handcuffs. He decided against it because the chance of Ailbhe being arrested as an accomplice was too great. The second was simpler and didn't involve anyone other than himself. He was uncharacteristically nervous at the thought of what was to come, so although he had a sleepless night, he pretended to be out for the count. At first light, when the ward was quiet, he began to moan softly, as if in pain. The dozing warder stood up and shook his shoulder. 'Winter, wake up.'

He stirred, as if from a deep sleep, and mumbled, 'Wassa marrer?'

'You were groaning. Are you alright?'

'I need the toilet. Can you take these cuffs off?'

'What do you take me for, an idiot?' Winter was shorter than him, and twenty years older. As far as he could tell, he posed no threat, but he wasn't about to remove the handcuffs completely. He produced a second pair, attaching one side to Winter's right wrist and the other to his own left. He unfastened the first pair from Winter's arm, leaving his left arm free. Had he bothered to check, he would have known that his prisoner was left-handed. It was an unexpected opportunity that wasn't part of his original plan, but Winter made the most of it. He pretended to stumble and went down on one knee, turning to his right at the same time.

The warder said, 'I've got you,' and started to lift him back to his feet. In so doing, he leant backwards, leaving his throat exposed. In that split second, Winter delivered a quick blow to his windpipe with the crook of his hand between thumb and index finger. It left the warder gasping for breath, and the punch that followed laid him unconscious on the floor. Working quickly, Winter freed himself with the key hanging from the warder's belt. Then he erected a screen around the bed to hide them from view. In less than thirty seconds, he was descending the hospital's rear stairs two at a time.

Konrad Weber had been Jürgen Schmidt's best friend for nigh on fifty years. Now pushing eighty, he hated the British almost as much as Winter. When Ailbhe turned up asking for his help, he didn't hesitate. He piloted *Jessica*, the narrowboat that had once belonged to Winter's grandfather, through the waterways of west Yorkshire to its current mooring, close to the junction of the Leeds and Burbeck Canal with the River Aire.

Ailbhe stubbed out her second cigarette of the morning and nervously checked her watch. It was five past seven. She stamped her feet and thrust her hands deep into her coat pockets to keep warm, hoping that Winter would be on time. Even if his plan worked, they could be in for a long, nerve-wracking wait. If he was being pursued, he wouldn't risk being seen near the canal. The boat was hardly his fastest means of escape. In fact, anyone walking along the towpath could easily keep up with it, which was precisely why he chose it. In his experience, the police would set up roadblocks and search woodland, on the assumption that an escaped convict would leave the area as quickly as possible. No one in their right mind would try to escape at four miles an hour.

Ailbhe needn't have worried. As she lit up another cigarette, a figure appeared in the distance, racing along the towpath towards them in his pyjamas.

'Start the engine!' she shouted to Weber.

Before climbing aboard, Winter checked that no one was watching. 'Good to see you again, Konrad,' he said, shaking his hand.

'Think nothing of it,' said the old man. 'Your papa would have done the same for me. That thing you wanted is on top of the wardrobe.'

'Thank you.'

'Get yourself inside before you're seen,' said Ailbhe. 'You'll find clothes and a pot of tea in there.'

Winter hugged her gratefully. 'I won't forget this, Ailbhe.'

'Get away with you. I owe you more than you will ever know.'

He went inside, and memories of childhood holidays came flooding back. His grandparents, sitting at the table, drinking schnapps, and playing cards. Him and his brother, sitting on single beds, reading. On top of the wardrobe was a double-bladed boot knife, left there by Konrad. The clothes and other items, bought by Ailbhe, were inside. Underneath them was a pile of old books. He picked one up and opened it. On the inside cover, he had scrawled his name when he was five years old. At that age the book, *Struwwelpeter* by Heinrich Hoffman, had scared him half to death.

In the galley, Ailbhe poured the tea, but Winter didn't return. She went to check on him and found him fast asleep in one of the single beds. When he woke, it was dark. He lifted his head from the pillow, but all he could hear was the *put-put-put* of the diesel engine.

'Hello, sleepyhead,' said Ailbhe, who was sitting on the other bed, watching him.

'How long have I been asleep?' he asked.

'A while. It's half past two.'

'In the morning? Surely Konrad needs a rest.'

'In the afternoon, Kevin. We're in a tunnel.'

'Ah, right. I'd better get dressed then.' Winter was beginning to wonder if his plan was actually going to work.

'I'll leave you to it. Do you want that cuppa now?'

'Yes, please. You know the drill if the police turn up?'

'Yes, stop worrying. We passed Huddersfield an hour ago. I'll get you that tea.'

'Don't go,' he said, taking her hand in his.

His touch sent a tingle through her body. Her heart began to race, and time seemed to stand still. There had been no one since Dieter. She closed the shutters on the windows before bending down and kissing him, and he put an arm around her slender waist, pulling her onto the bed.

An hour or so later, they were disturbed by a shout from Weber. 'Look sharp, the Bizzies are here!'

Ailbhe heard snippets of an exchange between Weber and another man. The words 'escaped prisoner' drifted over the sound of the engine, followed by something indistinct. She heard the man shout, 'Where from?' and Weber's reply, 'Huddersfield'. The engine stopped and she held her breath.

'Mind if I look around?'

'Please yourself, but my daughter's not well. She's in bed,' said Weber.

The door opened and she heard footsteps. She pretended to be asleep, but through half-closed eyes, she could see a uniformed man making his way through the darkened cabin. She stirred and said, 'Dad, is that you?'

'No, ma'am, it's the police.'

Too late, she saw Winter's prison-issue pyjamas, lying on the floor by the wardrobe. It never occurred to her that her eyes were accustomed to the dark, whereas the policeman could still see very little. He switched on his flashlight and saw that she was in bed, as Weber had said. Ailbhe thought it was only a matter of time before he saw the pyjamas, so she did the only thing she could think of. She sat up, allowing the sheets to fall to her waist. The young man blushed, but he didn't look away.

Ailbhe grabbed the sheet and covered herself, saying, 'Oops, sorry. Can I help you, officer?'

He became extremely flustered. 'Erm, I, er… I'm looking for a nipple… I mean, middle! Sorry! I'm looking for a middle-aged man, possibly wearing pyjamas, about five feet eight, with dark hair and a broken nose?'

'I see. Well, if you find him,' she said with a wink, 'could you send him my way?'

His cheeks burning with embarrassment, the policeman beat a hasty retreat, saying, 'Sorry to bother you, ma'am.' When he had gone, she got out of the bed and lifted the hinged base. Winter was lying naked in the underbed storage space with the knife in his hand.

'That was too close for comfort,' she said, handing him the pyjamas. 'You left these on the floor.'

The next day, as dusk was falling after fifty-four miles and thirty-one locks, Weber brought the *Jessica* to a halt at Burbeck, the western reach of the canal. Ailbhe was disappointed that this part of their adventure was over, for something amazing had happened. The greater part of the last twenty-four hours had been spent in the arms of her brother-in-law, and she had fallen in love. They talked more than they had in the previous twenty years, and it was such a thrill to be with someone who listened to her and seemed to be interested in what she had to say. Winter was very different to his brother, but he had been starved of female company. There was no way of knowing if he felt the same way about her.

They stayed below deck until they were ready to leave. To disguise himself, and because it was a cold day, Winter put on several layers of clothing under a greatcoat, scarf and flat cap, all purchased for him by Ailbhe. After saying goodbye to Konrad, they set off on foot towards the railway station in Macclesfield.

Once there, Winter remained in the shadows while Ailbhe bought the tickets. When the train arrived, they found an empty compartment where they could talk openly.

'Did you book the hotel?' he asked.

'I did,' she replied. 'A room in the name of Brown, paid in advance.'

'Good. We'll lay low for a couple of nights. By Tuesday, the police will think I'm long gone.'

'And after that?'

'If we make it to Ireland, I'll leave for the States from there.'

Ailbhe's face fell. 'America? For how long?'

'Forever. There's nothing left for me here, and I need to find my daughter.'

Tears filled her eyes. 'I t'ought that you and I…'

He put his arms around her and kissed her on the forehead. 'You don't understand. I want you to come with me.'

She looked up into his eyes. 'You do?'

'Yes! Wouldn't you like someone to take care of you for a change? While I was inside, I hated the thought that no one was waiting for me on the outside. If you'll have me, I'd like nothing better than to spend the rest of my life with you, Ailbhe. I think Dieter would be pleased.'

She was crying now, but they were tears of joy. 'Are you asking me to marry you?'

'I guess I am. What do you say?'

'Yes! But I'm not the one that needs looking after.'

'You may be right, but I know how hard things have been for you since Dieter died. You're an amazing woman, Ailbhe, and I'd like to make you happy. We'll be safe in America and I have money there. Once we're settled, we can send for your girls.'

'Ah no, I can't be leaving the girls behind,' she replied. 'They need their mam!'

'Well, if Kathleen can look after Esther until we find my daughter, I'll come back for them, I promise. What do you say?'

Ailbhe paused as she thought this over before coming to a decision. 'I'll have to talk to Kathleen, but yes, let's do it!' A sudden thought crossed her mind. 'Ah feck, I can't go! I don't have a passport.'

'Don't worry about that, you can travel on mine.'

'Won't the police be watching out for you?'

'Without a doubt,' he said. 'I can hardly travel under my own name, but I know someone in Dublin who can fix things.' Looking out of the window as the train slowed, Winter saw a sign that read Garston. It was the last stop before Liverpool Lime Street, where there was sure to be a police presence. 'Get your things together,' he said. 'We're getting off here.'

46

Liverpool, Lancashire
November 1925

The two fugitives checked into the Adelphi Hotel under the name Brown. Winter let himself into their room and placed a "Do Not Disturb" sign on the door, while Ailbhe went in search of room service. Their bed was a lot more comfortable than the one on the narrowboat, not that either of them really cared. The following morning, Winter turned his attention to the next part of the plan.

'How much money do you have?' he asked.

'On me? Probably enough to get us to Ireland,' she replied, 'but I've more at the cottage.'

'Good. I can't risk going to the bank. The police will be looking for us, but they'll be watching the ocean liners and the Dublin ferry. If we travel as Mr and Mrs Brown, we've a good chance of making it to Belfast.'

That afternoon, Ailbhe went on a recce. Winter was right, there was a definite police presence, but the docks stretched for seven miles and the police couldn't watch them all. She was scared and excited in equal measure. Scared at the thought that something could go wrong at any minute, but excited by the adventure that lay ahead. She found what she was looking for at the Prince's Dock office of Coast Lines Limited, where she bought two tickets for the overnight sailing to Belfast.

That night, Mr and Mrs Brown watched the English coastline recede into the distance before retiring to their cabin. In the morning, they were back on deck in time to watch the ferry arrive at Belfast Docks. From there, they decided to walk to the railway station to save what money they had left. They caught the early morning train to Derry, where they ate breakfast in a café near the station.

'How do we get to Tullybay from here?' asked Ailbhe.

'I'm about to find out,' said Winter. 'Wait here.' He returned in less than ten minutes, and she followed him to a nearby street, where several cars were parked. Within minutes, they were driving west out of the city in a stolen Model T Ford touring car. On the

Letterkenny Road, they used the last of Ailbhe's money to top up with fuel.

Rusholme, Manchester

James breathed in the fruity aromas of the Prunier cognac, swirling it around the glass before savouring the subtle, sweet taste of the amber liquid. He had once vowed never to drink again, but the recent discovery of several bottles in the pantry, left behind by Paul Lucas, was too much of a temptation. James reasoned that it wouldn't hurt to have the odd glass, but only on special occasions.

He decided to open a bottle when he saw the evening's programme of music listed in the Radio Times. It included a live radio broadcast of an orchestra performing at the Majestic Hotel in St Annes. Six years earlier, the hotel was known as the Imperial Hydro, the venue chosen for his wedding reception. The music, and the thought of what might have been, triggered memories that brought him to tears, but a loud knock snapped him out of his misery. He coughed and blew his nose before opening the front door. DCI Hughes was standing under the portico, trying to close his umbrella. 'Chief Inspector, what brings you out on a night like this?'

'I'm afraid I have some rather disturbing news that I wanted to share face-to-face, Mr Driscoll. May I come in?'

James' mind was racing as he led the way to the living room. 'This isn't a social visit, then? What's happened?'

'I thought you'd want to know that Kevin Winter escaped from Armley Gaol on Saturday.'

James' mental state was still fragile, and the pent-up feelings of fear and anxiety returned. He poured himself another brandy and downed it in one. 'Do you know where he is now?' he asked.

'We don't know, but we think he may try to return to America. He injured a prison warder while escaping, so we have to assume that he's armed and extremely dangerous. Every force in the country is on the lookout for him.'

'Do you think he might come for me, or my family?'

'I'm keeping an open mind. Anything I say would be pure speculation, but if he's still in the country, we don't expect him to be on the loose for long.'

'Then you're underestimating him, Inspector. You only caught him last time because he came after me.'

'True, but we'll be ready for him if he tries it again. With your permission, an officer is going to escort you to and from the university until the end of term. I've also contacted the Thurwell Valley Police, who are assigning an officer to keep an eye on your family.

James wasn't naive enough to think that the police could keep his family safe. 'That's very good of you,' he said, 'but if Winter's determined enough, there's really nothing the police can do to protect us, is there?'

'Quite honestly, no, sorry. The best we can hope for is to catch him in the act. Would you consider moving away from here until he's back inside?'

'Not for one moment. I wouldn't want to give him the satisfaction. Anyway, I have my work, so he could always find me on campus.'

'Fair enough. We will catch him, Mr Driscoll. It's just a matter of time.'

'Isn't everything?' said James. He couldn't sleep that night, but in the early hours he decided that enough was enough. Whatever Winter planned to do to him, it couldn't be any worse than living in fear of what he might do.

James had a gun in his bureau drawer, and from now on he would be sure to carry it with him at all times. His transformation from pacifist to would-be murderer was something he preferred not to think about.

James tried to live as normal a life as possible, which meant spending long hours at the university, or in his lab. In his spare time, he returned to his old routine of jogging in Platt Fields Park. Even though he wasn't yet fully fit, the middle-aged constable assigned to protect him couldn't keep up. Had he done so, he might have noticed James in tears whenever he ran past the bench where he proposed to Alice. He was still grieving for the loss of the love of his life, and he could still hear her laughter as Dalton ruined his proposal.

The presence of the policeman, and the constant fear that Winter might be lurking in the bushes made James extremely nervous. If that deranged criminal was planning an attack, there was little the officer could do to prevent it. It would be a relief when the autumn term ended, so that James could rejoin his family in Kirk Allerton.

Tullybay, County Donegal

The cottage was in darkness when Winter and Ailbhe arrived.

'Where are the girls?' he asked.

'They should be here,' she said with a worried look on her face. Inside, it was clear from the sinkful of dirty dishes that someone was living there. It was late when the door opened and in walked Kathleen, Ailbhe's eldest daughter.

'Where have you been till this hour?'

'Hello, Mammy. It's lovely to see you, too. Hi, Uncle Kevin.'

'Kathleen,' he replied.

'I'm working at O'Brien's now,' she said, referring to the only pub in the village.

'Ah, that's grand, so,' said her mother. 'Come here and give me a hug.'

They embraced, and Kathleen turned to her uncle. 'What are you doing here?' she asked. 'I t'ought you were in prison.'

Winter shared a look with Ailbhe, who said, 'He's out now and before you ask, we've become quite close recently.'

'Really? You and Uncle Kevin?'

'Yes. Where's Esther?' she asked, keen to change the subject.

'Gone.'

'What do you mean, gone? Gone where?'

'She left a note. Said she was going to Dublin to stay with a friend.'

'Mother of God! How? She has no money.'

'Well, she must have got some from somewhere.'

Ailbhe's face fell. Without saying a word, she turned on her heel and went into the other room. When she emerged, she was carrying an empty wooden box.

'It's all gone!' she said. 'The *sleveen*!'

She glanced at Winter, who asked, 'How much was in there?'

'I don't know exactly. A hundred or so.'

'Come here,' he said, putting his arms around her. 'Don't worry, we'll manage.'

'How? How are we going to get to America now?'

'America? What are you talking about?' asked Kathleen.

'A new life, for all of us. I was going to discuss it with you.'

Winter interrupted her. 'We can talk about that later. There are people in Dublin who owe me a favour or two. Why don't we go there together and look for Esther?'

Ailbhe nodded. Looking at Kathleen, she asked, 'What's the name of this friend?'

Kathleen picked up a letter from the table and handed it to her mother. It was an invitation from a schoolfriend whose family had moved to Dublin the previous year, and it included an address in the north of the city.

'Let's go and get her back,' said Winter.

'How?' asked Ailbhe. 'You can't keep driving round in a stolen car.'

'Don't worry about that. Model T Fords are like arses nowadays, everybody has one. I changed the plates to match one of the ones I saw in Derry, so as long as we don't go back there, it will look perfectly legal and above board, even if the Gardai stop me.'

'Something tells me you've done this before!'

'I just know better than to draw attention to myself. Now, do you have a recent photograph, Ailbhe? We'll need it for the passport anyway, and it might help to find her.'

'I do,' she said. 'It's about a year old.'

'That'll have to do,' he replied. 'We'll leave in the morning.'

'But we don't even have money for petrol,' said Ailbhe.

'I've a little put away,' said Kathleen. 'Not much, but you're welcome to it.'

Ailbhe hugged her daughter and began to cry. 'How can two girls be so different?'

'I'll pay you back, Kathleen,' said Winter. 'I have money. I just can't lay my hands on it right now.'

In Dublin, Winter parked the car in a quiet street in Killester and found the address in the letter. A heavyset man answered the door but denied knowing anything about Esther or her whereabouts. Ailbhe recognised him as the father of one of Esther's old schoolfriends.

'Dermot, it's me, Ailbhe.'

'I'm sorry, missus, I've never seen you before,' he lied. He tried to shut the front door, but Winter's boot was in the way.

'Get off my doorstep,' he growled aggressively, pushing Winter down the garden path. The next moment, he found himself lying on his back in a rose bush. It didn't take Winter long to persuade him to cooperate.

'Where is she, Dermot?' asked Ailbhe, who was mightily impressed by the way Winter had handled himself.

'She was here,' he grunted, 'but she left about a week ago. Said she'd met someone.'

'And you just let her go? She's the same age as your daughter!'

'I told her to go home. She was a bad influence on our Siobhan.'

Back at the car, Winter asked, 'What do you want to do?'

'I'm sorry, Kevin,' said Ailbhe. 'I'm not leaving until I know she's safe.'

He thought it unlikely that she would ever leave her girls alone again after this, but he could see the determination in her eyes.

'We both have a daughter to find,' he said, taking her hand in his. 'I know people. Let me ask around and see what I can find out.'

They checked into a room at Wynn's Hotel, the place where he had first met Sinéad McKenna. From there, they visited the city centre pubs, where Winter showed Esther's photograph to the bar staff. None of them had seen her.

Ailbhe was becoming frantic. 'What if something's happened to her, Kevin?' she asked.

'I'm sure she's alright,' he replied, 'But if you're worried that she might be hurt, why don't we try the local hospitals to see if she's been admitted?'

'Okay, anything's better than sitting around doing nothing.' She spoke to the hotel receptionist, who gave her a map of the city, on which she marked the main hospitals. They crossed the river and found Sir Patrick Dun's Hospital on Grand Canal Street. No one by the name of Esther Schmidt had been admitted. It was the same story at the Royal Hospital, Mercer's Hospital and St Kevin's, close to the Guinness Brewery. When they reached St Patrick's Hospital for Imbeciles, Ailbhe refused to go inside, waiting on the street while Winter spoke to the Medical Superintendent. It was getting late, so the hospitals on the north side of the river would have to wait until the morning. As luck would have it, their route back to the hotel took them past Dr Steevens' Hospital, which had not been marked on the map.

The Matron there looked at the photograph and said, 'I can't be sure, but we had a girl called Esther in here last weekend. She'd been badly beaten in Benburb Street, in the city centre. Unfortunately, she discharged herself before we could get her details.'

'Was she alright?' shouted Ailbhe as the Matron headed away down the corridor.

'They both were,' she called out as she hurried away.

'Both?' she queried, but the Matron had gone.

47

Dublin, Ireland
December 1925

Winter knew all about Benburb Street. It was about a mile to the west of their hotel, close to Collins Barracks, the home of the Eastern Command of the Irish Defence Forces. It was right in the middle of an infamous red-light district, and if Esther had been there late at night, he thought it could only mean one thing. When he shared his suspicions with Ailbhe, she became hysterical, blaming herself for not being there to protect her youngest child.

'We have to find her, Kevin,' she sobbed. 'Where is she?'

'If I was a betting man, I would say that her pimp wanted her back on the street, earning money, rather than lying in a hospital bed.'

'Oh Jaysus! She's only fifteen!'

'I'll have a drive along Benburb Street tonight and look for her. You'd better stay at the hotel.'

'No way. You go there on your own and you'll get yourself arrested!'

'Alright, but we have to be discreet. No giving out to anyone, no matter what you see.'

By half past ten, they were parked in a darkened side street with a view of the main road.

'If anyone walks past, we'll pretend to be canoodling,' said Ailbhe.

'Why pretend?' he asked, which helped to relieve the tension a little.

The street was full of working girls, particularly when the pubs shut, and large numbers of drunken soldiers passed through on their way back to their barracks. Things quietened down eventually and at midnight they gave up and returned to the hotel.

The following morning, Winter met an old friend for a drink, while Ailbhe walked the streets of Dublin, hoping to catch sight of Esther. When she returned, Winter had news.

'I've sold the cottage,' he said. 'We have enough money to get to the States.'

'What?' she replied. 'Who to?'

'Someone with plenty of money. He's always fancied a holiday home on the west coast.'

'But where are the girls going to live while we're away?'

'They can stay there until we get settled in America. The deal's already done.'

'You're full of surprises, Kevin Winter!'

'We needed money more than we needed the cottage. I'm just being practical.'

That evening, they returned to Benburb Street and sat in the car, watching and waiting. By midnight, most of the night's revellers had gone home. They were both thinking that this had been a huge waste of time, when they saw her being marched along the street against her will by a muscular, middle-aged man. She was struggling to break free when he turned and slapped her across the face. Ailbhe was out of the car and running across the road before Winter could stop her. She screamed and leapt on the man, clawing at his face and neck.

'Get your hands off me, bitch,' he shouted, grabbing her by the hair. He held her at arm's length before punching her hard in the face. She fell onto the stone pavement and lay there, semi-conscious. The man turned back towards Esther, just in time to catch the full force of Winter's boot between his legs. He sank to the ground, clutching his groin and rolling around in agony.

Winter helped Ailbhe to her feet and took his niece by the arm. 'Esther, it's Uncle Kevin,' he said. 'Come with us now and don't look back.'

She began to struggle and when he looked into her eyes, it was obvious that she'd been drugged. When she saw Ailbhe, she cried out, 'I'm sorry, Mammy!'

'You're safe now, sweetie,' she said. 'We're going to take you home.'

'Let's get you into the car,' said Winter. 'Who's that man?'

'We all work for him,' she mumbled. 'We work and he gets the money.'

'Right, wait here,' he said. Crossing the road again, he started to go through the man's pockets.

'I'm gonna kill you,' snarled the pimp, pulling a knife from his belt. Winter grabbed his arm and twisted, leaving him unable to move as he prised the knife from his grasp.

'I know what you are,' he hissed. 'One of your girls leaves, so you punish the others. Well, not this time. You really should have found a different profession, my friend.' With his back to the car, Winter plunged the knife deep into the man's chest, killing him almost instantly. He took a large wad of money from his jacket pocket and punched him hard on the jaw. From Ailbhe's seat in the vehicle, there was nothing to suggest that the man was anything other than unconscious.

When they got back to the hotel, Ailbhe made Esther put on her coat to cover up the fact that she was dressed like a hooker. Winter distracted the night porter and they smuggled her into their room.

In the morning, they let her sleep while they went down to breakfast.

'That's quite a shiner you've got there,' said Winter.

'I don't care,' replied Ailbhe. 'We got her back, that's all that matters.'

'What do you want to do now?' he asked.

'I have to talk to her. I want to know why she up and left the way she did.'

'I hope she's alright. I have to find Niamh, but if you'd rather stay here, I'll understand.'

'I don't know what to think right now. Can you give me a little time?'

'Of course,' he replied. They entered the lift to go back to their room, and she kissed him more passionately than she had ever kissed her late husband.

Winter responded, saying. 'I love you, Ailbhe.' That tipped her over the edge. Dieter had loved her in his own way, but he never said the words.

'I love you too,' she said, tears running down her cheeks. 'How can I ever repay you for what you've done, Kevin?'

'Oh, I can think of something,' he said with a cheeky smile. 'But maybe not with your daughter in the same room!'

While Esther had a much-needed bath, Ailbhe laid out some spare clothes for her to change into, before gathering up her old clothing and disposing of it in a large bin at the rear of the hotel. On the journey back to Tullybay, she sat beside Esther in the back of the car.

'How did this happen, darling?' she asked gently.

'What do you mean?'

'How did you end up working for that man?'

Esther began to cry. 'He found me on the street and said that, if I didn't do as he said, he would kill me and my family. Is he going to come after us?' she asked.

'No,' said Winter. 'I made sure of that.'

The rest of the journey was uneventful, although Esther cried for most of it. At one point they had to pull over so that she could throw up. Back at the cottage, thanks to Kathleen, a large pan of broth was keeping warm on the stove. When they had eaten, Winter asked them to listen to what he had to say.

'You girls deserve to know what I'm doing here after all this time, so I'm going to trust you not to repeat this to anybody. If you do, I could end up back inside.'

'Inside where?' asked Esther, who had regained some colour in her cheeks.

'Prison,' he replied. 'I escaped a few nights ago, and your mother helped me to get here.' Kathleen looked questioningly at Ailbhe, who looked down at the floor.

'Let me explain,' he continued. 'I found out that I have a daughter in America. She's only ten, and her mother's just died.'

'Why were you in prison?' asked Esther.

'It's a long story. My daughter doesn't know anything about me, but I have to find her.'

'So, what are you doing here?' asked Kathleen.

'I made your father a promise a long time ago that if anything happened to him, I would look after his family. I'm going to keep that promise.'

'What if we don't want your help?' she said.

'Kathleen!' exclaimed Ailbhe. 'Uncle Kevin has already helped us in ways you can't imagine.'

'How?' she asked.

'He's put a roof over your head for a start!' she shouted. 'This is his house.'

'Well, that's not exactly true,' said Winter.

'Sorry, I was forgetting. This was Uncle Kevin's house. He's just sold it so that we can afford to go to America.'

'We? What do you mean, we?' asked Kathleen indignantly.

'Well, I mean me and Uncle Kevin, for now?'

'Why would you leave us on our own while you go to the other side of the world with your brother-in-law?' asked Esther, tearfully.

'Because we love each other, and it's not the other side of the world!' she replied.

'Might as well be,' said Kathleen. 'Why didn't you ask us what we thought first?'

This was not going the way Ailbhe had hoped. 'We're asking you now,' she said.

'Where are we supposed to live, while you're off gallivanting?' replied Kathleen.

'You can stay here,' said Winter. 'I've rented the cottage back from its new owner for a year.'

'What happens after that?' she asked.

'Well, I'm hoping you'll both decide to come to America and live with us and my daughter. If I can find her, that is.'

'And if we don't want to?'

There was an awkward silence, until Ailbhe said, 'Then I'll come back, and we'll find somewhere else to live. I don't think you quite appreciate the opportunity you're being given here, but if you want to stay, rather than start a new life in America, that's up to you.'

Kathleen wasn't convinced. 'So, you would give up Uncle Kevin for us?'

'If I have to,' said Ailbhe, glancing at Winter and hoping he would understand.

'I really hope that doesn't happen,' he said, 'because since we've been together, your mam's been happier than I've ever seen her. Do you want to make her miserable again?'

'No, of course not,' said Kathleen, 'but this is all so sudden. Why do you want us to stay here for the time being? Why can't you take us with you?'

'Because we don't have anywhere to live yet. When we find Niamh, we'll get a place. Then your mam can stay to look after her, while I come back for you.'

Kathleen looked at Ailbhe. 'Is it what you want to do, Mammy?'

'Yes,' she said firmly. 'The only thing keeping me here is you two, but if you don't want to go, that's fine. It's up to you.'

'If you do come, you'll never have to worry about money again,' said Winter, 'and all the American boys will be beating a path to your door. What do you say?'

Kathleen turned to her sister and asked, 'What do you think to all this?'

Esther smiled. 'There's one tiny problem, as far as I can see.'

'What's that?' asked Ailbhe.
'I'm pregnant.'

Esther's announcement was a huge shock, but Ailbhe tried to stay calm. 'How do you know?' she asked.

'Someone punched me a week or so back and I ended up in hospital. They said that my baby was fine. That was the first I knew about it.'

Of course, thought Ailbhe, *the Matron said they were 'both' alright*. 'Who's the father?' she asked, but when she saw Winter roll his eyes, she realised it was a stupid question.

'How should I know?' said Esther. 'Some soldiers?'

'Don't get smart with me, young lady,' she said angrily. 'Something like this could ruin your life.'

'That's not very helpful, Mammy,' said Kathleen. 'It's what happens now that matters.'

As a devout Catholic, Ailbhe had no doubt what had to happen. 'Esther's fifteen. She's my responsibility, so she'll have the baby, and we'll put it up for adoption.'

'Oh no we won't!' shouted Esther. 'I'd rather die than have this… thing.'

'Everyone, just calm down,' said Winter. 'I think the best thing we can do is sleep on it. Things may seem different in the morning.'

He was right. When he woke, the bed was empty. He found Ailbhe sitting in her rocking chair by the fireplace in the front room. She'd been crying. He bent down and kissed her before putting more logs on the fire. 'What am I going to do, Kevin?' she asked.

It was freezing outside, or he would have suggested going for a walk. 'What can you do?' he asked. 'She's a headstrong lass, Ailbhe. The last thing you want is for her to go and pay someone to get rid of the baby.'

'You don't have to tell me that,' she said. 'That's how my sister died.'

'I'm sorry. I didn't know you had a sister.'

Ailbhe told him about her older sister Kathleen, who found herself pregnant and paid an old woman five pounds to take care of it. Three days later she died from an infection.

'I don't know what to do. The baby's done nobody any harm, Kevin. Getting rid of it is murder, plain and simple.'

'I don't think Esther would see it like that. Why don't you tell her about your sister? She's more likely to have the baby if she thinks it was her idea. If you try to force her to have it, she may never forgive you.'

Ailbhe did as he suggested. It was the first time she had ever told her daughters about her sister. Kathleen cried when she heard her mother talk fondly about the woman she was named after. Esther listened intently to the details of her aunt's death but said nothing. Quite wisely, Ailbhe didn't ask her to decide there and then.

An uneasy truce followed. As Christmas approached, Winter used some of the pimp's money to buy a tree. He took Ailbhe into Donegal, where they spent lavishly on food and presents. It made Christmas Day unforgettable. After opening their presents, they sat down to a traditional goose roast with all the trimmings.

'Thank you, Uncle Kevin,' said Esther.

'Think nothing of it,' he replied. 'Your dad would have done the same if he'd had the money. His family meant everything to him, you should know that.'

'We do,' said Kathleen.

Winter waited until the new year before mentioning America again. He discussed it with Ailbhe first. When they spoke to the girls, it was clear that Christmas had given them a taste of what their life could be like in the future. There was no argument when he told them that he and Ailbhe planned to leave the following week.

When Esther wasn't around, he gave Kathleen an envelope full of money. 'With what you earn at the pub, there should be enough there to tide you over until I can send more. Find somewhere safe to hide it. Somewhere Esther won't think of!'

'I will Uncle Kevin, thank you. What about the baby?'

'It's due in the summer,' said Ailbhe. 'There's a mother-and-baby home in Sligo, run by nuns. I want to know that everything's in place before we leave.'

'Esther might not be happy about that,' said Kathleen.

'I know,' said Ailbhe. 'I'm trusting you to keep a close eye on her. You know what I mean.'

'Yes, Mammy. Don't worry, we'll be fine.'

'Whatever happens, I'll be back before the baby's born,' said Winter.

While Ailbhe packed their suitcases, Winter drove to Dublin again, returning with a new passport. It had cost him fifty pounds and was indistinguishable from the real thing. When he showed it to Ailbhe, she had no idea it was fake, as it was the first one she'd ever seen. Inside the blue cardboard-covered booklet was Winter's photograph, along with those of Ailbhe and her daughters. Officially, they were now the Brown family, and three days later, after driving to Cobh, as Queenstown was now known, they disposed of the Model T and sailed for New York on the SS *Hagen*.

48

Kirk Allerton, Yorkshire
January 1926

In England, the Driscoll family Christmas had been lovely, but James couldn't get Winter out of his head. He hated living in fear of what might happen and never went anywhere without his gun. So that he was as prepared as he could be, he went running every morning, becoming stronger and fitter. When he returned to Manchester, DCI Hughes told him he was confident that Winter had left the country, but James wasn't so sure.

New York City

Winter was back on American soil for the first time in ten years. He hailed a cab to take Ailbhe to the Waldorf Astoria, where their luggage was due to arrive later that day. When she left, he made his way to Newark by ferry and bus. On Broad Street, he visited the National State Bank, where Moe had said there was an account in his name. He was now Kevin Brown, but he carried his old passport with him for identification.

At the counter, he asked one of the tellers what he needed to do to access his account, but he was unable to give a permanent address or details of employment. All he could really tell him was that he thought the account was set up in 1914, so the teller asked him to wait in a side room while he investigated. After ten minutes, Winter started to become anxious and was almost ready to leave when an older man entered the room carrying a ledger and a handwritten sheet.

'Mr Winter,' he said. 'I've managed to find an account in your name, but it has a co-signatory. Can you tell me who that might be?'

'The only person I can think of would be a Mr Varese,' he replied. The name seemed to do the trick.

'That all seems to be in order, sir. Now, how can I help you?'

'I'd like to know the balance of the account, please,' said Winter, 'and then I'd like to withdraw the funds.'

‘Very well,’ he said, as he consulted the sheet. ‘At close of business last night, there was precisely fifty-three dollars in the account. Would you like a cheque or cash?’

Winter was dumbstruck. When the man said fifty-three, he had expected the word thousand to follow. Someone had helped themselves to his money.

‘Mr Winter?’

‘Sorry, I, erm, there must be some mistake. I’d expected a much larger amount.’

The man consulted the ledger. ‘I can see here that your co-signatory withdrew 43,000 dollars in December,’ he said.

‘Who exactly is my co-signatory?’ asked Winter.

‘Massimo Varese. I assume that you know him?’

‘Of course,’ he said. Moe must have had a good reason for taking the money. ‘I’ll take the balance in cash, if that’s alright, and can I also exchange pounds for dollars?’

Winter left the bank with less than two thousand dollars in cash, having converted the last of the pimp’s money. It was enough to get them to California, but it would not last long. He needed to speak to Moe.

In Hoboken, the Varese estate was not as grand as he remembered. Cracked, peeling paintwork and overgrown gardens gave the place a ramshackle appearance.

‘Kevin Winter to see Mr Varese,’ he said to the guard at the main gate. He didn’t recognise any of the men patrolling the grounds.

One of them trotted up to the house and returned to confirm that he could enter, once he had been checked for weapons. Inside, he was kept waiting for almost an hour, before being ushered into Varese’s study. Nico’s younger brother Guido stayed seated as he entered the room.

‘Hello, Guido. I was hoping to speak to Moe.’

‘You know a *medianità*?’ he asked.

‘A what?’

‘A *medianità*. ’Ow you say, a medium? Papa died two months ago. I’m runnin’ things now.’

‘I’m sorry, I didn’t know. I wanted to say how sorry I was about Nico.’

‘Ah yes, Nico. Maybe you can tell me what the ’ell ’e was doin’, gettin’ ’imself killed in your backyard?’

'He wasn't in my backyard,' protested Winter. 'He was my best friend, and he was just trying to help me. They told me he was killed by the police, but I have no idea what happened, exactly.'

'Maybe not, but if it 'adn't been for you, my big brother would still be alive, ain't that so?'

'Perhaps.'

'Perhaps? Papa thought a lot of you, kid, but you're finished 'ere. You're gonna leave and never come back, *capisci*?'

'I'm sorry you feel that way, but there's another reason for my visit. My bank account has been emptied by someone using your father's name. I'm happy to take a cheque, if it's not too much trouble.'

'Really? How much are we talkin' about?'

'43,000 dollars.'

Guido laughed. He looked at the only other man in the room, who shook his head. 'I don't know nuttin' about an account.'

'Can I speak to Moe's bookkeeper? He's the one who set the account up.'

Guido shrugged. 'He disappeared after Papa died. Maybe he took your money.'

'What's his name?'

'You won't find him, 'e's gone.' The smile on Guido's face left Winter in no doubt that the bookkeeper had not disappeared voluntarily. It was clear that he was wasting his time.

'I tell you what, kid. Go talk to Fabrizio. If anyone knows anything, it'll be him.'

'I will, thank you. Goodbye, Godfather.'

Guido stood and turned his back on him. When Winter had gone, he turned to his associate and said, 'Give Lippi a call. I think we may 'ave found 'im 'is man.'

Fabrizio Lippi's office above the Havana Club looked out onto an alleyway off Broad Street. As one of Varese's trusted *capos*, he ran his Newark empire with little interference from the police. They made too much money from kickbacks to cause him any serious trouble. The call from Guido's *consigliere* alerted him to Winter's imminent arrival. Lippi remembered him as a likeable and trustworthy kid, who followed Nico Varese everywhere, more than thirty years ago. The rumour was that he had somehow caused Nico's death in England and would never be forgiven.

When Winter walked into the club, Tony Insalaco, his old *capo*, was sitting at the bar. The last time he'd seen him, he'd had jet black hair, slicked back to hide the fact that he was going bald. Now, there was not a hair on his head.

''Ow you doin,' kid?' he said. 'I 'eard you did a stretch.'

'I did,' he replied without going into detail. 'What happened to your hair?'

'It went south, like my wife.'

Winter laughed. 'That's terrible. I'll buy you a beer when I'm done upstairs.'

At the top of the stairs stood a man so wide that Winter wasn't sure he could fit through the doorway. 'Is Lippi in?' he asked.

'Dat's Mr Lippi to you, kid.'

'Is he in?'

'Wait there.'

'Come on in, kid' said a voice from the other side of the man-mountain.

'Fabrizio,' said Winter, once he could see him.

'Winter. What can I do for you?'

'I'm here for my money.'

'What money?'

'The money that was in my account, until someone took it out in December. 43,000 dollars.'

'That's news to me, kid. Who took it out?'

'According to the bank, it was Moe.'

'Moe's dead, kid. I don't know anythin' about an account.'

'I need that cash, Fabrizio.'

'Sorry, kid. I think the only person who could have helped you is six feet under. I tell you what, though. I've a job comin' up. It needs someone with your expertise, if you know what I mean. You up for it?'

'How much?'

'Ten grand. Interested?'

Interested? It was a huge amount. 'Possibly, but I need the cash now.'

''Ow about five now and the rest when the job is done?'

'Tell me more.'

Before he left, Winter met Insalaco for a drink. 'You ever heard of Newman Dean Studios, Tony?' he asked.

'The film studio? Sure. I like to keep an eye on the competition, *capisci*? There was a feature on this Newman guy in one of my wife's magazines a year or so back. Some big shot in LA, by all accounts. Why you askin'?'

'Maybe I'm looking to get into the film business in my old age.'

'You?' Insalaco laughed. 'Go for it, kid!'

'How would I find him?'

'Shouldn't be too difficult. He has one of those big mansions in the Santa Monica mountains, from what I recall.'

Winter left Newark with five thousand dollars and Insalaco's home telephone number. The job was challenging, but nothing he couldn't handle. He had time to plan it, and in the meantime, he would head out west with Ailbhe by his side. With luck, they would find Niamh and start to build a new life for her and Ailbhe's girls.

Los Angeles, California

Winter sat with Ailbhe in a rental car, watching the comings and goings at a snowy trailer park near Compton in south Los Angeles. Earlier that day, he had visited the office of Hadaway and White, Attorneys-at-Law in LA. The letter from Thaddeus J. White gave no clue as to Niamh's whereabouts, but Winter made him an offer he found hard to refuse. The appointment to change his will in favour of his daughter had been a ruse, allowing Winter to find the information he needed from a file that was conveniently left open on White's desk.

The Garbutts, Niamh's foster parents, lived in a trailer in Space 37, the location of which was marked on an information board at the park entrance. It backed onto a line of trees on the far side of the park, which was good news. It meant that Winter could get very close without being seen. The only vehicle on view was a wreck, in which a group of bored teenagers were playing a game of cops and robbers. Winter could only imagine what might become of his daughter if she remained in a place like this. He decided to come back later to speak to her foster parents.

When darkness fell, he parked the car on the far side of the trees and they worked their way to within ten feet of the trailer. From inside, they could hear raised voices.

'Wait here,' said Winter. 'If she comes out, take her back to the car.'

Silently, he approached the rear of the trailer. Through the window, he could see a middle-aged woman sitting at a table with her back to him. A child was curled up in a ball on a bench seat at the far end of the trailer, but his view was partly obscured by the man standing over her. Presumably, this was Mr Garbutt. He had taken off his belt, the buckle end of which hung loosely from his right hand.

'How many times you gotta be told?' he shouted drunkenly as he brought the belt down on the girl's back. She whimpered in pain, and he raised his arm again. He never got to deliver a second blow, for the trailer door flew open and he was pushed up against the wall by a man with a gun and a vicelike grip round his neck.

'What the …?' he gasped as he struggled to breathe.

Winter forced him onto a chair and pointed the gun at him. 'Sit down next to your wife,' he said. 'Move a muscle and I'll kill you.' He turned and looked at the girl, who had an angry-looking welt under her left eye.

She looked at him curiously with tears in her eyes and asked, 'What do you want?'

'He do that to you?' he asked. She nodded.

'What business is it of yours?' asked Garbutt.

'You were sent a letter about this girl from a solicitor. Why'd you ignore it?'

Garbutt squirmed 'I, er…, I don't remember no letter.'

'Sure you do. This girl's father wanted to contact her.'

'Who are you, Mister?' he asked.

Winter ignored him. 'Niamh, do you want to speak to your father?'

'Why would I?' she replied. 'He left us years ago.'

'Who did?' he asked.

'My father, Nico.'

Winter knew instantly why Nico had seemed reluctant to talk about Maureen all those years ago. 'Nico wasn't your father, Niamh, I am,' he said gently.

'What are you talking about?' she asked.

'My name is Kevin Winter and a long time ago I helped your mam get away from some very bad men. I brought her to New York and left her in good hands. I didn't know she was pregnant when I left her.'

'I don't believe you,' she said angrily.

‘It’s true. Your mother never told me about you. I got a letter from her attorney, look.’

Niamh grabbed Thaddeus White’s letter and read it. It seemed genuine enough, but she wasn’t convinced. ‘This doesn’t prove anything. How do I know you’re who you say you are?’

‘Ask me anything. Something no one else could know.’

Niamh thought back to the stories her mother told her when she was little. ‘She told me about a place in the mountains. What was it called?’

‘Glendalough. I’ll take you there one day, if you want.’

‘What was her real name?’

‘Maureen O’Neill. She owned a cottage in Donegal.

‘Supposing I believe you, what do you want?

‘If you’ll let me, I’d like to make it up to you.’

‘You got no right to do this,’ said Garbutt.

Ignoring him, Winter said, ‘These people treat you well?’

‘What does it look like?’ Looking at the couple, she said, ‘She can’t even look after herself, and when he’s not hitting me, he’s touching me. He makes me sick.’

Winter shut his eyes and saw Father McCarthy’s face. Rage boiled up inside, but he hid it well. ‘Right, here’s the deal,’ he said. ‘Come with me and you can go to school and have somewhere safe to live.’

‘That ain’t gonna happen,’ said the man. ‘She’s with us, all legal like.’

Niamh glared at him. ‘Don’t I get a say in this, Chuck?’

‘You shut your goddam mouth!’

Winter pointed the gun at him. ‘Talk to her like that again and I’ll blow your head off.’

‘Make your mind up, Niamh. You can stay here if you want, or you can pack a bag and no one will ever hurt you again. What’s it gonna be?’

‘What your doing is kidnapping,’ said the man.’ You’ll never get away with it.’

‘Niamh, take your things and go outside. There’s a nice lady out there who’ll look after you until I’m done here.’

‘You gonna kill him?’ she asked. Chuck let out an involuntary gasp and wet himself.

‘Wait outside.’ Niamh had already made her mind up. Whatever was about to happen couldn’t be any worse than the life she had here.

She stuffed what few possessions she had into a brown paper bag and went outside. Ailbhe came out of the shadows and signalled for her to follow.

There was terror in the eyes of Chuck Garbutt. 'What you gonna do?' he squealed.

'Well, I was going to give you quite a lot of money in exchange for my daughter, but …'

'Then you got yourself a deal, Mister.'

'You laid your hands on my daughter. I can't let that go.' Winter moved behind him and delivered a heavy blow to the back of his head with the gun. He was unconscious when his head hit the table. Winter opened a drawer next to the stove and pulled out a grubby kitchen knife. Without a second thought he lifted Garbutt's head and slit his throat. When he left the trailer, the bloody knife was in Mrs Garbutt's hand and hers were the only prints.

They drove east out of Compton for about an hour, until they arrived in a small town with only one hotel. Winter paid for two rooms, doubling the owner's takings for the night. Niamh hadn't said a word since leaving the Garbutts and he was worried that she might be having second thoughts, so he asked Ailbhe to share a room with her.

In the morning, Ailbhe went in search of a grocery store, leaving Winter to get to know his daughter. When she had left, Niamh asked, 'Is she your wife?'

'Not yet,' he replied, adding, 'she was my brother's wife, but he died.'

'She seems nice,' said Niamh.

'She is, but things have been tough for her and the girls.'

'She has daughters?'

'Yes, two. Kathleen and Esther.'

'Where are they?'

'Back in Ireland, waiting for me to go and fetch them,' he said. 'This is going to be a new life for all of us.'

'What if I don't like it?'

'Then you can go back to the Garbutts, if that's what you want,' he lied.

Niamh shook her head. 'I'm never going back there,' she said firmly.

Adopting a much softer tone, Winter said, 'Listen, Niamh, I'm sorry that I've missed seeing you grow up. I don't know why your mother kept you a secret, but if I'd known about you, I'd have been there, believe me.'

'Mommy told me that Nico was my father,' she said. 'I saw a lot of him when I was little, but then he cleared off and we never saw him again.'

'He didn't clear off, Niamh. He died.'

'What?' she cried. 'Mommy thought he'd left us for someone else.' The way she said it made Winter realise that Nico had been much more than just a friend to Maureen.

'I'm sorry, no. He came to see me in England and someone shot him.' He wondered if he should have invented a less distressing death, but he didn't want to lie to her.

Niamh was genuinely upset by the news. 'I liked him,' she said. 'He used to bring me presents.'

'Don't worry,' said Winter. 'There'll be plenty of presents as long as I'm around.'

'Do you have a job?' she asked.

'Yes, but I'm planning to retire.'

'What do you do?'

He had anticipated the question. 'I work for a big organisation. I'm what you might call a fixer.'

'What's that?' she asked.

'Someone who solves problems.'

'Like you did for my mom?'

He wondered whether she was being sarcastic but decided to give her the benefit of the doubt. 'Yes, like I did for your mom,' he said gently.

They sat in silence for a while, until Winter asked, 'When was the last time you went to school?'

'I don't remember,' she replied. 'I had to look after my mom when she got ill.' Although he had only just met her, Winter could see that this was one tough little kid.

'Right, well, we'll have to do something about that.'

'I didn't like school,' said Niamh. 'Girls used to make fun of me.'

'What for?' he asked.

'We were poor. Dirt poor. Mom did her best, but we didn't have much. I think she went hungry so that I didn't.'

'I'm sorry, Niamh. I wish I'd known.'

'It's not your fault,' she replied.

'Is there anything you really enjoy?' he asked. 'Anything you think you might want to do with your life?'

'I don't want to be an actress,' she said. 'That just made my mom unhappy.'

'Okay, but if you could do anything at all?'

'She wants to work with animals,' said Ailbhe, who had just returned. 'She told me last night.'

'I love animals,' said Niamh.

'Right, we'll have to see what we can do about that,' said Winter.

The three of them spent the following week looking for somewhere to live, before finally settling on a large, rented homestead in the small township of El Monte, to the east of LA. Winter wanted Niamh to receive an education, but he was concerned that sending her to school might alert the authorities to the fact that she was no longer with her foster parents. When he talked it over with Ailbhe, she came up with a solution.

'If you can afford it,' she said, 'I could teach her at home. I was always near the top of the class in most t'ings. I t'ink I could have gone to college if we'd had the money. Then I met Dieter and that was that.'

'Wow! You're not just a pretty face, then,' said Winter. 'Well, if you're sure, let's do it. I'm sure Niamh won't mind.'

49

El Monte, California
February 1926

When he was sure that Ailbhe was happy with her new life, he told her that he was going to Ireland to fetch her daughters. 'Can you write to them and ask them to be ready to leave by the end of the month?'

'Just be careful,' she said. 'You're a wanted man over there.'

'Don't worry about me,' he said. 'I'll be back before you know it.' He left her a thousand dollars and said goodbye to both of his girls. The next morning, he took a train to New York.

Early on a freezing cold Monday morning a week later, Winter was sitting in a Hertz rental car, down the street from a large house in a wealthy part of Essex County. Around his neck were his grandfather's old binoculars. By Thursday of the same week, he had discovered that on weekdays, its occupants were creatures of habit. Each morning, the man of the house would emerge before eight and sit on a rocking chair on his front porch to smoke a cigarette before a taxi took him to work. Less than half an hour later, his wife would leave in the family car with their two young children.

On that Thursday morning, when the street was quiet, Winter pulled a scarf over his face and tilted his hat to prevent anyone from being able to describe him. Then he got out of the car, fastened up his overcoat and strolled towards the house. When he got there, he sat down on the rocking chair and lifted the binoculars to his eyes. He soon found what he was looking for and left as casually as he had arrived.

Doyle Ferguson was the County Attorney for Essex County. Born in Allentown, Pennsylvania, and with degrees from Columbia University and the Carey Law School, he was determined to make a name for himself by tackling organised crime in Newark. Raids on the Varese's premises, including the Havana Club and several speakeasies, marked him out as a problem that needed to be taken care of.

On the Friday morning following Winter's visit, Ferguson's wife was getting her children ready for school when there was a frantic banging on the front door. The taxi driver had found Ferguson's lifeless body slumped on his rocking chair, his coat smouldering from a still-burning cigarette, and blood oozing from a hole in the centre of his forehead. Winter had shot him from a vantage point in a tree, some two hundred and fifty yards away.

It was two days before an eagle-eyed detective found Winter's footprints at the base of the tree. By then, he had collected the balance of his fee and was on a ship to Ireland.

Tullybay, County Donegal

When Winter arrived in Tullybay, the girls were expecting him, and the cottage was spick and span. Esther was now five months pregnant, so there was no time to lose. They left Donegal for the last time and made their way south to Cobh, where they boarded the SS *Bremen* and sailed for America. When they arrived in New York on a cold winter's morning, a taxi took them to Grand Central Terminal. Over the next four days, on the *Lake Shore Limited* train to Chicago and the *California Chief* to Los Angeles, they would discover just what a breathtaking country America was, as they travelled through the sweeping plains of the Midwest and on to the snow-covered Rockies and beyond.

That weekend, they arrived at LA's La Grande Station, where they were met by an emotional Ailbhe. The bright sunshine contrasted sharply with the west coast of Ireland.

Kirk Allerton, Yorkshire
April 1926

James walked through the village on his way home at the end of yet another term. He was carrying a battered old leather attaché case that had belonged to his father. As he passed The Fleece a man waved to him from the doorway, but his mind was elsewhere. He had no way of knowing that Winter was making a new life for himself on the far side of another continent. His only source of comfort, his gun, was nestled in the bottom of the case.

The arrival of spring saw James playing cricket for Rochdale once more, and he was clearly back to his best. He produced some match-winning performances, which brought him to the attention of the county selectors. In fact, he would have been chosen for the Lancashire Second XI in the Minor Counties Championship, if only the matches had been played at weekends. His opportunity came during the summer holidays, when he was selected to play for them in several matches. He impressed with bat and ball, but he was more interested in playing alongside one of his cricketing heroes. Johnny Tyldesley was a former Wisden Cricketer of the Year and had been a great batsman for Lancashire and England. In 1925, he was fifty-three years old and in ill health, but he loved the game and still played whenever he was able. Although James didn't know it at the time, a young teammate, Eddie Paynter, was destined to become a famous England international in the thirties.

Manchester University
June 1926

At the end of the following term, Lawrence Bragg asked James to pop in and see him.

'Come in and sit down,' he said. 'This won't take long.'

'That sounds ominous.'

'Relax, it's good news. You will be aware that Sir Henry Miers is retiring this summer. What you won't know is that one of his last actions as Vice Chancellor was to award you a professorship on my recommendation.'

James stared at him. 'I don't know what to say.'

'You don't have to say anything, Professor. You've earned it. In fact, if it hadn't been for your illness, it would've happened sooner.'

The following day, he was in celebratory mood as he headed home to see his mother. Walking from the station to the manor, the village seemed frozen in time. He paused on the bridge over the Thurwell to take in the scene. It looked exactly as it had a hundred years earlier, apart from the bright red postbox. He gazed at the sparkling waters of the river as they meandered their way to the coast. A lot of water had passed under that bridge in the nine years since George told him his future lay in engineering. He would have made a very good engineer, but in a dying industry. He could not have imagined then that fate would send him down a very different path. If only his father could see him now.

Old Trafford, Manchester
September 1926

By the end of the cricket season, Lancashire's star all-rounder had been injured, and James was selected to play in an end of season game against the MCC at Old Trafford.

Their opponents included England stars Percy Chapman, Maurice Tate, George Geary and Patsy Hendren, the man whose score had been predicted by Einstein six years earlier. In a close game, Lancashire struggled against the pace bowling of Tate and Geary. James acquitted himself well, scoring forty not out in the first innings and sharing a century partnership with opening batsman Harry Makepeace in the second. At tea on the final day, Lancashire had lost eight wickets and needed thirty-two runs for victory. James was still there on thirty-nine, but unless he could keep the county's less talented tailenders away from the MCC attack, a win looked unlikely.

Walking down the pavilion steps after tea, he saw his old friend Freddie Taylor, sitting in an aisle seat, looking very excited and proud as punch. He leapt to his feet and hugged James, saying, 'Show them what you can do, Jimmy,' They were both taken aback when an elderly gentleman sitting on the other side of the aisle thrust a folded sheet of paper into James' hand, saying, 'Mr Driscoll, you should read this when Geary bowls Woolley.'

James thought it was strange, but he pushed the piece of paper into his pocket and continued to the crease. Three overs later, with James on forty-six, and Lancashire still needing eighteen to win, Albert Woolley was clean bowled by the last ball of an over from Geary. James looked towards the pavilion, where Lancashire's last man, wicket-keeper George Duckworth, was making his way down the steps. When he saw him stop and speak to the old man, he remembered the piece of paper. Taking it from his pocket, he unfolded it, revealing a handwritten prediction. "Tate's next four balls will be a yorker and three bouncers."

James stared at the note. There was no way that anyone could know who was going to bowl the next over, let alone what Tate was going to do with the next four balls. Unless… Was this another message from Einstein?

James looked down the pitch as the ball was thrown to Tate. There was nothing particularly surprising about that. He was the best bowler in the MCC line-up, after all. However, just in case the old man did have a message from the future, or some other inside knowledge, he decided to watch out for the yorker. It was just as well that he did, for Tate's very first ball pitched right at his feet and would have bowled him had he not been ready for it. He looked over in the direction of the old man, who gave him a thumbs-up. Had he somehow overheard Tate discussing tactics? If that was the explanation, then he had better settle down and wait for a bouncer. Sure enough, a short-pitched ball followed. He stepped forward and clubbed it over long on for six. The crowd applauded both the shot and James reaching his fifty. He decided that he had nothing to lose. The third ball was another bouncer, down the leg side this time. He swayed to his right and helped it on its way, up and over the square leg boundary. The crowd went wild. Only six to win now.

Stomping back to his mark, Tate looked as though steam was about to come out of his ears. He turned and ran in, even faster than before. His right arm was a blur as he bowled yet another bouncer, straight down the middle of the pitch. James left his crease, leant back and gave it everything he had. It was a huge hit, the ball soaring over the bowler's head. It was still rising as it crossed the boundary, before landing on the upper balcony of the pavilion.

The crowd erupted in wild applause and began to pour onto the pitch. James had snatched victory from the jaws of defeat. Surprisingly, Maurice Tate had a wry smile on his face when he shook him by the hand. 'Well played, son,' he said. 'No one's ever done that to me before, not even the Aussies.'

'Thank you, sir. I got lucky.'

'Nonsense. You seemed to have all the time in the world to play those shots. I can see you playing for England one day if you carry on like that.'

As the players left the field to a rapturous reception, James searched for the old man's face in the crowd. There was no sign of him. He turned to Duckworth. 'What did that old codger say to you, George?'

‘Nothing that made any sense. He told me not to worry, Tate wouldn’t be bowling to me. I thought he meant that you would be out before I had to face a ball.’

‘Was that all he said?’

‘Not quite. He asked me to tell you not to give up. I thought he was talking about the match, but then he gave me this. I haven’t got a clue what it means.’

Duckworth passed James another sheet of paper, but at that moment a breathless Freddie emerged from the crowd.

‘That was flipping brilliant, James,’ he said. ‘I thought I was watching Percy Chapman for a minute!’ Chapman was a big-hitting Kent batsman who had recently captained England to Ashes victory.

‘Thanks, Freddie. If you want to wait by the players’ entrance, we can go for a pint later.’

As his friend trotted off in the direction of the pavilion, James looked at the sheet, on which was written, “Forget relativity. The answer lies in the quantum world. You can save them.”

Shocked by the message, James grabbed Duckworth by the shoulders. ‘Did you see which way he went?’

‘No, sorry,’ he replied.

‘Dammit!’ Still padded up, he started running clumsily towards the Talbot Road exit, only to be surrounded by a crowd of excited supporters, all wanting to shake his hand. Finding a needle in a haystack would be easier than finding the old man in this crowd, so he shook a few hands and turned back dejectedly.

‘Who is he?’ asked a bemused Duckworth.

‘I have no idea. I’ve never seen him before,’ said James, but he was asking himself a different question. What was he? A messenger, perhaps, delivering a ‘telegraph to the past?’

50

El Monte, California
September 1926

The spring and summer of 1926 were among the happiest times of Winter's life. He had enough money to free his new-found family from the need to work, although Kathleen chose to do so. She used her dressmaking skills to find employment as a tailoress, sewing or mending clothes for upper-class women. At eighteen, she was the spitting image of her mother and loved the attention she was getting from American boys. Winter hadn't been joking when he'd said they'd be beating a path to her door.

Esther had a baby girl in June. Not much more than a child herself, she couldn't face being a mother when the father was unknown and love had played no part in the girl's conception. Ailbhe understood completely and spoke to a priest at the Nativity Catholic Church in El Monte. He knew of a local couple who could not have children of their own, and with his help the baby was rehomed within a matter of weeks.

Niamh appeared to be adapting well to her new life and enjoyed being home-schooled by Ailbhe, who was patient and kind, and never told her what to do. They would talk for hours, and in time Niamh opened up about her mother. She had found Edith's body, the morning after she died from an overdose. Over the course of the summer, Ailbhe became as much of a mother to Niamh as Edith had ever been, but it took her time to get used to the fact that she now had a father who wanted to be there for her. Winter was generous with his money, yet she had no idea what he did. *How does he earn his money?* she wondered. *What does he do?*

One weekend, while Winter was at the local store with Ailbhe, Niamh sneaked into their bedroom to look for clues. She found Winter's handgun and ammunition in a shoebox on top of a wardrobe and lifted them down to have a closer look. At the back of a drawer, she found a locked metal box. Using skills acquired as a young child, she picked the lock with a hairpin and took out a pile of letters. Some of them were business-related, and contained cryptic messages with lists of dates, times and places. Others were love letters, which she read to see if they told her anything new about her father. They didn't, apart from the fact that someone named Sinéad had been important to him. She was about to return everything to its rightful place when she noticed the letter from Dame Ellen Terry. Niamh had no idea who she was, but the details of her mother's treatment at the hands of the head of Newman Dean Studios broke her heart. In a fit of rage, she picked up Winter's gun. It was too good an opportunity to miss, so she took it, a box of bullets and the letter to her own room, where she dressed hurriedly.

Later that day, Ailbhe emerged from Niamh's bedroom waving Ellen Terry's letter. 'What are you doing leaving this lying around?' she asked.

'I didn't,' said Winter, the surprise clear in his voice. 'It was locked away. Where did you find it?'

'In Niamh's room. She's gone.'

'Gone where?'

'I don't know, but she's not here.'

Winter went to their room, where the metal box was lying open on top of a chest of drawers next to an empty shoebox. 'Shit!' he cried. As he ran to the car, he shouted to Ailbhe, 'Stay here. If she comes back, don't let her leave!'

'Where are you going?'

'To stop her doing something stupid!'

Los Angeles, California

Newman Dean Studios lay just off Santa Monica Boulevard, some twenty miles west of El Monte. Winter drove there in less than twenty minutes. When he arrived, the studio appeared to be deserted. He parked as far from the entrance as possible and cut a hole in the outer fence with wire cutters. Once inside, he worked his way through the empty lots until he reached a cafeteria. He could hear voices coming from inside. The door had a small window in it, through which he could see two security guards with their backs to him. One was short and fat, the other tall and thin. In their black uniforms, they reminded him of Laurel and Hardy.

Winter's handgun was lying on a table, and sitting on a chair facing the door was a frightened ten-year-old girl. As he watched, the short, fat one shouted at her. 'I won't ask you again. Why'd you bring a gun in here?'

'And I already said, you big lummox,' replied Niamh. 'I want to speak to Mr Newman.'

'Less of your cheek,' snarled the guard, who grabbed her by the hair and slapped her hard across her bare legs.

Winter had seen enough. He walked into the room, saying, 'Is the café open, I'm starving?'

The guard let go of Niamh's hair and blocked Winter's path. 'Who let you in here?' he asked. Winter smiled and punched him hard in the stomach. He doubled up and sank to the floor, winded and struggling to breathe.

His colleague's mouth fell open, and he lunged for the table with the gun on it. As he did so, Niamh stuck out a leg and tripped him. He landed face first on the hard floor. Winter hauled him to his feet and grabbed him by the throat, pushing him up against a wall. The guard couldn't believe the strength of his attacker, who must have been thirty years his senior. 'The police are on their way,' he gasped, unconvincingly.

'Follow us and you'll be sorry,' growled Winter. A knee to the man's groin put paid to any thoughts he might have had of following them.

Winter grabbed Niamh by the hand and took her out the way he had come in. She sobbed bitterly as he drove her out of the city. When he was sure they weren't being followed, he stopped at a parking area and gave her the biggest hug. 'Are you alright?' he asked.

'Yes.'

'How did you get here?'

'On the bus.'

'You're ten years old! What on earth were you thinking of?'

'That man deserves to die for what he did to my mom,' she cried. 'Are you angry with me, daddy?'

It was the first time she'd ever called him that, and it took him by surprise. 'For going through my private things, yes, but not for wanting that man dead. I feel the same way.'

'Why don't you do it, then?'

He thought carefully before replying. 'You can't just go round killing people, Niamh. Anyway, wouldn't it be better to hit him where it hurts.'

'What do you mean?' she asked.

'I mean destroy his business and leave him penniless.'

'Wouldn't it be easier to kill him?'

'It might be simpler,' he said, 'but much less satisfying, believe me.'

'How would you know that?'

He paused. 'It's just what I think, that's all.'

'How could you destroy his business?'

'I'll have to have a think about that. Come on, let's get you home.'

Newman may have thought that his home in the hills was a fortress, given the four guards that he employed to patrol the compound surrounding the mansion, but he hadn't bargained with someone like Kevin Winter. Having told Ailbhe that he had a few days' work in San Diego for a former employer, he drove there and checked into a hotel for three nights. He chatted with the porter and gave him a generous tip before driving back to the Santa Monica hills. With his car parked where it couldn't be seen by passing traffic, he took his grandfather's old A-frame tent and a rifle from the boot and walked to a sheltered spot on a wooded hillside above Newman's mansion.

Contrary to what he had said to Niamh, Winter had decided that Newman had to die. He was an extremely powerful man, a very different kettle of fish to Driscoll. Destroying his business might take years, years that Winter didn't have. He wanted to spend as much time as possible with his new family, so he would end Newman's life with a single bullet. He knew that he might have to be patient, so he settled down for a long wait.

There was no sign of Newman that evening, but a limousine arrived early the following morning. Its driver went in through the main entrance and Winter waited for Newman to emerge. The hill behind him meant that there was hardly a breath of wind, so he only had to worry about the distance to the target, which he estimated to be a shade over three hundred yards. With a bullet in the chamber, he rested the rifle on a tree branch and waited.

It felt longer, but ten minutes later the driver reappeared with Newman a few paces behind, walking alongside a guard. The guard felt the pressure of a bullet passing very close to him, but by the time he heard the shot, his boss was lying dead in a pool of blood next to him. As all hell broke loose in the compound, Winter used the trees as cover to make good his escape. As he jogged back to his car, he couldn't help thinking that, had he been in charge, all four guards would have surrounded Newman, making him more or less invisible until he was in the car.

Two days later, Winter returned home with some unexpected news for Niamh. 'While I was in San Diego,' he said, 'I went to the zoo and met the manager. I mentioned your love of animals, and she told me about a new lion park, right here in El Monte.'

'That's right,' said Ailbhe. 'I heard someone talking about it at the store. They have that lion off the movies. You know, the one that sits there looking around at the start of the film.'

'Really? Can we go?' asked Niamh excitedly.

'I don't see why not,' said Winter. 'They call it Gay's Lion Farm. Who knows, they might even let you volunteer there in your spare time.'

The San Diego trip had been part of a well thought out alibi on Winter's part, but he had expected Niamh to be suspicious when she heard that Newman had been killed. It was clear from her reaction that news of his death had not yet reached El Monte.

With Newman dead, Winter turned his attention to the last piece of unfinished business, James Driscoll. In November, he placed a call to Tony Insalaco in Newark and arranged to meet him in New York the following week.

He left El Monte after telling Ailbhe that he had several weeks' work on the east coast, but that he hoped to be home in time for Christmas. In New York, he met Insalaco at Penn Street Station. 'Good to see you again, Tony,' he said.

''Ow you doin,' kid?' said Insalaco. 'What can I do for you?'

'I was hoping you could put a word in for me with the boss,' he replied. 'I'm moving to the west coast for good. I thought there might be something I could do for him out there.'

'I think we 'ave a casino in Vegas. That the sort of thing you 'ad in mind?'

'You know what I'm good at, Tony, but yeah, maybe. I fancy a fresh start.'

'Ok, I'll ask around and let you know. Where can I reach you?'

'I'm not sure where I'm gonna be for the next month or so,' said Winter. 'I'll contact you when I get back.'

51

Kirk Allerton, Yorkshire
December 1926

The ability to travel faster than light was the stuff of science fiction, a superpower if you like, but one that James now knew to be real. Even if it only applied to the smallest objects known to man, Einstein had harnessed that power to send messages, change the past and even save lives. Sadly, the limitations of his invention meant that nothing could be done for Alice or George but, since the old man's message, James couldn't help thinking that there might be another way. Quantum theory was in its infancy, and widely thought to be incompatible with relativity, but he couldn't help wondering if it might be the key to time travel. There was so much that scientists did not yet know about the way the world worked, and no knowing what discoveries lay in store.

Early one morning, as the first rays of the winter sun cast a golden hue across the valley, James prepared to set off on a run that was once again an integral part of his daily routine. In the hallway, he noticed an envelope on the mat that hadn't been there the night before. He picked it up and saw his name, neatly typed on the front, but there was no stamp. He opened the front door to check whether its bearer was still outside, but the lane was empty. In the kitchen, he sat down at the table, worried that this was exactly the sort of thing Winter would do.

He tore open the envelope and pulled out a letter. It was neatly typed on crisp, white paper, but there was something odd about it. He couldn't put his finger on it at first, but then it dawned on him. The text was flush with both margins, the way it was in books and newspapers. If there was a typewriter capable of such a thing, he had never seen or heard of it. No, it must have been produced on a printing press, but why would someone go to so much trouble? His curiosity piqued, he began to read.

Dear Professor Driscoll,

You don't know me, but our paths crossed briefly at Old Trafford. I don't need to tell you that the future is not set in stone, but too much information might change your fate in ways you would not like. Your future is inextricably linked with Einstein's, and you will need his help. Be patient and a solution will present itself when you least expect it. Remember Newton's words to Hooke and you may succeed in your quest. Good luck, and in case you were wondering, typewriters become very clever in the future.

Whoever sent this could read minds! James vividly remembered the day that he received Einstein's first letter. He thought it was an elaborate joke at first, but he had been wrong. Instinct told him that the latest letter was genuine, but if so, what on earth did it mean? "Remember Newton's words to Hooke," for example. Sir Isaac Newton and Robert Hooke were legendary figures in the Scientific Revolution of the seventeenth century, and James knew that they used to correspond with one another. In fact, one of Newton's most famous quotes could be found in a letter to Hooke. "If I have seen further, it is by standing on the shoulders of giants." That had to be the reference, but if Einstein was the giant, and James the pupil, how could he possibly stand on his shoulders and surpass his achievements? There had to be another explanation. No one in their right mind would compare him to Einstein.

His mind racing, he set off in the direction of Allerton Edge. After a punishing climb to the top, he stood on the promontory overlooking the village, wondering whether anywhere on earth was more beautiful. He loved this place, not least because he always seemed to have his best ideas here.

"Forget relativity," the original note had said. "The answer lies in the quantum world. You can save them." If that was true, then Hermes' limitations no longer mattered. Had he been looking in the wrong place all these years? If so, he was back to square one. So little was known about the quantum world, but what if the author of the letter had succeeded where James had failed? What if he had knowledge of a future in which quantum theory was better understood? A future in which typewriters had taken over from printing presses? It was an intriguing thought.

On Christmas Eve, Ellen Driscoll was in high spirits as she sipped a glass of eggnog while sorting through a pile of unopened cards. Since George's death, she had emerged from his shadow and made a huge success of Welbeck Ready-to-Wear. Not only was it now one of the most successful clothing companies in the country, with its products stocked in all the major department stores, but it had diversified to become a leading maker of footwear and accessories. Welbeck shoe shops were on every high street, and they had been awarded a Royal Warrant to supply goods and services to the Royal Household.

She giggled as she remembered James' reaction to the news. 'Cobblers to the King!' he had exclaimed. At dinner the night before, on what would have been George's sixty-fifth birthday, he had announced his Professorship. George would have been so proud to learn that one of his sons now had a title that had been earned through hard work.

Christmas had long since ceased to be a happy time for Ellen, but this year her boys had organised everything, from the huge tree in the hallway to a sumptuous Christmas dinner. Soon, Ralph would be arriving from Burnley with Molly's father, who was bringing a goose with all the trimmings. Harold Bradshaw would have spent Christmas alone, had the Driscolls not invited him to come and get to know Ruth, his six-month-old granddaughter.

The sound of a heavy envelope landing on the quarry tiles in the hallway startled Ellen. When she picked it up, it was addressed to James. She found him in the kitchen, munching on a slice of toast, drinking tea, and reading the Christmas Edition of the Radio Times.

'Listen to these predictions, Mother,' he said. 'It says that by 2026, the sky will be dark with aeroplanes queuing for runways. Compared with our primitive vehicles, cars will hardly be recognisable, and there will be so many of them that they won't be able to go anywhere!'

'That doesn't sound very likely, James,' she replied, 'But even if it's true, neither of us will be around to see it!' She handed him the envelope, saying, 'This came for you.'

He put the magazine down and examined the envelope. It bore a Liverpool postmark, and it dashed any hopes he may have had of an end to Winter's vendetta. Inside was a book by an Irish author, Abigail Moran. The title, *Time to Die,* was self-explanatory.

With a sinking feeling, James realised that if the title was to be believed, Winter was not in America and was coming for him. He went to his bedroom and took down his gun from its hiding place on top of a wardrobe. If Winter was coming, he wanted to be ready for him. Only a decade earlier, James believed that a human life should not be taken under any circumstances. Now, he just wanted Winter dead.

Allerton Edge, Yorkshire
December 1926

Alfie was hunched over, hands on knees and gasping for breath. James lay on his back, looking up at the wispy, feather-like clouds that dotted the blue December sky. The race had been Alfie's idea, a way of atoning for some of their Christmas excesses. It was the first time he had felt fit enough to tackle Allerton Edge since the war, but he reached the summit a full minute behind his brother. Sam, Alfie's Alsatian, had beaten them both, and lay there panting with his tongue hanging out.

'You okay, Alfie?' asked James as he took a canteen from his knapsack and poured some water into Sam's open mouth.

His brother was too breathless to speak but gave him a thumbs-up. James was well aware that only three years earlier, neither of them would have made it to the top. His overall level of physical and mental fitness had been so poor that he had been a danger to himself and others. Now, it seemed as though the events of 1923 had happened to someone else. Had it not been for Molly and his mother, he might be locked away in an asylum somewhere. Although the threat from Winter was undeniable, James no longer felt anxious. He was still preoccupied with the pursuit of time travel, but he didn't allow it to rule his life in the way it once had. He still believed he would succeed in the end, but thanks to Doctor Fraser, he could now accept the possibility that he might not.

He looked down on the village from his lofty vantage point. Allerton House, Alfie's new home, was resplendent in the Autumn sunshine. Next door, with their mother away in Wales visiting friends and family, the manor house stood empty. James waved at Molly, who was in their garden, looking up at him through a pair of binoculars. She waved back but appeared to be agitated. 'It looks as if Molly's on the warpath,' he said to Alfie.

'I'd better go and see what she wants,' he replied, hauling himself to his feet.

'You've only just got here,' said James.

'I know, but it might be important. Are you coming?'

'I'll follow you down in a bit,' said James. 'I like it up here.'

'Right. I'll see you later. Sam, heel.' The dog got to its feet and trotted obediently by his side as they started back down the hillside path.

James lay there for a few minutes more, breathing in the rarefied air. He got to his feet and noticed a discarded cigar butt on the ground. Bending down to pick it up, he heard a rustling in the bushes. 'Who's there?' he shouted.

Winter emerged from his hiding place, downwind from where the dog had been lying. 'Well, well, well,' he said. 'What have we got here?'

'You!' The shock was evident in James' voice. He cursed inwardly as he realised that Winter was standing between him and his gun, which was nestled in the bottom of his knapsack.

'Did you not get my message, *Englander*,' asked Winter. 'I told you, it's time to die.' He removed his knife from the sheath that was strapped to his left leg, adding, 'I'm going to enjoy this.'

James eyed the knife warily. 'Just what I'd expect from someone like you,' he said. 'Using your fists on a defenceless woman and a knife on an unarmed man. You're nothing but a coward.'

Winter saw red. 'You think I need this to finish you off?' He returned the knife to its sheath and moved menacingly towards his quarry. As the distance closed between them, he pushed out a right jab that James managed to dodge, countering with a right and left of his own and connecting with his assailant's already misshapen nose.

Winter grinned as he tasted his own blood running down the back of his throat. His boxing skills kicked in and he danced around James, using the fact that he was quicker and lighter on his feet to land punch after punch, while James was left chasing shadows. As cuts began to open up on his eyebrows and blood ran into his eyes, he realised that strength and guts were not going to be enough to win this fight. He still couldn't reach his knapsack, but he remembered his Uncle Mike saying something about discretion being the better part of valour when he had taken a beating from three older boys before the war. If he couldn't win this fight, as much as it would bruise his ego, he needed to get away and live to fight another day.

Despite the blood, Winter could see the fear in James' eyes and moved to cut off his only escape route. He knew that he could finish the fight whenever he wanted to, but he wanted James to suffer, so he toyed with him rather than pressing home his advantage. He tapped his knife with his hand and said, 'Don't even think about running away, unless you think you can outrun this knife. It'll be between your shoulder blades before you've gone ten yards.'

James eyesight was deteriorating and he was becoming desperate. *How the hell am I going to get out of this?* he wondered. Soon he would only be able to see shapes, so he launched himself at Winter and, through sheer brute strength, managed to drag him to the ground, dangerously close to the edge of the cliff. For a moment, James had him in a headlock, but an elbow to the stomach forced him to release his grip.

Winter wriggled free and got to his knees. Grabbing James by the hair, he took out the knife and said, 'This is for Sinéad. Time to die, *Engländer*.'

James could only think of Alice and how much he missed her. Winter pulled back James' head, exposing his throat. 'An eye for an eye, son,' he growled.

Spitting blood from his mouth, James grinned defiantly and said, 'Get on with it, then, you coward.'

Winter bristled at the jibe and hesitated as he shifted his weight slightly to deliver the fatal blow. James sensed rather than saw the arm raised above his head and managed to grab it. He gave it an almighty twist, forcing Winter to roll to his left. As he landed, Winter kicked out with his legs and caught James square in the chest, sending him staggering backwards. Blinded and with no idea where he was, he lost his footing and toppled backwards over the cliff-edge. As he fell, he felt strangely at peace, closing his eyes and waiting for the end that must surely come. The last thing he heard was someone far away calling his name.

52

Kirk Allerton, Yorkshire
December 1926

Am I dead? wondered James. He couldn't be sure, but nor could he see or feel anything. Only when he tried to move did he know that he was still very much alive. The pain in his chest was so intense that he blacked out. When he came to, Sam was licking his face.

'Where's Alfie?' he grunted. 'Go get him.' Sam ran off and he lay there on his back, wondering how long he had been lying there, and whether Winter was still around. He tried to turn his head, but the pain was unbearable. When he tried to breathe in, he passed out again.

'Jimmy! Jimmy, it's me!' Alfie was kneeling next to him.

'I can't breathe,' he gasped with difficulty, 'and I can't feel my legs.'

'Don't try to move. I think you may have broken your back and you've definitely broken your left arm. Molly's phoning for an ambulance.'

'Am I going to die?' asked James.

'No, of course not, but you're badly hurt. Don't try to speak. You need to stay perfectly still.' Alfie hoped that his face didn't betray his true feelings.

'Have you seen Winter?'

Alfie looked around in all directions. 'No sign of him.'

'He was up there, waiting for me,' gasped James.

'Then he could still be there. Sam and I are going to stay here with you until help arrives.'

'Where's Molly?'

'Waiting for the ambulance. She'll have called the police as well. She's…' Alfie stopped talking. He had seen his own car, making its way along the lane towards the village.

'What is it?' asked James.

'My car! That must be Winter, Molly can't drive!'

'The police will stop him.'

'That's not what I'm worried about! It was in the garage. He must have got into the house! I have to get down there.'

'Be careful.' Every word was painful now, but he had to warn his brother. 'He has a knife!'

'Stay here and try not to move.'

Alfie set off with Sam by his side. At the bottom of the hill, they ran across the fields towards Allerton House. A window was broken, and the back door was open. 'Molly!' he shouted frantically, running from room to room, terrified that Winter had taken her, or worse. He returned to the kitchen and lifted the telephone from its cradle. When the operator answered, he said, 'Police, please!'

'They're already on their way,' said a voice from behind him. He turned to find Molly standing in the doorway.

'Molly! Thank God,' he cried, taking her in his arms. 'Where were you?'

'Hiding in the bushes. I saw 'im coming. He was laughing. What 'appened up there?'

'He attacked Jimmy and pushed him off the cliff.'

'Is 'e alright?'

'No, he's very badly hurt!'

'You go back and look after 'im. I'll wait for the ambulance.'

Taking a bottle of Extract Cannabis from the pantry, he headed back up the hill.

When Sergeant Jenkins arrived on his bicycle, Molly explained what had happened. 'Right,' he said, 'I'll get on the blower and ask them to be on the lookout for Alfie's car. I suggest you stay inside and lock the doors until we catch this man.'

'That didn't keep 'im out before!'

It took the ambulancemen an hour and a half to reach James, and another forty minutes to bring him down the hillside on a stretcher. By then he was unconscious and in a very bad way. A bed was found for him in Driscoll Cottage Hospital, where his injuries were assessed and morphine was administered for the pain.

When Alfie and Molly arrived, they were taken into a private room, where a doctor told them to expect the worst.

'Don't be daft,' said Alfie. 'He's as strong as an ox.'

'I've no doubt of that, but quite frankly, knowing the height that he fell from, I'm amazed he survived the fall.'

'Are you sayin' 'e could die, doctor?' asked Molly.

'I'm afraid so. I'm very sorry. Is there anyone you need to call?'

Alfie had always assumed that his brother was indestructible. 'My mother's away in Wales,' he said. 'I can't see her being able to get back until tomorrow evening at the earliest.'

'I'll be surprised if he lives that long, but as you say, he's strong. You're welcome to stay for as long as you want, or we can telephone you if there's any change in his condition.'

'I wouldn't be here if it wasn't for Jimmy,' said Alfie, 'I'm not leaving him.' He felt completely helpless. James had saved his life, yet there was nothing he could do to help him.

'You stay, love,' said Molly. 'I'll ring your mother and fetch you summat to eat.'

When she returned, she brought sandwiches and a flask of tea. 'There were no answer from the number your mum gave us,' she said. 'I'll try again later.'

It was after ten when her call was answered by George's cousin, Olwen. They had spent the evening at the Coliseum Theatre in Aberystwyth, and Ellen had gone to bed shortly after arriving home. Olwen took the news very calmly and promised to call her back. An hour later, she rang to say her husband would drive Ellen home first thing in the morning. They should be there by lunchtime.

In his dream, James was running down a steep hillside, so fast that he was unable to stop. His stride became longer and longer, until he lost his footing and tumbled head over heels down the slope, before landing in a heap at the bottom. When he got to his feet, there was a train, and on it was Alice, holding out her hand and beckoning to him from the open carriage window. The faster he tried to run, the slower his progress. Somehow, he made it, and went from carriage to carriage, but Alice had disappeared. From the window, he saw a tunnel looming ahead, and everything went dark.

'Jimmy?'

He could hear Alfie's voice from somewhere in the darkness. If he was alive, he had no idea where he was, or how long he'd been there, but as he slowly regained consciousness, he tried to speak.

'Alfie, is that you?' he whispered.

'I'm here.'

'Where's here?'

'In hospital. You've had a bit of an accident.'

'Winter!' James tried to sit up, but the pain in his chest made him cry out. Alfie was also suffering from aches and pains, which was no surprise. He had shared his twin's pain since childhood, so he knew that James must be in agony.

'Don't try to move,' he said, 'you've a lot of broken bones. Stay still while I tell the nurse that you're awake.'

He went and found an elderly nurse, who gave James another dose of morphine. There was little else she could do for him other than try to make him comfortable.

James knew that he'd been dreaming about Alice, but he couldn't remember any of the details. He tried to piece together his memories of the previous day's events, but they were all jumbled up. Alfie noticed the nurse's face change as James told him about the dream. When she left the room, Alfie followed her into the corridor.

'What's wrong?' he asked.

'What do you mean?' she replied.

'You made a face while my brother was talking to me. I want to know why.'

'Alright, but you didn't hear this from me.'

Alfie wondered what on earth she was about to say. 'Hear what? What do you know?'

'I've been a nurse for a very long time,' she said. 'I can't explain it, but whenever a patient dreams about meeting their dead relatives or loved ones, they usually die within a few days. I'm sorry.'

'Poppycock! That sounds like an old wives' tale to me.'

'Well, you're right, I am an old wife, but I can only tell you what I've seen, too many times. I hope I'm wrong, I really do, but if I was you, I'd be thinking about saying goodbye while you can.'

The following day, Alfie was asleep in an armchair next to James' bed when someone gently shook his shoulder. He opened his eyes to see his mother looking tearfully down at him. Feeling helpless and hopeless, they hugged each other and cried as they stood beside James' bed.

'The doctor says that he's paralysed, and nothing can be done for him,' wept Ellen.

'I know, but he's a fighter, Mother. If anyone can get through this, Jimmy can.'

Throughout that second day, there was little change in his condition. Ellen, Alfie and Molly sat next to his bed with Paul Lucas, who had driven Ellen home. James would have been pleased to learn that he was now Olwen's husband. They all held hands in silent prayer as James drifted in and out of consciousness. When the doctor examined him late that afternoon, his expression was grave.

Addressing Ellen, he said, 'I think it's just a matter of time, Mrs Driscoll. Would you like me to fetch a priest?'

'Absolutely not. James never gave up on Alfie when he was at death's door, and I'm certainly not giving up on him now. So long as he has breath in his body, I'm praying for a miracle.'

The Driscoll family took it in turns to keep a vigil at James' bedside. Although he was unconscious, they talked to him constantly, hoping against hope that he could hear them and would find the strength to keep fighting. James exceeded all the doctor's expectations, and when he made it to midnight on New Year's Eve, they began to feel more optimistic about the outcome, even though he still hadn't woken up.

Their vigil continued into the new year. Early one morning, Alfie was half asleep when he felt a hand on his arm. He turned his head and saw that James was awake. Alfie was having difficulty breathing, so he knew that his brother had taken a turn for the worse.

'Listen to me,' gasped James.

'Don't try to speak,' said Alfie. 'Save your strength.'

'No, listen. If I die…'

'You're not going to die!' he exclaimed.

'If I die,' repeated James firmly, 'there's something I want you to do for me.'

'Don't talk like that,' said Alfie.

James grabbed his arm, and the look on his face told Alfie that he should listen. 'You're the only person I can trust,' he wheezed. He was having great difficulty talking now.

'Alright,' said Alfie. 'What is it?'

He listened intently, but James' breathing was extremely ragged, and he could only manage one or two words at a time. When he eventually lost consciousness, Alfie was unsure whether he had told him everything.

For the next twenty-four hours, with Alfie or his mother at his side, James was unresponsive. Ellen kept a vigil through the night until Alfie arrived to let her go home and get some sleep. He dozed in an armchair but was woken by a growing tightness in his chest. Out of the blue, James said, 'What day is it?'

'You're awake!' he replied. 'It's Sunday.'

‘The date?’

‘Erm, it’s the second of January.’

James visibly relaxed. ‘Eight years to the day.’

Alfie had to think. *January 1919?* ‘You mean Alice, don’t you?’ he said, but James did not reply. Was it really eight years since Alice had died?

Alfie stood up and crossed the room to open a window. When he realised that he no longer had the ache in his chest, he knew instinctively what it meant. He turned back to look at James and could see that the pain had left his face. His long struggle was over, and he was with his beloved Alice again, leaving Alfie to break the devastating news to his mother.

53

Schöneberg, Berlin
January 1927

Four years after Rathenau's assassination and the failed attempt to save him, Hermes was gathering dust in the corner of Einstein's study. He could not bring himself to repair it, and it served as a constant reminder of what might have been. He had last spoken to James when the young man telephoned, following his unanswered telegram after Walther died. Now he was dead and there was nothing anyone could do about it. Einstein had lost another friend, and the loss of such a humble man with so brilliant a mind, and at such a young age, before he'd had the opportunity to fulfil his potential, was difficult to accept. He withdrew to his study, from where he composed a heartfelt telegram to James' family.

Kirk Allerton, Yorkshire

Holy Trinity Church was packed for the funeral Mass, with James' flower-laden coffin standing in front of the altar and the parish priest presiding. To Ellen Driscoll, though six years had passed since her husband's death, it felt like only yesterday that his coffin had stood on the same spot. For the eulogy, the priest chose to read a selection of messages from some of the world's most eminent scientists. Lawrence Bragg was in the congregation, but telegrams had been received from Einstein, Rutherford and von Laue, to name but a few. Alfie listened with particular interest to Einstein's message.

WITH DEEPEST SYMPATHY STOP JAMES WAS A
GOOD MAN AND AN OUTSTANDING SCIENTIST
WHO NEVER STOPPED SEARCHING FOR
ANSWERS TO THE MOST CHALLENGING
QUESTIONS STOP HE KNEW THAT PAST
PRESENT AND FUTURE ARE AN ILLUSION
AND DEATH DOES NOT HAVE TO BE THE END

The priest said that Einstein's words reminded him of a verse from the Gospel According to St John, in which Jesus said, "He that believeth in me, though he were dead, yet shall he live: and whosoever liveth and believeth in me shall never die."

Alfie lowered his head to hide the smile that played across his lips. He was one of only two people in the congregation to have returned from the dead, and the only one to be aware of it. He knew that the priest had misunderstood Einstein's message, which referred to science, not faith. To Alfie, Einstein's words took on a completely different meaning. He remembered what his mother had said to the doctor at the hospital.

Well, Mother, he thought, remembering her prayers, *you just might get your miracle.*

James' family gathered at the graveside as the mourners made their way to The Fleece for the wake. After a short burial service, Ellen remained behind to speak to the priest, while the others headed for the pub. When there was no one within earshot, Molly put her arm around Alfie's waist and said, 'What were you smiling at in church, and don't say nothing?'

'It's hard to explain,' he replied, 'but before he died, Jimmy asked me to do something for him. He said it could change everything, but he swore me to secrecy. If I tell you, you have to promise not to breathe a word to another living soul.'

Intrigued, she said, 'I promise. What's the big secret?'

'It's how I'm going to save Jimmy's life.'

Molly looked at him as if he had taken leave of his senses. 'What on earth are you talking about?' There was a worried look on her face as she added, 'James is dead, you do know that, don't you?'

'Of course I do, but if you were listening to Einstein's message, he said that death is not the end.'

''E was talking spiritually, Alfie. You can't bring people back from the dead.'

'I can't, but Einstein can. He brought me back when I died, and my mother.'

Molly was scared now. 'Stop it! You 'ave to let James go, please,' she cried.

'I'm sorry, I didn't mean to upset you,' said Alfie. Any further discussion was interrupted by their arrival at the pub. 'Look,' he said gently, 'I'll explain later.'

When they returned to Allerton House that evening, he told her everything, including how Einstein's invention had brought him back from the dead and enabled James to warn the police about the plan to murder his mother.

The disbelief on Molly's face was clear to see. 'Are you joking, Alfie?' she asked, 'because it's not funny.'

'I swear to God, I'm telling the truth,' he replied. 'You have to believe me, Molly. Jimmy explained it all to me, and it makes perfect sense.'

She could see in his eyes that he was deadly serious. 'So, do you think it could save 'im?' she asked.

'I hope so, but I'll have to go to Berlin to find out,' he replied.

'I'll come wi' you, then,' she said.

'No, I'd rather not leave Mother on her own right now. Would you look after her while I'm away?'

Molly was disappointed but said, 'Of course. 'Ow long will you be gone?'

'A couple of weeks or so should be long enough,' he said. He decided not to mention the fact that he might never come back to this version of reality. A message from Hermes, sent to a time before Winter's prison break, would give James a second chance, but erase the last fourteen months of their lives.

In the morning, Alfie brought Molly breakfast in bed. 'Before I leave for Germany,' he said, 'I have to go to Jimmy's house in Rusholme. Would you like to come with me?'

'If it means I get to spend a bit more time with you, then yes please. Why do you 'ave to go there?'

'Jimmy asked me to, not long before he died. It was difficult to follow what he was saying at the end, so I'm not entirely sure why, but hopefully all will become clear when we get there.'

'Alright, just gi'me an hour or so to get ready,' she said. 'Can you put Ruth's cradle in the car for me?'

'Will do,' he replied. While he waited, he wedged the baby's cradle firmly behind the front passenger seat of his father's old Rolls-Royce and made a mental note to drive as gently as he could.

The road over the moors was closed due to snow, so Alfie had to take a more circuitous route to Manchester through Rochdale. The journey was uneventful, and when they arrived, he parked the car in front of Oakwood House and unlocked the front door with James' key. Stepping into the cold, forbidding hallway, he paused to pick up a pile of mail that had accumulated on the mat. He recalled the distressing circumstances of their earlier visit, when James was at his lowest ebb and almost beyond help.

Molly set a fire in the living room hearth and when the room was warm, she left the baby asleep in her cradle while Alfie turned his attention to James' request.

'Go to my house,' he had said. 'Go to the basement.' Alfie shuddered at the thought, wondering what he might find there, but he was pleased to have Molly for company. The temperature dropped noticeably as they carefully descended the stone steps by the light of a torch.

In James' laboratory, they wrinkled their noses at the musty smell. Alfie turned on the lights and saw that the room wasn't as big as he would have expected, judging by the size of the house above. A large island worktable stood in the centre of the room and there was a long run of cupboards against the far wall. To their left, a signed photograph of Einstein hung in a frame on the wall, behind a desk and chair. To their right was a large bookcase, filled with an eclectic mix of scientific textbooks and science fiction novels.

'So, this is where 'e worked?' said Molly.

'I guess so,' said Alfie.

Molly looked around the room. 'I wouldn't fancy being cooped up somewhere that didn't even 'ave a window to look out of.'

'Jimmy would have found that a distraction,' he replied. He moved the desk away from the wall so that he could examine the photograph more closely. He ran his left hand down the edge of the frame and found a catch, just where his brother had said it would be. When he pressed it, the frame swung outwards, revealing a wall safe behind. The combination was easy to remember, for it was Alfie's army number. He turned the dial one way and then the other, until there was a click and the door opened. He reached inside and removed a folder labelled Mercury, which he placed on the desk. The only other item was a shoebox bearing the distinctive Welbeck Shoes label. Someone had secured it with tape and written "Do Not Open" across the top, so he left it where it was. The folder contained a single sheet of paper and three documents, marked "Instructions," "Proofs" and "Codes" respectively. Alfie picked up the handwritten sheet and read aloud, 'In the other room, you will find everything you need.'

'What other room?' asked Molly.

Alfie wouldn't have known if James hadn't told him. He left the documents on the desk and looked around the laboratory. The door that led upstairs was the only one. His eyes settled on the bookcase as the only possible option, but it was flush against the wall, and despite his efforts, was too heavy to move. He felt around the sides and top, but there was nothing out of the ordinary.

'What are you doing?' asked Molly.

'Looking for the other room,' he replied. He started to read the titles of the books that filled the shelves, beginning with the novels. James' favourite book, *The Time Machine*, caught his eye, so he removed it from the shelf and examined it. It was well-thumbed but offered no clues. Nor did any of the others, so he turned his attention to the many science textbooks. Taking them from the shelves one at a time, he eventually came to an innocuous-looking volume, *Chemistry And Its Uses*, by McPherson and Henderson. As he lifted it from the top shelf, he heard a click and the bookcase moved slowly outwards.

Molly gasped. 'A secret door!' she exclaimed. ''Ow exciting.'

Alfie examined the book more closely and saw that there was a cord, securely attached to the spine. It ran through a hole in the back of the bookcase, where it was tied to a spring-loaded latch. With a mixture of excitement and trepidation, he squeezed through the opening.

Molly followed, saying, 'James wouldn't 'ave got through this gap the last time we were 'ere.'

Alfie had to agree. Once his eyes had adjusted to the darkness, he could see the outline of a light switch on the wall. He pressed it and a dim light appeared. He felt a faint draught on his face and looked up to see a vent in the ceiling, which must have been installed to provide a supply of fresh air.

The room was rectangular in shape and almost as big as the laboratory. There was a table and chair to the left and a sofa against the far wall, on which was a pillow and a pile of neatly folded sheets and blankets. To Alfie's right was a tall cupboard, next to a door that led to a toilet and sink. He looked inside the cupboard and saw that the shelves were stacked from top to bottom with canned meats, soups, fruit and vegetables.

'What is this place?' asked Molly.

‘A refuge, from what I can tell,’ he replied. If James had ever needed to hide from Winter, he could have survived in this room for many months, but Alfie wasn’t at all sure why he had wanted him to come here. He approached the table and saw for the first time that it stood against a screen rather than a wall. His heart skipped a beat as he realised that there was a gap at one end. When he peered behind it, he saw a large, triangular wooden frame, holding an array of glass tubes and other items of laboratory equipment. A notice on the wall read “Fragile – Do Not Touch.”

They returned to the laboratory, and Alfie picked up the document marked “Instructions.” Inside was a diagram showing the same apparatus that he had just been looking at. One of Jimmy’s latest inventions, no doubt. Alfie was no scientist, but the step-by-step instructions that accompanied the diagram seemed very clear.

Molly sat down at the desk and studied the document marked “Proofs.” It contained a list of dates and events, the significance of which was lost on her. The list began with an entry for the twelfth of April 1925 that read “Day One.” Henry Rider Haggard, the author of *King Solomon’s Mines*, died on the fourteenth of May 1925. Other entries included John Logie Baird demonstrating the world’s first television system in January 1926, and the General Strike in May of the same year. There were several references to that August’s cricketing highlights, including England beating Australia to win the Ashes, Jack Hobbs scoring 316 runs for Surrey against Middlesex and Lancashire beating Nottinghamshire to win the County Championship. One entry in particular attracted Molly’s attention. Against the twenty-first of November 1925 were the words “Winter escapes from prison.” They had been underlined.

‘Alfie, what does all of this mean?’ she asked.

He looked over her shoulder and read the same entry. His eyes were drawn to the top of the page, where a single word was written. He hadn’t taken much notice before, but now he understood.

‘Do you see what’s written there, Molly?’ he asked, pointing to the word with his finger.

‘Yes, Mercury. So what?’

‘Mercury was the Roman Messenger of the Gods. The same god that the Greeks called Hermes. I don’t have to go to Berlin after all!’

‘You don’t?’

‘No! Don’t you see? James has built his own device, right here in Rusholme!’

‘Well, I’ll be,’ she replied in amazement.

As she stood up, Alfie took her in his arms. She flung her arms around his neck and he lifted her off the floor, swinging her round the room and kissing her firmly on the lips.

‘Put me down, you daft ’apeth,’ she squealed.

He did as he was told and sat down on the chair. Looking at the picture of Einstein on the wall, he said, ‘If Jimmy is as clever as Einstein thinks he is, we might be able to warn him about Winter.’

Molly sat on his lap and ran her fingers through his hair. ‘Let’s find out, shall we?’

TO BE CONTINUED

A Sneak Peek

New York City
December 1930

Einstein enjoyed a commanding view of the New York skyline from his upper-deck suite on the *Belgenland.* It had changed in the nine years since his last visit and was now dominated by the Chrysler Building, a gleaming Art Deco skyscraper and the tallest building in the world at more than a thousand feet. This would be the Einsteins' view for the next five days, until they continued their journey to the west coast, where Albert had agreed to spend a couple of months as a visiting professor at the California Institute of Technology in Pasadena.

He couldn't help but think how different things could have been, had it not been for Hermes. After recovering from heart problems the previous year, he had planned to build a new lakeside summer house in Caputh to the south of Berlin. The Wall Street Crash happened just before it was completed, forcing him to abandon the purchase. His most recent message allowed him to move his money out of stocks and shares just before the crash, while the market was at its peak. He also warned his friend, Caroline Bamberger Fuld, before she sold the family's department store to Macy's in the summer. Along with her brother Louis, her intention was to use their fortune for more philanthropic causes, but they lost most of it in the crash. Einstein did not tell her how he knew what was coming, except that it was based on science. He swore her to secrecy and asked her to trust him. She agreed and was swayed by the stunning accuracy of his prediction of the St Valentine's Day Massacre, a week before it happened. When seven members and associates of Chicago's infamous North Side Gang were gunned down in a garage by men dressed as policemen, it was enough to persuade the Bambergers that Einstein had a conduit to the future. They kept the proceeds of their store sale in safety deposit boxes. In time, it proved to be a shrewd move on Einstein's part. The Bamberger siblings would eventually use their wealth to establish the Institute for Advanced Study in Princeton, where Einstein would spend the last twenty-two years of his life.

At some point on the voyage from Antwerp, he relented and agreed to meet the press when he arrived in New York. With more than fifty pressmen and a similar number of photographers crammed into the ship's lounge, nothing of any note came from the fifteen-minute free-for-all that was laughingly called a press conference. Danny Myers struggled to make himself heard.

Someone asked Einstein what he thought of Adolf Hitler, the leader of the second largest party in Germany. 'He is living on the empty stomach of Germany,' he said. 'As soon as economic conditions improve, he will no longer be important.'

The press conference was about to end when Myers shouted, 'How does it feel to be the smartest man alive, Professor?'

'I don't know,' he replied. 'You'd have to ask Nikola Tesla.'

Trudie found that getting to meet her old acquaintance was not as simple as she had thought. He was now an international celebrity and crowds followed him wherever he went. Towards the end of his New York stay, he returned to the *Belgenland* with Elsa after being given the keys to the city by Mayor Walker. Outside their stateroom, Trudie and Catherine were waiting. 'Hello, Albert,' said the older woman.

Einstein did not recognise her at first. Her weight had dropped by more than fifty pounds in the last couple of years. Then, a spark of recognition. 'Frau Lahm?' he replied. 'It's good to see you again.' Lahm was Trudie's family name before she left Germany.

While Elsa rummaged in her handbag for their door key, he joked, 'I have the keys to the city, and you can't even find the key to our room.'

'Do be quiet, Albert,' she said as she took the key from her bag.

He turned his attention to a wide-eyed Catherine, saying, 'I don't believe we've met.' Taking her hand, he kissed it as she looked at him, open-mouthed. 'It's a pleasure to meet you,' he said.

Before she could reply, Elsa said, 'Now, Albert, stop flirting and leave the poor girl alone. Will this take long? He's rather tired, I'm afraid.'

'Ah, don't listen to her,' said Einstein. 'Come in, please. See if you can organise some tea for our guests, *liebchen*,' he added, taking Trudie by the arm and leading her to a couch in their opulent stateroom. His attentiveness seemed out of place with his wife in the same room, but if Elsa noticed, then she chose to ignore it. Catherine wondered just how close they had been the last time they met.

For two hours that passed far too quickly, Trudie asked questions and Einstein answered, while asking questions of his own, so that at times it seemed as if he was the interviewer. Catherine took copious notes, gradually becoming less starstruck as she listened to this charming, witty man. She learnt that he hated press conferences, which he likened to being bitten by a pack of hungry wolves. He loved long walks in the rain. He had suffered heart problems two years earlier, which curtailed his activities but allowed him time to think. He believed in some sort of creator. He would like to see a democratic global government and thought the League of Nations might be the catalyst, if only America could be persuaded to join. When asked about time travel, he said it was an interesting concept but the stuff of science fiction. 'If it were possible, where are all the time travellers? Can you imagine what would happen if I were to travel back to a time before my grandfather had children and kill him?' he asked. 'I could never be born. No, such a paradox is simply not possible.'

'And what about travel to the future?' asked Trudie.

'I never think about the future,' he replied. 'I find it comes soon enough.'

Acknowledgements

Sincere thanks to Candida Bradford of A Place of Intent, for her excellent and insightful assessment of my draft manuscript.

I would also like to thank Bernadette, David, Catherine, Lauren, Michael and Storm, who all read my book and provided encouragement and support when it was most needed.

Last but by no means least, special mention should go to the members of the Thursday Book Club for their boundless enthusiasm and kindness.

About The Author

Ben Grantham is a writer of historical fiction who grew up in the south-west of England. His early career took him to the north-east, an industrial region dominated by steel, ships and coal. It could not have been more different to the rural tranquillity of Gloucestershire. He fell in love with the place, the people and Middlesbrough FC.

In the nineties, Ben was awarded an MBA from Newcastle Business School and worked throughout the UK as a business analyst, before taking a position in a large corporation that allowed him to spend more time with his young family. Several years ago, he gave up the world of business in order to write.

Telegraph To The Past is his first novel. He lives with his wife in County Durham and loves to travel.

Printed in Dunstable, United Kingdom

74402843R00217